Samuel Rutherford Crockett

The Black Douglas

Samuel Rutherford Crockett

The Black Douglas

ISBN/EAN: 9783743310322

Manufactured in Europe, USA, Canada, Australia, Japa

Cover: Foto ©Thomas Meinert / pixelio.de

Manufactured and distributed by brebook publishing software
(www.brebook.com)

Samuel Rutherford Crockett

The Black Douglas

" And at the last he . . . sailed over the seas to his own land."
Frontispiece

The Black Douglas

By

S. R. Crockett

Author of "The Raiders," "The Stickit Minister," etc.

New York
Doubleday & McClure Co.
1899

CONTENTS

CHAPTER I
The Black Douglas rides Home 1

CHAPTER II
My Fair Lady 12

CHAPTER III
Two riding together 20

CHAPTER IV
The Rose-red Pavilion 26

CHAPTER V
The Witch Woman 32

CHAPTER VI
The Prisoning of Malise the Smith 38

CHAPTER VII
The Douglas Muster 47

CHAPTER VIII
The Crossing of the Ford 53

CHAPTER IX
Laurence sings a Hymn 59

v

CHAPTER X

PAGE

The Braes of Balmaghie 66

CHAPTER XI

The Ambassador of France 75

CHAPTER XII

Mistress Maud Lindesay 82

CHAPTER XIII

A Daunting Summons 90

CHAPTER XIV

Captain of the Earl's Guard 95

CHAPTER XV

The Night Alarm 100

CHAPTER XVI

Sholto captures a Prisoner of Distinction 108

CHAPTER XVII

The Lamp is blown out 116

CHAPTER XVIII

The Morning Light 126

CHAPTER XIX

La Joyeuse baits her Hook 129

CHAPTER XX

Andro the Penman gives an Account of his Stewardship . 140

CHAPTER XXI

The Bailies of Dumfries 148

CHAPTER XXII

Wager of Battle 154

CHAPTER XXIII

Sholto wins Knighthood 162

CHAPTER XXIV

The Second Flouting of Maud Lindesay 167

CHAPTER XXV

The Dogs and the Wolf hold Council 173

CHAPTER XXVI

The Lion Tamer 179

CHAPTER XXVII

The Young Lords ride away 186

CHAPTER XXVIII

On the Castle Roof 192

CHAPTER XXIX

Castle Crichton 197

CHAPTER XXX

The Bower by yon Burnside 204

CHAPTER XXXI

The Gaberlunzie Man 209

CHAPTER XXXII

PAGE

"Edinburgh Castle, Tower, and Town" 215

CHAPTER XXXIII

The Black Bull's Head 223

CHAPTER XXXIV

Betrayed with a Kiss 231

CHAPTER XXXV

The Lion at Bay 242

CHAPTER XXXVI

The Rising of the Douglases 254

CHAPTER XXXVII

A Strange Meeting 261

CHAPTER XXXVIII

The MacKims come to Thrieve 270

CHAPTER XXXIX

The Gift of the Countess 278

CHAPTER XL

The Mission of James the Gross 288

CHAPTER XLI

The Withered Garland 299

CHAPTER XLII

Astarte the She-wolf 303

CONTENTS

CHAPTER XLIII

Malise fetches a Clout 314

CHAPTER XLIV

Laurence takes New Service 322

CHAPTER XLV

The Boasting of Gilles de Sillé 330

CHAPTER XLVI

The Country of the Dread 337

CHAPTER XLVII

Cæsar Martin's Wife 344

CHAPTER XLVIII

The Mercy of La Meffraye 352

CHAPTER XLIX

The Battle with the Were-wolves 358

CHAPTER L

The Altar of Iron 368

CHAPTER LI

The Marshal's Chamber 377

CHAPTER LII

The Jesting of La Meffraye 385

CHAPTER LIII

Sybilla's Vengeance 394

CHAPTER LIV

PAGE

The Cross under the Apron 405

CHAPTER LV

The Red Milk 414

CHAPTER LVI

The Shadow behind the Throne 424

CHAPTER LVII

The Tower of Death 433

CHAPTER LVIII

The White Tower of Machecoul 441

CHAPTER LIX

The Last Sacrifice to Barran-Sathanas 449

CHAPTER LX

His Demon hath deserted him 461

CHAPTER LXI

Leap Year in Galloway 471

LIST OF ILLUSTRATIONS

PAGE

"And at the last he . . . sailed over the seas to his own
    land" . . . . *Frontispiece*

William of Douglas reined up Darnaway underneath the
    whispering foliage of a great beech 15

"I am too young," he muttered; "I am not worthy" . 166

"But there cometh a night when every one of us watches
    the grey shallows to the east for those that shall
    return no more!" 195

A bright light as of a furnace burnt up before him, and
    the heat was overpowering as it rushed like a ruddy
    tide-race against his face 313

All the wild beasts appeared to be obeying the summons
    of the witch woman 361

The prisoners of the White Tower 383

It was like the sudden appearance of two white angels
    walking fearless and unscathed through the grim
    dominions of the Lords of Hell 448

THE BLACK DOUGLAS

CHAPTER I

THE BLACK DOUGLAS RIDES HOME

MERRY fell the eve of Whitsunday of the year 1439, in the fairest and heartsomest spot in all the Scottish southland. The twined May-pole had not yet been taken down from the house of Brawny Kim, master armourer and foster father to William, sixth Earl of Douglas and Lord of Galloway.

Malise Kim, who by the common voice was well named "The Brawny," sat in his wicker chair before his door, overlooking the island-studded, fairy-like loch of Carlinwark. In the smithy across the green bare-trodden road, two of his elder sons were still hammering at some armour of choice. But it was a ploy of their own, which they desired to finish that they might go trig and point-device to the Earl's weapon-showing to-morrow on the braes of Balmaghie. Sholto and Laurence were the names of the two who clanged the ringing steel and blew the smooth-handled bellows of tough tanned hide, that wheezed and puffed as the fire roared up deep and red before sinking to the right welding-heat in a little flame round the buckle-tache of the girdle brace they were working on.

B   1

And as they hammered they talked together in alternate snatches and silences — Sholto, the elder, meanwhile keeping an eye on his father. For their converse was not meant to reach the ear of the grave, strong man who sat so still in the wicker chair with the afternoon sun shining in his face.

"Hark ye, Laurence," said Sholto, returning from a visit to the door of the smithy, the upper part of which was open. "No longer will I be a hammerer of iron and a blower of fires for my father. I am going to be a soldier of fortune, and so I will tell him —"

"When wilt thou tell him?" laughed his brother, tauntingly. "I wager my purple velvet doublet slashed with gold which I bought with mine own money last Rood Fair that you will not go across and tell him now. Will you take the dare?"

"The purple velvet — you mean it?" said Sholto, eagerly. "Mind, if you refuse, and will not give it up after promising, I will nick that lying throat of yours with my gullie knife!"

And with that Sholto threw down his pincers and hammer, and valorously pushed open the lower door of the smithy. He looked with bold, dark blue eye at his father, and strode slowly across the grimy door-step. Brawny Kim had not moved for an hour. His great hands lay in his lap, and his eyes looked at the purple ridges of Screel, across the beautiful loch of Carlinwark, which sparkled and dimpled restlessly among its isles like a wilful beauty bridling under the gaze of a score of gallants.

But, even as he went, Sholto's step slowed, and lost its braggart strut and confidence. Behind him Laurence chuckled and laughed, smiting his thigh in his mocking glee.

"The purple velvet, mind you, Sholto! How well it will become you, coft from Rob Halliburton, our mother's own brother, seamed with red gold and lined with yellow satin and cramosie. Well indeed will it set you when Maud Lindesay, the maid who came from the north for company to the Earl's sister, looks forth from the canopy upon you as you stand in the archers' rank on the morrow's morn."

Sholto squared his shoulders, and with a little backward hitch of his elbow which meant "Wait till I come back, and I will pay you for this flouting," he strode determinedly across the green space towards his father.

The master armourer of Earl Douglas did not lift his eyes till his son had half crossed the road. Then, even as if a rank of spearmen at the word of command had lifted their glittering points to the "ready," Sholto MacKim stopped dead where he was, with a sort of gasp in his throat, like one who finds his defenceless body breast high against the line of hostile steel.

"The purple velvet!" came the cautious whisper from behind. But the taunt was powerless now.

The smith held his son a moment with his eyes.

"Well?" came in the deep low voice, more like the lowest tones of an organ than the speech of a man.

Sholto stood fixed, then half turning on his heel he began to walk towards the corner of the dwelling-house, over which a gay streamer of the early creeping convolvulus danced and swung in the stirring of the light breeze.

"You wish speech with me?" said his father, in the same level and thrilling undertone.

"No," said Sholto, hesitant in spite of himself, "but I thought — that is I desired — saw you my sister Magdalen pass this way? I have somewhat to give her."

"Ah, so," said Brawny Kim, without moving, "a steel breastplate, belike. Thou hast the brace-buckle in thy hand. Doth the little Magdalen go with you to the weapon-show to-morrow?"

"No, father," said Sholto, stammering, "but I was uneasy for the child. It is full an hour since I heard her voice."

"Then," said his father, "finish your work, put out the fire, and go seek your sister."

Sholto brought his hands together and made the little inclination of the head which was a sign of filial respect. Then, solemn as if he had been in his place in the ordered line of the Earl's first levy of archer men, he turned him about and went back to the smithy.

Laurence lay all abroad on the heap of charcoal of which the armourer's welding fire was made. He was fairly expiring with laughter, and when his brother angrily kicked him in the ribs, he only waggled an ineffectual hand and feebly crowed in his throat like a cock, in his efforts to stifle the sounds of mirth.

"Get up, fool," hissed his angry brother; "help me with this accursed hammer-striking, or I will make an end of such a giggling lout as you. Here, hold up."

And seizing his younger brother by the collar of his blue working blouse, he dragged him upon his feet.

"Now, by the saints," said Sholto, "if you cast your

gibes upon me, by Saint Andrew I will break every bone in your idiot's body."

"The purple velvet — oh, the purple velvet!" gasped Laurence, as soon as he could recover speech, "and the eyes of Maud Lindesay!"

"That will teach you to think rather of the eyes of Laurence MacKim!" cried Sholto, and without more ado he hit his brother with his clinched knuckles a fair blow on the bridge of his nose.

The next moment the two youths were grappling together like wild cats, striking, kicking, and biting with no thought except of who should have the best of the battle. They rolled on the floor, now tussling among the crackling faggots, anon pitching soft as one body on the peat dust in the corner, again knocking over a bench and bringing down the tools thereon to the floor with a jingle which might have been heard far out on the loch. They were still clawing and cuffing each other in blind rage, when a hand, heavy and remorseless, was laid upon each. Sholto found himself being dabbled in the great tempering cauldron which stood by his father's forge. Laurence heard his own teeth rattle as he was shaken sideways till his joints waggled like those of a puppet at Keltonhill Fair. Then it was his turn to be doused in the water. Next their heads were soundly knocked together, and finally, like a pair of arrows sent right and left, Laurence sped forth at the window in the gable end and found himself in the midst of a gooseberry bush, whilst Sholto, flying out of the door, fell sprawling on all fours almost under the feet of a horse on which a young man sat, smilingly watching the scene.

Brawny Kim scattered the embers of the fire on the

forge-hearth, and threw the breastplate and girdle-brace at which the boys had been working into a corner of the smithy. Then he turned to lock the door with the massive key, which stood so far out from the upper leaf that to it the horses waiting their turns to be shod were ordinarily tethered.

As he did so he caught sight of the young man sitting silent on the black charger. Instantly a change passed over his face. With one motion of his hand he swept the broad blue bonnet from his brow, and bowed the grizzled head which had worn it low upon his breast. Thus for the breathing of a breath the master armourer stood, and then, replacing his bonnet, he looked up again at the young knight on horseback.

"My lord," he said, after a long pause, in which he waited for the youth to speak, "this is not well — you ride unattended and unarmed."

"Ah, Malise," laughed the young Earl, "a Douglas has few privileges if he may not sometimes on a summer eve lay aside his heavy prisonment of armour and don such a suit as this! What think you, eh? Is it not a valiant apparel, as might almost beseem one who rode a-courting?"

The mighty master-smith looked at the young man with eyes in which reverence, rebuke, and admiration strove together.

"But," he said, wagging his head with a grave humorousness, "your lordship needs not to ride a-courting. You are to be married to a great dame who will bring you wealth, alliance, and the dower of provinces."

The young man shrugged his shoulders, and swung

lightly off his charger, which turned to look at him as he stood and patted its neck.

"Know you not, Malise," he said, "that the Earl of Douglas must needs marry provinces and the Lord of Galloway wed riches? But what is there in that to prevent Will Douglas going courting at eighteen years of his age as a young man ought. But have no fear, I come not hither seeking the favour of any, save of that lily flower of yours, the only true May-blossom that blooms on the Three Thorns of Carlinwark. I would look upon the angel smile on the face of your little daughter Magdalen. An she be here, I would toss her arm-high for a kiss of her mouth, which I would rather touch than that of lady or leman. For I do ever profess myself her vassal and slave. Where have you hidden her, Malise? Declare it or perish!"

The smith lifted up his voice till it struck on the walls of his cottage and echoed like thunder along the shores of the lake.

"Dame Barbara," he cried, and again, getting no answer, "ho, Dame Barbara, I say!"

Then at the second hallo, a shrill and somewhat peevish voice proceeded from within the house opposite.

"Aye, coming, can you not hear, great nolt! 'Deed and 'deed 'tis a pretty pass when a woman with the cares of an household must come running light-toe and clatter-heel to every call of such a lazy lout. Husband, indeed — not house-band but house-bond, I wot — house-torment, house-thorn, house-cross — "

A sonsy, well-favoured, middle-aged head, strangely at variance with the words which came from it, peeped out, and instantly the scolding brattle was stilled.

Back went the head into the dark of the house as if shot from a bombard.

Malise MacKim indulged in a low hoarse chuckle as he caught the words: "Eh, 'tis my Lord William! Save us, and me wanting my Ryssil gown that cost me ten silver shillings the ell, and no even so muckle as my white peaked cap upon my head."

Her husband glanced at the young Earl to see if he appreciated the savour of the jest. Then he looked away, turning the enjoyment over and over under his own tongue, and muttering: "Ah, well, 'tis not his fault. No man hath a sense of humour before he is forty years of his age — and, for that matter, 'tis all the riper at fifty."

The young man's eyes were looking this way and that, up and down the smooth pathway which skirted like a green selvage the shores of the loch.

"Malise," he said, as if he had already forgotten his late eager quest for the little Magdalen, "Darnaway here has a shoe loose, and to-morrow I ride to levy, and may also joust a bout in the tilt-yard of the afternoon. I would not ask you to work in Whitsuntide, but that there cometh my Lord Fleming and Alan Lauder of the Bass, bringing with them an embassy from France — and I hear there may be fair ladies in their company."

"Ah!" quoth Malise, grimly, "so I have heard it said concerning the embassies of Charles, King of France!"

But the young man only smiled, and dusted off one or two flecks of foam which had blown backwards from his horse's bit upon the rich crimson doublet of finest velvet, which, cinctured closely at the waist, fell half-way to his knees in heavy double pleats sewn with gold. A hunting horn of black and gold was suspended about his neck by a bandolier of dark leather, subtilely embroidered with bosses of gold. Laced boots of soft black hide, drawn together on the outside from ankle to mid-calf with a golden cord, met the scarlet " chausses " which covered his thighs and outlined the figure of him who was the noblest youth and the most gallant in all the realm of Scotland.

Earl William wore no sword. Only a little gold-handled poignard with a lady's finger ring set upon the point of the hilt was at his side, and he stood resting easily his hand upon it as he talked, drawing it an inch from its sheath and snicking it back again nonchalantly, with a sound like the clicking of a well-oiled lock.

"Clink the strokes strongly and featly, Malise, for tomorrow, when the Black Douglas rides upon Black Darnaway under the eyes of — well — of the ladies whom the ambassadors are bringing to greet me, there must be no stumbling and no mistakes. Or on the head of Malise MacKim the matter shall be, and let that wight remember that the Douglas does not keep a dule tree up there by the Gallows Slock for nothing."

The mighty smith was by this time examining the hoofs of the Earl's charger one by one with such instinctive delicacy of touch that Darnaway felt the kindly intent, and, bending his neck about, blew and snuffled into the armourer's tangled mat of crisp grey hair.

" Up there ! " exclaimed MacKim, as the warm breath tickled his neck, and at the burst of sound the steed shifted and clattered upon the hard-beaten floor of the smithy, tossing his head till the bridle chains rang again.

" Eh, my Lord William," an altered voice came from the doorstep, where Dame Barbara MacKim, now clothed and in her right mind, stood louting low before the young Earl, " but this is a blythe and calamitatious day for this poor bit bigging o' the Carlinwark — to think that your honour should visit his servants! Will you no come ben and sit doon in the house-place? 'Tis far from fitting for your feet to pass thereupon. But gin ye will so highly favour — "

" Nay, I thank you, good Dame Barbara," said the Earl, very courteously taking off the close-fitting black cap with the red feather in it which was upon his head. " I must bide but a moment for your husband to set right certain nails in the hoofs of Darnaway here, to ready me for the morrow. Do you come to see the sport? So buxom a dame as the mistress of Carlin-wark should not be absent to encourage the lads to do their best at the sword-play and the rivalry of the butts."

And as the dame came forth courtesying and bowing her delighted thanks, Earl William, setting a forefinger under her triple chin, stooped and kissed her in his gay-est and most debonair manner.

" Eh, only to think on't," cried the dame, clapping her hands together as she did at mass, " that I, Barbara MacKim, that am marriet to a donnert auld carle like Malise there, should hae the privileege o' a salute frae the bonny mou' o' Yerl William — (Thank ye kindly, my lord!) — and be inveeted to the weepen-shawing to sit amang the leddies and view the sport. Malise, my man, caa' ye no that an honour, a privileege? Is that no owing to me being the sister — on my faither's side —

o' Ninian Halliburton, merchant and indweller in Dumfries ? "

"Nay, nay, good dame," laughed the Earl, " 'tis all for the sake of your own very sufficient charms ! I trust that your good man here is not jealous, for beauty, you well do ken, ever sends the wits of a Douglas woolgathering. Nevertheless, let us have a draught of your home-brewed ale, for kissing is but dry work, after all, and little do I think of it save " (he set his cap on his head with a gallant wave of his hand) "in the case of a lady so fair and tempting as Dame Barbara MacKim ! "

At this the dame cast up her hands and her eyes again. " Eh, what will Marget Ahanny o' the Shankfit say noo — this frae the Yerl William. Eh, sirce, this is better than an Abbot's absolution. I declare 'tis mair sustainin' than a' the consolations o' religion. Malise, do you hear, great dour cuif that ye are, what says my lord ? And you to think so little of your married wife as ye do ! Think shame, you being what ye are, and me the ain sister to that master o' merchandise and Bailie o' Dumfries, Maister Ninian Halliburton o' the Vennel ! "

And with that she vanished into the black oblong of the door opposite the smithy.

CHAPTER II

MY FAIR LADY

The strong man of Carlinwark made no long job of the horseshoeing. For, as he hammered and filed, he marked the eye of the young Earl restlessly straying this way and that along the green riverside paths, and his fingers nervously tapping the ashen casing of the smithy window-sill. Malise MacKim smiled to himself, for he had not served a Douglas for thirty years without knowing by these signs that there was the swing of a kirtle in the case somewhere.

Presently the last nail was made firm, and Black Darnaway was led, passaging and tossing his bridle reins, out upon the green sward. Malise stood at his head till the Douglas swung himself into the saddle with a motion light as the first upward flight of a bird.

He put his hand into a pocket in the lining of his "soubreveste" and took out a golden "Lion" of the King's recent mintage. He spun it in the air off his thumb and then looked at it somewhat contemptuously as he caught it.

"I think you and I, Master-Armourer, could send out a better coinage than that with the old Groat press over there at Thrieve!" he said.

Malise smiled his quiet smile.

"If the Earl of Douglas deigns to make me the master

12

of his mint, I promise him plenty of good, sound, broad pieces of a noble design — that is, till Chancellor Crichton hangs me for coining in the Grassmarket of Edinburgh."

"That would he never, with the Douglas lances to prick you a way out and the Douglas gold to buy the good-will of traitorous judges!"

Half unconsciously the Earl sighed as he looked at the fair lake growing rosy in the light of the sunset. His boyish face was overspread with care, and for the moment seemed all too young to have inherited so great a burden. But the next moment he was himself again.

"I know, Malise," he said, "that I cannot offer you gold in return for your admirable handicraft. But 'tis nigh to Keltonhill Fair, do you divide this gold Lion betwixt those two brave boys of yours. Faith, right glad was I to be Earl of Douglas and not a son of his master armourer when I saw you disciplining for their souls' good Messires Sholto and Laurence there!"

The smith smiled grimly.

"They are good enough lads, Sholto and Laurence both, but they will be for ever gnarring and grappling at each other like messan dogs round a kirk door."

"They will not make the worse soldiers for that, Malise. I pray you forgive them for my sake."

The master armourer took the hand of his young lord on which he was about to draw a riding glove of Spanish leather. Very reverently he kissed the signet ring upon it.

"My dear lord," he said, "I can refuse naught to any of your great and gracious house, and least of all to you,

the light and pleasure of it—aye, and the light of a
surly old man's heart, more even than the duty he owes
to his own married wife! Oh, be careful, my lord, for
you are the desire of many hearts and the hope of all
this land."

He hesitated a moment, and then added with a kind
of curious bashfulness—

"But I am concerned about ye this nicht, William
Douglas—I fear that ye could not—would not permit
me—"

"Could not permit what—out with it, old grumble-
pate?"

"That I should saddle my Flanders mare and ride
after you. Malise MacKim would not be in the way
even if ye went a-trysting. He kens brawly, in such a
case, when to turn his head and look upon the hills
and the woods and the bonny sleeping waters."

The Earl laughed and shook his head.

"Na, na, Malise," he said, "were I indeed on such a
quest the sight of your grey pow would fright a fair
lady, and the mere trampling of that club-footed she-
elephant of yours put to flight every sentiment of love.
Remember the Douglas badge is a naked heart. Can I
ride a-courting, therefore, with all my fighting tail behind me as though I besought an alliance with the King
of England's daughter?"

Silently and sadly the strong man watched the young
Earl ride away to the south along that fair lochside.
He stood muttering to himself and looking long under
his hand after his lord. The rider bowed his head as
he passed under the rich blazonry of the white May-blossom, which, like creamy lace, covered the Three Thorns

WILLIAM OF DOUGLAS REINED UP DARNAWAY UNDERNEATH THE WHIS-
PERING FOLIAGE OF A GREAT BEECH.

of Carlinwark, now deeply stained with rose colour from the clouds of sunset.

"Aye, aye," he said, "the Douglas badge is indeed a heart — but it is a bleeding heart. God avert the omen, and keep this young man safe — for though many love him, there be more that would rejoice at his fall."

The rider on Black Darnaway rode right into the saffron eye of the sunset. On his left hand Carlinwark and its many islets burned rich with spring-green foliage, all splashed with the golden sunset light. Darnaway's well-shod hoofs sent the diamond drops flying, as, with obvious pleasure, he trampled through the shallows. Ben Gairn and Screel, boldly ridged against the southern horizon, stood out in dark amethyst against the glowing sky of even, but the young rider never so much as turned his head to look at them.

Presently, however, he emerged from among the noble lakeside trees upon a more open space. Broom and whin blossom clustered yellow and orange beneath him, garrisoning with their green spears and golden banners every knoll and scaur. But there were broad spaces of turf here and there on which the conies fed, or fought terrible battles for the meek ear-twitching does, "spat-spatting" at each other with their fore paws and springing into the air in their mating fury.

William of Douglas reined up Darnaway underneath the whispering foliage of a great beech, for all at unawares he had come upon a sight that interested him more than the noble prospect of the May sunset.

In the centre of the golden glade, and with all their faces mistily glorified by the evening light, he saw a group of little girls, singing and dancing as they performed some quaint and graceful pageant of child-hood.

Their young voices came up to him with a wistful, dying fall, and the slow, graceful movement of the rhythmic dance seemed to affect the young man strangely. Involuntarily he lifted his close-fitting feathered cap from his head, and allowed the cool airs to blow against his brow.

> " *See the robbers passing by, passing by, passing by,*
>   *See the robbers passing by,*
>   *My fair lady !* "

The ancient words came up clearly and distinctly to him, and softened his heart with the indefinable and exquisite pathos of the refrain whenever it is sung by the sweet voices of children.

"These are surely but cottars' bairns," he said, smiling a little at his own intensity of feeling, "but they sing like little angels. I daresay my sweetheart Magdalen is amongst them."

And he sat still listening, patting Black Darnaway meanwhile on the neck.

> " *What did the robbers do to you, do to you, do to you,*
>   *What did the robbers do to you,*
>   *My fair lady ?* "

The first two lines rang out bold and clear. Then again the wistfulness of the refrain played upon his heart as if it had been an instrument of strings, till the tears came into his eyes at the wondrous sorrow and yearning with which one voice, the sweetest and purest of all, replied, singing quite alone:

" They broke my lock and stole my gold, stole my gold, stole my gold,
Broke my lock and stole my gold,
My fair lady !"

The tears brimmed over in the eyes of William Douglas, and a deep foreboding of the mysteries of fate fell upon his heart and abode there heavy as doom.

He turned his head as though he felt a presence near him, and lo! sudden and silent as the appearing of a phantom, another horse was alongside of Black Darnaway, and upon a white palfrey a maiden dressed also in white sat, smiling upon the young man, fair to look upon as an angel from heaven.

Earl William's lips parted, but he was too surprised to speak. Nevertheless, he moved his hand to his head in instinctive salutation; but, finding his bonnet already off, he could only stare at the vision which had so suddenly sprung out of the ground.

The lady slowly waved her hand in the direction of the children, whose young voices still rang clear as cloister bells tolling out the Angelus, and whose white dresses waved in the light wind as they danced back and forth with a slow and graceful motion.

"You hear, Earl William," she said, in a low, thrilling voice, speaking with a foreign accent, "you hear? You are a good Christian, doubtless, and you have heard from your uncle, the Abbot, how praise is made perfect 'out of the mouths of babes and sucklings.' Hark to them; they sing of their own destinies — and it may be also of yours and mine."

And so fascinated and moved at heart at once by her beauty and by her strange words, the Douglas listened.

c

> "*What did the robbers do to you, do to you, **do to you**,*
> *What did the robbers do to you,*
>   ***My fair lady?***"

The lady on the delicately pacing palfrey turned the
darkness of her eyes from the white-robed choristers
to the face of the young man. Then, with an impetuous
motion of her hand, she urged him to listen for the next
words, which swept over Earl William's heart with a
cadence of unutterable pain and inexplicable melancholy.

> "*They broke my lock and stole my gold, stole my gold, stole my gold,*
> *Broke my lock and stole my gold,*
>   ***My fair lady!***"

He turned upon his companion with a quick energy,
as if he were afraid of losing himself again.

"Who are you, lady, and what do you here?"

The girl (for in years she was little more) smiled and
reined her steed a little back from him with an air at
once prettily petulant and teasing.

"Is that spoken as William Douglas or as the Justicer
of Galloway — a country where, as I understand, there
is no trial by jury?"

The light of a radiant smile passed from her lips
into his soul.

"It is spoken as a man speaks to a woman beautiful
and queenly," he said, not removing his eyes from her
face.

"I fear I may have startled you," she said, without
continuing the subject. "Even as I came I saw you
were wrapped in meditation, and my palfrey going
lightly made no sound on the grass and leaves."

Her voice was so sweet and low that William Douglas, listening to it, wished that she would speak on for ever.

"The hour grows late," he said, remembering himself. "You must have far to ride. Let me be your escort homewards if you have none worthier than I."

"Alas," she answered, smiling yet more subtly, "I have no home near by. My home is very far and over many turbulent seas. I have but a maiden's pavilion in which to rest my head. Yet since I and my company must needs travel through your domains, Earl William, I trust you will not be so cruel as to forbid us?"

"Yes,"—he was smiling now in turn, and catching somewhat of the gay spirit of the lady,—"as overlord of all this province I do forbid you to pass through these lands of Galloway without first visiting me in my house of Thrieve!"

The lady clapped her hands and laughed, letting her palfrey pace onwards through the woodland glades bridle free, while Black Darnaway, compelled by his master's hand, followed, tossing his head indignantly because it had been turned from the direction of his nightly stable on the Castle Isle.

CHAPTER III

TWO RIDING TOGETHER

"Joyous," she cried, as they went, 'Oh, most joyous would it be to see the noble castle and to have all the famous two thousand knights to make love to me at once! To capture two thousand hearts at one sweep of the net! What would Margaret of France herself say to that?"

"Is there no single heart sufficient to satisfy you, fair maid?" said the young man, in a low voice; "none loyal enough nor large enough for you that you desire so many?"

"And what would I do with one if it were in my hands," she said wistfully; "that is, if it were a worthy heart and one worth the taking. Ever since I was a child I have always broken my toys when I tired of them."

The voices of the singing children on the green came more faintly to their ears, but the words were still clear to be understood.

"Off to prison you must go, you must go, you must go,
Off to prison you must go,
My fair lady!"

"You hear? It is my fate!" she said.

"Nay," answered the Earl, passionately, still looking in her eyes. "Mine, mine — not yours! Gladly I would go to prison or to death for the love of one so fair!"

"My lord, my lord," she laughed, with a tolerant protest in her voice, " you keep up the credit of your house right nobly. How goes the distich? My mother taught it me upon the bridge of Avignon, where also as here in Scotland the children dance and sing.

> "First in the love of Woman,
>   First in the field of fight,
>   First in the death that men must die,
>   Such is the Douglas' right!"

"Here and now," he said, still looking at her, " 'tis only the first I crave."

"Earl William, positively you must come to Court!" she shrilled into sudden tinkling laughter; "there be ladies there more worthy of your ardour than a poor errant maiden such as I."

"A Court," cried Earl William, scornfully, "to the Seneschal's court! Nay, truly. Could a Stewart ever keep his faith or pay his debts? Never, since the first of them licked his way into a lady's favour."

"Oh," she answered lightly, "I meant not the Court of Stirling nor yet the Chancellor's Castle of Edinburgh. I meant the only great Court — the Court of France, the Court of Charles the Seventh, the Court which already owns the sway of its rarest ornament, your own Scottish Princess Margaret."

"Thither I cannot go unless the King of France grants me my father's rights and estates!" he said, with a certain sternness in his tone.

"Let me look at your hand," she answered, with a

gentle inclination of her fair head, from which the lace
that had shrouded it now streamed back in the cool
wind of evening.

Stopping Darnaway, the young Earl gave the girl his
hand, and the white palfrey came to rest close beneath
the shoulder of the black war charger.

" To-morrow," she said, looking at his palm, " to-morrow you will be Duke of Touraine.   I promise it to you
by my power of divination.   Does that satisfy you ? "

" I fear you are a witch, or else a being compound of
rarer elements than mere flesh and blood," said the Earl.

" Is that a spirit's hand," she said, laughing lightly
and giving her own rosy fingers into his, " or could even
the Justicer of Galloway find it in his heart to burn
these as part of the body of a witch ? "

She shuddered and pretended to gaze piteously up at
him from under the long lashes which hardly raised
themselves from her cheek.

" Spirit-slender, spirit-white they are," he replied, " and
as for being the fingers of a witch — doubtless you are
a witch indeed.   But I will not burn so fair things as
these, save as it might be with the fervours of my lips."

And he stooped and pressed kiss after kiss upon her
hand.

Gently she withdrew her fingers from his grasp and
rode further apart, yet not without one backward glance
of perfectest witchery.

" I doubt you have been overmuch at Court already,"
she said.   " I did not well to ask you to go thither."

" Why must I not go thither ? " he asked.

" Because I shall be there," she replied softly, courting
him yet again with her eyes.

As they rode on together through the rich twilight dusk, the young man observed her narrowly as often as he could.

Her skin was fair with a dazzling clearness, which even the gathering gloom only caused to shine with a more perfect brilliance, as if a halo of light dwelt permanently beneath its surface. Faint responsive roses bloomed on either cheek and, as it seemed, cast a shadow of their colour down her graceful neck. Dark eyes shone above, fresh and dewy with love and youth, and smiled out with all ancientest witcheries and allurements in their depths. Her lithe, slender body was simply clad in a fair white cloth of some foreign fabric, and her waist, of perfectest symmetry, was cinctured by a broad ring of solid silver, which, to the young man, looked so slender that he could have clasped it about with both his hands.

So they rode on, through the woods mostly, until they reached a region which to the Earl appeared unfamiliar. The glades were greener and denser. The trees seemed more primeval, the foliage thicker overhead, the interspaces of the golden evening sky darker and less frequent.

"In what place may your company be assembled?" he asked. "Strange it is that I know not this spot. Yet I should recognise each tree by conning it, and of every rivulet in Galloway I should be able to tell the name. Yet with shame do I confess that I know not where I am."

"Ah," said the girl, her face growing luminous through the gloom, "you called me a witch, and now you shall see. I wave my hands, so — and you are no more in Galloway. You are in the land of faëry. I blow you a kiss, so — and lo! you are no more William, sixth Earl of Douglas and proximate Duke of Touraine, but you are even as True Thomas, the Beloved of the Queen of the Fairies, and the slave of her spell!"

"I am indeed well content to be Thomas Rhymer," he answered, submitting himself to the wooing glamour of her eyes, "so be that you are the Lady of the milk-white hind!"

"A courtier indeed," she laughed; "you need not to seek your answer. You make a poor girl afraid. But see, yonder are the lights of my pavilion. Will it please you to alight and enter? The supper will be spread, and though you must not expect any to entertain you, save only this your poor Queen Mab" (here she made him a little bow), "yet I think you will not be ill content. They do not say that Thomas of Ercildoune had any cause for complaint. Do you know," she continued, a fresh gaiety striking into her voice, "it was in this very wood that he was lost."

But William Douglas sat silent with the wonder of what he saw. Their horses had all at once come out on a hilltop. The sequestered boskage of the trees had gradually thinned, finally dwarfing into a green drift of fern and birchen foliage which rose no higher than Black Darnaway's chest, and through which his rider's laced boots brushed till the Spanish leather of their gold-embossed frontlets was all jetted with gouts of dew.

Before him swept horizonwards a great upward drift of solemn pine trees, the like of which for size he had never seen in all his domain. Or so, at least, it seemed in that hour of mystery and glamour. For behind them the evening sky had dulled to a deep and solemn wash of blood red, across which lay one lonely bar of black cloud, solid as spilled ink on a monkish page. But under the trees themselves, blazing with lamps and breathing odours of all grace and daintiness, stood a lighted pavilion of rose-coloured silk, anchored to the ground with ropes of sendal of the richest crimson hue.

"Let your horse go free, or tether him to a pine; in either case he will not wander far," said the girl. "I fear my fellows have gone off to lay in provisions. We have taken a day or two more on the way than we had counted on, so that to-night's feast makes an end of our store. But still there is enough for two. I bid you welcome, Earl William, to a wanderer's tent. There is much that I would say to you."

CHAPTER IV

THE ROSE-RED PAVILION

As the young Earl paused a moment without to tether Black Darnaway to a fallen trunk of a pine, a chill and melancholy wind seemed to rise suddenly and toss the branches dark against the sky. Then it flew off moaning like a lost spirit, till he could hear the sound of its passage far down the valley. An owl hooted and a swart raven disengaged himself from the coppice about the door of the pavilion, and fluttered away with a croak of disdainful anger. Black Darnaway turned his head and whinnied anxiously after his master.

But William Douglas, though little more than a boy if men's ages are to be counted by years, was yet a true child of Archibald the Grim, and he passed through the mysterious encampment to the door of the lighted pavilion with a carriage at once firm and assured. He could faintly discern other tents and pavilions set further off, with pennons and bannerets, which the passing gust had blown flapping from the poles, but which now hung slackly about their staves.

"I would give a hundred golden St. Andrews," he muttered, "if I could make out the scutcheon. It looks most like a black dragon couchant on a red field, which is not a Scottish bearing. The lady is French, doubtless, and passes through from Ireland to visit the Chancellor's Court at Edinburgh."

The Black Douglas paused a moment at the tent-flap, which, being of silken fabric lined with heavier material, hung straight and heavy to the ground.

"Come in, my lord," cried the low and thrilling voice of his companion from within. "With both hands I bid you welcome to my poor abode. A traveller must not be particular, and I have only those condiments with me which my men have brought from shipboard, knowing how poor was the provision of your land. See, do you not already repent your promise to sup with me?"

She pointed to the table on which sparkled cut glass of Venice and rich wreathed ware of goldsmiths' work. On these were set out oranges and rare fruits of the Orient, such as the young man had never seen in his own bleak and barren land.

But the Douglas did no more than glance at the luxury of the providing. A vision fairer and more beautiful claimed his eyes. For even as he paused in amazement, the lady herself stood before him, transformed and, as it seemed, glorified. In the interval she had taken off the cloak which, while on horseback, she had worn falling from her shoulders. A thin robe of white silk broidered with gold at once clothed and revealed her graceful and gracious figure, even as a glove covers but does not conceal the hand upon which it is drawn. Whether by intent or accident, the collar had been permitted to fall aside at the neck and showed the dazzling whiteness of the skin beneath, but at the bosom it was secured by a button set with black pearls which constituted the lady's only ornament.

Her arms also were bare, and showed in the lamplight whiter than milk. She had removed the silver belt, and

was tying a red silken scarf about her waist in a manner
which revealed a swift grace and lithe sinuosity of movement, making her beauty appear yet more wonderful and
more desirable to the young man's eyes.

On either side the pavilion were placed folding couches
of rosy silk, and in the corner, draped with rich blue
hangings, glimmered the lady's bed, its fair white linen
half revealed. Two embroidered pillows were at the
foot, and on a little table beside it a crystal ball on a
black platter.

No crucifix or *prie-dieu,* such as in those days was in
every lady's bower, could be discerned anywhere about
the pavilion.

So soon as the tent-flap had fallen with a soft rustle
behind him, the Earl William abandoned himself to the
strange enchantment of his surroundings. He did not
stop to ask himself how it was possible that such dainty
providings had been brought into the midst of his wide,
wild realm of Galloway. Nor yet why this errant damsel
should in the darksome night-time find herself alone on
this hilltop with the tents of her retinue standing empty
and silent about. The present sufficed him. The soft
radiance of dark eyes fell upon him, and all the quick-
running, inconsiderate Douglas blood rushed and sang
in his veins, responsive to that subtle shining.

He was with a fair woman, and she not unwilling to
be kind. That was ever enough for all the race of the
Black Douglas. What the Red Douglas loved is another
matter. Their ambitions were more reputable, but
greatly less generous.

"My lord," said the lady, giving him her hand, "will
you lead me to the table? I cannot offer you the re-

freshment of any elaborate toilet, but here, at least, is wheaten bread to eat and wine of a good vintage to drink."

"You yourself scarce need such earthly sustenance," he answered gallantly, "for your eyes have stolen the radiance of the stars, and 'tis evident that the night dews visit your cheek only as they do the roses — to render them more fresh and fair."

"My lord flatters well for one so young;" she smiled as she seated herself and motioned him to sit close beside her. "How comes it that in this wild place you have learned to speak so chivalrously?"

"When one answers beauty the words are somehow given," he said, "and, moreover, I have not dwelt in grey Galloway all my days."

"You speak French?" she queried in that tongue.

"Ah," she said when he answered, "the divine language. I knew you were perfect." And so for a long while the young man sat spellbound, watching the smiles coming and going upon her red and flower-like lips, and listening to the fast-running ripple of her foreign talk. It was pleasure enough to hearken without reply.

It seemed no common food of mortal men that was set before William Douglas, served with the sweep of white arms and the bend of delicate fingers upon the chalice stem. He did not care to eat, but again and again he set the wine cup down empty, for the vintage was new to him, and brought with it a haunting aroma, instinct with strange hopes and vivid with unknown joys.

The pavilion, with its cords of sendal and its silver hanging lamps, spun round about him. The fair woman herself seemed to dissolve and reunite before his eyes.

She had let down the full-fed river of her hair, and it flowed in the Venetian fashion over her white shoulders, sparkling with an inner fire — each fine silken thread, as it glittered separate from its fellows, twining like a golden snake.

And the ripple of her laughter played upon the young man's heart carelessly as a lute is touched by the hands of its mistress. Something of the primitive glamour of the night and the stars clung to this woman. It seemed a thing impossible that she should be less pure than the air and the waters, than the dewy grass beneath and the sky cool overhead. He knew not that the devil sat from the first day of creation on Eden wall, that human sin is all but as eternal as human good, and that passion rises out of its own ashes like the phœnix bird of fable and stands again all beautiful before us, a creature of fire and dew.

Presently the lady rose to her feet, and gave the Earl her hand to lead her to a couch.

"Set a footstool by me," she bade him, "I desire to talk to you."

"You know not my name," she said, after a pause that was like a caress, "though I know yours. But then the sun in mid-heaven cannot be hidden, though name-less bide the thousand stars. Shall I tell you mine? It is a secret; nevertheless, I will tell you if such be your desire."

"I care not whether you tell me or no," he answered, looking up into her face from the low seat at her feet. "Birth cannot add to your beauty, nor sparse quarter-ings detract from your charm. I have enough of both, good lack! And little good they are like to do me."

"Shall I tell you now," she went on, "or will you wait till you convoy me to Edinburgh?"

"To Edinburgh!" cried the young man, greatly astonished. "I have no purpose of journeying to that town of mine enemies. I have been counselled oft by those who love me to remain in mine own country. My horoscope bids me refrain. Not for a thousand commands of King or Chancellor will I go to that dark and bloody town, wherein they say lies waiting the curse of my house."

"But you will go to please a woman?" she said, and leaned nearer to him, looking deep into his eyes.

For a moment William Douglas wavered. For a moment he resisted. But the dark, steadfast orbs thrilled him to the soul, and his own heart rose insurgent against his reason.

"I will come if you ask me," he said. "You are more beautiful than I had dreamed any woman could be."

"I do ask you!" she continued, without removing her eyes from his face.

"Then I will surely come!" he replied.

She set her hand beneath his chin and bent smilingly and lightly to kiss him, but with an imprisoned passionate cry the young man suddenly clasped her in his arms. Yet even as he did so, his eyes fell upon two figures, which, silent and motionless, stood by the open door of the pavilion.

CHAPTER V

THE WITCH WOMAN

ONE of these was Malise the Smith, towering like a giant. His hands rested on the hilt of a mighty sword, whose blade sparkled in the lamplight as if the master armourer had drawn it that moment from the midst of his charcoal fire.

A little in front of Malise there stood another figure, less imposing in physical proportions, but infinitely more striking in dignity and apparel. This second was a man of tall and spare frame, of a countenance grave and severe, yet with a certain kindly power latent in him also. He was dressed in the white robe of a Cistercian, with the black scapulary of the order. On his head was the mitre, and in his hand the staff of the abbot of a great establishment which he wears when he goes visiting his subsidiary houses. More remarkable than all was the monk's likeness to the young man who now stood before him with an expression of indignant surprise on his face, which slowly merged into anger as he understood why these two men were there.

He recognised his uncle the Abbot William Douglas, the head of the great Abbey of Dulce Cor upon Solway side.

This was he who, being the son and heir of the brother of the first Duke of Touraine, had in the flower

of his age suddenly renounced his domains of Nithsdale
that he might take holy orders, and who had ever since
been renowned throughout all Scotland for high sanctity
and a multitude of good works.

The pair stood looking towards the lady and William
Douglas without speech, a kind of grim patience upon
their faces.

It was the Earl who was the first to speak.

"What seek you here so late, my lord Abbot?" he
said, with all the haughtiness of the unquestioned head
of his mighty house.

"Nay, what seeks the Earl William here alone so
late?" answered the Abbot, with equal directness.

The two men stood fronting each other. Malise leaned
upon his two-handed sword and gazed upon the ground.

"I have come," the Abbot went on, after vainly waiting for the young Earl to offer an explanation, "as your
kinsman, tutor, and councillor, to warn you against this
foreign witch woman. What seeks she here in this land
of Galloway but to do you hurt? Have we not heard
her with our own ears persuade you to accompany her
to Edinburgh, which is a city filled with the power and
deadly intent of your enemies?"

Earl William bowed ironically to his uncle, and his
eye glittered as it fell upon Malise MacKim.

"I thank you, Uncle," he said. "I am deeply indebted
for your so great interest in me. I thank you too, Malise,
for bringing about this timely interference. I will pay
my debts one day. In the meantime your duty is done.
Depart, both of you, I command you!"

Outside the thunder began to growl in the distance.
An extraordinary feeling of oppression had slowly filled

D

the air. The lamps, swinging on the pavilion roof tree, flickered and flared, alternately rising and sinking like the life in the eyes of a dying man.

All the while the lady sat still on the couch, with an expression of amused contempt on her face. But now she rose to her feet.

"And I also ask, in the name of the King of France, by what right do you intrude within the precincts of a lady's bower. I bid you to leave me!"

She pointed imperiously with her white finger to the black, oblong doorway, from which Malise's rude hand had dragged the covering flap to the ground.

But the churchman and his guide stood their ground.

Suddenly the Abbot reached a hand and took the sword on which the master armourer leaned. With its point he drew a wide circle upon the rich carpets which formed the floor of the pavilion.

"William Douglas," he said, "I command you to come within this circle, whilst in the right of my holy office I exorcise that demon there who hath so nearly beguiled you to your ruin."

The lady laughed a rich ringing laugh.

"These are indeed high heroics for so plain and poor an occasion. I need not to utter a word of explanation. I am a lady travelling peaceably under escort of an ambassador of France, through a Christian country. By chance, I met the Earl Douglas, and invited him to sup with me. What concern, spiritual or temporal, may that be of yours, most reverend Abbot? Who made you my lord Earl's keeper?"

"Woman or demon from the pit!" said the Abbot, sternly, "think not to deceive William Douglas, the aged, as you have cast the glamour over William Douglas, the boy. The lust of the flesh abideth no more for ever in this frail tabernacle. I bid thee, let the lad go, for he is dear to me as mine own soul. Let him go, I say, ere I curse thee with the curse of God the Almighty!"

The lady continued to smile, standing meantime slender and fair before them, her bosom heaving a little with emotion, and her hair rippling in red gold confusion down her back.

"Certainly, my lord Earl came not upon compulsion. He is free to return with you, if he yet be under tutors and governors, or afraid of the master's stripes. Go, Earl William, I made a mistake; I thought you had been a man. But since I was wrong I bid you get back to the monk's chapter house, to clerkly copies and childish toys."

Then black and sullen anger glared from the eyes of the Douglas.

"Get hence," he cried. "Hence, both of you — you, Uncle William, ere I forget your holy office and your kinsmanship; you, Malise, that I may settle with to-morrow ere the sun sets. I swear it by my word as a Douglas. I will never forgive either of you for this night's work!"

The fair white hand was laid upon his wrist.

"Nay," said the lady, "do not quarrel with those you love for my poor sake. I am indeed little worth the trouble. Go back with them in peace, and forget her who but sat by your side an hour neither doing you harm nor thinking it."

"Nay," he cried, "that will I not. I will show them that I am old enough to choose my company for myself.

Who is my uncle that he should dictate to me that am an earl of Douglas and a peer of France, or my servant that he should come forth to spy upon his master?"

"Then," she whispered, smiling, "you will indeed abide with me?"

He gave her his hand.

"I will abide with you till death! Body and soul, I am yours alone!"

"By the holy cross of our Lord, that shall you not!" cried Malise; "not though you hang me high as Haman for this ere the morrow's morn!"

And with these words he sprang forward and caught his master by the wrist. With one strong pull of his mighty arm he dragged him within the circle which the Abbot had marked out with the sword's point.

The lady seemed to change colour. For at that moment a gust of wind caused the lamps to flicker, and the outlines of her white-robed figure appeared to waver like an image cast in water.

"I adjure and command you, in the name of God the One and Omnipotent, to depart to your own place, spirit or devil or whatever you may be!"

The voice of the Abbot rose high above the roaring of the bursting storm without. The lady seemed to reach an arm across the circle as if even yet to take hold of the young man. The Abbot thrust forward his crucifix.

And then the bolt of God fell. The whole pavilion was illuminated with a flash of light so intense and white that it appeared to blind and burn up all about. The lady was seen no more. The silken covering blazed up. Malise plunged outward into the darkness of the storm, carrying his young master lightly as a child in his arms, while the Abbot kept his feet behind him like a boat in a ship's wake. The thunder roared overhead like the sea bellowing in a cave's mouth, and the great pines bent their heads away from the mighty wind, straining and creaking and lashing each other in their blind fury.

Malise and the Abbot seemed to hear about them the plunging of riderless horses as they stumbled downwards through the night, their path lit by lightning flashes, green and lilac and keenest blue, and bearing between them the senseless form of William Earl of Douglas.

CHAPTER VI

THE PRISONING OF MALISE THE SMITH

[Now these things, material to the life and history of William, sixth Earl of Douglas, are not written from hearsay, but were chronicled within his lifetime by one who saw them and had part therein, though the part was but a boy's one. His manuscript has come down to us and lies before the transcriber. Sholto MacKim, the son of Malise the Smith, testifies to these things in his own clerkly script. He adds particularly that his brother Laurence, being at the time but a boy, had little knowledge of many of the actual facts, and is not to be believed if at any time he should controvert anything which he (Sholto) has written. So far, however, as the present collector and editor can find out, Laurence MacKim appears to have been entirely silent on the subject, at least with his pen, so that his brother's caveat was superfluous.]

* * * * * *

The instant Lord William entered his own castle of Thrieve over the drawbridge, and without even returning the salutations of his guard, he turned about to the two men who had so masterfully compelled his return.

" Ho, guard, there ! " he cried, " seize me this instant the Abbot of the New Abbey and Malise MacKim."

And so much surprised but wholly obedient, twenty

archers of the Earl's guard, commanded by old John of
Abernethy, called Landless Jock, fell in at back and
front.

Malise, the master armourer, stood silent, taking the
matter with his usual phlegm, but the Abbot was
voluble.

"William," he said, holding out his hands with an
appealing gesture, "I have laboured with you, striven
with, prayed for you. To-night I came forth through
the storm, though an old man, to deliver you from the
manifest snares of the devil —"

But the Earl interrupted his recital without compunc-
tion.

"Set Malise MacKim in the inner dungeon," he cried.
"Thrust his feet into the great stocks, and let my lord
Abbot be warded safely in the castle chapel. He is little
likely to be disturbed there at his devotions."

"Aye, my lord, it shall be done!" said Landless Jock,
shaking his head, however, with gloomy foreboding, as
the haughty young Earl in his wet and torn disarray
flashed past him without further notice of the two men
whom the might of his bare word had committed to
prison. The Earl sprang up the narrow turret stairs,
passing as he did so through the vaulted hall of the
men-at-arms, where more than a hundred stout archers
and spearmen sat carousing and singing, even at that
advanced hour of the night, while as many more lay
about the corridors or on the wooden shelves which they
used for sleeping upon, and which folded back against
the wall during the day. At the first glimpse of their
young master, every man left awake among them struggled to his feet, and stood stiffly propped, drunk or sober

according to his condition, with his eyes turned towards the door which gave upon the turnpike stair. But with a slight wave of his hand the Earl passed on to his own apartment.

Here he found his faithful body-servant, René le Blesois, stretched across the threshold. The staunch Frenchman rose mechanically at the noise of his master's footsteps, and, though still soundly asleep, stood with the latch of the door in his hand, and the other held stiffly to his brow in salutation.

Left to his own devices, Lord William Douglas would doubtless have cast himself, wet as he was, upon his bed had not Le Blesois, observing his lord's plight even in his own sleep-dulled condition, entered the chamber after his master and, without question or speech, silently begun to relieve him of his wet hunting dress. A loose chamber gown of rich red cloth, lined with silk and furred with "cristy" grey, hung over the back of an oaken chair, and into this the young Earl flung himself in black and sullen anger.

Le Blesois, still without a word spoken, left the room with the wet clothes over his arm. As he did so a small object rolled from some fold or crevice of the doublet, where it had been safely lodged till displaced by the loosening of the belt, or the removing of the banderole of his master's hunting horn.

Le Blesois turned at the tinkling sound, and would have stopped to lift it up after the manner of a careful servitor. But the eye of his lord was upon the fallen object, and with an abrupt wave of his hand towards the door, and the single word "Go!" the Earl dismissed his body-servant from the room.

Then rising hastily from his chair, he took the trinket in his hand and carried it to the well-trimmed lamp which stood in a niche that held a golden crucifix.

The Lord Douglas saw lying in his palm a ring of singular design. The main portion was formed of the twisting bodies of a pair of snakes, the jewel work being very cunningly interlaced and perfectly finished. Their eyes were set with rubies, and between their open mouths they carried an opal, shaped like a heart. The stone was translucent and faintly luminous like a moonstone, but held in its heart one fleck of ruby red, in appearance like a drop of blood. By some curious trick of light, in whatever position the ring was held, this drop still appeared to be on the point of detaching itself and falling to the ground.

Earl William examined it in the flicker of the lamp. He turned it every way, narrowly searching inside the golden band for a posy, but not a word of any language could he find engraved upon it.

"I saw the ring upon her hand — I am certain I saw it on her hand!" He said these words over and over to himself. "It is then no dream that I have dreamed."

There came a low knocking at the door, a rustling and a whispering without. Instantly the Earl thrust the ring upon his own finger with the opal turned inward, and, with the dark anger mark of his race strongly dinted upon his fair young brow, he faced the unseen intruder.

"Who is there?" he cried loudly and imperiously.

The door opened with a rasping of the iron latch, and a little girlish figure clothed from head to foot in a white night veil danced in. She clapped her hands at sight of him.

"You are come back," she cried; "and you have so fine a gown on too. But Maud Lindesay says it is very wrong to be out of doors so late, even if you are Earl of Douglas, and a great man now. Will you never play at 'Catch-as-catch-can' with David and me any more?"

"Margaret," said the young Earl, "what do you away from your chamber at all? Our mother will miss you, and I do not want her here to-night. Go back at once!"

But the little wilful maiden, catching her skirts in her hands at either side and raising them a little way from the ground, began to dance a dainty *pas seul*, ending with a flashing whirl and a low bow in the direction of her audience.

At this William Douglas could not choose but smile, and soon threw himself down on the bed, setting his clasped hands behind his head, and contenting himself with looking at his little sister.

Though at this time but eight years of age, Margaret of Douglas was possessed of such extraordinary vitality and character that she seemed more like eleven. She had the clear-cut, handsome Douglas face, the pale olive skin, the flashing dark eyes, and the crisp, blue-black hair of her brother. A lithe grace and quickness, like those of a beautiful wild animal, were characteristic of every movement.

"Our mother hath been anxious about you, brother mine," said the little girl, tiring suddenly of her dance, and leaping upon the other end of the couch on which her brother was reclining. Establishing herself opposite him, she pulled the coverlet up about her so that presently only her face could be seen peeping out from under the silken folds.

"Oh, I was so cold, but I am warmer now," she cried. "And if Maid Betsy A'hannay comes to take me away, I want you to stretch out your hand like this, and say: 'Seneschal, remove that besom to the deep dungeon beneath the castle moat,' as we used to do in our plays before you became a great man. Then I could stay very long and talk to you all through the night, for Maud Lindesay sleeps so sound that nothing can awake her."

Gradually the anger passed out of the face of William Douglas as he listened to his sister's prattle, like the vapours from the surface of a hill tarn when the sun rises in his strength. He even thought with some self-reproach of his treatment of Malise and of his uncle the Abbot. But a glance at the ring on his finger, and the thought of what might have been his good fortune at that moment but for their interference, again hardened his resolution to adamant within his breast.

His sister's voice, clear and high in its childish treble, recalled him to himself.

"Oh, William, and there is such news; I forgot, because I have been so overbusied with arranging my new puppet's house that Malise made for me. But scarcely were you gone away on Black Darnaway ere a messenger came from our granduncle James at Avondale that he and my cousins Will and James arrive to-morrow at the Thrieve with a company to attend the wappenshaw."

The young man sprang to his feet, and dashed one hand into the palm of the other.

"This is ill tidings indeed!" he cried. " What does

the Fat Flatterer at Castle Thrieve? If he comes
to pay homage, it will be but a mockery. Neither he
nor Angus had ever any good-will to my father, and they
have none to me."

"Ah, do not be angry, William," cried the little maid.
"It will be beautiful. They will come at a fitting time.
For to-morrow is the great levy of the weapon-showing,
and our cousins will see you in your pride. And they
will see me, too, in my best green sarcenet, riding on a
white palfrey at your side as you promised."

"A weapon-showing is not a place for little girls,"
said the Earl, mollified in spite of himself, casting himself down again on the couch, and playing with the serpent ring on his finger.

"Ah, now," cried his sister, her quick eyes dancing
everywhere at once, "you are not attending to a single
word I say. I know by your voice that you are not.
That is a pretty ring you have. Did a lady give it to
you? Was it our Maudie? I think it must have been
our Maud. She has many beautiful things, but mostly
it is the young men who wish to give her such things.
She never sends any of them back, but keeps them in
a box, and says that it is good to spoil the Egyptians.
And sometimes when I am tired she will tell me the
history of each, and whether he was dark or fair. Or
make it all up just as good when she forgets. But, oh,
William, if I were a lady I should fall in love with
nobody but you. For you are so handsome — yes,
nearly as handsome as I am myself — (she passed her
hands lightly through her curls as she spoke). And
you know I shall marry no one but a Douglas — only
you must not ask me to wed my cousin William of

Avondale, for he is so stern and solemn; besides, he has always a book in his pocket, and wishes me to learn somewhat out of it as if I were a monk. A Douglas should not be a monk, he should be a soldier."

So she lay snugly on the bed and prattled on to her brother, who, buried in his thoughts and occupied with his ring, let the hours slip on till at the open door of the Earl's chamber there appeared the most bewitching face in the world, as many in that castle and elsewhere were ready to prove at the sword's point. The little girl caught sight of it with a shrill cry of pleasure, instantly checked and hushed, however, at the thought of her mother.

"O Maudie," she cried, "come hither into William's room. He has such a beautiful ring that a lady gave him. I am sure a lady gave it him. Was it you, Maud Lindesay? You are a sly puss not to tell me if it was. William, it is wicked and provoking of you not to tell me who gave you that ring. If it had been some one you were not ashamed of, you would be proud of the gift and confess. Whisper to me who it was. I will not tell any one, not even Maudie."

Her brother had risen to his feet with a quick movement, girding his red gown about him as he rose.

"Mistress Maud," he said respectfully, "I fear I have given you anxiety by detaining your charge so late. But she is a wilful madam, as you have doubtless good cause to know, and ill to advise."

"She is a Douglas," smiled the fair girl, who stood at the chamber door refusing his invitation to enter, with a flash of the eye and a quick shake of the head which betokened no small share of the same qualities; "is not that enough to excuse her for being wayward and headstrong?"

Earl William wasted no more words of entreaty upon his sister, but seized her in his arms, and pulling the coverlet in which she had huddled herself up with her pert chin on her knees, more closely about her, he strode along the passage with her in his arms till he stopped at an open door leading into a large chamber which looked to the south.

"There," he said, smiling at the girl who had followed behind him, "I will lock her in with you and take the key, that I may make sure of two such uncertain charges."

But the girl had deftly extracted the key even as she passed in after him, and as the bolts shot from within she cried: "I thank you right courteously, Lord William, but mine apothecary, fearing that the air of this isle of Thrieve might not agree with me, bade me ever to sleep with the key of the door under my pillow. Against fevers and quinsies, cold iron is a sovereign specific."

And for all his wounded heart, Earl William smiled at the girl's sauciness as he went slowly back to his chamber, taking, in spite of his earldom, pains to pass his mother's door on tiptoe.

CHAPTER VII

THE day of the great weapon-showing broke fair and clear after the storm of the night. The windows of heaven had had all their panes cleaned, and even after it was daylight the brighter stars appeared — only, however, to wink out again when the sun arose and shone on the wet fields, coming forth rejoicing like a bridegroom from his chamber.

And equally bright and strong came forth the young Earl, every trace of the anger and disappointment of the night having been removed from his face, if not from his mind, by the recreative and potent sleep of youth and health.

In the hall he called for Sir John of Abernethy, nick-named Landless Jock.

"Conduct my uncle the Abbot from the chapel where he has been all night at his devotions, to his chamber, and furnish him with what he may require, and bring up Malise the Smith from the dungeon. Let him come into my presence in the upper hall."

William Douglas went into a large oak-ceiled chamber, wide and high, running across the castle from side to side, and with windows that looked every way over the broad and fertile strath of Dee.

Presently, with a trampling of mailed feet and the double rattle which denoted the grounding of a pair of

47

steel-hilted partisans, Malise was brought to the door by two soldiers of the Earl's outer guard.

The huge bulk of Brawny Kim filled up the doorway almost completely, and he stood watching the Douglas with an unmoved gravity which, in the dry wrinkles about his eyes, almost amounted to humorous appreciation of the situation.

Yet it was Malise who spoke first. For at his appearance the Earl had turned his back upon his retainer, and now stood at the window that looks towards the north, from which he could see, over the broad and placid stretches of the river, the men putting up the pavilions and striking spears into the ground to mark out the spaces for the tourney of the next day.

"A fair good morrow to you, my lord," said the smith. "Grievous as my sin has been, and just as is your resentment, give me leave to say that I have suffered more than my deserts from the ill-made chains and uncouth manacles wherewith they confined me in the black dungeon down there. I trow they must have been the workmanship of Ninian Lamont the Highlandman, who dares to call himself house-smith of Thrieve. I am ready to die if it be your will, my lord; but if you are well advised you will hang Ninian beside me with a bracelet of his own rascal handiwork about his neck. Then shall justice be satisfied, and Malise MacKim will die happy."

The Earl turned and looked at his ancient friend. The wrinkles about the brow were deeply ironical now, and the grey eyes of the master armourer twinkled with appreciation of his jest.

"Malise," cried his master, warningly, "do not play at

cat's cradle with the Douglas. You might tempt me to
that I should afterwards be sorry for. A man once dead
comes not to life again, whatever monks prate. But tell
me, how knew you whither I had gone yester-even?
For, indeed, I knew not myself when I set out. And in
any event, was it a thing well done for my foster father
to spy upon me the son who was also his lord?"

The anger was mostly gone now out of the frank
young face of the Earl, and only humiliation and resentment, with a touch of boyish curiosity, remained.

"Indeed," answered the smith, "I watched you not
save under my hand as you rode away upon Black Darnaway, and then I turned me to the seat by the wall to
listen to the cavillings of Dame Barbara, the humming
of the bees, and the other comfortable and composing
sounds of nature."

"How then did you come to follow me in the unde-
sirable company of my uncle the Abbot?"

"For that you are in the debt of my son Sholto, who,
seeing a lady wait for you in the greenwood, climbed a
tree, and there from amongst the branches he was witness
of your encounter."

"So —" said the Douglas, grimly, "it is to Master
Sholto that I am indebted somewhat."

"Aye," said his father, "do not forget him. For he
is a good lad and a bold, as indeed he proved to the
hilt yestreen."

"In what consisted his boldness?" asked the Earl.

"In that he dared come home to me with a cock-and-
bull story of a witch lady, who appeared suddenly where
none had been a moment before, and who had immediately enchanted my lord Earl. Well nigh did I

E

twist his neck, but he stuck to it.   Then came riding
by my lord Abbot on his way to Thrieve, and I judged
that the matter, as one of witchcraft, was more his affair
than mine."

"Now hearken," cried the Earl, in quick, high tones
of anger, "let there be no more of such folly, or on your
life be it.   The lady whom you insulted was travelling
with her company through Galloway from France.   She
invited me to sup with her, and dared me to adventure
to Edinburgh in her company.   Answer me, wherein
was the witchcraft of that, saving the witchery natural
to all fair women?"

"Did she not prophesy to you that to-day you would
be Duke of Touraine, and receive the ambassadors of
the King of France?"

"Well," said the Earl, "where is your wit that you
give ear to such babblings?   Did she not come from
that country, as I tell you, and who should hear the
latest news more readily than she?"

The smith looked a little nonplussed, but stuck to it
stoutly that none but a witch woman would ride alone
at nightfall upon a Galloway moor, or unless by enchantment set up a pavilion of silk and strange devices
under the pines of Loch Roan.

"Well," said Earl William, feeling his advantage
and making the most of it, "I see that in all my little
love affairs I must needs take my master armourer
with me to decide whether or no the lady be a witch.
He shall resolve for me all spiritual questions with his
forehammer.   Malise MacKim a witch pricker!   Ha
— this is a change indeed.   Malise the Smith will make
the censor of his lord's love affairs, after what certain

comrades of his have told me of his own ancient love-makings. Will he deign to come to the weapon-showing to-day, and instead of examining the swords and halberts, the French arbalasts and German fusils, demit that part of his office to Ninian the Highlandman, and go peering into ladies' eyes for sorceries and scanning their lips for such signs of the devil as lurk in the dimples of their chins? In this he will find much employment and that of a congenial sort."

Malise was vanquished, less by the sarcasm of the Earl than by the fear that perhaps the Highlandman might indeed have his place of honour as chief military expert by his master's right hand at the examination of weapons that day on the green holms of Balmaghie.

"I may have been overhasty, my lord," he said hesitatingly, "but still do I think that the woman was far from canny."

The Earl laughed and, turning him about by the shoulders, gave him a push down the stair, crying, "Oh, Malise, Malise, have you lived so long in the world without finding out that a beautiful woman is always uncanny!"

The levy that day of clansmen owning fealty to the Douglas was no hasty or local one. It was not, indeed, a "rising of the countryside," such as took place when the English were reported to be over the border, when the beacon fires were thrown west from Criffel to Screel, from Screel to Cairnharrow, and then tossed northward by the three Cairnsmuirs and topmost Merrick far over the uplands of Kyle, till from the sullen brow of Brown Carrick the bale fire set the town drum of Ayr beating its alarming note. Still this muster was a day on which

every Douglas vassal must ride in mail with all his
spears behind him — or bide at home and take the
consequences.

All the night from distant parishes and outlying
valleys horsemen had been riding, clothed in complete
panoply of mail. These were the knights, barons, free-
holders, who owned allegiance to the house of Douglas.
Each lord was followed by his appointed tail of esquires
and men-at-arms; behind these dense clusters of heavily
armed spearmen marched steadily along the easiest
paths by the waterside and over the lower hill passes.
Light running footmen slung their swords over their
backs by leathern bandoliers and pricked it briskly
southwards over the bent so brown. Archers there
were from the border towards the Solway side — lithe
men, accustomed to spring from tussock to tuft of shaking grass, whose long strides and odd spasmodic side
leapings betrayed even on the plain and unyielding
pasture lands the place of their amphibious nativity.

"The Jack herons of Lochar," these were named by
the men of Galloway. But there was no jeering to their
faces, for not one of those Maxwells, Sims, Patersons,
and Dicksons would have thought twice of leaping behind
a tree stump to wing a cloth-yard shaft into a scoffer's
ribs at thirty yards, taking his chance of the dule tree
and the hempen cord thereafter for the honour of
Lochar.

CHAPTER VIII

THE CROSSING OF THE FORD

It was still early morning of the great day, when Sholto and Laurence MacKim, leaving their mother in the kitchen, and their young sister Magdalen trying a yet prettier knot to her kerchief, took their way by the fords of Glen Lochar to an eminence then denominated plainly the Whinny Knowe, the same which afterwards gained and has kept to this day the more fatal designation of Knock Cannon. The lads were dressed as became the sons of so prosperous a craftsman (and master armourer to boot) as Malise MacKim of the Carlinwark.

Laurence, the younger, wore his archer's jack over the suit of purple velvet, high boots of yellow leather, and, withal, a dainty cap set far back on his head, from which sprouted the wing of a blackcock in as close imitation as Master Laurence dared compass of the Earl Douglas himself. His bow was slung at his back all ready for the inspection. A sash of orange silk was twisted about his slim waist, and in this he would set his thumb knowingly, and stare boldly as often as the pair of brothers overtook a pretty girl. For Master Laurence loved beauty, and thought not lightly of his own.

Sholto, though, as we shall soon see, despised not love, had eyes more for the knights and men-at-arms, and considered that his heaven would be fully attained as soon as he should ride one of those great prancing horses, and carry a lance with the pennon of the Douglas upon it.

Meanwhile he wore the steel cap of the home guard, the ringed neck mail, the close-fitting doublet of blue dotted over with red Douglas hearts and having the white cross of St. Andrew transversely upon it. About his waist was a peaked brace of shining plate armour, damascened in gold by Malise himself, and filling out his almost girlish waist to manlier proportions. From this depended a row of tags of soft leather. Close chain-mail covered his legs, to which at the knees were added caps of triple plate. A sheaf of arrows in a blue and gold quiver on his right side, a sword of metal on his left, and a short Scottish bow in his hand completed the attire of a fully equipped and efficient archer of the Earl's guard.

The lads were soon at the fords of Lochar, where in the dry summers the stones show all the way across — one in the midst being named the Black Douglas, noted as the place where, as tradition affirms, Archibald the Grim used to pause in crossing the ford to look at his new fortress of Thrieve, rising on its impregnable island above the rich water meadows.

Now neither Sholto nor Laurence wished to wet their leg array before the work and pageant of the day began. This was the desire of Laurence, because of the maids who would assemble on the Boreland Braes, and of Sholto inasmuch as he hoped to win the prize for the best accoutrement and the most point-device attiring among all the archers of the Earl's guard. The young

men had asked crusty Simon Conchie, the boatman at
the Ferry Croft, to set them over, offering him a groat
for his pains. But he was far too busy to pay any attention to mere silver coin on such an occasion, only pausing long enough to cry to them that they must e'en cross
at the fords, as many of their betters would do that day.

There was nothing for it, therefore, but either to strip
to the waist or to wait the chances of the traffic. Both
Sholto and Laurence were exceedingly loath to take the
former course. They had not, however, long to hesitate,
for a train of sumpter mules, belonging to the Lord Herries of Terregles, whose father had been with Archibald
the Tineman in France, came up laden with the choicest
products of the border country which he designed to offer
as part of the "Service-Kane" to his overlord, the Earl
of Douglas.

Now mules are all of them snorting, ill-conditioned
brutes, and are ever ready to run away upon the least
excuse, or even without any. So as soon as those of Lord
Herries' train caught the glint of Sholto's blue baldric
and shining steel girdle-brace appearing suddenly from
behind a knoll, they incontinently bolted every way with
noses to the ground, scattering packs and brandishing
heels like young colts turned out to grass. It chanced
that one of the largest mules made directly towards the
fords of Lochar, and the youths, catching the flying bridle
at either side, applied a sort of brake which sufficiently
slowed the beast's movements to enable such agile skip-
jacks as Sholto and Laurence to mount. But as they
were concerned more with their leaping from the ground
than with what was already upon the animal's back, their
heads met with a crash in the midst, in which collision

the superior weight of the younger had very naturally
the better of the encounter.

Sholto dropped instantly back to the ground. He was
somewhat stunned by the blow, but the sight of his
brother triumphantly splashing through the shallows
aroused him. He arose, and seizing the first stone that
came to hand hurled it after Laurence, swearing frater-
nally that he would smite him in the brisket with a dirk
as soon as he caught him for that dastard blow. The
first stone flew wide, though the splash caused the mule
to shy into deeper water, to the damping of his rider's
legs. But the second, being better aimed, took the animal fairly on the rump, and, fetching up on a fly-galled
spot, frightened it with bumping bags and loud squeals
into the woods of Glen Lochar, which come down close
to the fords on every side. Here presently Laurence
found himself, like Absalom, caught in the branches of
a beech, and left hanging between heaven and earth.
A rider in complete plate of black mail caught him down,
still holding on to his bow, and, placing him across the
saddle, brought down the flat of his gauntleted hand
upon a spot of the lad's person which, being uncovered
by mail, responded with a resounding smack. Then,
amid the boisterous laughter of the men-at-arms, he let
Laurence slip to the ground.

But the younger son of Brawny Kim, master armourer
of Carlinwark, was not the lad to take such an insult
meekly, even from a man-at-arms riding on horseback.
He threw his bow into the nearest thicket, and seizing
the most convenient ammunition, which chanced to be
in great plenty that day upon the braes of Balmaghie,
pursued his insulter along the glade with such excellent

aim and good effect that the black unadorned armour of
the horseman showed disks of defilement all over, like a
tree trunk covered with toadstool growths.

"Shoot down the intolerable young rascal! Shall he
thus beard my Lord Maxwell?" cried a voice from the
troop which witnessed the chase. And more than one
bow was bent, and several hand-fusils levelled from the
company which followed behind.

But the injured knight threw up his visor.

"Hold, there!" he cried, "the boy is right. It was I
who insulted him, and he did right to be revenged, though
the rogue's aim is more to be admired than his choice of
weapons. Come hither, lad. Tell me who thou art, and
what is thy father's quality?"

"I am Laurence MacKim, an archer of my lord's
guard, and the younger son of Malise MacKim, master
armourer to the Douglas."

Laurence, being still angry, rang out his titles as if
they had been inscribed in the book of the Lion-King-at-
Arms.

"Saints save us," cried the knight in swart armour,
"all that!"

Then, seeing the boy ready to answer back still more
fiercely, he continued with a courteous wave of the
hand.

"I humbly ask your pardon, Master Laurence. I am
glad the son of Brawny Kim hath no small part of his
father's spirit. Will you take service and be my esquire,
as becomes well a lad of parts who desires to win his
way to a knighthood?"

The heart of Laurence MacKim beat quickly — a horse
to ride — an esquire — perhaps if he had luck and much

fighting, a knighthood. Nevertheless, he answered with a bold straight look out of his black eyes.

"I am an archer of my lord Douglas' outer guard. I can have no promotion save from him or those of his house — not even from the King himself."

"Well said!" cried the knight; "small wonder that the Douglas is the greatest man in Scotland. I will speak to the Earl William this day concerning you."

Lord Maxwell rode on at the head of his company with a courteous salutation, which not a few behind him who had heard the colloquy imitated. Laurence stood there with his heart working like yeast within him, and his colour coming and going to think what he had been offered and what he had refused.

"God's truth," he said to himself, "I might have been a great man if I had chosen, while Sholto, that old sober sides, was left lagging behind."

Then he looked about for his bow and went swaggering along as if he were already Sir Laurence and the leader of an army.

But Nemesis was upon him, and that in the fashion which his pride would feel the most.

"Take that, beast of a Laurence!" cried a voice behind him.

And the lad received a jolt from behind which loosened his teeth in their sockets and discomposed the dignified stride with which in imagination he was commanding the armies of the Douglas.

CHAPTER IX

LAURENCE SINGS A HYMN

LAURENCE turned and beheld his brother. In another
instant the two young men had clinched and were rolling
on the ground, wrestling and striking according to their
ability. Sholto might easily have had the best of the
fray, but for the temper aroused by Laurence's recent
degradation, for the elder brother was taller by an inch,
and of a frame of body more lithe and supple. Moreover, the accuracy of Sholto MacKim's shape and the
severe training of the smithy had not left a superfluous
ounce of flesh on him anywhere.

In a minute the brothers had become the centre of a
riotous, laughing throng of varlets — archers seeking
their corps, and young squires sent by their lords to find
out the exact positions allotted to each contingent by the
provost of the camp. For as the wappenshaw was to be
of three days' duration in all its nobler parts, a wilderness of tents had already begun to arise under the scattered white thorns of the great Boreland Croft which
stretched up from the river.

These laughed and jested after their kind, encouraging
the youths to fight it out, and naming Laurence the
brock or badger from his stoutness, and the slim Sholto
the whitterick or, as one might say, weasel.

"At him, Whitterick — grip him! Grip him! Now
you have him at the pinch! Well pulled, Brock! 'Tis

a certainty for Brock — good Brock! Well done — well
done! Ah, would you? Hands off that dagger! Let
fisticuffs settle it! The Whitterick hath it — the Whitterick!"

And thus ran the comment. Sholto being cumbered
with his armour, Laurence might in time have gotten the
upper grip. But at this moment a diversion occurred
which completely altered the character of the conflict.
A stout, reddish young man came up, holding in his
hand a staff painted with twining stripes of white and
red, which showed him to be the marshal of that part
of the camp which pertained to the Earl of Angus. He
looked on for a moment from the skirts of the crowd,
and then elbowed his way self-importantly into the
centre, till he stood immediately above Laurence and
Sholto.

"What means this hubbub, I say? Quit your hold
there and come with me; my Lord of Angus will settle
this dispute."

He had come up just when the young men were in the
final grips, when Sholto had at last gotten his will of his
brother's head, and was, as the saying is, giving him
"Dutch spice" in no very knightly fashion.

The Angus marshal, seeing this, seized Sholto by the
collar of his mailed shirt, and drawing him suddenly
back, caused him to lose hold of his brother, who as
quickly rose to his feet. The red man began to beat
Sholto about the headpiece right heartily with his staff,
which exercise made a great ringing noise, though naturally, the skull cap being the work of Malise MacKim,
little harm ensued to the head enclosed therein.

But Master Laurence was instantly on fire.

"Here, Foxy-face," he cried, "let my brother a-be! What business is it of yours if two gentlemen have a difference? Go back to your Angus kernes and ragged craw-bogle Highland folk!"

Meanwhile Sholto had recovered from his surprise, and the crowd of varlets was melting apace, thinking the Angus marshal some one of consequence. But the brothers MacKim were not the lads to take beating with a stick meekly, and the provost, who indeed had nothing to do with the Galloway part of the encampment, had far better have confined his officiousness to his own quarters.

"Take him on the right, Sholto," cried Laurence, "and I will have at him from this side." The Red Angus drew his sword and threatened forthwith to slay the lads if they came near him. But with a spring like that of a grey Grimalkin of the woods, Sholto leapt within his guard ere he had time to draw back his arm for thrust or parry, and at the same moment Laurence, snatching the red and white staff out of his hand, dealt him so sturdy a clout between the shoulders that, though he was of weight equal to both of his opponents taken together, he was knocked breathless at the first blow and went down beneath the impetus of Sholto's attack.

Laurence coolly disengaged his brother, and began to thrash the Angus man with his own staff upon all exposed parts, till the dry wood broke. Then he threw the pieces at his head, and the two brothers went off arm in arm to find a woody covert in which to repair damages against the weapon-showing, and the inspection of their lord and his keen-eyed master armourer.

As soon as they had discovered such a sequestered

holt, Laurence, who had frequent experience of such rough-and-tumble encounters, stripped off his doublet of purple velvet, and, turning the sleeve inside out, he showed his brother that it was lined with a rough-sur- faced felt cloth almost of the nature of teasle. This being rubbed briskly upon any dusty garment or fouled armour proved most excellent for restoring its pristine gloss and beauty. The young men, being as it were born to the trade and knowing that their armament must meet their father's inexorable eye, as he passed along their lines with the Earl, rubbed and polished their best, and when after half an hour's sharp work each examined the other, not a speck or stain was left to tell of the various casual incidents of the morning. Two bright, fresh-coloured youths emerged from their thicket, immaculately clad, and with countenances of such cherubic innocence, that my lord the Abbot William of the great Cistercian Abbey of Dulce Cor, looking upon them as with bare bowed heads they knelt reverently on one knee to ask his bless- ing, said to his train, "They look for all the world like young angels! It is a shame and a sin that two such fair innocents should be compelled to join in aught ruder than the chanting of psalms in holy service."

Whereat one of his company, who had been witness to their treatment of the Angus provost and also of Lau- rence's encounter with the knight of the black armour, was seized incontinently with a fit of coughing which almost choked him.

"Bless you, my sons," said the Abbot, "I will speak to my nephew, the Earl, concerning you. Your faces plead for you. Evil cannot dwell in such fair bodies. What are your names?"

The younger knelt with his fingers joined and his eyes meekly on the grass, while Sholto, who had risen, stood quietly by with his steel cap in his hand.

"Laurence MacKim," answered the younger, modestly, without venturing to raise his eyes from the ground, "and this is my brother Sholto."

"Can you sing, pretty boy?" said the Abbot to Laurence.

"We have never been taught," answered downright Sholto. But his brother, feeling that he was losing chances, broke in:

"I can sing, if it please your holiness."

"And what can you sing, sweet lad?" asked the Abbot, smiling with expectation and setting his hand to his best ear to assist his increasing deafness.

"Shut your fool's mouth!" said Sholto under his breath to his brother.

"Shut your own! 'Tis ugly as a rat-trap at any rate!" responded Laurence in the same key. Then aloud to the Abbot he said, "An it please you, sir, I can sing 'O Mary Quean!'"

The Abbot smiled, well pleased.

"Ah, exceeding proper, a song to the honour of the Queen of Heaven (he devoutly crossed himself at the name), — I knew that I could not be mistaken in you."

"Your pardon, most reverend," interjected Sholto, anxiously, "please you to excuse my brother; his voice hath just broken and he cannot sing at present." Then, under his breath, he added, "Laurie MacKim, you God-forgotten fool, if you sing that song you will get us both stripped in a thrice and whipped on the bare back for insolence to the Earl's uncle!"

"Go to," said his brother, "I *will* sing.   The old cock is monstrous deaf at any rate."

"Sing," said the Abbot, "I would hear you gladly. So fair a face must be accompanied by the pipe of a nightingale.   Besides, we sorely need a tenor for the choir at Sweetheart."

So, encouraged in this fashion, the daring Laurence began :

> " *Nae priests aboot me shall be seen*
> *To mumble prayers baith morn and e'en,*
> *I'll swap them a' for Mary Quean !*
> *I'll bid nae mess for me be sung,*
> *Dies ille, dies iræ,*
> *Nor clanking bells for me be rung,*
> *Sic semper solet fieri !*
> *I'll gang my ways to Mary Quean.*"

"Ah, very good, very good, truly," said the Abbot, thrusting his hand into his pouch beneath his gown, "here are two gold nobles for thee, sweet lad, and another for your brother, whose countenance methinks is somewhat less sweet.   You have sung well to the praise of our Lady !   What did you say your name was ?   Of a surety, we must have you at Sweetheart.   And you have the Latin, too, as I heard in the hymn.   It is a thing most marvellous.   Verily, the very unction of grace must have visited you in your cradle ! "

Laurence held down his head with all his native modesty, but the more open Sholto grew red in the face, hearing behind him the tittering and shoulder-shaking of the priests and lay servants in the Abbot's train, and being sure that they would inform their master as soon as he passed on concerning the true import of Master Laurence's song.   He was muttering in a rapid recitative,

"Oh, wait — wait, Laurie MacKim, till I get you on the Carlinwark shore. A sore back and a stiff skinful of bones shalt thou have, and not an inch of hide on thee that is not black and blue. Amen!" he added, stopping his maledictions quickly, for at that moment the Abbot came somewhat abruptly to the end of his speech.

The great churchman rode away on his fair white mule, with a smile and a backward wave of his hand.

"I will speak to my nephew concerning you this very day, my child," he cried.

And the countenance of that most gentle youth kept its sweet innocence and angelic grace to the last, but that of Sholto was more dark and frowning than ever.

F

CHAPTER X

By ten of the clock the braes of Balmaghie were a sight most glorious to look upon. Well nigh twelve thousand men were gathered there, of whom five thousand were well-mounted knights and fully equipped men-at-arms, every man of them ready and willing to couch a lance or ride a charge.

The line of the tents which had been set up extended from opposite the Castle island of Thrieve to the kirk hill of Balmaghie. Every knight's following was strictly kept within its own pale, or fence of green wands set basket-wise, pointed and thrust into the earth like the spring traps of those who catch mowdiewarts. Many also were the quarrels and bickerings of the squires who had been sent forward to choose and arrange the several encampments. Nor were rough and tumble fights such as we have seen the MacKims indulging in, thought derogatory to the dignity of any, save belted knights only.

Each camp displayed the device of its own lord, but higher than all, from the top of every mound and broomy hillock floated the banner of the overlord. This was the lion of Galloway, white on a ground of blue, and beneath it, but on the same staff, a pennon whereon was the bleeding heart of the Douglas family.

The lists were set up on the level meadow that is called the Boat Croft. At either end a pavilion had been erected, and the jousting green was strongly fenced in, with a rising tier of seats for the ladies along one side, and a throne in the midst for the Douglas himself, as high and as nobly upholstered as if the King of Scots had been presiding in person.

At ten by the great sun-dial of Thrieve, the Earl, armed in complete armour of rare work, damascened with gold, and bearing in his hand the truncheon of commander, rode first through the fords of Lochar, and immediately after him came his brother David, a tall handsome boy of fourteen, whose olive skin and high-bred beauty attested his Douglas birth.

Next rode the Earl of Angus, a red, foxy-featured man, with mean and shifty eyes. He sat his horse awkwardly, perpetually hunching his shoulders forward as if he feared to fall over his beast's head. And saving among his own company, no man did him any honour, which caused him to grin with wicked sidelong smiles of hate and envy.

Then amid the shouting of the people there appeared, on a milk-white palfrey, Margaret, the Earl's only sister, already famous over all Scotland as " The Fair Maid of Galloway." With her rode one who, in the esteem of most who saw the pair that day, was a yet rarer flower, even Maud Lindesay, who had come out of the bleak North to keep the lonely little maid company. For Margaret of Douglas was yet no more than a child, but Maud Lindesay was nineteen years of age and in the first perfect bloom of her beauty.

Behind these two came the whole array of the knights

and barons who owned allegiance to the Douglas, —
Herons and Maxwells, Ardwell Macullochs, Gordons from
the Glen of Kells, with Agnews and MacDowalls from the
Shireside. But above all, and outnumbering all, there
were the lesser chiefs of the mighty name — Douglases of
the North, the future Moray and Ormond among them,
the noble young sons of James the Gross of Avondale,
who rode nearest their cousin, the head of the clan. Then
came Douglases of the Border, Douglases of the Hermit-
age, of Renfrew, of Douglasdale. Every third man in
that great company which splashed and caracoled
through the fords of Lochar, was a William, a James, or
an Archibald Douglas. The King himself could not
have raised in all Scotland such a following, and it is
small wonder if the heart of the young man expanded
within him.

Presently, soon after the arrival of the cavalcade, the
great wappenshaw was set in array, and forming up company by company the long double line extended as far as
the eye could reach from north to south along the side of
the broad and sluggish-moving river.

Sholto, who in virtue of his courage and good marks-
manship had been placed over the archer company
which waited on the right of the ford, fell in immediately behind the cortège of the Earl. He was first man
of all to have his equipment examined, and his weapons
obtained, as they deserved, the commendation of his
liege lord, and the grim unwilling approval of Malise,
the master armourer, whose unerring eye could not
detect so much as a speck on the shirt of mail, or a grain
of rust on the waist brace of shining steel.

Then the Earl rode down the lines, and Sholto, re-

membering the encounter amidst the dust of the road-
way, breathed more freely when he saw his father's back.

And surely that day the heart of the Douglas must
have beat proud and high within him, for there they
stood, company behind ordered company, the men on
whom he could count to the death. And truly the lad
of eighteen, who in Scotland was greater than the King,
looked upon their steadfast thousands with a swelling
heart.

The Abbot had made particular inquiries where Laurence was stationed, which was in the archer company
of the Laird of Kelton. Most of the monkish band had
been made too happy by the deception practised on their
Abbot concerning "Mary Quean," and were too desirous
to have such a rogue to play his pranks in the dull abbey,
to tell any tales on Laurence MacKim. But one, Ber-
guet, a Belgian priest who had begged his way to Scotland, and whose nature was that of the spy and sycophant,
approached and volunteered the information to the Abbot
that this lad to whom he was desirous of showing favour,
was a ribald and hypocritical youth.

"Eh, what?" said the Abbot, "a bodle for thy ill-set
tongue, false loon, dost think I did not hear him sing his
fair and seemly orisons? I tell thee, rude outland jab-
berer, that I am a Douglas, and have ears better than
those of any Frenchman that ever breathed. For this
thou shalt kneel six nights on the cold stone of the holy
chapel house, and say of paternosters ten thousand and
of misereres thou shall sing three hundred. And this
shall chance to teach thee to be scanter with thy foul
breath when thou speakest to the Abbot of the Foundation of Devorgill concerning better men than thyself."

The Belgian priest gasped and fell back, and none
other was found to say aught against Master Laurence,
which, considering the ten thousand paternosters and the
three hundred misereres, was not unnatural.

As the Earl passed along the line he was annoyed by
the iterated requests of his uncle to be informed when
they should come to the company of the Laird of Kelton.
And the good Abbot, being like all deaf men apt to speak
a little loud, did not improve matters by constantly making remarks behind his hand, upon the appearance or
character (as known to him) of the various dependents
of the Douglas House who had come out to show their
loyalty and exhibit their preparedness for battle.

As thus it was. The young Earl would come in his
inspection to a company of Solway-side men — stiff-
jointed fishers of salmon nets out of the parishes of
Rerrick or Borgue — or, as it might be, rough colts from
the rock scarps of Colvend, scramblers after wild birds'
nests on perilous heuchs, and poachers on the deer preserves of Cloak Moss, as often as they had a chance.
Then the Earl, having zealously commended the particular Barnbacle or Munches who led them, all would be
peace and concord, till out of the crowd behind would
issue the growling comment of his uncle, the Abbot of
Dulce Cor.

"A close-fisted old thief! The saints pity him not!
He will surely fry in Hell! Last Shrovetide did he not
drive off five of our best milch cows, and hath steadfastly
refused to restore them? *Anathema maranatha* to his
vile body and condemned be his huckstering soul!"

Needless to add, every word of this comment and
addition was heard by the person most concerned.

Or it might be, " Henry A'milligan — his mother's son,
God wot. And his father's, too, doubtless — if only one
could know who his father was. The devil dwell in his
fat belly ! *Exorciso te* — "

So it went on till the temper of the young lord of Galloway was strained almost to the breaking point, for he
wished not to cause a disturbance among so great a
company and on a day of such renown.

At last they came to the muster of the clean-run limber
lads of Kelton, artificers mostly, and stated retainers of
the castle and its various adjacent bourgs of Carlinwark,
Rhonehouse, Gelston, and Mains of Thrieve.

Some one at this point took the Abbot by the elbow
and shouted in his ear that this was the company he
desired to see. Then he rode forward to the left hand
of his nephew, as Malise and he passed slowly down the
line examining the weapons.

" Laurence MacKim, I would see Laurence MacKim ! "
cried the Abbot, holding up his hand as if in the chapel
of his monastery. The Earl stopped, and Malise turned
right about on his heel in great astonishment.

" What wants old marrowbones with our Laurie ? " he
muttered ; " surely he cannot have gotten into mischief
with the lasses already. But I kenna — I kenna. When
I was sixteen I can mind — I can mind. And the loon
may well be his father's own son."

And Malise, the man of brawn, watched out of his
quiet grey eyes the face of the Abbot William, wondering what was to come next.

Laurence stood forth at a word of command from the
Earl. He saluted, and then dropped the point of his
sword meekly upon the ground. His white-and-rose

cherub's face expressed the utmost goodness and innocence.

"Dear kinsman," said the Abbot to his nephew, "I
have a request to prefer which I hope you will grant,
though it deprive you of one retainer. This sweet youth
is not fit company for rude soldiers and ill-bred rufflers
of the camp. His mind is already on higher things. He
hath good clerkly Latin also, being skilled in the humanities, as I have heard proven with mine own ears. His
grace of language and deportment is manifest, and he
can sing the sweetest and most spiritual songs in praise
of Mary and the saints. I would have him in our choir
at Sweetheart Abbey, where we have much need both of
a voice such as his, and also of a youth whose sanctity
and innocence cannot fail to leaven with the grace of the
spirit the neophytes of our college, and the consideration
of whom may even bring repentance into older and more
hardened hearts."

Malise MacKim could not believe his ears as he
listened to the Abbot's rounded periods. But all the
same his grey eyes twinkled, his mouth slowly drew
itself together into the shape of an O, from which issued
a long low whistle, perfectly audible to all about him
except the Abbot. "Lord have mercy on the innocence
and cloistered quiet of the neophytes if they get our
Laurie for an example!" muttered Malise to himself as
he turned away.

Even the young Earl smiled, perhaps remembering the
last time he had seen the youth beside him, clutching
and tearing like a wild cat at his brother's throat in the
smithy of Carlinwark.

"You desire the life of a clerk?" said Lord William

pleasantly to Laurence. He would gladly have purchased his uncle's silence at even greater price.

"If your lordship pleases," said Laurence, meekly, adding to himself, "it cannot be such hard work as hammering at the forge, and if I like it not, why then I can always run away."

"You think you have a call to become a holy clerk?"

"I feel it here," quoth Master Laurence, hypocritically, indicating correctly, however, the organ whose wants have made clerks of so many — that is, the stomach.

Earl William smiled yet more broadly, but anxious to be gone he said: "Mine Uncle, here is the lad's father, Malise MacKim, my master armourer and right good servant. Ask him concerning his son."

"'Tis all up a rotten tree now," muttered Laurence to himself; "my father will reveal all."

Malise MacKim smiled grimly, but with a salutation to the dignitary of the church and near relative of his chief, he said: "Truly, I had never thought of this my son as worthy to be a holy clerk. But I will not stand in the way of his advancement nor thwart your favour. Take him for a year on trial, and if you can make a monk of him, do so and welcome. I recommend a leathern strap, well hardened in the fire, for the purpose of encouraging him to make a beginning in the holy life."

"He shall indeed have penance if he need it. For the good of the soul must the body suffer!" said Abbot William, sententiously.

"Saints' bones and cracklings," muttered Laurence, "this is none so cheerful! But I can always run away if the strap grows overlimber, and then let them catch me if they can. Sholto will help me."

"Fall out!" commanded the Earl, sharply, "and join yourself to the company of the Abbot William. Come, Malise, we lose our time."

Thus was one of our heroes brought into the way of becoming a learned and holy clerk. But all those who knew him best agreed that he had a far road to travel.

CHAPTER XI

THE Earl had almost arrived at the pavilion erected at the southern end of the jousting meadow, when a gust of cheering borne along the lines announced the arrival of a belated company. The young man glanced northward with intent to discover, by their pennons, who his visitors might be. But the distance was too great, and identification was made more difficult by the swarming of the populace round the newcomers. So, being unable to make the matter out, Earl William despatched his brother David to bring him word of their quality.

Presently, however, and before David Douglas' return, shouts of "Avondale, Avondale!" from the men of Lanarkshire informed the young Earl of the name of one at least of those who had arrived. A frown so quick and angry darkened his brow that it showed the consideration in which the Douglas held his granduncle James the Gross, Earl of Avondale.

"I hope, at least," he said in a low voice to Malise, who stood half a step behind him, "that my cousins Will and James have come with him. They are good metal for a tourney, and worth breaking a lance with."

By this time the banners of the visitors were discernible crossing the fords of Lochar, while high advanced above all private pennons two standards could be seen, the banner royal of Scotland, and close beside the rampant lion the white lilies of France.

"Saint Bride!" cried the Earl, "have they brought the King of Scots to visit me? His Majesty had been better at his horn-book, or playing ball in the tennis court of Stirling."

Then came David back, riding swiftly on his fine dark chestnut, which, being free from the mantle wherein the horses of knights were swathed, and having its mane and tail left long, made a gallant show as the lad threw it almost on its haunches in his boyish pride of horsemanship.

"William," said David Douglas, "a word in your ear, brother. The whole tribe are here,—fat Jamie and all his clan."

The brothers conferred a little apart, for in those troubled times men learned caution early, and though the Douglas was the greatest lord in Scotland, yet, surrounded by meaner men as he was, it behoved him to be jealous and careful of his life and honour.

Earl Douglas came out of the sparred enclosure of the tilt-ring in order to receive his guests.

First, as an escort to the ambassador royal of France and Scotland who came behind, rode the Earl of Avondale and his five sons, noble young men, and most unlikely to have sprung from such a stock. James the Gross rode a broad Clydesdale mare, a short, soft unwieldy man, sitting squat on the saddle like a toad astride a roof, and glancing slily sideways out of the pursy recesses of his eyes.

Behind him came his eldest son William, a man of a true Douglas countenance, quick, high, and stern.

Then followed James, whose lithe body and wonderful
dexterity in arms were already winning him repute as
one of the bravest knights in all Christendom in every
military and manly exercise.

Behind the Avondale Douglases rode two men abreast,
with a lady on a palfrey between them.

The first to take the eye, both by his stature and
his remarkable appearance, rode upon a charger covered
from head to tail in the gorgeous red-and-gold diamonded
trappings pertaining to a marshal of France. He was
in complete armour, and wore his visor down. A long
blue feather floated from his helmet, falling almost
upon the flank of his horse; a truncheon of gold and
black was at his side. A pace behind him the lilies
of France were displayed, floating out languidly from
a black and white banner staff held in the hands of a
young squire.

The knight behind whom the banner royal of Scotland fluttered was a man of different mould. His
spare frame seemed buried in the suit of armour that
he wore somewhat awkwardly. His pale ascetic countenance looked more in place in a monkish cloister
than on a knightly tilting ground, and he glanced this
way and that with the swift and furtive suspicion of
one who, while setting one trap, fears to be taken in
another.

But the lady who rode on a white palfrey between
these two took all men's regard, even in the presence
of a marshal of France and a herald extraordinary of
the King of Scots.

The Earl Douglas, having let his eyes once rest upon
her, could not again remove them, being, as it were,

fixed by the very greatness of the wonder which he saw.

It was the lady of the pavilion underneath the pines, the lady of the evening light and of the midnight storm.

She was no longer clothed in simple white, but arrayed like a king's daughter. On her head was a high-peaked coiffure, from which there flowed down a graceful cloud of finest lace. This, even as the Earl looked at her, she caught at with a bewitching gesture, and brought down over her shoulder with her gloved hand. A close-fitting robe of palest blue outlined the perfections of her body. A single fleur-de-lys in gold was embroidered on the breast of her white bodice, and the same device appeared again and again on the white housing of her palfrey.

She sat in the saddle, gently smiling, and looking down with a sweetness which was either the perfection of finished coquetry or the expression of the finest natural modesty.

Strangely enough, the first thought which came to the Earl Douglas after his surprise was one in which triumph was blended with mirth.

"What will the Abbot and Malise think of this?" he said, half aloud. And he turned him about in order to look upon the face of his master armourer.

He found Malise MacKim ashen-pale and drawn of countenance, his mouth open and squared with wonder. His jaw was fallen slack, and his hands gripped one upon the other like those of a suppliant praying to the saints.

The Earl smiled, and bidding Malise unlace his helmet in compliment to his guests, he stood presently bareheaded before them, his head appearing above the blackness of his armour, bright as a flower with youth and instinct with all the fiery beauty of his race.

It was James the Gross who came forward to act as herald. "My well-beloved nephew," he began in somewhat whining tones, "I bring you two royal embassies, one from the King of France and the other from the King of Scotland. I have the honour to present to you the Marshal Gilles de Retz, ambassador of the most Christian King, Charles the Seventh, who will presently deliver his master's message to you."

The marshal, who till now had kept his visor down, slowly raised it, and revealed a face which, being once seen, could never afterwards be banished from the memory.

It was a large grey-white countenance, with high cheek-bones and colourless lips, which were continually working one upon the other. Black eyes were set close together under heavy brows, and a long thin nose curved between them like the beak of an unclean bird.

"Earl William," said the marshal, "I give you greeting in the name of our common liege lord, Charles, King of France, and also in that of his son, the Dauphin Louis. I bring you also a further token of their good-will, in that I hail you heir to the great estates and dignities of your father and grandfather, sometime Dukes of Touraine and vassals premier of the King of France."

The young man bowed, but in spite of the interest of his message, the marshal caught his eyes resting upon the face of the lady who rode beside him.

"To this I add that which, save for the message

of the King, my master, ought fitly to have come first. I present you to this fair lady, my sister-in-law, the Damosel Sybilla de Thouars, maid of honour to your high princess Margaret of Scotland, who of late hath expanded into a yet fairer flower under the sun of our land of France."

The Earl dismounted and threw the reins of his horse to Malise, whose face wore an expression of bitterest disappointment and instinctive hatred. Then he went to the side of the Lady Sybilla, and taking her hand he bowed his head over it, touching the glove to his lips with every token of respect. Still bareheaded, he took the reins of her palfrey and led her to the stand reserved for the Queen of Beauty.

Here the Earl invited her to dismount and occupy the central seat.

"Till your arrival it lacked an occupant, saving my little sister; but to-day the gods have been good to the house of Douglas, and for the first time since the death of my father I see it filled."

Smilingly the lady consented, and with a wave of his hand the Earl William invited the Marshal de Retz to take the place on the other side of the Lady Sybilla.

Then turning haughtily to the herald of the King of Scots, who had been standing alone, he said:—

"And now, sir, what would you with the Earl Douglas?"

The ascetic, monkish man found his words with little loss of time, showing, however, no resentment for Earl William's neglect of any reverence to the banner under whose protection he came.

"I am Sir James Irving of Drum," he said, "and I stand here on behalf of Sir Alexander Livingston, tutor and guardian of the King of Scots, to invite your friendship and aid. The Lord Crichton, sometime Chancellor of this realm, hath rebelled against the royal authority and fortified him in Edinburgh Castle. So both Sir Alexander Livingston and the most noble lady, the Queen Mother, desire the assistance of the great power of the Earl of Douglas to suppress this revolt."

Scarcely had these words been uttered when another knight stepped forward out of the train which had followed the Earl of Avondale.

"I am here on behalf of the Chancellor of Scotland, who is no rebel against any right authority, but who wishes only to bring this distracted realm back into some assured peace, and to deliver the young King out of the hands of flatterers and lechers. I have the honour, therefore, of requesting on behalf of the Chancellor of Scotland, Sir William Crichton, the true representative of royal authority, the aid and alliance of my Lord of Douglas."

A smile of haughty contempt passed over the face of the Earl, and he dismissed both heralds, uttering in the hearing of all those words which afterwards became so famous over Scotland:

"Let dog eat dog! Wherefore should the lion care?"

G

CHAPTER XII

MISTRESS MAUD LINDESAY

THE sports of the first day of the great wappenshaw were over. The Lord James Douglas, second son of the Gross One, had won the single tourneying by unhorsing all his opponents without even breaking a lance. For the second time Sholto MacKim wore on his cap the golden buckle of archery, and took his way happily homeward, much uplifted that the somewhat fraudulent eyes of Mistress Maud Lindesay had smiled upon him whilst the French lady was fastening it there.

The knightly part of the great muster had already gone back to their tents and lodgings. The commonalty were mostly stringing away through the vales and hill passes to their homes, no longer in ordered companies, but in bands of two or three. Disputes and misunderstandings arose here and there between men of different provinces. The Galloway men called " Annandale thieves" at those border lads who came at the summons of the hereditary Warden of the Marches. The borderers replied by loud bleatings, which signified that they held the Galwegians of no better understanding than their native sheep.

It was a strange and varied company which rode home to Thrieve to receive the hospitality of the young Earl of Douglas and Duke of Touraine. The castle itself, being no more than a military fortress, containing in addition to the soldiers' quarters only the apartments designed for the family (and scant enough even of those) could not, of course, accommodate so great a company.

But as was the custom at all great houses, though more in England and France than in poverty-stricken Scotland, the Earl of Douglas had in store an abundant supply of tents, some of them woven of arras and ornamented with cloth of gold, others of humbler but equally serviceable material.

His mother, the Countess of Douglas, who knew nothing of the occurrences of the night of the great storm, nor guessed at the suspicions of witchcraft and diablerie which made a hell of the breast of Malise, the master armourer, received her son's guests with distinguished courtesy.   Malise himself had gone to find the Abbot, so soon as ever he set eyes on the companion of the Marshal de Retz, that they might consult together — only, however, to discover that the gentle churchman had quitted the field immediately after he had obtained the consent of his nephew to the possession of the new chorister, to whom he had taken so sudden and violent a fancy.

The hoofs of the whole cavalcade were erelong sounding hollow and dull upon the wooden bridge, which the Earl's father had erected from the left bank to the southernmost corner of the Isle of Thrieve, a bridge which a single charge of powder, or even a few strokes of a woodman's axe, had been sufficient to remove and disable, but which nevertheless enabled the castle-dwellers to avoid the extreme inconvenience of passing through the ford at all states of the river.

Sholto MacKim, throwing all the consciousness of a shining success into the stiffness of the neck which upheld the slight additional weight of the Earl's gold buckle in his cap, found himself, not wholly by accident, in the neighbourhood of his heart's beloved, Maud Lindesay. For, like a valiant seneschal, she had kept her place all day close beside the Fair Maid of Galloway.

And now the little girl was more than ever eager to keep near to her friend, for the ambassador of the King of France had bent one look upon her, so strange and searching that Margaret, though not naturally timid, had cried aloud involuntarily and clasped her friend's hand with a grasp which she refused to loosen, till Sholto had promised to walk by the side of her pony and allow her to net her trembling fingers into the thick of his clustering curls.

For the armourer's son was, in those simple days, an ancient ally and playmate of the little noble damsel, and he dreamed, and not without some excuse, that in an age when every man's strong arm and brave heart constituted his fortune, the time might come when he might even himself to Maud Lindesay, baron's daughter though she were. For both his father and himself were already high in favour with their master the Earl, who could create knighthoods and dispose lordships as easily as (and much more effectually and finally than) the King himself.

The emissaries of the Chancellor and Sir Alexander Livingston did not accompany the others back to the castle after the short and haughty answer which they had received, but with their followers returned the way they had come to their several headquarters, giving, as was natural between foes so bitter, a wide berth to each other on their northward journeys to Edinburgh and Stirling.

"What think you of this day's doings, Mistress Lindesay?" asked Sholto as he swung along beside the train with little Margaret Douglas's hand still clutching the thick curls at the back of his neck.

The maid of honour tossed her shapely head, and, with a little pretty upward curl of the lip, exclaimed: "'Twas as stupid a tourney as ever I saw. There was not a single handsome knight nor yet one beautiful lady on the field this day."

"What of James of Avondale when knights are being judged?" said Sholto, with a kind of gloomy satisfaction, boyish and characteristic; "he at least looked often enough in your direction to prove that he did not agree with you about the lack of the beautiful lady."

At this Maud Lindesay elevated her pretty nostrils yet further into the air. "James of Avondale, indeed —" she said, "he is not to be compared either for dignity or strength with the Earl himself, nor yet with many others whom I know of lesser estate."

"Sholto MacKim," cried the clear piping voice of the little Margaret, "how in the world am I to keep hold of your hair if you shake and jerk your head about like that? If you do not keep still I will send for that pretty boy over there in the scarlet vest, or ask my cousin James to ride with me. And he will, too, I know — for he likes bravely to be beside my dear, sweet Maud Lindesay."

After this Sholto held his head erect and forth-looking, as if he had been under the inspection of the Earl and were doubtful of his weapons passing muster.

There came a subtle and roguish smile into the eyes of
Mistress Maud Lindesay as she observed the stiffening
of Sholto's bearing.

"Who were those others of humbler estate?" he
queried, sending his words straight out of his lips like
pellets from a pop-gun, being in fear lest he should
unsettle the hand of the small tyrant upon his hair.

"Your brother Laurence for one," replied the minx,
for no other purpose than to see the flush of disappointment tinge his brow with sudden red.

"I wish my brother Laurence were in —" he began.
But the girl interrupted him.

"Hush," she said, holding up her finger, "do not
swear, especially at a son of the holy church. Ha, ha!
A fit clerk and a reverend will they make of Laurence
MacKim! I have heard of your ploys and ongoings, both
of you. Think not I am to be taken in by your meek-
ness and pretence of dutiful service. You go athwart
the country making love to poor maidens, and then,
when you have won their hearts, you leave them
lamenting."

And she affected to heave a deep sigh.

"Ah, Maudie," said the little girl, reproachfully, "now
you are being bad. I know it by your voice. Do not be
unkind to my Sholto, for his hair is so pleasant to touch.
I wish you could feel it. And, besides, when you are
wicked to him, you make him jerk, and if he does it
often I shall have to send him away."

The Maid of Galloway was indeed entirely correct.
For Maud Lindesay, accustomed all her life to the
homage of many men, and having been brought up in
a great castle in an age when chivalrous respect to

women had not yet given place to the licence of the Revival of Letters, practised irritation like a fine art. She was brimful of the superfluity of naughtiness, yet withal as innocent and playful as a kitten.

But Sholto, both from a feeling that he belonged to an inferior rank, and also being exceedingly conscious of his youth, chose to be bitterly offended.

"You mistake me greatly, Mistress Lindesay," he said in an uneven schoolboy's voice, to which he tried in vain to add a touch of worldly coldness; "I do not make love to every girl I meet, nor yet do I love them and leave them as you say. You have been most gravely misinformed."

"Nay," tripped the maid of honour, with arch quickness of reply, "I said not that you were naturally equipped for such amorous quests. I meant to designate your brother Laurence. 'Tis pity he is to be a clerk. Though one day doubtless he will make a very proper and consolatory father confessor —"

Sholto walked on in silence, his eyes fixed before him, and in such high dudgeon that he pretended to be unconscious of what the girl had been saying. Then the little Margaret began to prattle in her pretty way, and the youth answered "yes" and "no" sulkily and at random, his thoughts being alternately on the doing of some great deed to make his mistress repent her cruelty, and on a leap into the castle pool, in whose unsunned deeps he might find oblivion from all the flouts of hard-hearted beauty.

Maud kept her eyes upon him, a smile of satisfaction on her lips so long as he was not looking at her. She liked to play her fish as satisfactorily as she could before grassing it at her feet.

"Besides, it will do him good," she said to herself.
"He hath lately won the gold badge of archery, and, like
all men, is apt to think overmuch of himself at such
times. Moreover, I can always make it up to him after —
if I like, that is."

But as often as Sholto dropped a little behind, keeping
pace with Maid Margaret's slower palfrey so that Maud
was sure he looked at her, the pretty coquette cast down
her eyes in affected humility and sorrow. Whereupon
immediately Sholto felt his resentment begin to melt like
snow off a dike top when the sun of April is shining.

But neither of them uttered another word till they
reached the drawbridge which crossed the nether moat
and conducted to the noble gateway of Thrieve. Then,
at the foot of the stairway to the hall, Sholto, having
swung the little maid from her pony, after a moment of
sullen hesitation went across to assist Mistress Maud
Lindesay out of her saddle.

As he lifted the girl down his heart thundered tumultuously in his breast, for he had never so touched her
before. Her lashes rested modestly on her cheek — long,
black, and upcurled a little at the ends. As her foot
touched the ground, she raised them a moment, and
looked at him with one swift flash of violet eyes made
darker by the seclusion from which she had released
them. Then in another moment she had dropped them
again, detaching them from his with a mighty affectation
of confusion.

"Please, Sholto, I am sorry. I did not mean it." She
spoke like a child that is sorry for a fault and is fearful
of being chidden.

And even though knowing full well by bitter experience all her naughtiness and hypocrisy, Sholto, gulping his heart well down into his throat, could not do otherwise than forgive a thing so pretty and so full of the innocent artifices which make mown hay of the hearts of men.

With a touch of his lips upon the hand of Margaret the Maid in token of fealty, Sholto MacKim turned on his heel and went away towards the fords of Thrieve, muttering to himself, "No, she does not mean it, I do believe. But I have ever heard that of all women she who never means it is the most dangerous."

And this is a dict which no wise man can gainsay.

CHAPTER XIII

A DAUNTING SUMMONS

Not far before them had ridden the Earl and the Lady Sybilla. Behind these two came the Marshal de Retz and the fat Lord of Avondale. They were telling each other tales of the wars of La Pucelle, the latter laughing and shaking shoulders, but at the end of every side-splitting legend the Frenchman would glance over his shoulder at Maud Lindesay and the little maiden Margaret.

As Sholto passed them on his return he stood aside, poised at the salute, looking meanwhile with awe on the great and notable French soldier. Yet at the first glimpse of his unvisored face there fell upon the young man a dislike so fierce and instinctive that he grasped his bow and fumbled in his quiver for an arrow, in order to send it through the unlaced joints of the Marshal's gorget, which for ease's sake his squire had undone when they left the field.

Sholto MacKim was at the fords waiting the chance of crossing and the pleasure of the surly keeper of the bridge, Elson A'Cormack, who sat in his wheelhouse, grunting curses on all who passed that way.

"Foul feet, slow bellies, fushionless and slack ye are to run my lord's errands! But quick enow to return home upon your trampling clattering ruck of horses, and every rascal of you expecting to ride over my bridge of good pine planking instead of washing the dirt from your hoofs in honest Dee water."

The long files of horsemen threaded their way across the green plain of the isle towards the open space in front of Thrieve Castle, the points of their spears shining high in the air, and the shafts so thick underneath that, seen from a distance, they made a network of slender lines reticulated against the brightness of the sun.

The great island strength of the Douglases was then in its highest state of perfection as a fortress and of dignity as a residence. Archibald the Grim, who built the keep, could not have foreseen the wondrous beauty and strength to which Thrieve would attain under his successors. This night of the wappenshaw the lofty grey walls were hung with gaily coloured tapestries draped from the overhanging gallery of wood which ran round the top of the castle. From the four corners of the roof flew the banners of four provinces which owned the sway of the mighty house, — Galloway, Annandale, Lanark, and the Marches, — while from the centre, on a flagstaff taller than any, flew their standard royal, for so it might be called, the heart and stars of the Douglases' more than royal house.

While the outer walls thus blazed with colour, the woods around gave back the constant reverberation of cannon, as with hand guns and artillery of weight the garrison greeted the return of the Earl and his guests. The green castle island from end to end was planted thick with tents and gay with pavilions of many hues and various design, their walls covered with intricate devices, and each flying the colours of its owner, while on poles without dangled shields and harness of various kinds, ready for the younger squires to clean and oil for the use of their masters on the remaining days of the tournament.

Sholto waited at the bridge-head, impatient of the press, and eager to be left alone with his own thoughts, that he might con over and over the words and looks of his heart's idol, and suck all the sweet pain he could out of her very hardheartedness. Suddenly tossed backwards like a ball from lip to lip, according to the universal and, indeed, obligatory custom of the time, there reached him the "passing of the word." He heard his own name repeated over and over in fifty voices and tones, waxing louder as the "word" neared him.

"Sholto MacKim — Sholto MacKim, son of Malise, the armourer, wanted to speak with the Earl. Sholto MacKim. Sholto — "

A great nolt of a Moray Highlandman, with a mouth like a gash, shouted it in his very ear.

Surprised and somewhat anxious at heart, Sholto cast over in his mind all the deeds, good and evil, which might procure him the honour of an interview with Earl William Douglas, but could think of nothing except his having involuntarily played the spy at the young lord's meeting with the lady in the wood. It was therefore with some natural trepidation that the young man obeyed the summons.

"At any rate," he meditated with a slight return of complacency, as he butted and shoved his way castle-wards, "he can scarcely mean to have my head. For he was all day with my father at his elbow, and at the worst I shall have another chance of seeing" — he did not call the beloved by her Christian name even to him-

self, so he compromised by adding somewhat lamely—
"*her.*"

Thus Sholto, putting speed in his heels and swinging
along over the trampled sward with the easy tireless trot
of a sleuthhound, threaded his way among the groups of
villein prickers and swearing men-at-arms who cumbered
the main approaches of the castle.

He found the Earl walking swiftly up and down a
little raised platform which extended round three sides
of Thrieve, outside the main defences, but yet within
the nether moat, the sluggish water of which it over-
looked on its inner side.

Earl William was manifestly discomposed and excited
by the events of the day, and especially by the fact that
the Lady Sybilla seemed utterly unconscious of ever
having set eyes upon him before, appearing entirely
oblivious of having received him in a pavilion of rose-
coloured silk under the shelter of a grove of tall pines.
The young lord instinctively recoiled from any communication with his master armourer, whose grave and
impassive face revealed nothing which might be passing
in his mind.   Then the Earl's thoughts turned upon
Sholto, who had been the first to observe his beauteous
companion of the Carlinwark woods.

Earl William was even younger than Sholto, but the
cares and dignities of a great position had rendered him
far less boyish in manner and carriage than the son of
Malise MacKim.

His head, now released from his helm, rose out from the
richly ornamented collar of his armour with the grace of
a flower and the strength of a tree rooted among rocks.
He had already laid aside his gorget, and when Sholto

was announced, the Earl's ancient retainer, old Landless
Jock of Abernethy, was bringing him a cap of soft velvet which he threw on the back of his head with an air
of supreme carelessness. Then he rose and walked up
and down, carrying his armour as if it had been a mere
feather weight, whereas it was tilting harness of double
plate and designed only for wearing on horseback.

Sholto marked in the young lord a boyish eagerness
equal to his own. Indeed, his impatient manner recalled
his late feelings, as he had stood on the bridge and
desired to be left alone with his thoughts of Maud
Lindesay.

Sholto stood still and quiet on the topmost step of the
ascent from the moat-bridge waiting for the Earl to
signify his will.

CHAPTER XIV

"Sholto MacKim," said the Earl of Douglas, abruptly, "saw you the lady who arrived with the foreign ambassador?"

"She is indeed wondrous fair to look on," answered Sholto, the whole heart in him instantly wary, while outwardly he seemed more innocent than before.

"Have your eyes ever lighted on that lady before?"

"Nay, my lord, of a surety no. In what manner should they, seeing that I have never been in France in my life, nor indeed more than a score of miles from this castle of Thrieve?"

"Thou art a good lad, and also ready of wit, Master Sholto," said the Earl, looking at the armourer's son musingly. "Clear of eye and true of hand, so they tell me. Did you not win the arrow prize this day?"

Lord William raised his eyes to where in the bonnet of the youth his own golden badge of archery glistened.

"And I also won the swording prize at the last wappenshaw on the moot hill of Urr," said Sholto, taking courage, and being resolved that if his fortune stood not now on tiptoe, it should not be on account of any superfluity of modesty on his own part.

"Ah," said the Earl, "I remember. It was two golden hearts joined together with an arrow and a star in the midst — a fitting Douglas emblem, by the bones of Saint Bride! Where hast thou left that badge that thou dost not wear it along with the other?"

Sholto blushed and muttered that he had forgotten it at home. He was all of a breaking perspiration lest he should have to tell the Earl that he had given it to Maud Lindesay, as indeed he meant to do presently, along with the golden buckle of archery, — that is if the dainty, mischievous-hearted maiden could be persuaded to accept thereof.

"Ah," said the Earl, smiling, "I comprehend. There is some maid in the question, and if I advance you to the command of my house-guard and give you an officer's responsibility, you will of a surety be ever desiring to go gadding to the greenwood — and around the loch of Carlinwark are most truly dangerous glades."

"Nay, indeed nay," cried Sholto, eagerly. "If it is my lord's will to appoint me to his guard, by Saint Bride and all the other saints I swear never to leave the island, unless it be sometimes of a Sunday afternoon for an hour or two — just to see my mother."

"Your mother!" quoth the Earl, laughing heartily. "So then my two golden hearts are in your mother's keeping. Art a good lad, Sholto, and as for guile it is simply not in thee!"

Sholto looked modestly down upon the earth, as if conscious of his own exceeding merits, but willing for the nonce to say nothing about them. But the young Earl came over to him, and dealing him a sound buffet on the back, cried: "Nay, lad, that lamb-like look I have seen tried on mine uncle the Abbot of Sweetheart. Thy brother Laurence is in the way of clerkly advancement on account of that same sweetly innocent regard, which he hath in even greater perfection. But I am a young man, remember — and one youth flings not glamour easily into the eyes of another. Sholto, neither you nor I are any better than we should be, and if we are not so evil as some others, let us not set up as overwhelmingly virtuous. For at twenty virtue is mostly but lack of opportunity."

Sholto blushed so becomingly at this accusation that if the Earl had not seen the brothers locked in the death grip like crabs in a fishwife's creel, even he might have been deceived.

"Nevertheless," continued the Earl, "in spite of your claims to virtue, I am resolved to make you officer of my castle-guard — if not in name, at least in fact. For old Landless Jock of Abernethy must keep the name while he lives, and stand first when my steward pays out the chuckling golden Lions at Whitsun and eke Lady Day. But you shall have enough and be no longer a charge upon your father. Malise should be a proud man, having both his sons provided for in one day."

The Earl turned him about with his usual quick imperiousness. "Malise," he cried, "Malise MacKim!"

And again the "word" ran through the castle, escaped the gate, circumnavigated the moat, and ran round the circle of the tents till the shouts of "Malise, Malise," could have been heard almost at the deserted fords of Lochar, where sundry varlets were watching for a chance to search the deserted pavilions for anything left behind therein by the knights and squires. ·

Presently there was seen ascending to the moat platform the huge form of the master armourer himself.

He stood waiting his master's pleasure, with a knife which he had been sharpening in his hand. It was a curious weapon, long, thin, and narrow in the blade, which was double-edged and ground fine as a razor on both sides.

"Ah, Malise," said the Earl, "you have not taught your son amiss. He threatens to turn out a most marvellous lad, for not only can he make weapons, but he can excel the best of my men-at-arms in their use. Have you any objection that he be attached to my guard?"

The strong man smiled with his usual calm, and kept his humorous grey eyes fixed shrewdly on the Earl.

"Aye," he said, "it is indeed more fitting that Sholto, my son, should ride behind my Lord of Douglas than stiff old Malise upon his Flanders mare."

The Earl blushed a little, for he remembered how the armourer had offered to ride behind him after he had shod Black Darnaway at the Carlinwark. He went on somewhat hastily.

"I have resolved to make your son, Sholto, officer of the castle-guard. It is perhaps over-responsible a post for so young a man, yet I myself am younger and have heavier burdens to bear. Also Landless Jock is growing old and stiff, and will not suffer to be spoken to. For my father's sake I cannot be severe with him. He will die in his charge if he will, but on Douglasdale and not at Thrieve. So now I would have your son do my bidding without question, which is more than his father ever did before him."

"I can answer for Sholto," said Malise MacKim. "He is afraid of nothing save perhaps the strength of his father's right arm. He is cool enough in danger.

Nothing daunts him except the flutter of a farthingale. But then my lord knows well that is a fault most commendable in this castle of Thrieve. Sholto will be an honest captain of your house-carls, if you see to it that the steward locks up his loaves of sugar and his most toothsome preserves."

"Faith," cried the Earl, heartily, "I know not but what I would join Master Sholto in a raid on these dainties myself."

In this fashion was Sholto MacKim placed in command of the house-guard of the castle of Thrieve.

CHAPTER XV

THE NIGHT ALARM

AT parting with his father, the young captain received many wise and grave instructions, all of which he resolved to remember and profit by — a resolution which he did not fail to keep for full five minutes.

"Be douce in deportment," said his father, speaking quietly and yet with a certain sternness of demeanour. "Think three times before you give an order, but let no man think even once before obeying it. Set him astraddle the wooden horse with a spear shaft at either foot to teach him that a soldier's first duty is not to think. Keep your eyes more on the alert for the approach of an enemy than for the ankles of the women-folk at the turnings of the turret stairs."

To these and many other maxims out of the incorporate wisdom of the elders, Sholto promised most faithful attendance, and, for the time being, he fully intended to keep his word. But no sooner was his father gone, and he introduced to his new quarters and duties by David Douglas, the Earl's younger brother, than he began to wonder which was the window of Maud Lindesay's chamber and speculate on how soon he would see her thereat.

In the castle of Thrieve that night there was little sleeping room to spare. The Earl and his brother lay

100

wrapped in their plaids in one of the round towers of
the outer defences. In the castle hall the retainers of
the French ambassador slept side by side, or heads and
tails with the archers of the house-guard. Lights
flickered on the turnpike stair which led to the upper
floors. The servitors had cleared the great hall, and
here on a dais, raised above the "marsh" and sheltered
by an arras curtain hastily arranged, James the Gross
slept on a soft French bed, which he had caused to be
brought all the way from his castle of Strathavon on the
moors of Lanarkshire.

In the Earl's chamber on the third floor was lodged
the Marshal de Retz. Next him ranged the apartment
of the countess. Here also was the Lady Sybilla at the
end of the passage in the guest chamber which looked to
the north, and from the windows of which she could see
the broad river dividing itself about the castle island,
and flowing as calmly on as if the stern feudal pile had
been a peaceful monastery and the waving war banners
no more than so many signs of holy cross.

Above, in the low-roofed chambers, which gave upon
the wooden balcony, were the apartments of Maud
Lindesay and her charge, little Margaret Douglas, the
Fair Maid of Galloway.

Now the single postern stair of the castle was shut at
the foot, where it opened out upon the hall of the guard
by a sparred iron gate, the key of which was put into
Sholto's charge. The night closed early upon the castle-
ful of wearied folk. The marshals of the camps caused
the lights to be put out at nine-of-the-clock in all the
tents and pavilions, but the lamps and candles burned
longer in the castle itself, where the Earl had been

giving a banquet to his guests, of the best that his
estates could afford. Nevertheless, it was yet long before midnight when the cheep of the mouse in the wain-
scot, the restless stir or muffled snore of a crowded sleeper
in the guardroom, was the only sound to be heard
from dungeon to banner-staff of the great castle.

Sholto's heart throbbed tumultuous and insurgent
within him. And small is the wonder. Never in his
wildest dreams had he imagined such a fate as this, to
be actual captain of the Earl's own body-guard, even
though neither title nor emolument was yet wholly his;
better still, that he should dwell night and day within
arm's reach almost of the desire of his heart, flinty-
bosomed and mischievous as she was — these were heights
of good fortune to which his imagination had never
climbed in its most daring ascents.

No longer did he envy his brother's good fortune, as
he had been somewhat inclined to do earlier in the day,
when he thought of returning to wield the forehammer
all alone in his father's smithy.

The first night of Captain Sholto's responsibility in
the castle of Thrieve was destined to be a memorable
one. To the youth himself it would have appeared so in
any case. Only a panelled door divided him from the
girl who, wayward and scornful as she had ever been
to him, yet kept his heart dangling at her waist-belt as
truly as if it had been the golden key of her armoire.

The ancient Sir John of Abernethy, dubbed Landless
Jock, would not be separated from his masters, and slept
with two sergeants of the guard in the turret adjacent
to that in which the brothers of Douglas, William and
David, lay in the first sleep of youth and an easy mind.

Sholto therefore found himself left with the undivided responsibility for the safety of the castle and all who dwelt within it. He was also the only man who, by reason of his charge and in virtue of his master-key, was permitted to circulate freely through all the floors and passages of the vast feudal pile.

Sholto went out to the barred gate of the castle, where in a little cubbyhole dark even at noonday, and black as Egypt now, the warder slept with his hand upon his keys, and his head touching the lever of the gear wherewith he drew the creaking portcullis up and rolled back the iron doors which shut the keep off from the world of the wide outer courtyard and the garrison which manned the turrets.

The porter, Hugh MacCalmont, sat up on his elbow at Sholto's salutation, only enough to see his visitor by the glint of the little iron "cruisie" lamp hanging upon the wall. He knew him by the golden chain of office which the Earl had given Sholto.

"Captain of the guard," he muttered, "Lord, here's advancement indeed. My lord might have remembered me that have served him faithfully these thirty years, opening and shutting without mistake. He might have named me captain of the guard, and not this limber Jack. But the young love the young, and in truth 'tis natural. But what Landless Jock will say when he comes to have this sprat set over him, I know not but I can guess!"

Satisfied that all was safe there, Sholto stepped gingerly over the reclining forms of the first relief guard, who lay wrapped in their cloaks, every man grasping his arms. Most of these were lying in the dead sleep

of tired men, whilst others restlessly moved about this
way and that, as if seeking an easier adaptation of their
bones to the corners of the blue whinstones and rough
shell lime than had been provided for when the castle
was built by Archibald the Grim, Lord of Thrieve and
Galloway.

Close by the last turn of the turret staircase yawned
the iron-sparred mouth of the dungeon, in which in its
time many a notable prisoner had been immured. It
was closed with a huge grid of curved iron bars, each
as thick as a man's arm, cunningly held together by a
gigantic padlock, the key of which was nightly taken to
the sleeping-room of the Earl — whether, as was now
the case, the cell stood empty, or whether it contained
an English lord waiting ransom or a rebellious baron
expectant of his morning summons to the dule tree of
the Black Douglas.

Then taking the master-key from his belt, Sholto unlocked the sparred gate leading from the *salle de garde*
into the turret stair which was the sole communication
with the upper floors of the castle.

Slowly, and with a step no louder than the beating of
his own heart, he went upwards, glancing in midway
upon the banquet hall, where the dim light from the postern without revealed a number of dark forms wrapped
in slumber lying on the dining-table and on the floor;
ascending yet higher he came to the floor where slept
the Countess of Douglas, the Lady Sybilla, and in the
Earl's own chamber the Marshal de Retz, ambassador
of the King of France.

Sholto stood a moment with his hand raised in a
listening attitude, before he ventured to ascend those

narrower stairs which led to the uppermost floor of all, on which were the chambers occupied by the little Maid Margaret and her companion and gossip Mistress Maud Lindesay.

He told himself that it was his duty to see to the safety of the whole castle; that he had special instructions to visit three times, during the course of each night of duty, all the passages and corridors of the fortress. But nevertheless it needed all his courage to enable Sholto to perform the task which had been laid upon him. As he dragged one foot after the other up the turret stairs, it seemed as if a leaden clog had been attached to each pointed shoe.

He had also a vague sense of being watched by presences invisible to him, but malign in their nature. Again and again he caught himself listening for footsteps which seemed to dog his own. He heard mysterious whisperings that flouted his utmost vigilance, and mocking laughter that lurked in unseen crevices and broke out so soon as he had passed.

Sholto set his hand firmly upon his sword handle and bit his lips, lest even to himself he should own his uneasiness. It was not seemly that the captain of the Douglas guard should be frightened by shadows.

Passing the corridor which led towards the sleeping rooms of the maid and her companion, he ascended to the roof of the castle, thrusting aside the turret door and issuing upon the wide, open spaces with an assured step. The cool breeze from the west restored him to himself in a moment. The waning moon cast a pale light across the landscape, and he could see the tents on the castle island glimmer greyish white beneath him. Beyond that again was the shining confluence of the sluggish river about the isle, and the dark line of the woods of Balmaghie opposite. He had begun to meditate on the rapid changes of circumstance which had overtaken him, when suddenly a shrill and piercing shriek rang out, coming up through the castle beneath, again and again repeated. It was like the cry of a child in the grip of instant and deadly terror.

Sholto's heart gave a great bound. That something untoward should happen on this the first night of his charge was too disastrous. He drew his sword and set in his lips the silver call which depended from the chain of office the Earl had thrown about his neck when he made him captain of his guard.

His feet hardly touched the stone stairs as he flew downwards, and wings were added to his haste by the sounds of fear which continued to increase. In another moment he was upon the last step of the turnpike and at the entrance of the corridor which led to the rooms of the little Lady Margaret and Maud Lindesay.

As Sholto came rushing down the steep descent from the roof he caught sight of a dark and shaggy beast running on all fours just turning out of the corridor, and taking the first step of the descent towards the floor beneath. Without pausing to consider, Sholto lunged forward with all his might, and his sword struck the fugitive quadruped behind the shoulder. He had time to see in the pale bluish flicker of the *cruisie* lamp that the beast he had wounded was of a dark colour, and that its head seemed immensely too large for its body.

Nevertheless, the thing did not fall, but ran on and

vanished out of Sholto's sight. The young man again set the silver call to his lips and blew. The next moment he could hear the soldiers of the guard clattering upward from their hall, and he himself ran along the corridor towards the place whence the screams of terror seemed to proceed.

CHAPTER XVI

SHOLTO CAPTURES A PRISONER OF DISTINCTION

He found that the noise came from the chamber occupied by the little Lady Margaret. When he arrived at the door it stood open to the wall. The child was sitting up on her bed, clothed in the white garmentry of the night. Bending over her, with her arms round the heaving shoulders of the little girl, Sholto saw Maud Lindesay, clad in a dark, hooded mantle thrown with the appearance of haste about her. The door of the next chamber also stood wide, and from the coverlets cast on the floor it was obvious that its occupant had left it hastily in order to fly to her friend's assistance.

At the sound of hasty footsteps Maud Lindesay turned about, and was instantly stricken pale and astonished by the sight of the young man with his sword bare. She cried aloud with a stern and defiant countenance, "Sholto MacKim, what do you here?"

And before he had time to answer, the little girl looked at him out of her friend's arms and called out: "O Sholto, Sholto, I am so glad you are come. I woke to find such a terrible thing looking at me out of the night. It was shaped like a great wolf, but it was rough of hide, and had upon it a head like a man's. I was so terrified that at first I could not cry out. But when it came nearer, and gazed at me, then I cried. Do not go away, Sholto. I am so glad, so glad that you are here."

Maud Lindesay had again turned towards Margaret.

"Hush," she said soothingly, "it was a dream. You were frighted by a vision, by a nightmare, by a succubus of the night. There is no beast within the castle."

"But I saw it plainly," the maid cried. "It opened the door as if it had hands— I saw it stand there by the bed and look at me—oh, so terribly! I saw its teeth glisten and heard them snap together!"

"Little one, be still, it was but a dream," said Sholto, untruthfully; "nevertheless I will go and search the rest of the castle."

And with these words he went along the corridor, finding the men whom he had summoned by means of his captain's silver call clustered upon the landing of the turret stair which communicated with the third floor. As he glanced along the oak-panelled corridor, it seemed to Sholto that he discerned a figure vanishing at the further end. Instantly he resolved on searching, and summoning his men to follow, he led the way down the passage, sword in hand. As he went he snatched the lamp from its pin on the wall, and held it in his left high above his head.

At the further end of the corridor was the door of a little chamber, and it seemed to Sholto that the shape he had seen must have disappeared at this point.

He knocked loudly on the door with the hilt of his sword, and cried, " If any be within, open — in the name of the Earl ! "

No voice replied, and Sholto boldly set his foot against

the lower panelling, and drove the door back to the wall with a clang.

Then at sight of a something dark, wrapped in a cloak, standing motionless against the window, the young captain of the guard elevated his lamp, and let the flicker of the light fall on the erect figure and haughty face of a young man, who, with his hand on his hip, stood considering the rude advance of his pursuers with a calm and questioning gaze.

It was the Earl of Douglas himself.

Sholto stood petrified at sight of him, and for a long minute could in no wise recover his self-control nor regain any use of his tongue.

"Well," said the Earl, haughtily, "whence this unseemly uproar? What do you here, Sholto?"

Then the spirit of his father came upon the young captain of the guard. He knew that he had only done his duty in its strictness, and he boldly answered the Earl: "Nay, my lord, were it not for courtesy, I have more right to ask you that question. Your sister hath been frighted, and at sound of her terror all we who were dispersed throughout the castle rushed to the spot. As I came down the stairs from the roof at speed, I saw something like to a great wolf about to descend the turret before me. With my sword I struck at it, and to all appearance wounded it. It vanished, and after searching the castle I can find neither wolf nor dog. But I saw, as it seemed, a figure enter this room, and upon opening it I find — the Earl of Douglas. That is all I know, and I leave the matter in my lord's own hands."

The haughty look gradually disappeared from the face of the Earl as Sholto spoke.

Smilingly he dismissed the guard with a word, saying that he would inquire into the cause of the disturbance in person, and then turned to Sholto.

"You are right," he said, "you have entirely done your duty and justified my appointment."

He paused, looked this way and that along the corridor, and continued:

"It chanced that in the tower without I could not sleep, and feeling uneasy concerning my guests, I entered the castle by the private door and staircase which leads into the apartment corresponding to this on the floor beneath. I was assuring myself that you were doing your duty when, being disturbed by the sudden hubbub, and judging it needless that the men-at-arms should know of my presence in the castle, I came in hither till the matter should have blown over. And so, but for your good conscience and the keenness of your vision, the matter would have ended."

Sholto bowed coldly.

"But, my lord," he said, ignoring the Earl's explanation, "the matter grows more mysterious than ever. Your sister, the little Lady Margaret, hath been grievously frighted by an appearance like a great beast which (so she affirms) opened the door of her chamber and looked within."

"She but dreamed," said the Earl, carelessly; "such visions come from supping late."

"But, with all respect, your lordship," continued Sholto, "I also saw the appearance even as I ran down the stairs from the roof at the noise of her crying."

"You were startled — excited, and but thought you saw."

Sholto reversed his sword, which he had held with the point towards the ground while he was speaking with his lord the Earl.

Holding the blade midway with much deference, he presented the hilt to William Douglas.

"Will you examine the point of this sword?" he said.

The Earl came a step nearer to him and Sholto advanced the steel till it was immediately beneath the lamp. There was blood upon the last inch or so of the blade. The Earl suddenly became violently agitated.

"This is indeed passing strange. There is no hound within the castle nor has there been for years. Even the presence of a lap-dog will fret my mother, so in my father's time they were every one removed to the kennels at the further end of the isle of Thrieve, whence even their howling cannot be heard. But let us proceed to the Lady Margaret, and on our way examine the place where you saw the apparition."

Sholto stood aside for the Earl to pass, but with a wave of his hand the latter said courteously, "Nay, but do you lead the way, captain of the guard."

They passed the door of the chamber where lay the Lady Sybilla. The niece of the ambassador must have been a heavy sleeper, for there was no sound within. Opposite was the chamber of the Earl's mother. She also appeared to be undisturbed, but the increasing deafness of the Countess offered a complete explanation of her tranquillity.

Next the two young men came to the door of the marshal's chamber. As they were about to pass, it opened silently, and a man-servant with a closely cropped obsequious head appeared within. He unclosed the door no further than would permit of his exit, and then he shut it again behind him, and stood holding the latch in his hand.

"His Excellency, being overfatigued, hath need of a little strong spirit," he said, with a curious gobbling movement of his throat as if he himself had been either thirsty or in deadly and overmastering fear.

The Earl ordered Sholto to wake the cellarer and bid him bring the ambassador of France that which he required. He himself would go onward to his sister's chamber. Sholto somewhat sullenly obeyed, for his heart was hot and angry within him. He thought that he began to see clearly the motive of the Earl's presence in the castle. The youth was himself so deeply and hopelessly in love with Mistress Maud Lindesay that he could not understand any other of his sex being insensible to the charm of her beauty and myriad winsome graces.

As he went down the stairs he recalled a thousand circumstances to mind which now seemed capable of but one explanation. It was evident that the Earl William came to visit some one by means of the private staircase under cloud of night. Nay, more, Maud Lindesay and he might be already privately married, and the matter kept secret on account of the pride of his family, who devised another match for him. For though the daughter of a knight, Maud Lindesay was assuredly no fit mate for the head of the more than regal house of Douglas. He remembered how on Sundays and saints' days Earl William always rode to and from the kirk with his sister on one side and Maud Lindesay on the other. That the young Earl was by no means insensible to

I

beauty, Sholto knew well, and he remembered his words to his own father, when he had asked to be allowed to accompany him on his Flanders mare, that such attendance was not seemly when a man was going a-courting.

As is always the case, he grew more and more confirmed in his ill humour, so soon as the eye of jealousy began to view everything in the light of prepossession.

Sholto awaked the cellarer out of his crib, who, presently, with snorts of disdain and much jangling of steel keys, drew half a tankard from a keg of spirit in the cellar on the dungeon floor and handed it grudgingly to the captain of the guard.

"The Frenchman wants it, does he?" he growled. "Had the messenger been old Landless Jock, I had known down whose Scottish throat it had gone, but this one is surely too young for such tricks. See that you spill it not by the way, Master Sholto," he called out after him, as that youth betook himself up to the chamber of the ambassador of France.

At the shut portal he paused and knocked. His hand was on the pin to enter with the tankard as was the custom. But the door opened no more than an inch or two, and the dark face of the cropped servitor appeared in the crevice.

"In a moment, sir," he said, and again vanished within, while a strong animal odour disengaged itself almost like something tangible from the chinks of the doorway.

Sholto stood in astonishment with the *eau de vie* in his hand, till presently the door was opened again very quickly. The form of the servitor was seen, and with a swift edging motion he came out, drawing the door behind him as before. He held a bar of iron in his hand like the fastening of a window, and a little breath of heat told the smith's son that though black it was still warm from the fire.

"Take this iron," he said abruptly, "and bring it to me fully heated. I am finishing a little device which his Excellency needs for the combat of the morrow."

The captain of the guard was nettled at the man's tone. Also he desired much to know what his master was doing on the floor above.

"Heat it at your own nose, fellow," he said rudely; "I am captain of the castle-guard, and must attend to my own business. Take the spirit out of my hand if you do not want it thrown in your face."

The swarthy, bullet-headed man glared at him with eyes like burning coals, but Sholto cared no jot for his anger. Forthwith he turned his back upon him, glad at heart to have found some one to quarrel with, and hoping that the ambassador's squire might prove courageous and challenge him to fight on the morrow.

But the man only replied: "I am Henriet, servant of the marshal. I bid you remember that I shall make you live to regret these words."

CHAPTER XVII

THE LAMP IS BLOWN OUT

THE door of Margaret Douglas's chamber still stood open, and Sholto found Earl William seated upon the foot of the bed, endeavouring by every means in his power to distract his sister's attention from her fears. Maud Lindesay, now more completely dressed than when he had first seen her, sat on the other side of the little lady's couch. She was laughing as he entered at some merry jest of the Earl's. And at the sound of her tinkling mirth Sholto's heart sank within him. So soon as she caught sight of the new captain of the guard the gladness left her face, and she became grave and sober, like a gossip long unconfessed when the holy father comes knocking at the door.

At sight of her emotion Sholto resolved that if his fears should prove to be well founded, he would resign his honourable office. For to abide continually in the castle, and hourly observe Maud Lindesay's love for another, was more than his philosophy could stand.

In the meantime there was only his duty to be done. So he saluted the Earl, and in a few words told him that which he had seen. But the soul of William Douglas was utterly devoid of suspicion, both because he held himself so great that none could touch him, and also because, being high of spirit and open as the sky, he read into the acts of others his own straightforwardness and unsuspicion.

The Earl rose smilingly, declaring to Margaret that to-morrow he would hang every dog and puppy in Galloway on the dule tree of Thrieve, whereupon the child began to plead for the life of this cur and that other of her personal acquaintances with a tearful earnestness which told of a sorely jangled mind.

" Well, at least," cried Earl Douglas, " I will not have such brutes prowling about my castle of Thrieve even in my sister's dreams. Captain Sholto, do you station a man of your guard in the angle of the staircase where it looks along each corridor. Pick out your prettiest crossbowmen, for it were not seemly that my guests should be disturbed by the rude shots and villanous reek of the fusil."

Sholto bowed stiffly and waited the further pleasure of his master. Then the two young men went out without Maud Lindesay having uttered a word, or manifested the least surprise at the advancement which had befallen the heir of the master armourer of Carlinwark.

As soon as the door had closed upon the two maidens, the Earl turned a face suddenly grave and earnest on his young captain of the guard.

" What think you," he said, " was this appearance real ? "

" Real enough to leave these upon the floor," answered Sholto, pointing to sundry gouts and drops of blood upon the turret stairs.

The Earl took the lamp from his hand and earnestly scrutinised each step in a downward direction. The spots ran irregularly as if the wounded beast had shaken his head from side to side as he ran. They turned along towards the corridor where at the first alarm Sholto had found the Earl, and in the very midst of it abruptly stopped. While Sholto and William Douglas were examining the floor, they both looked over their shoulders, uneasily conscious of a regard upon them, as if some one, unseen himself, had been looking down from behind.

"Do you place your men as I told you," said the Earl, abruptly, "and bring me a truckle bed out of the guard-room. I shall remain in this closet till morning. But do you keep a special lookout on the floor above, that the repose of my sister and her friend be not again disturbed."

Sholto bowed without speech, and hastening down to the guardroom he commanded two of his best bowmen to follow him with their apparatus, while he himself snatched up the low truckle couch which custom assigned to the captain of the guard should he desire to rest himself during the night, and on which Landless Jock had always passed the majority of his hours of duty. This he carried to the Earl, and placing it in the angle he saw his youthful master stretch himself upon it, wrapped in his cloak and with a naked sword ready to his hand.

"A good and undisturbed slumber to you, my lord," said Sholto, curtly, as he went out.

He saw that his two men were duly posted upon the lower landing of the stair, and then betook himself to the upper floor where slept the little Maid of Galloway.

He walked slowly to the end of the passage scrutinising every recess and closet door, every garde-robe and wall press from which it was possible that the beast he had seen might have emerged. He was wholly unsuccessful

in discovering anything suspicious, and had almost resolved to station himself at the turn of the staircase
which led down from the roof, when, looking back, at
the sharp click of a latch, he saw Maud Lindesay coming
out of the chamber of the little Maid of Galloway.

Softly closing the door behind her, she paused a
moment as if undecided, and then more with her chin
than with her finger she beckoned him to approach.

"She sleeps," said the girl, softly, "but so uncertainly
and with so many startings of terror, that I will not leave
her alone. Will you aid me to remove the mattress
of my couch and lay it on the floor beside her?"

Sholto signified his willingness. His mind was more
than ever oppressed by the thought that the Earl of
Douglas loved this girl, whom he had found listening to
his jests with such frank joyousness.

Maud stayed him with one of the long looks out from
under her eyelashes. The dark violet orbs rested upon
him a moment reproachfully with a hurt expression in
their depths, and were then dropped with a sigh.

"You are still angry with me," she said, a little wistfully, "and I wanted to tell you how happy it made me
— made us, I mean — when we heard that you were to
be captain of the castle-guard instead of that grumbling
old curmudgeon, Jock of Abernethy."

The heart of Sholto was instantly melted, more by her
looks than by her words, though deep within him he had
still an angry feeling that he was being played with.
All the same, and in spite of his resolves, the eyeshot
from under those dark and sweeping lashes did its usual
and deadly work.

"I did not know that aught which might befall me

could be anything to Mistress Maud Lindesay," said Sholto, with the last shreds of dignity in his voice.

"I said not to me, but to *us*," she corrected, smiling; "but tell me what think you of this appearance which has so startled our Margaret. Was it ghost or goblin or dream of the night? We have never had either witch or warlock about the house of Thrieve since the old Abbot Gawain laid the ghost of Archibald the Grim with four-and-forty masses, said without ever breaking his fast, down there in the castle chapel."

"Nay, ask me not," answered Sholto, "I am little skilled in matters spiritual. I should try sword point and arrowhead on such gentry, and if these do them no harm, why then I think they will not distress me much."

But all the same he said nothing to the girl about the red blood on his sword or the splashed gouts on the steps of the staircase.

He followed Maud Lindesay into her chamber, and being arrived there, lifted couch and all in his arms, with an ease born of long apprenticeship to the forehammer. The girl regarded him with admiration which she was careful not to dissemble.

"You are very strong," she said. Then, after a pause, she added, "Margaret and I like strong men."

The heart of the youth was glad within him, thus to be called a man, even though he kept saying over and over to himself: "She means it not! She means it not! She loves the Earl! I know well she loves the Earl!"

Maud Lindesay paused a moment before the chamber door of her little charge, finger on lip, listening.

"She sleeps — go quietly," she whispered, holding the

door open for him. He set down the bed where she
showed him — by the side of the small slumbering figure
of the Maid of Galloway.

Then he went softly to the door. The girl followed
him. "You will not be far away," she said doubtfully
and with a perilous sort of humility, "if this dreadful
thing should come back again? I — that is we, would
feel safer if we knew that you — that any one strong and
brave was near at hand."

Then the heart of Sholto broke out in quick anger.

"Deceive me not," he cried, "I know well that the
Earl loves you, and that you love him in return."

"Well, indeed, were it for my lord Earl if he loved as
honest a woman," said Maud Lindesay, pouting disdainfully. "But what is such a matter, yea or nay, to
you?"

"It is all life and happiness to me," said Sholto, earnestly. "Ah, do not go — stay a moment. I shall never
sleep this night if you go without giving me an answer."

"Then," said the girl, "you will be the more in the
line of your duty, which allows not much sleep o' nights.
You are but a silly, petulant boy for all your fine cap-
taincy. I wish it had been Landless Jock. He would
never have vexed me with foolish questions at such a
time."

"But I love you, and I demand an answer," cried
Sholto, fuming. "Do you love the Earl?"

"What do you think yourself now?" she said, looking
up at him with an inimitable slyness, and pronouncing
her words so as to imitate the broad simplicity of countryside speech.

Sholto vented a short gasp or inarticulate snort of

anger, at which Maud Lindesay started back with affected terror.

"Do not fright a poor maid," she said. "Will you put me in the castle dungeon if I do not answer? Tell me exactly what you want me to say, and I will say it, most mighty captain."

And she made him the prettiest little courtesy, turning at the same time her eyes in mock humility on the ground.

"Oh, Maud Lindesay," said Sholto, with a little conflicting sob in his throat, ill becoming so noted a warrior as the captain of the castle-guard of the Black Douglas, "if you knew how I loved you, you would not treat me thus."

The girl came nearer to him and laid a white and gentle hand on the sleeve of his blue archer's coat.

"Nay, lad," she said more soberly, lifting a finger to his face, "surely you are no milksop to mind how a girl flouts you. Love the Earl — say you? Well, is it not our duty to the bread we eat? Is he not worthy? Is he not the head of our house?"

"Cheat me not with words. The Earl loves you," said Sholto, lifting his head haughtily out of her reach. (To have one's chin pushed this way and that by a girl's forefinger, and as it were considered critically from various points of view, may be pleasant, but it interferes most seriously with dignity.)

"He may, indeed," drolled the minx, "one can never tell. But he has never said so. He is perhaps afraid, being born without the self-conceit of some people — archers of the guard, fledgling captains, and such-like gentrice."

"Do you love him?," reiterated Sholto, determinedly.

"I will tell you for that gold buckle," said Maud, calmly pointing with her finger.

Instantly Sholto pulled the cap from his head, undid the pin of the archery prize, and thrust it into his wicked sweetheart's hands.

She received it with a little cry of joy, then she pressed it to her lips. Sholto, rejoicing at heart, moved a step nearer to her. But, in spite of her arch delight, she was on the alert, for she retreated deftly and featly within the chamber door of the Fair Maid of Galloway. There was still more mirthful wickedness in her eyes.

"Love the Earl? — Of course I do. Indeed, I doat upon him," she said. "How I shall love this buckle, just because his hand gave it to you!"

And with that she shut to the door.

Sholto, in act to advance, stood a moment poised on one foot like a goose. Then with a heart blazing with anger, and one of the first oaths that had ever passed his lips, he turned on his heel and strode away.

"I will never think of her again — I will never see her. I will go to France and perish in battle. I will throw me in the castle pool. I will — "

So the poor lad retreated, muttering hot and angry words, all his heart sore within him because of the cruelty of this girl.

But he had not proceeded twenty steps along the corridor, when he heard the door softly open and a low voice whispered, "Sholto! Sholto! I want you, Sholto!"

He bent his brows and strode manfully on as if he had not heard a word.

"Sholto! — dear Sholto! Do not go, I need you."

Against his will he turned, and, seeing the head of
Maud Lindesay, her pouting lips and beckoning finger,
he went sulkily back.

"Well?" he said, with the stern curtness of a military
commander, as he stood before her.

She held the iron lamp in her hand. The wick had
fallen aside and was now wasting itself in a broad, unequal yellow flame. The maid of honour looked at it
in perplexity, knitting her pretty brows in a mock frown.

"It burned me as I was ordering my hair," she said.
"I cannot blow it out. I dare not. Will you — will you
blow it out for me, Captain Sholto?"

She spoke with a sweet childlike humility.

And she held the lamp up so that the iron handle was
almost touching her soft cheek. There was a dancing
challenge in her dark eyes and her lips smiled danger-
ously red. She could not, of course, have known that
the light made her look so beautiful, or she would have
been more careful.

Sholto stood still a moment, at wrestle with himself,
trying to conquer his dignity, and to retain his attitude
of stern disapproval.

But the girl swept her lashes up towards him, dropped
them again dark as night upon her cheek, and anon
looked a second time at him.

"I am sorry," she said, more than ever like a child.
"Forgive me, and — the lamp is so hot."

Now Sholto was young and inexperienced, but he was
not quite a fool. He stooped and blew out the light, and
the next moment his lips rested upon other lips which,
as it had been unconsciously, resigned their soft sweetness to his will.

Then the door closed, and he heard the click of the lock as the bolts were shot from within. The gallery ran round and round about him like a clacking wheel. His heart beat tumultuously, and there was a strange humming sound in his ears.

The captain of the guard stumbled half distracted down the turret stair.

The old world had been destroyed in a moment and he was walking in a new, where perpetual roses bloomed and the spring birds sang for evermore. He knew not, this poor foolish Sholto, that he had much to learn ere he should know all the tricks and stratagems of this most naughty and prettily disdainful minx, Mistress Maud Lindesay.

But for that night at least he thought he knew her heart and soul, which made him just as happy.

CHAPTER XVIII

THE MORNING LIGHT

In the morning Sholto MacKim had other views of it. Even when at last he was relieved from duty he never closed an eye. The blowing out of the lamp had turned his ideas and hopes all topsy-turvy. His heart sang loud and turbulent within him. He had kissed other girls indeed before at kirns and country dances. He laughed triumphantly within him at the difference. They had run into corners and screamed and struggled, and held up ineffectual hands. And when his lips did reach their goal, it was generally upon the bridge of a nose or a tip of an ear. He could not remember any especial pleasure accompanying the rite.

But this! The bolt of an arbalast could not have given him a more instant or tremendous shock. His nerves still quivered responsive to the tremulous yielding of the lips he had touched for a moment in the dark of the doorway. He felt that never could he be the same man he had been before. Deep in his heart he laughed at the thought.

And then again, with a quick revulsion, the return wave came upon him. "How, if she be as untouched as her beauty is fresh, has she learned that skill in caressing?"

He paused to think the matter over.

"I remember my father saying that a wise man should always mistrust a girl who kisses overwell."

Then again his better self would reassert itself.

"No," he would argue, tramping up and down the corridor, wheeling in the short bounds of the turnpike head, and again returning upon his own footsteps, "why should I belie her? She is as pure as the air—only, of course, she is different to all others. She speaks differently; her eyes are different, her hair, her hands—why should she not be different also in this?"

But when Maud Lindesay met Sholto in the morning, coming suddenly upon him as he stood, with a pale face and dark rings of sleeplessness about his eyes, as he looked meditatively out upon the broad river and the blue smoke of the morning campfires, there was yet another difference to be revealed to him. He had expected that, like others, she would be confused and bashful meeting him thus in the daylight, after—well, after the volcanic extinguishing of the lamp.

But there she stood, dainty and calm under the morning sunshine, in fresh clean gown of lace and varied whiteness, her face grave as a benediction, her eyes deep and cool like the water of the castle well.

Sholto started violently at sight of her, recovered himself, and eagerly held out both his hands.

"Maud," he said hoarsely, and then again, in a lower tone, "sweetest Maud."

But pretty Mistress Lindesay only gazed at him with a certain reserved and grave surprise, looking him straight in the face and completely ignoring his outstretched hands.

"Captain Sholto," she said steadily and calmly, "the

Lady Margaret desires to see you and to thank you for your last night's care and watchfulness. Will you do me the honour to follow me to her chamber?"

There was no yielding softness about this maiden of the morning hours, no conscious droop and a swift up-lifting of penitent eyelids, no lingering glances out of love-weighted eyes. A brisk and practical little lady rather, her feet pattering most purposefully along the flagged passages and skipping faster than even Sholto could follow her. But at the top of the second stairs he was overquick for her. By taking the narrow edges of the steps he reached the landing level with his mistress.

His desire was to put out his hand to circle her lithe waist, for nothing is so certainly reproductive of its own species as a first kiss. But he had reckoned with-out the lady's mutual intent and favour, which in mat-ters of this kind are proverbially important. Mistress Maud eluded him, without appearing to do so, and stood farther off, safely poised for flight, looking down at him with cold, reproachful eyes.

"Maud Lindesay, have you forgotten last night and the lamp?" he asked indignantly.

"What may you mean, Captain Sholto?" she said, with wonderment in her tone, "Margaret and I never use lamps. Candles are so much safer, especially at night."

CHAPTER XIX

LA JOYEUSE BAITS HER HOOK

On the morrow, the ambassador of France being confined to his room with a slight quinsy caught from the marshy nature of the environment of Thrieve, the Earl escorted the Lady Sybilla to the field of the tourney, where, as Queen of Beauty, her presence could not be dispensed with.

The Maid Margaret, the Earl's sister, remained also in the castle, not having yet recovered from her fright of the preceding evening.

With her was Maud Lindesay and her mother — "the Auld Leddy," as she was called throughout all the wide dominions of her son.

In spite of his weariness Sholto led his archer guard in person to the field of the tournament. For this day was the day of the High Sport, and many lances would be splintered, and often would the commonalty need to be scourged from the barriers.

But ere he went Sholto summoned two of the staunchest fellows of his company, Andro, called the Penman, and his brother John. Then, having posted them at either end of the corridor in which were the chambers occupied by the two girls, he laid a straight charge, and a heavy, upon them.

"On your heads be it if you fail, or let one soul pass,"

he said. "Stand ready with your hands on the wheel of
your crossbows, and if any man come hither, challenge
him to stand, and bid him return the way he came. But
if any dog or thing running on four feet ascend or descend the stair, make no sound, ask no question, cry no
warning, but whang the steel bolt through his ribs, in at
one side and out at the other."

Then Andro the Penman and his brother John, being
silent capable fellows, said nothing, but spat on their
hands, smiled at each other well pleased, and made the
wheels of their crossbows sing a clear whirring note.

"I would not like to be that dog —" said Andro the
Swarthy.

"Whose foul carcase I pray God to send speedily,"
echoed John the Blond.

Sholto had hoped that whilst he was at the guard-
setting, he might have had occasion to see once more the
tantalising mischief-maker whom he yet loved with all
his heart, in spite of, or perhaps because of, the distrac-
tion to which she continually reduced his spirit by means
of her manifold and incalculable contrarieties.

Nevertheless, it was with an easier heart that Sholto
wended his way out of the castle yett, all arrayed in the
new suit of armour his lord had sent him. It was made
of chain of the finest, composed of many rings set alternately thick and thin, and the whole was flexible as the
deer leather which he wore underneath it. Over this a
doublet of blue silk carried the Lion of Galloway done
in white upon it, and all the cerulean of the ground was
dotted over with the Douglas heart. But, greatest joy
of all, there was brought to him by command of the
Earl a suitable horse, not heavily armed like a charger

for the tilt, but light of foot, and answering easily to the
hand. Blue and red were the silken housings, fringed
with long silver lace, through which could be seen here
and there as the wind blew the sheen of the glossy skin.
The buckles and bits were also of massive silver, and at
sight of them the cup of Sholto's happiness was full.
For a space, as he gazed upon his steed, he forgot even
Maud Lindesay.

Then when he was mounted and out upon the green,
waiting for the coming forth of his lord, what delight it
was to feel the noble dark grey answer to each touch of
the rein, obeying his master's thought more than the
strength of his wrist or the prick of his heel.

As he waited there, his predecessor in office, old Sir
John of Abernethy, Landless Jock as he was nicknamed,
came out from the main doorway. He carried a gleaming headpiece from which the blue feather of the Douglas fell over his arm half-way to the ground. On its
front was a lion crest which ramped among golden *fleur-
de-lys*. The old man held it up for Sholto to take.

"Hae," he said in a surly tone, "this is his lordship's
new helmet just brought as a present frae the Dauphin
of France. So he has cast off the well-tried one, and
with it also the auld servant that hath served him these
many years."

"Nay, Sir John," said Sholto, with courtesy, taking
the helmet which it was his duty as his master's esquire
to carry before him on a velvet-covered placque, "nay
— well has the good servant deserved his rest, and to
take his ease. The young to the broil and the moil,
the old to the inglenook and the cup of wine beneath
the shade."

"Ah, lad, I envy ye not, think not that of puir Landless Jock," said the mollified old man, sadly shaking his
head; "I also have tried the new office, the shining armour, and felt the words of command rise proudly in the
throat. I envy you not, though your advancement hath
been sudden—and well—for my own son John I had
hoped, though indeed the loon is paper backed and feck-
less. But now there remains for me only to go to the
Kirk of Saint Bride in Douglasdale, and there set me
down by my auld master's coffin till I die."

At that moment there issued forth from the gateway
the young Earl, holding by the hand the Lady Sybilla.
His mother, the Countess, came to the door to see them
ride away. The Queen of the Sports was in a merry
mood, and as she tripped down the steps she turned,
and looking over her shoulder she called to the Lady
Douglas, "Fear not for your son, I will take good care
of him!"

But the elder woman answered neither her smile nor
yet her word, but stood like a mother who sees a first-
born son treading in places perilous, yet dares not warn
him, knowing well that she would drive him to giddier
and yet more dangerous heights.

The pennons of the escort fluttered in the breeze as
the men on horseback tossed their lances high in the
air, in salutation of their lord. The archer guard stood
ranked and ready, bows on their shoulders and arrows
in quiver. Horses neighed, armour clanked and sparkled, and from the moat platform twenty silver trumpets blared a fanfare as the Lady Sybilla, the arbiter
of this day's chivalry, mounted her palfrey with the help
of Earl Douglas. She thanked him with a low word in

his ear, audible only to himself, as he set her in the
saddle and bent to kiss her hand.

A right gallant pair were Douglas and Sybilla de
Thouars as they rode away, their heads close together,
over the green sward and under the tossing banners of
the bridge. Sholto was behind them giving great heed to
the managing of his horse, and wondering in his heart
if indeed Maud Lindesay were looking down from her
chamber window. As they passed the drawbridge he
turned him about in his saddle, as it were, to see that
his men rode all in good order. A little jet of white
fluttered quickly from the sparred wooden gallery which
clung to the grey walls of Thrieve, just outside the
highest story. And the young man's heart told him
that this was the atonement of Mistress Maud Lindesay.

Earl Douglas was in his gayest humour on this second
day of the great tourneying. He had got rid of his most
troublesome guests. His uncle James of Avondale, his
red cousin of Angus, the grave ill-assorted figure of the
Abbot of Dulce Cor, had all vanished. Only the young
and chivalrous remained, — his cousins, William and
James, Hugh and Archibald, good lances all and excellent fellows to boot. It was also a most noble chance
that the French ambassador was confined by the quinsy,
for it was certainly pleasant to ride out alone with that
beauteous head glancing so near his shoulder, to watch
at will the sun crimsoning yet more the red lips, sparkling in the eyes that were bright as sunshine slanting
through green leaves on a water-break, and to mark as
he fell a pace behind how every hair of that luxuriant
coif rippled golden and separate, like a halo of Floren-
tine work about the head of a saint.

The Lady Sybilla de Thouars was merry also, but
with what a different mirth to that of Mistress Maud
Lindesay — at least so thought Captain Sholto MacKim,
with a conscious glow of pride in his own Scottish sweetheart.

True, Sholto was scarce a fair judge in that he loved
one and did not love the other. He owned to himself in
a moment of unusual candour that there might be something in that. But when the gay tones of the lady's
laughter floated back on the air, as his master and she
rode forward by the edge of Dee towards the Lochar
Fords, the first fear with which he had looked upon her
in the greenwood returned upon the captain of the guard.

Earl William and the Lady Sybilla talked together
that which no one else could hear.

"So after all you have not become a churchman and
gone off to drone masses with the monks of your good
uncle?" she said, looking up at him with one of her
lingering, drawing glances.

"Nay," Earl William answered; "surely one Douglas
at the time is gift enough to holy church. At least, I
can choose my own way in that, though in most things
I am as straitly constrained as the King himself."

"Speaking of the King," she said, "my uncle the
Marshal must perforce ride to Edinburgh to deliver his
credentials. Would it not be a most mirthful jest to
ride with equipage such as this to that mongrel poverty-
stricken Court, and let the poor little King and his
starved guardian see what true greatness and splendour
mean?"

"I have sworn never again to enter Edinburgh town,"
said the Earl, slowly; "it was prophesied that there

one of my race must meet a black bull which shall trample the house of Douglas into ruins."

"Of course, if the Earl of Douglas is afraid—" mused the lady. The young man started as if he had been stung.

"Madame," he said with a sudden chill hauteur, "you come from far and do not know. No Douglas has ever been afraid throughout all their generations."

The lady turned upon him with a sweet and moving smile. She held out her fair hand.

"Pardon—nay, a thousand pardons. I knew not what I said. I am not acquainted with your Scottish speech nor yet with your Scottish customs. Do not be angry with me; I am a stranger, young, far from my own people and my own land. Think me foolish for speaking thus freely if you like, but not wilfully unkind."

And when the Earl looked at her, there were tears glittering in her beautiful eyes.

"I *will* go to Edinburgh," he cried. "I am the Douglas. The Tutor and the Chancellor are but as two straws in my hand, a longer and a shorter. I fling them from me—thus!"

The Lady Sybilla clapped her hands joyously and turned towards the young man. "Will you indeed go with me?" she cried. "Will you truly? I could kiss your hand, my Lord Douglas, you make me so glad."

"Your kiss will keep," said the Earl, with a quiet passion quivering in his voice.

"Nay, I meant it not thus—not as you mean it. I knew not what I said. But it will indeed change all things for me if you do but come. Then I shall have some one to speak with—some one with whom to laugh

at their pitiful Court mummery, their fiasco of dignity.
You are not like these other beggarly Scots, my Lord
Duke of Touraine."

"They are brave men and loyal gentlemen," said the
generous young Earl. "They would die for me."

"Nay, but so I declare would I," gaily cried the
lady, glancing at his handsome head with a quick admiring regard. "So would I — if I were a man. Besides, there is so little worth living for in a country such
as this."

The Earl was silent and she proceeded.

"But how joyous we shall be at Edinburgh! Know
you that at the Court of Charles that was my name —
La Joyeuse they called me. We will keep solemn
countenances, you and I, while we enter the presence
of the King. We will bow. We will make obeisances.
Then, when all is over, we will laugh together at the
fatted calf of a Tutor, the cunning Chancellor with his
quirks of law, and the poor schoolboy scarce breeched
whom they call King of Scotland. But all the while
I shall be thinking of the true King of Scots — who
alone shall ever be King to me —"

At this point La Joyeuse broke off short, as if her
feelings were hurrying her to say more than she had
intended.

"I did wrong to flout their messengers yesterday,"
said William Douglas, his boyish heart misgiving him at
dispraise of others; "perhaps they meant me well. But
I am naturally quick and easily fretted, and the men
annoyed me with their parchments royal, their heralds-
of-the-Lion, and the 'King of Scots' at every other
word."

"Who is the youth who rides at the head of your company?" said the Lady Sybilla.

"His name is Sholto MacKim, and it was but yesterday that I made him captain of my guard," answered the Earl.

"I like him not," said the Lady Sybilla; "he is full of ignorance and obstinacy and pride. Besides which, I am sure he loves me not."

"Save that last, I am not sure that a Douglas has a right to dislike him for any such faults. Ignorance, obstinacy, and pride are, indeed, good old Galloway virtues of the ancientest descent, and not to be despised in the captain of an archer guard."

"And pray, sir, what may be the ill qualities which, in Captain Sholto, make up for these excellent Scottish virtues?" asked the lady, disdainfully.

"He is faithful —" began the Earl.

"So is every dog!" interjected Sybilla de Thouars.

The Earl laughed a little gay laugh.

"There is one dog somewhere about the castle, licking an unhealed sword-thrust, that wishes our Sholto had been a trifle less faithful."

The Lady Sybilla sat silent in her saddle for a space; then, striking abruptly into a new subject, she said, "Do you defend the lists to-day?"

"Nay," answered the Earl, "to-day it is my good fortune to sit by your side and hold the truncheon while others meet in the shock. But the knight who this day gains the prize, to-morrow must choose a side against me and fight a *mêlée*."

"Ah," cried the girl, "I would that my uncle were healed of his quinsy. He loveth that sport. He says that he is too old to defend his shield all day against every comer, but in the *mêlée* he is still as good a lance as when he rode by the side of the Maid over the bridge of Orleans."

"That is well thought of," cried the Earl; "he shall lead the Knights of the Blue in my place."

"Nay, my Lord Duke," cried the Lady Sybilla, "more than anything on earth I desire to see you bear arms on the field of honour."

"Oh, I am no great lance," replied the Douglas, modestly; "I am yet too young and light. As things go now, the butterfly cannot tilt against the beef barrel when both are trussed into armour. But with the bare sword I will fight all day and be hungry for more. Aye, or rattle a merry rally with the quarter-staff like any common varlet. But at both Sholto there is my master, and doth ofttimes swinge me tightly for my soul's good."

The lady went on quickly, as if avoiding any further mention of Sholto's name.

"Nevertheless, to-morrow I must see you ride in the lists. My uncle says that your father was a mighty lance when he rode at Amboise, on the famous day of the Thirteen Victories."

"Ah, but my father was twice the man that I am," said the Earl, who had not taken his eyes from her face since she began to speak.

"Great alike in love and war?" she queried, smiling.

"So, at least, it is reported of him in Touraine," answered his son, smiling back at her.

"He loved and rode away, like all your race!" cried the girl, with a strange sudden flicker of passion which died as suddenly. "But I think it not of you, Lord

William. I know you could be true — that is, where you truly loved."

And as she spoke she looked at him with a questioning eagerness in her eyes which was almost pitiful.

" I do love and I am loyal," said the young man, with a grave quiet which became him well, and ought to have served him better with a woman than many protestations.

CHAPTER XX

In the fighting of that day James Douglas, the second son of the fat Earl of Avondale, won the prize, worsting his elder brother William in the final encounter. The victor was a nobly formed youth, of strength and stature greater than those of his brother, but without William of Avondale's haughty spirit and stern self-discipline.

For James Douglas had the easy popular virtues which would drink with any drawer or pricker at a tavern board, and made him ready to clap his last gold Lion on the platter to pay for the draught — telling, as like as not, the good gossip of the inn to keep the change, and (if well favoured) give him a kiss therefor. The Douglas *cortège* rode home amid the shoutings of the holiday makers who thronged all the approaches to the ford in order to see the great nobles and their trains ride by, and Sholto and his men had much trouble to keep these spectators as far back as was decent and seemly.

The Earl summoned his victorious cousins, William and James, to ride with him and the tourney's Queen of Beauty. But William proved even more silent than usual, and his dark face and upright carriage caused him to sit his charger as if carved in iron. Jolly James, on the other hand, attempted a jest or two which

140

savoured rustically enough. Nevertheless, he received
the compliments of the Lady Sybilla on his courage and
address with the equanimity of a practised soldier. He
was already, indeed, the best knight in Scotland, even as
he was twelve years after when in the lists of Stirling he
fought with the famous Messire Lalain, the Burgundian
champion.

Earl William dropped behind to speak a moment with
Sholto, and to give him the orders which he was to con-
vey to the provost of the games with regard to the
encounter of the morrow.

La Joyeuse took the opportunity of addressing her
nearer and more silent companion.

" You are, I think, the head of the other Douglas
House," said the Lady Sybilla, glancing up at the stern
and unbending Master of Avondale.

" There is but one house of Douglas, and but one head
thereof," replied Lord William, with a certain severity,
and without looking at her. The lady had the grace to
blush, either with shame or with annoyance at the
rebuff.

" Pardon," she said, " you must remember that I am a
foreigner. I do not understand your genealogies. I
thought that even in France I had heard of the Black
Douglas and the Red."

" The Red and the Black alike are the liegemen of
William of Douglas, whom Angus and Avondale both
have the honour of serving," answered he, still more
uncompromisingly.

" Aye," cried the jovial James, " cousin Will is the
only chief, and will make a rare lance when he hath
eaten a score or two more bolls of meal."

The Earl William returned even as James was speaking.

"What is that I hear about bolls of meal?" he said; "what wots this fair damosel of our rude Scots measures for oats and bear? You talk like the holder of a twenty-shilling land, James."

"I was saying," answered James Douglas, "that you would be a proper man of your lance when you had laid a score or two bolls of good Galloway meal to your ribs. English beef and beer are excellent, and drive a lance home into an unarmed foe; but it needs good Scots oats at the back of the spear-haft to make the sparks fly when knight meets with knight and iron rings on iron."

"Indeed, cousin Jamie," said the Earl, "you have some right to your porridge, for this day you have over-turned well nigh a score of good knights and come off unhurt and unashamed. Cousin William, how liked you the whammel you got from James' lance in your final course?"

"Not that ill," said the silent Master; "I am indeed better at taking than at giving. James is a stouter lance than I shall ever be —"

"Not so," cried jolly James. "Our Will never doth himself justice. He is for ever reading Deyrolles and John Froissard in order to learn new ways and tricks of fence, which he practises on the tilting ground, instead of riding with a tight knee and the weight of his body behind the shaft of ash. That is what drives the tree home, and so he gets many a coup. Yet to fall, and to be up and at it again, is by far the truer courage."

The Lady Sybilla laughed, as it seemed, heartily, yet with some little bitterness in the sound of it.

"I declare you Douglases stick together like crabs in a basket. Cousins in France do not often love each other so well. You are fortunate in your relations, my Lord Duke."

"Indeed, and that I am," cried the young man, joyously. "Here be my cousins, William and James — Will ever ready to read me out of wise books and advise me better than any clerk, Jamie aching to drive lance through any man's midriff in my quarrel."

"Lord, I would that I had the chance!" cried James. "Saint Bride! but I would make a hole clean through him and out at the back, though my elbuck should dinnle for a week after."

So talking together, but with the lady riding more silent and somewhat constrainedly in their midst, the three cousins of Douglas passed the drawbridge and came again to the precincts of the noble towers of Thrieve.

*   *   *   *   *   *

In an hour Sholto followed them, having ridden fast and furious across the long broomy braes of Boreland, and wet the fringes of his charger's silken coverture by vaingloriously swimming the Dee at the castle pool instead of going round by the fords. This he did in the hope that Maud Lindesay might see him. And so she did; for as he came round by the outside of the moat, making his horse caracole and thinking no little of himself, he heard a voice from an upper window call out: "Sholto MacKim, Maudie says that you look like a draggled crow. No, I will not be silent."

Then the words were shut off as if a hand had been set over the mouth which spoke. But presently the

voice out of the unseen came again : "And I hate you,
Sholto MacKim.   For we have had to keep in our chamber this livelong day, because of the two men you have
placed over us, as if we had been prisoners in Black
Archibald.[1] This very day I am going to ask my brother
to hang Black Andro and John his brother on the dule
tree of Carlinwark."

"Yes, indeed, and most properly," cried another voice,
which made his very heart flutter, "and set his new
captain of the guard a-dangle in the midst, decked out
from head to foot in peacocks' feathers."

Sholto was very angry, for like a boy he took not
chaffing lightly, and had neither the harshness of hide
which can endure the rasping of a woman's tongue, nor
the quickness of speech to give her the counter retort.

So he cast the reins of his horse to a stable varlet and
stamped indoors, carrying his master's helmet to the
armoury.   Then still without speech to any he brushed
hastily up the stairs towards the upper floor, which he
had set Andro the Penman and his brother to guard.

At the turning of the staircase David Douglas, the
Earl's brother, stopped him.   Sholto moved in salute
and would have passed by.

But David detained him with an impetuous hand.

"What is this ? " he said ; "you have set two archers
on the stairs who have shot and almost killed the ambassador's two servants, Poitou the man-at-arms, and
Henriet the clerk, just because they wished to take the
air upon the roof.   Nay, even when I would have visited
my sister, I was not permitted — 'None passes here save

---

[1] The pet name of the deepest dungeon of Castle Thrieve, yet extant
and plain to be seen by all.

the Earl himself, till our captain takes his orders off
us!' That was the word they spoke. Was ever the
like done in the castle of Thrieve to a Master of Douglas
before?"

"I am sorry, my Lord David," said Sholto, respectfully, "but there were matters within the knowledge of
the Earl which caused him to lay this heavy charge upon
me."

"Well," said the lad, quickly relenting, "let us go and
see Margaret now. She must have been lonely all this
fair day of summer."

But Sholto smiled, well pleased, thinking of Maud
Lindesay.

"I would that I had a lifetime of such loneliness as
Margaret's hath been this day," he said to himself.

At the turning of the stair they were stayed, for there,
his foot advanced, his bow ready to deliver its steel bolt
at the clicking of a trigger, stood Andro the Swarthy.

From his stance he commanded the stair and could
see along the corridor as well.

David Douglas caught his elbow on something which
stood a few inches out of the oaken panelling of the
turnpike wall. He tried to pull it out. It was the steel
quarrel of a cross-bow wedged firmly into the wood and
masonry. He cried: "Whence came this? Have you
been murdering any other honest men?"

The archer stood silent, glancing this way and that
like a sentinel on duty. The two young men went on
up the stair.

As their feet were approaching the sixth step, a sudden word came from the Penman like a bolt from his
bow.

L

"Halt!" he cried, and they heard the *gur-r-r-r* of his steel ratchet.

Sholto smiled, for he knew the nature of the man.

"It is I, your captain," he said. "You have done your duty well, Andro the Penman. Now get down to your dinner. But first give an account of your adventures."

"Do you relieve us from our charge?" said the archer, with his bow still at the ready.

"Certainly," quoth Sholto.

"Come, Jock, we are eased," cried Andro the Swarthy up the stair, and he slid the steel bolt out of its grip with a little click; "faith, my belly is toom as a last year's beef barrel."

"Did any come hither to vex you?" asked Sholto.

"Not to speak of," said the archer; "there were, indeed, two varlets of the Frenchmen, and as they would not take a bidding to stand, I had perforce to send a quarrel buzzing past their lugs into the wall. You can see it there behind you."

"Rascal," cried David Douglas, indignantly, "you do not say that first of all you shot it through the arm of the poor clerk Henriet."

"It is like enough," said Andro, coolly, "if his arm were in the way."

Then came a voice down the stairs from above.

"And the wretches would neither let any come to visit us nor yet permit us to go into the hall that we might speak with our gossips."

"How should we be responsible with our lives for the lasses if we had let them gad about?" said Andro, preparing to salute and take himself off.

At this moment the little maid and her elder companion came forward meekly and kneeled down before Sholto.

"We are your humble prisoners," said Maud Lindesay, "and we know that our offences against your highness are most heinous; but why should you starve us to death? Burn us or hang us, — we will bear the extreme penalty of the law gladly, — but torture is not for women. For dear pity's sake, a bite of bread. We have had nothing to eat all day, except two lace kerchiefs and a neck riband."

"Lord of Heaven," cried Sholto, swinging on his heel and darting down towards the kitchen, "what a fool unutterable I am!"

CHAPTER XXI

THE BAILIES OF DUMFRIES

The combat of the third day was, by the will of the Earl, to be of a peculiar kind. It was the custom at that time for the *mêlée* to be fought between an equal number of knights in open lists, each being at liberty to carry assistance to his friends as soon as he had disposed of his own man. On this occasion, however, the fight was to be between three knights with their several squires on the one side, and an equal number of knights and squires on the other.

As the combat of the previous day had decided, young James Douglas of Avondale was to lead one party, being the successful tilter of the day of single combat, while the Earl himself was to head the other.

The chances of battle must be borne, and whatever happened in the shock of fight was to be endured without complaint. But no blow was to be struck at either knight or squire in any way disabled by wound.

To Sholto's great and manifest joy the Earl, his master, chose the new captain of his guard to support him in the fray, and told him to make choice of the best battle-axe and sword he could find, as well as to provide himself with the shield which most suited the strength of his left arm.

"By your permission I will ask my father," said Sholto.

"He also fights on our side as the squire of Alan Fleming," said the Earl; "if Laurence had not been a monk, he might have made a third MacKim."

Then was Sholto's heart high and uplifted within him, to think of the victory he would achieve over his brother less than two days after they had parted, and he hastened off to choose his arms under the direction of his father.

The party of James of Avondale consisted of his brother William and young John Lauder, called Lauder of the Bass. These three had already entered their pavilion to accoutre themselves for the combat when a trumpet announced the arrival from the castle of the ambassador of France, who, being recovered from his sickness, had come in haste to see the fighting of the last and greatest day of the tourney.

As soon as he heard the wager of battle the marshal cried: "I also will strike a blow this day for the honour of France. My quinsy has altogether left me, and my blood flows strong after the rest. I will take part with James of Avondale."

And, without waiting to be asked, he went off followed by his servant Poitou towards the pavilion of the Avondale trio.

Now as the Marshal de Retz was the chief guest, it was impossible for James of Avondale to refuse his offer. But there was anger and blasphemy in his heart, for he knew not what the Frenchman could do, and though he had undoubtedly been a gallant knight in his day, yet in these matters (as James Douglas whispered to his brother) a week's steady practice is worth a lifetime of theory. Still there was nothing for the brothers from Douglasdale but to make the best of their bargain. The person most deserving of pity, however, was the young laird of the Bass, who, being thus dispossessed, went out to the back of the lists and actually shed tears, being little more than a boy, and none looking on to see him.

Then he came back hastily, and besought James of Douglas to let him fight as his squire, saying that as he had never taken up the knighthood which had been bestowed on him by the Earl for his journey to France, there could be nothing irregular in his fighting once more as a simple esquire. And thus, after an appeal to the Earl himself, it was arranged, much to John Lauder's content.

For his third knight the Douglas had made choice of his cousin Hugh, younger brother of his two opponents, and at that William and James of Avondale shook their heads.

"He pushes a good tree, our Hughie," said James. "If he comes at you, Will, mind that trick of swerving that he hath. Aim at his right gauntlet, and you will hit his shield."

The conflict on the Boat Croft differed much from the chivalrous encounters of an earlier time and a richer country. And of this more anon.

It chanced that on the borders of the crowd which that day begirt the great enclosure of the lists two burgesses of Dumfries stood on tiptoe, — to wit, Robert Semple, merchant dealing in cloth and wool, and Ninian Halliburton, the brother of Barbara, wife of Malise MacKim, master armourer, whose trade was only conditioned by the amount of capital he could find to lay out and the probability he had of disposing of his purchase within a reasonable time.

It would give an entirely erroneous impression of
the state of Scotland in 1440 if the sayings and doings
of the wise and shrewd burghers of the towns of Scotland were left wholly without a chronicler. The burghs
of Scotland were at once the cradles and strongholds of
liberty. They were not subject to the great nobles.
They looked with jealousy on all encroachments on
their liberties, and had sharp swords wherewith to en-
force their objection. They had been endowed with
privileges by the wise and politic kings of Scotland,
from William the Lion down to James the First, of
late worthy memory. For they were the best bulwark
of the central authority against the power of the great
nobles of the provinces.

Now Robert Semple and Ninian Halliburton were
two worthy citizens of Dumfries, men of respectability,
well provided for by the success of their trade and the
saving nature of their wives. They had come westward
to the Thrieve for two purposes: to deliver a large
consignment of goods and gear, foreign provisions and
fruits, to the controller of the Earl's household, and to
receive payment therefor, partly in money and partly in
the wool and cattle, hides and tallow, which have been the
staple products of Galloway throughout her generations.

Their further purposes and intents in venturing so
far west of the safe precincts of their burgh of Dumfries may be gathered from their conversation herein-
after to be reported.

Ninian Halliburton was a rosy-faced, clean-shaven
man, with a habit of constantly pursing out his lips
and half closing his eyes, as if he were sagely deciding
on the advisability of some doubtful bargain. His com-

panion, Robert Semple, had a similar look of shrewdness, but added to it his face bore also the imprint of a sly and lurking humour not unlike that of the master armourer himself. In time bygone he had kept his terms at the college of Saint Andrews, where you may find on the list of graduates the name of Robertus Semple, written by the foundational hand of Bishop Henry Wardlaw himself. And upon his body, as the Bailie of Dumfries would often feelingly recall, he bore the memory, if not the marks, of the disciplining of Henry Ogilvy, Master in Arts — a wholesome custom, too much neglected by the present regents of the college, as he would add.

"This is an excellent affair for us," said Ninian Halliburton, standing with his hands folded placidly over his ample stomach, only occasionally allowing them to wander in order to feel and approve the pile of the brown velvet out of which the sober gown was constructed. "A good thing for us, I say, that there are great lords like the Earl of Douglas to keep up the expense of such days as this."

"It were still better," answered his companion, dryly, "if the great nobles would pay poor merchants according to their promises, instead of threatening them with the dule tree if they so much as venture to ask for their money. Neither you nor I, Bailie, can buy in the lowlands of Holland without a goodly provision of the broad gold pieces that are so hard to drag from the nobles of Scotland."

The rosy-gilled Bailie of Dumfries looked up at his friend with a quick expression of mingled hope and anxiety.

"Does the Earl o' Douglas owe you ony siller?" he asked in a hushed whisper, "for if he does, I am willing to take over the debt — for a consideration."

"Nay," said Semple, "I only wish he did. The Douglases of the Black were never ill debtors. They keep their hand in every man's meal ark, but as they are easy in taking, they are also quick in paying."

"Siller in hand is the greatest virtue of a buyer," said the Bailie, with unction. "But, Robert Semple, though I was willing to oblige ye as a friend by taking over your debt, I'll no deny that ye gied me a fricht. For hae I no this day delivered to the bursar o' the castle o' Thrieve sax bales o' pepper and three o' the best spice, besides much cumin, alum, ginger, seatwell, almonds, rice, figs, raisins, and other sic thing. Moreover, there is owing to me, for wine and vinegar, mair than twa hunder pound. Was that no enough to gar me tak a 'dwam' when ye spoke o' the great nobles no payin'!"

"I would that all our outlying monies were as safe," said Semple; "but here come the knights and squires forth from their tents. Tell me, Ninian, which o' the lads are your sister's sons."

"There is but one o' the esquires that is Barbara Halliburton's son," answered the Bailie; "the ither is her ain man — and a great ram-stam, unbiddable, unhallowed deevil he is — Guid forbid that I should say as muckle to his face!"

CHAPTER XXII

WAGER OF BATTLE

THE knights had moved slowly out from their pavilions on either side, and now stood waiting the order to charge. My Lord Maxwell sat by the side of the Lady Sybilla, and held the truncheon, the casting down of which was to part the combatants and end the fight. The three knights on the southern or Earl's side were a singular contrast to their opponents. Two of them, the Earl William and his cousin Hugh, were no more than boys in years, though already old in military exercises; the third, Alan Fleming of Cumbernauld, was a strong horseman and excellent with his lance, though also slender of body and more distinguished for dexterity than for power of arm. Yet he was destined to lay a good lance in rest that day, and to come forth unshamed.

The Avondale party were to the eye infinitely the stronger, that is when knights only were considered. For James Douglas was little less than a giant. His jolly person and frank manners seemed to fill all the field with good humour, and from his station he cried challenges to his cousin the Earl and defiances to his brother Hugh, with that broad rollicking wit which endeared him to the commons, to whom "Mickle Lord Jamie" had long been a popular hero.

"Bid our Hugh there rin hame for his hippen clouts lest he make of himself a shame," he cried; "'tis not fair that we should have to fight with babes."

"Mayhap he will be as David to your Goliath, thou great gomeril!" replied the Earl with equal good humour, seeing his cousin Hugh blush and fumble uncomfortably at his arms.

Then to the lad himself he said: "Keep a light hand on your rein, a good grip at the knee, and after the first shock we will ride round them like swallows about so many bullocks."

The other two Avondale knights, William Douglas and the Marshal de Retz, were also large men, and the latter especially, clothed in black armour and with the royal ermines of Brittany quartered on his shield, looked a stern and commanding figure.

The squires were well matched. These fought on foot, armed according to custom with sword, axe, and dagger — though Sholto would much have preferred to trust to his arrow skill even against the plate of the knights.

The trumpets blew their warning from the judge's gallery. The six opposing knights laid their lances in rest. The squires leaned a little forward as if about to run a race. Lord Maxwell raised his truncheon. The trumpets sounded again, and as their stirring *tarantara* rang down the wide strath of Dee, the riders spurred their horses into full career. It so chanced that, as they had stood, James of Avondale was opposite the Earl, each being in the midst as was their right as leaders. The Master of Avondale opposed his brother Hugh, and the Marshal de Retz couched spear against

young Alan Fleming. In this order they started to ride
their course. But at the last moment, instead of riding
straight for his man, the Frenchman swerved to the
left, and, raising his lance high in the air, he threw it
in the manner of his country straight at the visor bars
of the young Earl of Douglas. The spear of James of
Avondale at the same time taking him fair in the middle
of his shield, the double assault caused the young man
to fall heavily from his saddle, so that the crash sounded
dully over the field.

"Treachery !   Treachery !— A foul false stroke ! A
knave's device !" cried nine-tenths of those who were
crowded about the barriers. "Stop the fight ! Kill the
Frenchman !"

"Not so," cried Lord Maxwell, "they were to fight
as best they could, and they must fight it to the
end !"

And this being a decision not to be gainsaid, the combat
proceeded on very unequal terms. Sholto, who had been
eagerly on the stretch to match himself with the squire
of James of Avondale, the young knight of the Bass,
found himself suddenly astride of his lord's body and
defending himself against both the French ambassador
and his squire Poitou, who had simultaneously crossed
over to the attack. For the Marshal de Retz, if not
in complete defiance of the written rule of chivalry, at
least against the spirit of gallantry and the rules of the
present tourney, would have thrust the Earl through
with his spear as he lay, crying at the same time,
"À outrance ! À outrance !" to excuse the foulness of
his deed.

It was lucky for himself that he did not succeed,

for, undoubtedly, the Douglases then on the field would have torn him to pieces for what they not unnaturally considered his treachery. As it was, there sounded a mighty roar of anger all about the barriers, and the crowd pressed so fiercely and threateningly that it was as much as the archers could do to keep them within reasonable bounds.

"Saints' mercy!" puffed stout Ninian Halliburton, "let us get out of this place. I am near bursen. Haud off there, varlet, ken ye not that I am a Bailie of Dumfries? Keep your feet off the tail o' my brown velvet gown. It cost nigh upon twenty silver shillings an ell!"

"A Douglas! A Douglas! Treachery! Treachery!" yelled a wild Minnigaff man, thrusting a naked brand high into the air within an inch of the burgess's nose. That worthy citizen almost fell backwards in dismay, and indeed must have done so but for the pressure of the crowd behind him. He was, therefore, much against his will compelled to keep his place in the front rank of the spectators.

"Well done, young lad," cried the crowd, seeing Sholto ward and strike at Poitou and his master, "God, but he is fechtin' like the black deil himself!"

"It will be as chancy for him," cried the wild Minnigaff hillman, "for I will tear the harrigals oot o' Sholto MacKim if onything happen to the Earl!"

But the captain of the guard, light as a feather, had easily avoided the thrust of the marshal's spear, taking it at an angle and turning it aside with his shield. Then, springing up behind him, he pulled the French knight down to the ground with the hook of his axe, by that trick of attack which was the lesson taught once for all to the Scots of the Lowlands upon the stricken field of the Red Harlaw.

The marshal fell heavily and lay still, for he was a man of feeble body, and the weight of his armour very great.

"Slay him! Slay him!" yelled the people, still furious at what, not without reason, they considered rank treachery.

Sholto recovered himself, and reached his master only in time to find Poitou bending over Earl Douglas with a dagger in his hand.

With a wild yell he lashed out at the Breton squire, and Sholto's axe striking fair on his steel cap, Poitou fell senseless across the body of Douglas.

"Well done, Sholto MacKim — well done, lad!" came from all the barrier, and even Ninian Halliburton cried: "Ye shall hae a silken doublet for that!" Then, recollecting himself, he added, "At little mair than cost price!"

"God in heeven, 'tis bonny fechtin!" cried the man from Minnigaff. "Oh, if I could dirk the fause hound I wad dee happy!"

And the hillman danced on the toes of the Bailie of Dumfries and shook the barriers with his hand till he received a rap over the knuckles from the handle of a partisan directed by the stout arms of Andro the Penman.

"Haud back there, heather-besom!" cried the archer, "gin ye want ever again to taste 'braxy'!"

Over the rest of the field the fortune of war had been somewhat various. William of Douglas had unhorsed his brother Hugh at the first shock, but immediately

foregoing his advantage with the most chivalrous courtesy, he leaped from his own horse and drew his sword.

On the right Alan Fleming, being by the marshal's
action suddenly deprived of his opponent, had wheeled
his charger and borne down sideways upon James of
Douglas, and that doughty champion, not having fully
recovered from the shock of his encounter with the Earl,
and being taken from an unexpected quarter, went down
as much to his own surprise as to that of the people at
the barriers, who had looked upon him as the strongest
champion on the field.

It was evident, therefore, that, in spite of the loss of
their leader, the Earl's party stood every chance to win
the field. For not only was Alan Fleming the only
knight left on horseback, but Malise MacKim had disposed of the laird of Stra'ven, squire to William of
Avondale, having by one mighty axe stroke beaten the
Lanarkshire man down to his knees.

"A Douglas! A Douglas!" shouted the populace;
"now let them have it!"

And the adherents of the Earl were proceeding to
carry out this intent, when my Lord Maxwell unexpectedly put an end to the combat by throwing down his
truncheon and proclaiming a drawn battle.

"False loon!" cried Sholto, shaking his axe at him in
the extremity of his anger, "we have beaten them fairly.
Would that I could get at thee! Come down and fight
an encounter to the end. I will take any Maxwell here
in my shirt!"

"Hold your tongue!" commanded his father, briefly,
"what else can ye expect of a border man but broken
faith?"

The archers of the guard rushed in, as was their duty, and separated the remaining combatants. Hugh and his brother William fought it to the last, the younger with all his vigour and with a fierce energy born of his brother James's taunts, William with the calm courtesy and forbearance of an old and assured knight towards one who has yet his spurs to win.

The stunned knights and squires were conveyed to their several pavilions, where the Earl's apothecaries were at once in attendance. William of Douglas was the first to revive, which he did almost as soon as the laces of his helm had been undone and water dashed upon his face. His head still sang, he declared, like a hive of bees, but that was all.

He bent with the anxiety of a generous enemy over the unconscious form of the Marshal de Retz, from whom they were stripping his armour. At the removal of the helmet, the strange parchment face with its blue-black stubbly beard was seen to be more than usually pale and drawn. The upper lip was retracted, and a set of long white teeth gleamed like those of a wild beast.

The apothecary was just commencing to strip off the leathern under-doublet from the ambassador's body to search for a wound, when Poitou, his squire, happened to open his eyes. He had been laid upon the floor, as the most seriously wounded of the combatants, though being the least in honour he fell to be attended last.

Instantly he cried out a strange Breton word, unintelligible to all present, and, leaping from the floor, he flung himself across the body of his master, dashing aside the astonished apothecary, who had only time to discern on the marshal's shoulder the scar of a recent cautery before Poitou had restored the leathern under-doublet to its place.

"Hands off! Do not touch my master. I alone can bring him to. Leave the room, all of you."

"Sirrah!" cried the Earl, sternly, striding towards him, "I will teach you to speak humbly to more honourable men."

"My lord," cried Poitou, instantly recalled to himself, "believe me, I meant no ill. But true it is that I only can recover him. I have often seen him taken thus. But I must be left alone. My master hath a blemish upon him, and one great gentleman does not humiliate another in the presence of underlings. My Lord Douglas, as you love honour, bid all to leave me alone for a brief space."

"Much cared he for honour, when he threw the lance at my master!" growled Sholto. "Had I known, I would have driven my bill-point six inches lower, and then would there have been a most satisfactory blemish in the joining of his neck-bone."

M

CHAPTER XXIII

SHOLTO WINS KNIGHTHOOD

THE ambassador recovered quickly after he had been
left with his servant Poitou, according to the latter's
request. The Lady Sybilla manifested the most tender
concern in the matter of the accident of judgment which
had been the means of diverting her kinsman from his
own opponent and bringing him into collision with the
Earl Douglas.

"Often have I striven with my lord that he should
ride no more in the lists," she said, "for since he received the lance-thrust in the eye by the side of La
Pucelle before the walls of Orleans, he sees no more
aright, but bears ever in the direction of the eye which
sees and away from that wherein he had his wound."

"Indeed, I knew not that the Marshal de Retz had
been wounded in the eye, or I should not have permitted
him to ride in the tourney," returned the Earl, gravely.
"The fault was mine alone."

The Lady Sybilla smiled upon him very sweetly and
graciously.

"You are great soldiers — you Douglases. Six knights
are chosen from the muster of half a kingdom to ride a
mêlée. Four are Douglases, and, moreover, cousins
germain in blood."

"Indeed, we might well have compassed the sword-
162

play," said the Earl William, "for in our twenty generations we never learned aught else. Our arms are strong enough and our skulls thick enough, for even mine uncle, the Abbot, hath his Latin by the ear. And one Semple, a plain burgher of Dumfries, did best him at it — or at least would have shamed him, but that he desired not to lose the custom of the Abbey."

"When you come to France," replied the girl, smiling on him, "it will indeed be stirring to see you ride a bout with young Messire Lalain, the champion of Burgundy, or with that Miriadet of Dijon, whose arm is like that of a giant and can fell an ox at a blow."

"Truly," said the young Earl, modestly, "you do me overmuch honour. My cousin James there, he is the champion among us, and alone could easily have overborne me to-day, without the aid of your uncle's blind eye. Even William of Avondale is a better lance than I, and young Hugh will be when his time comes."

"Your squire fought a good fight," she went on, "though his countenance does not commend itself to me, being full of all self-sufficience."

"Sholto — yes; he is his father's son and fought well. He is a MacKim, and cannot do otherwise. He will make a good knight, and, by Saint Bride, I will dub him one, ere this sun set, for his valiant laying on of the axe this day."

The great muster was now over. The tents which had been dotted thickly athwart the castle island were already mostly struck, and the ground was littered with miscellaneous débris, soon to be carried off in trail carts with square wooden bodies set on boughs of trees, and flung into the river, by the Earl's varlets and stablemen.

The multitudinous liegemen of the Douglas were by this time streaming homewards along every mountain pass. Over the heather and through the abounding morasses horse and foot took their way, no longer marching in military order, as when they came, but each lance taking the route which appeared the shortest to himself. North, east, and west spear-heads glinted and armour flashed against the brown of the heather and the green of the little vales, wherein the horses bent their heads to pull at the meadow hay as their riders sought the nearest way back again to their peel-towers and forty-shilling lands.

It was at the great gate of Thrieve that the Earl called aloud for Sholto. He had been speaking to his cousin William, a strong, silent man, whose repute was highest for good counsel among all the branches of the house of Douglas.

Sholto came forward from the head of his archer guard with a haste which betrayed his anxiety lest in some manner he had exceeded his duty. The Earl bade him kneel down. A little behind, the young Douglases of Avondale, William, James, and Hugh, sat their horses, while the boy David, who had been left at home to keep the castle, looked forth disconsolately from the window of the great hall. On the steps stood the little Maid Margaret and her companion, Maud Lindesay, who had come down to meet the returning train of riders. And, truth to tell, that was what Sholto cared most about. He did not wish to be disgraced before them all.

So as he knelt with an anxious countenance before his lord, the Earl took his cousin William's sword out of his hand, and, laying it on the shoulder of Sholto MacKim,

he said, "Great occasions bring forth good men, and
even one battle tries the temper of the sword. You,
Sholto, have been quickly tried, but thy father hath
been long tempering you. Three days agone you were
but one of the archer guard, yesterday you were made its
captain, to-day I dub you knight for the strong courage of the heart that is within, and the valiant service
which this day you did your lord. Rise, Sir Sholto!"

But for all that he rose not immediately, for the head
of the young man whirled, and little drumming pulses
beat in his temples. His heart cried within him like
the overword of a song, "Does she hear? Will she
care? Will this bring me nearer to her?" So that,
in spite of his lord's command, he continued to kneel,
till lusty James of Avondale came and caught him by
the elbow. "Up, Sir Knight, and give grace and good
thank to your lord. Not your head but mine hath a
right to be muzzy with the coup I gat this day on the
green meadow of the Boat Croft."

And practical William of Avondale whispered in his
cousin's ear, "And the lands for the youth that we
spoke of."

"Moreover," said the Earl, "that you may suitably
support the knighthood which your sword has won, I
freely bestow on you the forty-shilling lands of Aireland
and Lincolns with Screel and Ben Gairn, on condition
that you and yours shall keep the watch-fires laid ready
for the lighting, and that in time you rear you sturdy
yeomen to bear in the Douglas train the banneret of
MacKim of Aireland."

Sholto stood before his generous lord trembling and
speechless, while James Douglas shook him by the elbow

and encouraged him roughly, "Say thy say, man; hast lost thy tongue?"

But William Douglas nodded approval of the youth.

"Nay," he said, "let alone, James! I like the lad the better that he hath no ready tongue. 'Tis not the praters that fight as this youth hath fought this day!"

So all that Sholto found himself able to do, was no more than to kneel on one knee and kiss his master's hand.

"I am too young," he muttered. "I am not worthy."

"Nay," said his master, "but you have fairly won your spurs. They made me a knight when I was but two years of my age, and I cried all the time for my nurse, your good mother, who, when she came, comforted me with pap. Surely it was right that I should make a place for my foster-brother within the goodly circle of the Douglas knights."

"I AM TOO YOUNG," HE MUTTERED; "I AM NOT WORTHY."

CHAPTER XXIV

THE SECOND FLOUTING OF MAUD LINDESAY

SHOLTO MACKIM stood on the lowest step of the ascent into the noble gateway of Thrieve, hardly able to believe in his own good fortune. But these were the days when no man awaked without having the possibility of either a knighthood or the gallows tree to encourage him to do his duty between dawn and dark.

The lords of Douglas had gone within, and were now drinking the Cup of Appetite as their armour was being unbraced by the servitors, and the chafed limbs rubbed with oil and vinegar after the toils of the tourney. But still Sholto stood where his master had left him, looking at the green scum of duckweed which floated on the surface of the moat of Thrieve, yet of a truth seeing nothing whatever, till a low voice pierced the abstraction of his reverie.

"Sir Sholto!" said Mistress Maud Lindesay, "I bid you a long good-by, Sir Sholto MacKim! Say farewell to him, Margaret, as you hear me do!"

"Good-by, kind Sir Sholto!" piped the childish voice of the Maid of Galloway, as she made a little courtesy to Sholto MacKim in imitation of her companion. "I know not where you are going, but Maudie bids me, so I will!"

"And wherefore say you good-by to me?" cried Sholto, finding his words at once in the wholesome atmosphere of raillery which everywhere accompanied that quipsome damosel, Mistress Maud Lindesay.

"Why, because we are humble folk, and must get our ways upstairs out of the way of dignities. Permit me to kiss your glove, fair lord!" and here she tripped down the steps and pretended to take his hand.

"Hold off!" he cried, snatching it away angrily, for her tone vexed and thwarted him.

The girl affected a great terror, which merged immediately into a meek affectation of resignation.

"No—you are right—we are not worthy even to kiss your knightly hand," she said, "but we will respectfully greet you." Here she swept him a full reverence, and ran up the steps again before he could take hold of her. Then, standing on the topmost step, and holding her friend's hand in hers, she spoke to the Maid of Galloway in a tone hushed and regretful, as one speaks of the dead.

"No, Margaret," she said, "he will no more play with us. Hide-and-seek about the stack-yard ricks at the Mains is over in the gloamings. Sir Sholto cares no more for us. He has put away childish things. He will not even blow out a lamp for us with his own honourable lips. No, he will call his squire to do it!"

Sholto looked the indignation he would not trust himself to speak.

"He will dine with the Earl in hall, and quaff and stamp and shout with the best when they drink the toasts. But he has become too great a man to carry you and me any more over the stepping-stones at the

ford, or pull with us the ripe berries when the briars
are drooping purple on the braes of Keltonhill.   Bid
him good-by, Margaret, for he was our kind friend
once.   And when he rides out to battle, perhaps, if
we are good and respectful, he may again wave us a
hand and say: 'There are two lassies that once I
kenned!'"

At this inordinate flouting the patience of the new
knight, growing more and more angry at each word, came
quickly to the breaking point; for his nerves were jarred
and jangled by the excitement of the day. He gave vent
to a short sharp cry, and started up the steps with the
intention of making Mistress Lindesay pay in some
fashion for her impertinence. But that active and gamesome maid was most entirely on the alert. Indeed, she
had been counting from the first upon provoking such
a movement. And so, with her nimble charge at her
heels, Mistress Lindesay was already at the inner port,
and through the iron-barred gate of the turret stair,
before the youthful captain of the guard, still cumbered with his armour, could reach the top of the outer
steps.

As soon as Sholto saw that he was hopelessly dis-
tanced, he slackened his gait, and, with a sober tread
befitting a knight and officer of a garrison, he walked
along the passage which led to the chamber allotted to
the captain of the guard, from which that day Landless
Jock had removed his effects.

The soldiers of the guard, who had heard of the honours which had so swiftly come upon the young man,
rose and respectfully saluted their chief. And Sholto,
though he had been silent when the sharp tongue of the

mirth-loving maid tormented him, found speech readily enough now.

"I thank you," he said, acknowledging their salutations. "We have known each other before. Fortune and misfortune come to all, and it will be your turns one day. But up or down, good or ill, we shall not be the worse comrades for having kept the guard and sped the bolt together."

Then there came one behind him who stood at the door of his chamber, as he was unhelming himself, and said: "My captain, there stand at the turret stair the ladies Margaret and Maud with a message for you."

"A message for me — what is it?" said Sholto, testily, being (and small blame to him) a trifle ruffled in his temper.

"Nay, sir," said the man, respectfully, "that I know not, but methinks it comes from my lord."

It will not do to say to what our gallant Sholto condemned all tricksome queans and spiteful damosels in whose eyes dwelt mischief brimming over, and whose tongues spoke softest words that yet stung and rankled like fairy arrows dipped in gall and wormwood.

But since the man stood there and repeated, "I judge the message to be one from my lord," Sholto could do no less than hastily pull on his doublet and again betake himself along the corridor to the foot of the stair.

When he arrived there he saw no one, and was about to depart again as he had come, when the head of Maud Lindesay appeared round the upper spiral looking more distractedly mischievous and bewitching than ever, her head all rippling over with dark curls and her eyes fairly scintillating light. She nodded to him and leaned a little farther over, holding tightly to the baluster meanwhile.

"Well," said Sholto, roughly, "what are my lord's commands for me, if, indeed, he has charged you with any?"

"He bids me say," replied Mistress Maud Lindesay, "that, since lamps are dangerous things in maidens' chambers, he desires you to assist in the trimming of the waxen tapers to-night — that is, if so menial a service shame not your knighthood."

"Pshaw!" muttered Sholto, "my lord said naught of the sort."

"Well then," said Maud Lindesay, smiling down upon him with an expression innocent and sweet as that of an angel on a painted ceiling, "you will be kind and come and help us all the same?"

"That I will not!" said Sholto, stamping his foot like an ill-tempered boy.

"Yes, you will — because Margaret asks you?"

"*I will not!*"

"Then because *I* ask you?"

Spite of his best endeavours, Sholto could not take his eyes from the girl's face, which seemed fairer and more desirable to him now than ever. A quick sob of passion shook him, and he found words at last:

"Oh, Maud Lindesay, why do you treat thus one who loves you with all his heart?"

The girl's face changed. The mischief died out of it, and something vague and soft welled up in her eyes, making them mistily grey and lustrous. But she only said: "Sholto, it is growing dark already! It is time the tapers were trimmed!"

Then Sholto followed her up the stairs, and though I do not know, there is some reason for thinking that he forgave her all her wickedness in the sweet interspace between the gloaming and the mirk, when the lamps were being lighted on earth, and in heaven the stars were coming out.

CHAPTER XXV

THE DOGS AND THE WOLF HOLD COUNCIL

IT was a week or two after the date of the great wappenshaw and tourneying at the Castle of Thrieve, that in the midmost golden haze of a summer's afternoon four men sat talking together about a table in a room of the royal palace of Stirling.

No one of the four was any longer young, and one at least was immoderately fat. This was James, Earl of Avondale, granduncle of the present Earl of Douglas, and, save for young David, the Earl's brother, nearest heir to the title and all the estates and honours pertaining thereto, with the single exception of the Lordship of Galloway.

The other three were, first, Sir Alexander Livingston, the guardian of the King's person, a handsome man with a curled beard, who was supposed to stand high in the immediate favours of the Queen, and who had long been tutor to his Majesty as well as guardian of his royal person. Opposite to Livingston, and carefully avoiding his eye, sat a man of thin and foxy aspect, whose smooth face, small shifty mouth, and perilous triangular eyes marked him as one infinitely more dangerous than either of the former — Sir William Crichton, the Chancellor of the realm of Scotland.

The fourth was speaking, and his aspect, strange and

ofttimes terrifying, is already familiar to us. But the pallid corpse-like face, the blue-black beard, the wild-beast look, in the eyes of the Marshal de Retz, ambassador of the King of France, were now more than ever heightened in effect by the studied suavity of his demeanour and the graciousness of language with which he was clothing what he had to say.

"I have brought you together after taking counsel with my good Lord of Avondale. I am aware, most noble seigneurs, that there have been differences between you in the past as to the conduct of the affairs of this great kingdom; but I am obeying both the known wishes and the express commands of my own King in endeavouring to bring you to an agreement. You will not forget that the Dauphin of France is wedded to the Scottish princess nearest the throne, and that therefore he is not unconcerned in the welfare of this realm.

"Now, messieurs, it cannot be hid from you that there is one overriding and insistent peril which ought to put an end to all your misunderstandings. There is a young man in this land, more powerful than you or the King, or, indeed, all the powers legalised and established within the bounds of Scotland.

"Who is above the law, gentlemen? I name to you the Earl of Douglas. Who hath a retinue ten times more magnificent than that with which the King rides forth? The Earl of Douglas! Who possesses more than half Scotland, and that part the fairest and richest? Who holds in his hands all the strong castles, is joined by bond of service and manrent with the most powerful nobles of the land? Who but the Earl of Douglas, Duke of Touraine, Warden of the Marches, hereditary Lieutenant-General of the Kingdom ? ''

At this point the crafty eyes of Crichton the Chancellor were turned full upon the speaker. His hand tugged nervously at his thin reddish beard as if it had been combing the long goat's tuft which grew beneath his smooth chin.

"But did not you yourself come all the way from France to endue him with the duchy of Touraine ? " he said. " Doth that look like pulling him down from his high seat ? "

The marshal moved a politic hand as if asking silence till he had finished his explanation.

"Pardon," he said; "permit me yet a moment, most High Chancellor — but have you heard so little of the skill and craft of Louis, our most notable Dauphin, that you know not how he ever embraces men with the left arm whilst he pierces them with the dagger in his right ? "

The Chancellor nodded appreciation. It was a detail of statecraft well known to him, and much practised by his house in all periods of their history.

"Now, my lords," the ambassador continued, "you are here all three — the men who need most to end this tyranny — you, my Lord of Avondale, will you deign to deliver your mind upon this matter ? "

The fat Earl hemmed and hawed, clearing his throat to gain time, and knitting and unknitting his fingers over his stomach.

"Being a near kinsman," he said at last, "it is not seemly that I should say aught against the Earl of Douglas; but this I do know — there will be no peace in Scotland till that young man and his brother are both cut off."

The Chancellor and De Retz exchanged glances. The anxiety of the next-of-kin to the title of Earl of Douglas for the peace and prosperity of the realm seemed to strike them both as exceedingly natural in the circumstances.

"And now, Sir Alexander, what say you?" asked the Sieur de Retz, turning to the King's guardian, who had been caressing the curls of his beard with his white and signeted hand.

"I agree," he replied in a courtly tone, "that in the interests of the King and of the noble lady whose care for her child hath led her to such sacrifices, we ought to put a limit to the pride and insolence of this youth!"

The Chancellor bent over a parchment to hide a smile at the sacrifices which the Queen Mother had made for her son.

"It is indeed, doubtless," said Sir William Crichton, "a sacrifice that the King and his mother should dwell so long within this Castle of Stirling, exposed to every rude blast from off these barren Grampians. Let her bring him to the mild and equable climate of Edinburgh, which, as I am sure your Excellency must have observed, is peculiarly suited to the rearing of such tender plants."

He appealed to the Sieur de Retz.

The marshal bowed and answered immediately, "Indeed, it reminds me of the sunniest and most favoured parts of my native France."

The tutor of the King looked somewhat uncomfortable at the suggestion and shook his head. He had no idea of putting the King of Scots within the power of his arch enemy in the strong fortress of Edinburgh.

But the Frenchman broke in before the ill effects of the Chancellor's speech had time to turn the mind of the King's guardian from the present project against the Earl of Douglas.

"But surely, gentlemen, it should not be difficult for two such honourable men to unite in destroying this curse of the commonweal — and afterwards to settle any differences which may in the past have arisen between themselves."

"Good," said the Chancellor, "you speak well. But how are we to bring the Earl within our danger? Already I have sent him offers of alliance, and so, I doubt not, hath my honourable friend the tutor of the King. You know well what answer the proud chief of Douglas returned."

The lips of Sir Alexander Livingston moved. He seemed to be taking some bitter and nauseous drug of the apothecary.

"Yes, Sir Alexander, I see you have not forgot. The words, 'If dog eat dog, what should the lion care?' made us every caitiff's scoff throughout broad Scotland."

"For that he shall yet suffer, if God give me speed," said the tutor, for the answer had been repeated to the Queen, who, being English, laughed at the wit of the reply.

"I would that my boy should grow up such another as that Earl Douglas," she had said.

The tutor stroked his beard faster than ever, and there was in his eyes the bitter look of a handsome man whose vanity is wounded in its weakest place.

N

"But, after all, who is to cage the lion?" said the Chancellor, pertinently.

The marshal of France raised his hand from the table as if commanding silence. His suave and courtier-like demeanour had changed into something more natural to the man. There came the gaunt forward thrust of a wolf on the trail into the set of his head. His long teeth gleamed, and his eyelids closed down upon his eyes till these became mere twinkling points.

"I have that at hand which hath already tamed the lion," he said, "and is able to lead him into the cage with cords of silk."

He rose from the table, and, going to a curtain that concealed the narrow door of an antechamber, he drew it aside, and there came forth, clothed in a garment of gold and green, close-fitting and fine, clasped about the waist with a twining belt of jewelled snakes, the Lady Sybilla.

CHAPTER XXVI

THE LION TAMER

On this summer afternoon the girl's beauty seemed more wondrous and magical than ever. Her eyes were purple-black, like the berries of the deadly nightshade seen in the twilight. Her face was pale, and the scarlet of her lips lay like twin geranium petals on new-fallen snow.

Gilles de Retz followed her with a certain grim and ghastly pride, as he marked the sensation caused by her entrance.

"This," he said, "is my lion tamer!"

But the girl never looked at him, nor in any way responded to his glances.

"Sybilla," said De Retz, holding her with his eyes, "these gentlemen are with us. They also are of the enemies of the house of Douglas—speak freely that which is in your heart!"

"My lords," said the Lady Sybilla, speaking in a level voice, and with her eyes fixed on the leaf-shadowed square of grass, which alone could be seen through the open window, "you have, I doubt not, each declared your grievance against William, Earl of Douglas. I alone have none. He is a gallant gentleman. France I have travelled, Spain also, and Portugal, and have explored the utmost East,—wherever, indeed, my Lord

179

of Retz hath voyaged thither I have gone. But no braver or more chivalrous youth than William Douglas have I found in any land. I have no grievance against him, as I say, yet for that which hath been will I deliver him into your hands."

One of the men before her grew manifestly uneasy.

"We did not come hither to listen to the praises of the Earl of Douglas, even from lips so fair as yours!" sneered Crichton the Chancellor, lifting his eyes one moment from the parchment before him to the girl's face.

"He is our enemy," said the tutor of the King, Alexander Livingston, more generously, "but I will never deny that he is a gallant youth; also of his person proper to look upon."

And very complacently he smoothed down the lace ruffles which fell from the neck of his silken doublet midway down its front.

"The young man is a Douglas," said James the Gross, curtly; "if he were of coward breed, we had not needed to come hither secretly!"

"It needeth not four butchers to kill a sheep!" said De Retz. "Concerning that, we agree. Proceed, my Lady Sybilla."

The girl was now breathing more quickly, her bosom rising and falling visibly beneath her light silken gown.

"Yet because of those that have been of the house of Douglas before him, shall I have no pity upon William, sixth Earl thereof! And because of two dead Dukes of Touraine, will I deliver to you the third Duke, into whose mouth hath hardly yet come the proper gust of living. This is the tale I have heard a thousand times.

There was in France, it skills not where, a vale quiet as
a summer Sabbath day. The vines hung ripe-clustered
in wide and pleasant vineyards. The olives rustled grey
on the slopes. The bell swung in the monastery tower.
The cottage in the dell was safe as the château on the
hill. Then came the foreign leader of a foreign army,
and lo! in a day, there were a hundred dead men in the
valley, all honourable men slain in defence of their own
doors. The smoky flicker of flames broke through the
roof in the daylight. There was heard the crying of
many women. And the man who wrought this was an
Earl of Douglas."

The girl paused, and in a low whisper, intense as the
breathing of the sea, she said:

"*And for this will I deliver into your hands his grand-
son, William of Douglas!*"

Then her voice came again to the ears of the four lis-
teners, in a note low and monotonous like the wind that
goes about the house on autumn evenings.

"There was also one who, being but a child, had escaped from that tumult and had found shelter in a white
convent with the sisters thereof, who taught her to pray,
and be happy in the peace of the hour that is exactly
like the one before it. The shadow of the dial finger
upon the stone was not more peaceful than the holy
round of her life.

"Then came one who met her by the convent wall,
met her under the shade of the orchard trees, met her
under cloud of night, till his soul had power over hers.
She followed him by camp and city, fearing no man's
scorn, feeling no woman's reproach, for love's sake and
his. Yet at the last he cast her away, like an empty

husk, and sailed over the seas to his own land. She
lived to wed the Sieur de Thouars and to become my
mother.

"*And for this will I reckon with his son William, Duke
of Touraine.*"

She ceased, and De Retz began to speak.

"By me this girl has been taught the deepest wisdom
of the ancients. I have delved deep in the lore of the
ages that this maiden might be fitted for her task. For
I also, that am a marshal of France and of kin to my
Lord Duke of Brittany, have a score to settle with
William, Earl of Douglas, as hath also my master,
Louis the Dauphin!"

"It is enough," interjected Crichton the Chancellor,
who had listened to the recital of the Lady Sybilla with
manifest impatience, "it is the old story — the sins of
the fathers are upon the children. And this young man
must suffer for those that went before him. They drank
of the full cup, and so he hath come now to the drains.
It skills not why we each desire to make an end of him.
We are agreed on the fact. The question is *how*."

It was again the voice of De Retz which replied, the
deep silence of afternoon resting like a weight upon all
about them.

"If we write him a letter inviting him to the Castle
of Edinburgh, he will assuredly not come; but if we
first entertain him with open courtesy at one of your
castles on the way, where you, most wise Chancellor,
must put yourself wholly in his hands, he will suspect
nothing. There, when all his suspicions are lulled, he
will again meet the Lady Sybilla; it will rest with her
to bring him to Edinburgh."

The Chancellor had been busily writing on the parchment before him whilst De Retz was speaking. Presently he held up his hand and read aloud that which he had written.

"To the most noble William, Earl of Douglas and Duke of Touraine, greeting! In the name of King James the Second, whom God preserve, and in order that the realm may have peace, Sir William Crichton, Chancellor of Scotland, and Sir Alexander Livingston, Governor of the King's person, do invite and humbly intreat the Earl of Douglas to come to the City of Edinburgh, with such following as shall seem good to him, in order that he may be duly invested with the office of Lieutenant-General of the Kingdom, which office was his father's before him. So shall the realm abide in peace and evil-doers be put down, the peaceable prevented with power, and the Earl of Douglas stand openly in the honourable place of his forebears."

The Chancellor finished his reading and looked around for approbation. James of Avondale was nodding gravely. De Retz, with a ghastly smile on his face, seemed to be weighing the phrases. Livingston was admiring, with a self-satisfied smile, the pinkish lights upon his finger-nails, and the girl was gazing as before out of the window into the green close wherein the leaves stirred and the shadows had begun to swim lazily on the grass with the coming of the wind from off the sea.

"To this I would add as followeth," continued Crichton. "The Chancellor of Scotland to William, Earl of Douglas, greeting and homage! Sir William Crichton ventures to hope that the Earl of Douglas will do him the great honour to come to his new Castle of Crichton, there to be entertained as beseemeth his dignity, to the healing of all ancient enmities, and also that they both may do honour to the ambassador of the King of France ere he set sail again for his own land."

"It is indeed a worthy epistle," said James the Gross, who, being sleepy, wished for an end to be made.

"There is at least in it no lack of 'Chancellor of Scotland!'" sneered Livingston, covertly.

"Gently, gently, great sirs," interposed De Retz, as the Chancellor looked up with anger in his eye; "have out your quarrels as you will — after the snapping of the trap. Remember that this which we do is a matter of life or death for all of us."

"But the Douglases will wash us off the face of Scotland if we so much as lay hand on the Earl," objected Livingston. "It might even affect the safety of his Majesty's person!"

James the Gross laughed a low laugh and looked at Crichton.

"Perhaps," he said; "but what if the gallant boy David go with his brother? Whoever after that shall be next Earl of Douglas can easily prevent that. Also Angus is for us, and my Lord Maxwell will move no hand. There remains, therefore, only Galloway, and my son William will answer for that. I myself am old and fat, and love not fighting, but to tame the Douglases shall be my part, and assuredly not the least."

All this while the Lady Sybilla had been standing motionless gazing out of the window. De Retz now motioned her away with an almost imperceptible signal of his hand, whereat Sir Alexander Livingston, seeing the girl about to leave the chamber of council, courteously rose to usher her out. And with the very slightest acknowledgment of his profound obeisance, Sybilla de Thouars went forth and left the four men to their cabal of treachery and death.

CHAPTER XXVII

THE YOUNG LORDS RIDE AWAY

THIS was the letter which, along with the Chancellor's invitations, came to the hand of the Earl William as he rode forth to the deer-hunting one morning from his Castle of Thrieve:

" My lord, if it be not that you have wholly forgotten me and your promise, this comes to inform you that my uncle and I purpose to abide at the Castle of Crichton for ten days before finally departing forth of this land. It is known to me that the Chancellor, moved thereto by One who desires much to see you, hath invited the Earl of Douglas to come thither with what retinue is best beseeming so great a lord.

" But 'tis beyond hope that we should meet in this manner. My lord hath, doubtless, ere this forgot all that was between us, and hath already seen others fairer and more worthy of his courteous regard than the Lady Sybilla. This is as well beseems a mighty lord, who taketh up a cup full and setteth it down empty. But a woman hath naught to do, save only to remember the things that have been, and to think upon them. Grace be to you, my dear lord. And so for this time and it may be for ever, fare you well! "

When the Earl had read this letter from the Lady Sybilla, he turned himself in his saddle without delay and said to his hunt-master:

"Take back the hounds, we will not hunt the stag this day."

The messenger stood respectfully before him waiting to take back an answer.

"Come you from the town of Edinburgh?" asked the Earl, quickly.

"Nay," said the youth, "let it please your greatness, I am a servant of my Lord of Crichton, and come from his new castle in the Lothians."

"Doth the Chancellor abide there at this present?" asked the Earl.

"He came two noons ago with but one attendant, and bade us make ready for a great company who were to arrive there this very day. Then he gave me these two letters and set my head on the safe delivery of them."

"Sholto," cried the young lord, "summon the guard and men-at-arms. Take all that can be spared from the defence of the castle and make ready to follow me. I ride immediately to visit the Chancellor of Scotland at his castle in the Lothians."

It was Sholto's duty to obey, but his heart sank within him, both at the thought of the Earl thus venturing among his enemies, and also because he must needs leave behind him Maud Lindesay, on whose wilful and wayward beauty his heart was set.

"My lord," he stammered, "permit me one word. Were it not better to wait till a following of knights and gentlemen beseeming the Earl of Douglas should be brought together to accompany you on so perilous a journey?"

"Do as I bid you, Sir Captain," was the Earl's short rejoinder; "you have my orders."

"O that the Abbot were here —" thought Sholto, as he moved heavily to do his master's will; "he might reason with the Earl with some hope of success."

On his way to summon the guard Sholto met Maud Lindesay going out to twine gowans with the Maid on the meadows about the Mains of Kelton. For, as Margaret Douglas complained, " All ours on the isle were trodden down by the men who came to the tourney, and they have not grown up again."

"Whither away so gloomy, Sir Knight ?" cried Maud, all her winsome face alight with pleasure in the bright day, and because of the excellent joy of living.

"On a most gloomy errand, indeed," said Sholto. " My lord rides with a small company into the very stronghold of his enemy, and will hear no word from any !"

" And do you go with him ? " cried Maud, her bright colour leaving her face.

"Not only I, but all that can be spared of the men-at-arms and of the archer guard," answered Sholto.

Maud Lindesay turned about and took the little girl's hand.

"Margaret," she said, "let us go to my lady. Perhaps she will be able to keep my Lord William at home."

So they went back to the chamber of my Lady of Douglas. Now the Countess had never been of great influence with her son, even during her husband's lifetime, and had certainly none with him since. Still it was possible that William Douglas might, for a time at least, listen to advice and delay his setting out till a suitable retinue could be brought together to protect him. Maud and Margaret found the Lady of Douglas busily em-

broidering a vestment of silk and gold for the Abbot of
Sweetheart. She laid aside her work and listened with
gentle patience to the hasty tale told by Maud Lindesay.

"I will speak with William," she answered, with a
certain hopelessness in her voice, "but I know well he
will go his own gait for aught that his mother can say.
He is his father's son, and the men of the house of
Douglas, they come and they go, recking no will but
their own. And even so will my son William."

"But he is taking David with him also!" cried Margaret. "I met him even now on the stair, wild in haste
to put on his shirt of mail and the sword with the golden
hilt which the ambassador of France gave him."

A quick flush coloured the pale countenance of the
Lady Countess.

"Nay, but one is surely enough to meet the Chancellor.
David shall not go. He is but a lad and knows nothing
of these things."

For this boy was ever his mother's favourite, far more
than either her elder son or her little daughter, whom
indeed she left entirely to the care and companionship
of Maud Lindesay.

My Lady of Douglas went slowly downstairs. The
Earl, with Sholto by his side, was ordering the accoutrement of the mounted men-at-arms in the courtyard.

"William," she called, in a soft voice which would not
have reached him, busied as he was with his work, but
that little Margaret raised her childish treble and called
out: "William, our mother desires to speak with you.
Do you not hear her?"

The Earl turned about, and, seeing his mother, came
quickly to her and stood bareheaded before her.

"You are not going to run into danger, William?" she said, still softly.

"Nay, mother mine," he answered, smiling, "do not fear, I do but ride to visit the Chancellor Crichton in his castle, and also to bid farewell to the French ambassador, who abode here as our guest."

A sudden light shone in upon the mind of Maud Lindesay.

"'Tis all that French minx!" she whispered in Sholto's ear, "she hath bewitched him. No one need try to stop him now."

His mother went on, with an added anxiety in her voice.

"But you will not take my little David with you? You will leave me one son here to comfort me in my loneliness and old age?"

The Earl seemed about to yield, being, indeed, careless whether David went with him or no.

"Mother," cried David, coming running forth from the castle, "you must not persuade William to make me stay at home. I shall never be a man if I am kept among women. There is Sholto MacKim, he is little older than I, and already he hath won the archery prize and the sword-play, and hath fought in a tourney and been knighted — while I have done nothing except pull gowans with Maud Lindesay and play chuckie stones with Margaret there."

And at that moment Sholto wished that this fate had been his, and the honours David's. He told himself that he would willingly have given up his very knighthood that he might abide near that dainty form and witching face. He tortured himself with the thought that Maud would listen to others as she had listened to him; that she would practise on others that heart-breaking slow droop and quick uplift of the eyelashes which he knew so well. Who might not be at hand to aid her to blow out her lamp when the guards were set of new in the corridors of Thrieve?

"Mother," the Earl answered, "David speaks good sense. He will never make a man or a Douglas if he is to bide here within this warded isle. He must venture forth into the world of men and women, and taste a man's pleasures and chance a man's dangers like the rest."

"But are you certain that you will bring him safe back again to me?" said his mother, wistfully. "Remember, he is so young and eke so reckless."

"Nay," cried David, eagerly, "I am no younger than my cousin James was when he fought the strongest man in Scotland, and I warrant I could ride a course as well as Hughie Douglas of Avondale, though William chose him for the tourney and left me to bite my thumbs at home."

The lady sighed and looked at her sons, one of them but a youth and the other no more than a boy.

"Was there ever a Douglas yet who would take any advice but from his own desire?" she said, looking down at them like a douce barndoor fowl who by chance has reared a pair of eaglets. "Lads, ye are over strong for your mother. But I will not sleep nor eat aright till I have my David back again, and can see him riding his horse homeward through the ford."

CHAPTER XXVIII

ON THE CASTLE ROOF

MAUD LINDESAY parted from Sholto upon the roof of the keep. She had gone up thither to watch the cavalcade ride off where none could spy upon her, and Sholto, noting the flutter of white by the battlements, ran up thither also, pretending that he had forgotten something, though he was indeed fully armed and ready to mount and ride.

Maud Lindesay was leaning over the battlements of the castle, and, hearing a step behind her, she looked about with a start of apparent surprise.

The after dew of recent tears still glorified her eyes.

" Oh, Sholto," she cried, " I thought you were gone; I was watching for you to ride away. I thought—"

But Sholto, seeing her disorder, and having little time to waste, came quickly forward and took her in his arms without apology or prelude, as is (they say) wisest in such cases.

"Maud," he said, his utterance quick and hoarse, " we go into the house of our enemies. Thirty knights and no more accompany my lord, who might have ridden out with three thousand in his train."

" 'Tis all that witch woman," cried the girl; " can you not advise him ? "

" The Earl of Douglas did not ask my advice," said

Sholto, a little dryly, being eager to turn the conversation upon his own matters and to his own advantage. "And, moreover, if he rides into danger for the sake of love — why, I for one think the more of him for it."

"But for such a creature," objected Maud Lindesay. "For any true maid it were most right and proper! Where is there a noble lady in Scotland who would not have been proud to listen to him? But he must needs run after this mongrel French woman!"

"Even Mistress Maud Lindesay would accept him, would she?" said Sholto, somewhat bitterly, releasing her a little.

"Maud Lindesay is no great lady, only the daughter of a poor baron of the North, and much bound to my Lord Douglas by gratitude for that which he hath done for her family. As you right well know, Maud Lindesay is little better than a tiremaiden in the house of my lord."

"Nay," said Sholto, "I crave your pardon. I meant it not. I am hasty of words, and the time is short. Will you pardon me and bid me farewell, for the horses are being led from stall, and I cannot keep my lord waiting?"

"You are glad to go," she said reproachfully; "you will forget us whom you leave behind you here. Indeed, you care not even now, so that you are free to wander over the world and taste new pleasures. That is to be a man, indeed. Would that I had been born one!"

"Nay, Maud," said Sholto, trying to draw the girl again near him, because she kept him at arm's length by the unyielding strength of her wrist, "none shall ever come near my heart save Maud Lindesay alone! I would

o

that I could ride away as sure of you as you are of Sholto MacKim!"

"Indeed," cried the girl, with some show of returning spirit, "to that you have no claim. Never have I said that I loved you, nor indeed that I thought about you at all."

"It is true," answered Sholto, "and yet — I think you will remember me when the lamps are blown out. God speed, belovedst, I hear the trumpet blow, and the horses trampling."

For out on the green before the castle the Earl's guard was mustering, and Fergus MacCulloch, the Earl's trumpeter, blew an impatient blast. It seemed to speak to this effect:

> *Hasten ye, hasten ye, come to the riding,*
> *Hasten ye, hasten ye, lads of the Dee —*
> *Douglasdale come, come Galloway, Annandale,*
> *Galloway blades are the best of the three!*"

Sholto held out his arms at the first burst of the stirring sound, and the girl, all her wayward pride falling from her in a moment, came straight into them.

"Good-by, my sweetheart," he said, stooping to kiss the lips that now said him not nay, but which quivered pitifully as he touched them, "God knows whether these eyes shall rest again on the desire of my heart."

Maud looked into his face steadily and searchingly.

"You are sure you will not forget me, Sholto?" she said; "you will love me as much to-morrow when you are far away, and think me as fair as you do when you hold me thus in your arms upon the battlements of Thrieve?"

Before Sholto had time to answer, the trumpet rang

"But there cometh a night when every one of us watches the grey shallows to the east for those that shall return no more!"

out again, with a call more instant and imperious than before.

Sholto clasped her close to him as the second summons shrilled up into the air.

"God keep my little lass!" he said; "fear not, Maud, I have never loved any but you!"

He was gone. And through her tears Maud Lindesay watched him from the top of the great square keep, as he rode off gallantly behind the Earl and his brother.

"In time past I have dreamed," she thought to herself, "that I loved this one and that; but it was not at all like this. I cannot put him out of my mind for a moment, even when I would!"

As the brothers William and David Douglas crossed the rough bridge of pine thrown over the narrows of the Dee, they looked back simultaneously. Their mother stood on the green moat platform of Thrieve, with their little sister Margaret holding up her train with a pretty modesty. She waved not a hand, fluttered no kerchief of farewell, only stood sadly watching the sons with whom she had travailed, like one who watches the dear dead borne to their last resting-place.

"So," she communed, "even thus do the women of the Douglas House watch their beloveds ride out of sight. And so for many times they return through the ford at dawn or dusk. But there cometh a night when every one of us watches the grey shallows to the east for those that shall return no more!"

"See, see!" cried the little Margaret, "look, dear mother, they have taken off their caps, and even Sholto hath his steel bonnet in his hand. They are bidding us farewell. I wish Maudie had been here to see. I wonder

where she has hidden herself. How surprised she will
be to find that they are gone!"

It was a true word that the little Maid of Galloway
spoke, for, according to the pretty custom of the young
Earl, the cavalcade had halted ere they plunged into the
woods of Kelton. The Douglas lads took their bonnets
in their hands. Their dark hair was stirred by the
breeze. Sholto also bared his head and looked towards
the speck of white which he could just discern on the
summit of the frowning keep.

"Shall ever her eyelashes rise and fall again for me,
and shall I see the smile waver alternately petulant and
tender upon her lips?"

This was his meditation. For, being a young man in
love, these things were more to him than matins and
evensong, king or chancellor, heaven or hell—as indeed
it was right and wholesome that they should be.

CHAPTER XXIX

CASTLE CRICHTON

CRICHTON CASTLE was much more a defenced château and less a feudal stronghold than Thrieve. It stood on a rising ground above the little Water of Tyne, which flowed clear and swift beneath from the blind "hopes" and bare valleys of the Moorfoot Hills. But the site was well chosen both for pleasure and defence. The ground fell away on three sides. Birch, alder, ash, girt it round and made pleasant summer bowers everywhere.

The fox-faced Chancellor had spent much money on beautifying it, and the kitchens and larders were reported to be the best equipped in Scotland. On the green braes of Crichton, therefore, in due time the young Douglases arrived with their sparse train of thirty riders. Sir William Crichton had ridden out to meet them across the innumerable little valleys which lie around Temple and Borthwick to the brow of that great heathy tableland which runs back from the Moorfoots clear to the Solway.

With him were only the Marshal de Retz and his niece, the Lady Sybilla.

Not a single squire or man-at-arms accompanied these three, for, as the Chancellor well judged, there was no way more likely effectually to lull the suspicions of a gallant man like the Douglas than to forestall him in generous confidence.

The three sat their horses and looked to the south for their guests at that delightsome hour of the summer gloaming when the last bees are reluctantly disengaging themselves from the dewy heather bells and the circling beetles begin their booming curfew.

"There they come!" cried De Retz, suddenly, pointing to a few specks of light which danced and dimpled between them and the low horizon of the south, against which, like a spacious armada, leaned a drift of primrose sunset clouds.

"There they come — I see them also!" said the Lady Sybilla, and suddenly sighed heavily and without cause.

"Where, and how many?" cried the Chancellor, in a shrill pipe usually associated with the physically deformed, but which from him meant no more than anxious discomposure.

The marshal pointed with the steady hand of the practised commander to the spot at which his keen eye had detected the cavalcade.

"Yonder," he said, "where the pine tree stands up against the sky."

"And how many? I cannot see them, my eyesight fails. I bid you tell me how many," gasped the Chancellor.

The ambassador looked long.

"There are, as I think, no more than twenty or thirty riders."

Instantly the Chancellor turned and held out his hand.

"We have him," he muttered, withdrawing it again as soon as he saw that the ambassador did not take it, being occupied gazing under his palm at the approaching train of riders.

The Lady Sybilla sat silent and watched the company which rode towards them — with what thoughts in her heart, who shall venture to guess? She kept her head studiously averted from the Marshal de Retz, and once when he touched her arm to call attention to something, she shuddered and moved a little nearer to the Chancellor. Nevertheless, she obeyed her companion implicitly and without question when he bade her ride forward with them to receive the Chancellor's guests.

Crichton took it on himself to rally the girl on her silence.

"Of what may you be thinking so seriously?" he said.

"Of thirty pieces of silver," she replied instantly.

And at these words the marshal turned upon the girl a regard so black and relentless that the Chancellor, happening to encounter it, shrank back abashed, even as some devilkin caught in a fault might shrink from the angry eyes of the Master of Evil.

But the Lady Sybilla looked calmly at her kinsman.

"Of what do you complain?" he asked her.

"I complain of nothing," she made him answer. "I am that which I am, and I am that which you have made me, my Lord of Retz. Fear not, I will do my part."

Right handsome looked the young Earl of Douglas, as with a flush of expectation and pleasure on his face he rode up to the party of three who had come out to meet him. He made his obeisance to Sybilla first, with a look of supremest happiness in his eyes which many women would have given their all to see there. As he came close he leaped from his horse, and advancing to his lady he bent and kissed her hand.

"My Lady Sybilla," he said, "I am as ever your loyal servant."

The Chancellor and the ambassador had both dismounted, not to be outdone in courtesy, and one after the other they greeted him with what cordiality they could muster. The narrow, thin-bearded face of the Chancellor and the pallid death-mask of De Retz, out of which glittered orbs like no eyes of human being, furnished a singular contrast to the uncovered head, crisp black curls, slight moustache, and fresh olive complexion of the young Earl of Douglas.

And as often as he was not looking at her, the eyes of the Lady Sybilla rested on Lord Douglas with a strange expression in their deeps. The colour in her cheek came and went. The vermeil of her lip flushed and paled alternate, from the pink of the wild rose-leaf to the red of its autumnal berry.

But presently, at a glance from her kinsman, Sybilla de Thouars seemed to recall herself with difficulty from a land of dreams, and with an obvious effort began to talk to William Douglas.

"Whom have you brought to see me?" she said.

"Only a few men-at-arms, besides Sholto my squire, and my brother David," he made answer. "I did not wait for more. But let me bring the lad to you. Sholto you did not like when he was a plain archer of the guard, and I fear that he will not have risen in your grace since I dubbed him knight."

David Douglas willingly obeyed the summons of his brother, and came forward to kiss the hand of the Lady Sybilla.

"Here, Sholto," cried his lord, "come hither, man. It

will do your pride good to see a lady who avers that conceit hath eaten you up."

Sholto came at the word and bowed before the French damosel as he was commanded, meekly enough to all outward aspect. But in his heart he was saying over and over to himself words that consoled him mightily: "A murrain on her! The cozening madam, she will never be worth naming on the same day as Maud Lindesay!"

"Nay," cried the Lady Sybilla, laughing; "indeed, I said not that I disliked this your squire. What woman thinks the worse of a lad of mettle that he does not walk with his head between his feet. But 'tis pity that there is no fair cruel maid to bind his heart in chains, and make him fetch and carry to break his pride. He thinks overmuch of his sword-play and arrow skill."

"He must go to France for that humbling," said the Earl, gaily, "or else mayhap some day a maid may come from France to break his heart for him. The like hath been and may be again."

"I would that I had known there were such gallant blades as you three, my Lords of Douglas and their knight, sighing here in Scotland to have your hearts broke for the good of your souls. I had then brought with me a tierce of damsels fair as cruel, who had done it in the flashing of a swallow's wing. But 'tis a contract too great for one poor maid."

"Yet you yourself ventured all alone into this realm of forlorn and desperate men," answered the Earl, scarcely recking what he said, nor indeed caring so that her dark eyes should continue to rest on him with the look he had seen in them at his first coming.

"All alone — yes, much, much alone," she answered

with a strange glance about her. "My kinsman loves not womankind, and neither in his castles nor yet in his company does he permit any of the sex long to abide."

The men now mounted again, and the three rode back in the midst of the cavalcade of Douglas spears, the Chancellor talking as freely and confidently to the Earl as if he had been his friend for years, while the Earl of Douglas kept up the converse right willingly so long as, looking past the Chancellor, his eyes could rest also upon the delicately poised head and graceful form of the Lady Sybilla.

And behind them a horse's length the Marshal de Retz rode, smiling in the depths of his blue-black beard, and looking at them out of the wicks of his triangular eyes.

Presently the towers of the Castle of Crichton rose before them on its green jutting spur. The Tyne Valley sank beneath into level meads and rich pastures, while behind the Moorfoots spread brown and bare without prominent peaks or distinguished glens, but nevertheless with a certain large vagueness and solemnity peculiarly their own.

The *fêtes* with which the Chancellor welcomed his guests were many and splendid. But in one respect they differed from those which have been described at Castle Thrieve. There was no military pomp of any kind connected with them. The Chancellor studiously avoided all pretence of any other distinction than that belonging to a plain man whom circumstances have raised against his will to a position of responsibility.

The thirty spears of the Earl's guard, indeed, constituted the whole military force within or about the Castle of Crichton.

"I am a lawyer, my lord, a plain lawyer," he said; "all Scots lawyers are plain. And I must ask you to garrison my bit peel-tower of Crichton in a manner more befitting your own greatness, and the honour due to the ambassador of France, than a humble knight is able to do."

So Sholto was put into command of the court and battlements of the castle, and posted and changed guard as though he had been at Thrieve, while the Chancellor bustled about, affecting more the style of a rich and comfortable burgess than that of a feudal baron.

"'Tis a snug bit hoose," he would say, dropping into the countryside speech; "there's nocht fine within it from cellar to roof tree, save only the provend and the jolly Malmsey. And though I be but a poor eater myself, I love that my betters, who do me the honour of sojourning within my gates, should have the wherewithal to be merry."

And it was even as he said, for the tables were weighted with delicacies such as were never seen upon the boards of Thrieve or Castle Douglas.

CHAPTER XXX

AND ever as he gazed at her the Earl of Douglas grew more and more in love with the Lady Sybilla. There was no covert side through which a burn plunged downward from the steep side of Moorfoot, but they wandered it alone together. Early and late they might have been met, he with his face turned upon her, and she looking straight forward with the same inscrutable calm. And all who saw left them alone as they took their way to gather flowers like children, or, as it might be, stood still and silent like a pair of lovers under the evening star. For in these summer days and nights bloomed untiringly the brief passion-flower of William Douglas's life.

Meanwhile Sholto gritted his teeth in impotent rage, but had nothing to do save change guard and keep a wary eye upon the Chancellor, who went about rubbing his hands and glancing sidelong as the copses closed behind the Earl of Douglas and the Lady Sybilla. As for the ambassador of France, he was, as was usual with him, much occupied in his own chamber with his servants Poitou and Henriet, and save when dinner was served in hall appeared little at the festivities.

Sholto wished at times for the presence of his father; but at others, when he saw William Douglas and Sybilla

return with a light on their faces, and their eyes large
and vague, he bethought him of Maud Lindesay, and was
glad that, for a little at least, the sun of love should
shine upon his lord.

It was in the gracious fulness of the early autumn,
when the sheaves were set up in many a park and
little warded holt about the Moorfoot braes, that William Douglas and Sybilla de Thouars stood together
upon a crest of hill, crowned with dwarf birch and
thick foliaged alder — a place in the retirement of
whose sylvan bower they had already spent many tranced
hours.

The Lady Sybilla sat down on a worn grey rock which
thrust itself through the green turf. William Douglas
stood beside her pulling a blade of bracken to pieces.
The girl had been wearing a broad flat cap of velvet,
which in the coolness of the twilight she had removed
and now swung gently to and fro in her hand as she
looked to the north, where small as a toy and backed by
the orange glow of sunset, the Castle of Edinburgh
could be seen black upon its wind-swept ridge. The girl
was speaking slowly and softly.

"Nay, Earl Douglas," she said, "marriage must not
be named to Sybilla de Thouars, certainly never by
an Earl of Douglas and Duke of Touraine. He must
wed for riches and fair provinces. His house is regal
already. He is better born than the King, more powerful also. The daughter of a Breton squire, of a forlorn
and deserted mother, the kinswoman of Gilles de Retz
of Machecoul and Champtocé, is not for him."

"A Douglas makes many sacrifices," said the young
man with earnestness; "but this is not demanded of

him.   Four generations of us have wedded for power.
It is surely time that one did so for love."

The girl reached him her hand, saying softly: "Ah,
William, would that it had been so.   Too late I begin
to think on those things which might have been, had
Sybilla de Thouars been born under a more fortunate
star.   As it is I can only go on — a terror to myself and
a bane to others."

The young man, absorbed in his own thoughts, did not
hear her words.

"The world itself were little to give in order that in
exchange I might possess you," he answered.

The girl laughed a strange laugh, and drew back her
hand from his.

"Possess me, well — but marry me — no.   Honest men
and honourable like Earl Douglas do not wed with the
niece of Gilles de Retz.   I had thought my heart within
me to be as flint in the chalk, yet now I pray you on my
knees to leave me.   Take your thirty lances and your
young brother and ride home.   Then, safe in your island
fortress of Thrieve, blot out of your heart all memory
that ever you found pleasure in a creature so miserable
as Sybilla de Thouars."

"But," said the young Earl, passionately, "tell me
why so, my lady.   I do not understand.   What obstacle
can there be ?   You tell me that you love me, that you
are not betrothed.   Your kinsman is an honourable man,
a marshal and an ambassador of France, a cousin of the
Duke of Brittany, a reigning sovereign.   Moreover, am
not I the Douglas ?   I am responsible to no man.   William Douglas may wed whom he will — king's daughter
or beggar wench.   Why should he not join with the

honourable daughter of an honourable house, and the one woman he has ever loved?"

The girl let her velvet cap fall on the ground, and sank her face between her hands. Her whole body was shaken with emotion.

"Go — go," she cried, starting to her feet and standing before him, "call out your lances and ride home this night. Never look more upon the face of such a thing as Sybilla de Thouars. I bid you! I warn you! I command you! I thought I had been of stone, but now when I see you, and hear your words, I cannot do that which is laid upon me to do."

William of Douglas smiled.

"I cannot go," he said simply, "I love you. Moreover, I will not go — I am Earl of Douglas."

The girl clasped her hands helplessly.

"Not if I tell you that I have deceived you, led you on?" she said. "Not if I swear that I am the slave of a power so terrible that there are no words in any language to tell the least of the things I have suffered?"

The Earl shook his head. The girl suddenly stamped her foot in anger. "Go — go, I tell you," she cried; "stay not a day in this accursed place, wherein no true word is spoken and no loyal deed done, save those which come forth from your own true heart."

"Nay," said William Douglas, with his eyes on hers, "it is too late, Sybil. I have kissed the red of your lips. Your head hath lain on my breast. My whole soul is yours. I cannot now go back, even if I would. The boy I have been, I can be no more for ever."

The girl rose from the stone on which she had been sitting. There was a new smile in her eyes. She held out her hands to the youth who stood so erect and proud before her. "Well, at the worst, William Douglas," she said, "you may never live to wear a white head, but at least you shall touch the tree of the knowledge of good and evil, taste the fruitage and smell the blossoms thereof more than a hundred greybeards. I had not thought that earth held anywhere such a man, or that aught but blackness and darkness remained this side of hell for one so desolate as I. I have bid you leave me. I have told you that which, were it known, would cost me my life. But since you will not go, — since you are strong enough to stand unblenching in the face of doom, — you shall not lose all without a price."

She opened her arms wide, and her eyes were glorious.

"I love you," she said, her lips thrilling towards him, "I love you, love you, as I never thought to love any man upon this earth."

CHAPTER XXXI

THE GABERLUNZIE MAN

THE next morning the Chancellor came down early from his chamber, and finding Earl Douglas already waiting in the courtyard, he rubbed his hands and called out cheerfully: "We shall be more lonely to-day, but perhaps even more gay. For there are many things men delight in which even the fairest ladies care not for, fearing mayhap some invasion of their dominions."

"What mean you, my Lord Chancellor?" said the Douglas to his host, eagerly scanning the upper windows meanwhile.

"I mean," said the Chancellor, fawningly, "that his Excellency, the ambassador of France, hath ridden away under cloud of night, and hath taken his fair ward with him."

The Earl turned pale and stood glowering at the obsequious Chancellor as if unable to comprehend the purport of his words. At last he commanded himself sufficiently to speak.

"Was this resolution sudden, or did the Lady Sybilla know of it yesternight?"

"Nay, of a surety it was quite sudden," replied the Chancellor. "A message arrived from the Queen Mother to the Marshal de Retz requesting an immediate meeting on business of state, whereupon I offered my Castle of

Edinburgh for the purpose as being more convenient
than Stirling. So I doubt not that they are all met
there, the young King being of the party. It is, indeed,
a quaint falling out, for of late, as you may have heard,
the Tutor and the Queen have scarce been of the number
of my intimates."

The Earl of Douglas appeared strangely disturbed.
He paid no further attention to his host, but strode to
and fro in the courtyard with his thumbs in his belt, in
an attitude of the deepest meditation.

The Chancellor watched him from under his eyebrows
with alternate apprehension and satisfaction, like a
timid hunter who sees the lion half in and half out of
the snare.

"I have a letter for you, my Lord Douglas," he said,
after a long pause.

"Ah," cried Douglas, with obvious relief, "why did
you not tell me so at first. Pray give it me."

"I knew not whether it might afford you pleasure or
no," answered the Chancellor.

"Give it me!" cried Douglas, imperiously, as though
he spoke to an underling.

Sir William Crichton drew a square parcel from beneath his long-furred gown, and handed it to William
Douglas, who, without stepping back, instantly broke
the seal.

"Pshaw," cried he, contemptuously, "it is from the
Queen Mother and Alexander Livingston!"

He thought it had been from another, and his disappointment was written clear upon his face.

"Even so," said the Chancellor, suavely; "it was delivered by the same servant who brought the message

which called away the ambassador and his companion."

The Earl read it from beginning to end. After the customary greetings and good wishes the letter ran as follows:

"The King greatly desires to see his noble cousin of Douglas at the castle of Edinburgh, presently put at his Majesty's disposal by the High Chancellor of Scotland. Here in this place are now assembled all the men who desire the peace and assured prosperity of the realm, saving the greatest of all, my Lord and kinsman of Douglas. The King sends affectionate greeting to his cousin, and desires that he also may come thither, that the ambassador of France may carry back to his master a favourable report of the unity and kindly governance of the kingdom during his minority."

The Chancellor watched the Earl as he read this letter. To one more suspicious than William Douglas it would have been clear that he was himself perfectly acquainted with the contents.

"I am bidden meet the King at the Castle of Edinburgh," said Douglas; "I will set out at once."

"Nay, my lord," said Crichton, "not this day, at least. Stay and hunt the stag on the braes of Borthwick. My huntsmen have marked down a swift and noble buck. To-morrow to Edinburgh an you will!"

"I thank you, Sir William," the Douglas answered, curtly enough; "but the command is peremptory. I must ride to Edinburgh this very day."

"I pray you remember that Edinburgh is a turbulent city and little inclined to love your great house. Is it, think you, wise to go thither with so small a retinue?"

The Earl waved his hand carelessly.

"I am not afraid," he said; "besides, what harm can

befall when I lodge in the castle of the Lord Chancellor of Scotland ? ”

Crichton bowed very low.

“What harm, indeed ? ” he said; “I did but advise your lordship to bethink himself. I am an old man, pray remember — fast growing feeble and naturally inclined to overmuch caution. But the blood flows hot through the veins of eighteen.”

Sholto, who knew nothing of these happenings, had just finished exercising his men on the smooth green in front of the Castle of Crichton, and had dismissed them, when a gaberlunzie or privileged beggar, a long lank rascal with a mat of tangled hair, and clad in a cast-off leathern suit which erstwhile some knight had worn under his mail, leaped suddenly from the shelter of a hedge. Instinctively Sholto laid his hand on his dagger.

“Nay,” snuffled the fellow, “I come peaceably. As you love your lord hasten to give him this letter. And, above all, let not the Crichton see you.”

He placed a small square scrap of parchment in Sholto’s hand. It was sealed in black wax with a serpent’s head, and from the condition of the outside had evidently been in places both greasy and grimy. Sholto put it in his leathern pouch wherein he was used to keep the hone for sharpening his arrows, and bestowed a silver groat upon the beggar.

“Thy master’s life is surely worth more than a groat,” said the man.

“I warrant you have been well enough paid already,” said Sholto, “that is, if this be not a deceit. But here is a shilling. On your head be it, if you are playing with Sholto MacKim ! ”

So saying the captain of the guard strode within.   He had already acquired the carriage and consequence of a veteran old in the wars.

His master was still pacing up and down the courtyard, deep in meditation.   Sholto saluted the young Earl and asked permission to speak a word with him.

"Speak on, Sholto — well do you know that at all times you may say what you will to me."

"But this I desire to keep from prying eyes.   My lord, there is a letter in my wallet which was given me even now by a gaberlunzie man.   He declares that it concerns your life.   I pray you take out my hone stone as if to look at it, and with it the letter."

The Earl nodded, as if Sholto had been making a report to him.   Then he went nearer and began to finger his squire's accoutrements, finally opening his belt pouch and taking out the stone that was therein.

"Where gat you this hone!" he said, holding it to the light; "it looks not the right blue for a Water-of-Ayr stone."

Sholto answered that it came from the Parton Hills, and, as the Earl replaced it, he possessed himself of the square letter and thrust it into the bosom of his doublet.

As soon as William Douglas was alone, he broke the seal and tore open the parchment.   It was written in a delicate foreign script, the characters fine and small:

"My lord, do not, I beseech you, come to Edinburgh or think of me more.   Last night my Lord of Retz spied upon us and this morning he hath carried me off.   Wherever you are when you receive this, turn instantly and ride with all speed to one of your strong castles.   As you love me, go!   We can never hope to see one another again.   Forget an unfortunate girl who can never forget you."

There was no signature saving the impression of the joined serpents' heads, which he remembered as the signet of the ring he had found and given back to her on the day of the tournament.

"I will never give her up. I must see her," cried the Earl of Douglas, "and this very day. Aye, and though I were to die for it on the morrow, see her I will!"

CHAPTER XXXII

"EDINBURGH CASTLE, TOWER, AND TOWN"

It was with an anxious heart that Sholto rode out behind his master over the bald northerly slopes of the Moorfoots. For a long time David Douglas kept close to his brother, so that the captain of the guard could speak no private word. For, though he knew that nothing was to be gained by remonstrance, Sholto was resolved that he would not let his reckless master run unwarned into danger so deadly and certain.

He rode up, therefore, and craved permission to speak to the Earl, seizing an occasion when David had fallen a little behind.

"Thou art a true son of Malise MacKim, whatever thy mother may aver," cried the Earl. "I'll wager a gold angel thou art going to say something shrewdly unpleasant. That great lurdain, thy father, never asks permission to speak save when he has stilettos rankling where his honest tongue should be."

"My lord," said Sholto, "bear a word from one who loves you. Go not into this town of Edinburgh. Or at least wait till you can ride thither with three thousand lances as did your father, and his father before him."

The Earl laughed merrily and clapped his young knight on the shoulder.

"Did you not tell me the same ere we came to the
Castle of Crichton, and lo! there we were ten days in
the place and not a man-at-arms within miles except
your own Galloway varlets! Sholto, my lad, we might
have sacked the castle, rolled all the platters down the
slopes into the Tyne, and sent the cooks trundling after
them, for all that any one could have done to stop us.
Yet here are we riding forth, feathers in our bonnets,
swords by our sides, panged full of the Chancellor's
good meat and drink, and at once, as soon as we are
gone, Sholto MacKim begins the same old discontented
corbie's croak!"

"But, my lord, 'tis a different matter yonder. The
Castle of Edinburgh is a strong place with many courts
and doors — a hostile city round about, not a solitary
castle like Crichton. They may separate you from us,
and we may be able neither to save you nor yet to die
with you, if the worst comes to the worst."

"I may inform you as well soon as syne, you waste
your breath, Sholto," said Earl Douglas, "and it ill
becomes a young knight, let me tell you, to be so
chicken-hearted. The next time I will leave you at
home to hem linen for the bed-sheets. Malise is a
licensed croaker, but I thought better of you, Master
Sholto MacKim!"

The captain of the Earl's guard looked on the ground
and his heart was distressed within him. Yet, in spite
of the raillery of the Douglas, he resolved to make one
more effort.

"My lord," he said, "you know not the full hatred
of these men against your house. What other object
save the destruction of the Douglas can have drawn

together foes so deadly as Crichton and Livingston?
At least, my lord, if you are set on risking your own life,
send back one of us with your brother David!"

Then cried out David Douglas, who had joined them
during the converse, against so monstrous a proposal.

"I will not go back in any case," said the lad; "William has the earldom and the titles. I may at least be
allowed part of the fun. Sholto, if William dies without heirs and I become Earl, my first act will be to hang
you on the dule tree with a raven on either side, for a
slow-bellied knave and prophet of evil!"

The Earl looked at his brother and seemed to hesitate.

"There is something in what you say, Sholto."

"My lord, if the blow fall, let not your line be wholly
cut off. I pray you let five good lads ride straight for
Douglasdale with David in the midst —"

"Sholto," cried the boy, "I will not go back, nor
be a palterer, all because you are afraid for your own
skin!"

"My place is with my master," said Sholto, curtly,
and the boy looked ashamed for a moment; but he soon
recovered himself and returned to the charge.

"Well, then, 'tis because you want to see Maud Linde-
say that you are so set on returning. I saw you kiss
Maud's hand in the dark of the stairs. Aha! Master
Sholto, what say you now?"

"Hold your tongue, David," cried his brother; "you
might have seen him kiss yet more pleasantly, and yet
do no harm. But, after all, you and I are Douglases
and our star is in the zenith. We will fall together, if
fall we must. Not a word more about it. David, I
will race you to yonder dovecot for a golden lion."

"Done with you !" cried his brother, joyously, and in an instant spurs were into the flanks of their horses, and the young men flew thundering over the green turf, riding swiftly into the golden haze from which rose ever higher and higher the dark towers of the Castle of Edinburgh.

Past grey peel and windswept fortalice the young Lords of Douglas rode that autumn day, gaily as to a wedding, on their way to place themselves in the power of their house's enemies. The sea plain pursued them, flecked green and purple on their right hand. Little ships floated on the smooth surface of the firth, hardly larger in size than the boats of fisher folk, yet ships withal which had adventured into far seas and brought back rich produce into the barren lands of the Scots.

At last they entered the demesne of Holyrood, and saw the deer crouching and basking about the copses or scampering over the broomy knowes of the Nether Hill. As they came near to the Canongate Port, they saw a gallant band gaily dressed coming forth to meet them, and the Earl's eye brightened as it caught in the midst the glint of ladies' attiring.

"See, Sholto," he cried, "and repent! Yonder is not a single lance shining, and you cannot turn your grumbling head but you will see nigh two score, with a stout Douglas heart bumping under each."

"Ah," said Sholto, without joy or conviction, "but we are neither in nor yet out of this weary town of Edinburgh!"

As the cavalcade approached, there came a boy on a pony at speed towards them. He carried a switch in his hand, and with it he urged his little beast to still greater endeavours.

"The King!" cried David, cheerfully. "I heard he was a sturdy brat enough!"

And in another moment the two young men of the dominant house were taking off their bonnets to the boy who, in name at least, was their sovereign and over-lord.

"Hurrah!" cried the lad, as he circled about them, reckless and irresponsible as a sea-gull, "I am so glad, so very glad you have come. I like you because you are so bold and young. I have none about me like you. You will teach me to ride a tourney. I have been hearing all about yours at Thrieve from the Lady Sybilla. I wish you had asked me. But now we shall be friends, and I will come and stay long months with you all together — that is, if my mother will let me."

All this the young King shouted as he ranged along-side of the two brothers, and rode with them towards the city.

King James II. of Scotland was at this time an open-hearted boy, with no evident mark of the treachery and jealous fury which afterwards distinguished him as a man. The schooling of Livingston, his tutor, had not yet perverted his mind (as it did too soon afterwards), and he welcomed the young Douglases as the embodiment of all that was great and knightly, noble and gallant, in his kingdom.

"Yesterday," he began, as soon as he had subdued the ardour of his frolicsome little steed to a steadier gait, varied only by an occasional curvet, "yesterday I was made to read in the Chronicles of the Kings of Scotland,

and lo, it was the Douglas did this and the Douglas said that, till I cried out upon Master Kennedy, 'Enough of Douglases — I am a Stewart. Read me of the Stewarts.' Then gave Master Kennedy a look as when he laughs in his sleeve, and shook his head. 'This book concerneth battles,' said he, 'and not gear, plenishing, and tocher. The Douglas won for King Robert his crown, the Stewart only married his daughter — though that, if all tales be true, was the braver deed!' Now that was no reverent speech to me that am a Stewart, nor yet very gallant to my great-grandmother, was it, Earl Douglas?"

"It was no fine courtier's flattery, at any rate," said the Douglas, his eyes wandering hither and thither across the cavalcade which they were now meeting, in search of the graceful figure and darkly splendid head of the girl he loved.

The Lady Sybilla was not there.

"They have secluded her," he muttered, in sharp jealous anger; "'tis all her kinsman's fault. He hath the marks of a traitor and worse. But they shall not spite nor flout the Douglas."

So with a countenance grave and unresponsive he saluted Livingston the tutor, who came forth to meet him. The Chancellor was expected immediately, for he had ridden in more rapidly by the hill way in order that he might welcome his notable guests to the metropolitan residence of the Kings of Scotland.

The Castle of Edinburgh was at that time in the fulness of its strength and power. The first James had greatly enlarged and strengthened its works defensive. He had added thirty feet to the height of David's Tower, which now served as a watch-station over all the rock, and in his last days he had begun to build the great hall which the Chancellor had but recently finished.

It was here that presently the feast was set. The banquet-hall ran the width of the keep, and the raised dais in the centre was large enough to seat the whole higher baronage of Scotland, among whom (as the Earl of Douglas thought with some scorn) neither of his entertainers, Crichton and Livingston, had any right to place themselves.

But the question where the Lady Sybilla was bestowed soon occupied the Douglas more than any thought of his own safety or of the loyalty of his entertainers. Sybilla, however, was neither in the courtly cavalcade which met them at the entrance of the park, nor yet among the more numerous ladies who stood at the castle yett to welcome to Edinburgh the noble and handsome young lords of the South.

Douglas therefore concluded that De Retz, discovering some part of the love that was between them, or mayhap hearing of it from some spy or other at Crichton Castle, had secluded his sweetheart. He loosened his hand on the rein to lay it on the sword-hilt, as he thought of this cruelty to a maid so pure and fair.

Sholto kept his company very close behind him as they rode up the High-street, a gloomy defile of tall houses dotted from topmost window to pavement with the heads of chattering goodwives, and the flutter of household clothing hung out to dry.

At the first defences of the castle Douglas called Sholto and said: "Your fellows are to be lodged here on the Castle Hill. The Chancellor hath sent word that there is no room in the castle itself. For the tutor's men and King's men have already filled it to the brim."

These tidings agonised Sholto more than ever.

"My lord," he said, in a tortured whisper, "turn about your rein and we will cut our way out even yet. Do you not see that the devils would separate you from all who love you? And I shall be blamed for this in Galloway. At least, let me accompany you with half a dozen men."

"Nay," said the Earl, "such suspicion were a poor return for the Chancellor's putting himself in our hands all the days we spent with him at his Castle of Crichton. To your lodgings, Sholto, and give God thanks if there be therein a pretty maid or a dame complaisant, according to the wont of young squires and men-at-arms."

In this fashion rode the Earl of Douglas to take his first dinner in the Castle of Edinburgh. And Sholto MacKim went behind him, no man saying him nay. For his master had eyes only for one face, and that he could not see.

"But I shall find her yet," he said over and over in his heart. It was but a boyish heart, and simple, too; but all so brave and high that the gallantest and greatest gentleman in the world had not one like to it for loyalty and courage.

CHAPTER XXXIII

THE BLACK BULL'S HEAD

THE banqueting-hall of Edinburgh Castle, but lately out of artificers' hands, was a noble oblong chamber reaching from side to side of the south-looking keep, begun by James I. It was decorated in the French manner with oak ceilings and panellings, all bossed and cornered with massive silver-gilt mouldings.

Save in the ordering of the repast itself there was a marked absence of ostentation. Only a soldier or two could be seen, mostly on guard at the outer gates, and Sholto, who till now had been uneasy and fearful for his master, became gradually more reassured when he saw with what care every want of the Earl and his brother was attended to, and if possible even forestalled.

The young King was in jubilant spirits, and could scarcely be persuaded to let the brothers Douglas remain a moment alone. He was resolved, he said, to have his bed brought into their chamber that he might talk to them all night of tourneys and noble deeds of arms. Never had he met with any whom he loved so much, and on their part the young Lords of Douglas became boys again, in this atmosphere of frank and boyish admiration.

It was a state banquet to which they sat down. That is, there was no hungry crowd of hangers-on clustered

223

below the salt.   To each gentleman was allotted a
silver trenchard for his own use, instead of one betwixt
two as was the custom.   The service was ordered in the
French manner, and there was manifest through all a
quiet observance and good taste which won upon the
Earl of Douglas.   Nevertheless, his eyes still continued
to range this way and that through the castle, scanning
each tower, glancing up at every balcony and archway,
in search of the Lady Sybilla.

In the banquet-hall the little King sat on his high
chair in the midst, with the brothers of Douglas one on
either side of him.   He spoke loudly and confidently
after the manner of a pampered boy of high spirits.

" I will soon come and visit you in return at the Castle
of Thrieve.   The Lady Sybilla hath told me how strong
it is and how splendid are the tourneys there, as grand,
she swears, as those of France."

"The Lady Sybilla is peradventure gone to her own
land ? " ventured Douglas, not wishing to ask a more
direct question.   He spoke freely, however, on all other
subjects with the King, laughing and talking mostly with
him, and finding little to say to the tutor Livingston or
the Chancellor, who, either from humility or from fear,
had taken care to interpose half a dozen knights between
himself and his late guests.

" Nay," cried the young King, looking querulously at
his tutor, "but, indeed, I wot not what they have done
with my pretty gossip, Sybilla; I have not seen her for
three weeks, save for a moment this morning.   And
before she went away she promised to teach me to dance
a coranto in the French manner, and the trick of the
handkerchief to hide a dagger in the hand."

As the Earl listened to the boy's prattle, he became more and more convinced that the Marshal de Retz, having in some way discovered their affection for each other, had removed Sybilla out of his reach. Her letter, indeed, showed clearly that she was in fear of ill-treatment both for himself and for her.

The banquet passed with courtesies much more elaborate than was usual in Scotland, but which indicated the great respect in which the Douglases were held. Between each course a servant clad in the royal colours presented a golden salver filled with clear water for the guests to wash their hands. Through the interstices of the ceiling strains of music filtered down from musicians hidden somewhere above, which sounded curiously soothing and far away.

The Chancellor bowed and drank every few minutes to the health of the Earl and his brother across the board, while the tutor sat smiling upon all with the polish of a professional courtier. In his high seat at the table end the little King chatted incessantly of the times when he could do as he pleased, and when he and his cousin of Douglas would ride together to battle and tourney, or feast together in hall.

"Be sure, then, I will not keep all these grey-beard sorners about me," he said, lowering his voice cautiously; "I will only have young gallant men like you and David there. But what comes here?"

There was a stir among the servitors at the upper end of the room. Sholto, who stood behind his master's chair, heard the skirl of the war-pipes approach nearer. It grew louder, more insistent, finally almost oppressive. The doors at either end were filled with armed men.

Q

They filed silently into the hall in dark armour, all carrying shining Lochaber axes.

Douglas leaned back in his chair, and looked nonchalantly on like a spectator of a pageant. He continued to talk to the King easily and calmly, as if he were in his own Castle of Thrieve. But Sholto saw the white and ghastly look on the face of the Chancellor, and noted his hands nervously grip the table. He observed him also lean across and confer with Livingston, who nodded like one that agrees that the moment of action has come.

At the upper end of the hall were wide folding doors which till now had been shut. These were opened swiftly, either half falling back to the wall. And through the archway came two servitors in black habits, carrying between them on a huge platter of silver a black bull's head, ghastly and ominous even in death, with staring eyeballs and matted frontlet of ensanguined hair.

"Treachery!" instantly cried Sholto, and ere the men could approach he had drawn his sword and stood ready to do battle for his lord. For throughout all Scotland a bull's head served at table is the symbol of death.

The Earl did not move or speak. He watched the progress of the men in black, who staggered under their heavy burden. David also had risen to his feet with his hand on his sword, but William Douglas sat still. Alarm, wonder, and anxiety chased each other across the face of the young King.

"What is this, Chancellor—why is the room filled with armed men?" he cried.

But Crichton had withdrawn himself behind the partisans of his soldiers, and down the long table there was not a man but had risen and bared his sword. Every eye was turned upon the young Earl. A score of men-at-arms came forward to seize him.

"Stand back on your lives!" cried Sholto, sweeping his blade about him to keep a space clear about his youthful master.

But still the Earl William sat calm and unmoved, though all others had risen to their feet and held arms in their hands.

"What means this mumming?" he said, high and clear. "If a mystery is to be played, surely it were better to put it off till after dinner."

Then through the open doorway came a voice piercing and reedy.

"The play is played indeed, William of Douglas, and the lion is now safe in the power of the dogs. How like you our kennel, most mighty lion?"

It was the voice of the Chancellor Crichton.

The young King came running from his place and threw his arms about the Earl's neck.

"I am the King," he cried; "not one of you shall touch or hurt my cousin Douglas!"

"Stand back, James," said the tutor Livingston; "the Douglas is a traitor, and you shall never reign while he rules. He and his brother must be tried for treason. They have claimed the King's throne, and usurped his authority."

Sholto MacKim turned about. In all that threatening array of armed men no friendly eye met his, and none of all he had trusted drew a blade for the Douglas. Sholto stood calculating the chances. To die like a man was easy, but how to die to some purpose seemed more difficult. He saw the King with his arm about the neck of William Douglas, who remained quietly in his place with a pale but assured countenance.

It was Sholto's only chance. With his left hand he seized the young King by the collar of his doublet, and set the point of his sword to his back between the shoulder-blades.

"Now," he cried, "let a man lay hand on my Lord Douglas and I will slay the King!"

At this there was great consternation, and but for fear of Sholto's keeping his word half a score would have rushed forward to the assistance of the boy. The scream of a woman from some concealed portal showed that the Queen Mother was waiting to witness the downfall of the mighty house which, as she had been taught, alone threatened her boy's throne.

Sholto's arm was already drawn back for the thrust, when the voice of the Earl of Douglas was heard. He had risen to his feet, and now stood easy and careless as ever, with his thumb in the blue silken sash which girt his waist.

"Sholto," he said calmly, "you forget your place. Let the King go instantly, and ask his Majesty's pardon. Set your sword again in its sheath. I am your lord. I dubbed you knight. Do as I command you."

Most unwillingly Sholto did as he was bidden, and the King, instead of withdrawing, placed himself still closer to William of Douglas.

"And now," cried the Earl, facing the array of armed men who thronged the banquet-hall, "what would ye with the Douglas? Do ye mean my death, as by the Bull's Head here on the table ye would have me believe?"

"For black treason do we apprehend you, Earl of Douglas," creaked the voice of the Chancellor, still speaking from behind his array of men-at-arms, "and because you have set yourself above the King. But we are no butchers, and trial shall ye have by your peers."

"And who in this place are the peers of the Earl of Douglas?" said the young man, haughtily.

"I will not bandy words with you, my Lord Douglas. You are overmastered. Yield yourself, therefore, as indeed you must without remeed. Deliver your weapons and submit; 'tis our will."

"My brave Chancellor," said the Earl William, still in a voice of pleasant irony, "you have well chosen your time to shame yourself. We are your invited guests, and the guests of the King of Scotland. We are here unarmed, sitting at meat with you in your own house. We have come hither unattended, trusting to the honour of these noble knights and gentlemen. Therefore my brother and I have no swords to deliver. But if, being honourable men, you stand, as is natural, upon a nice punctilio, I can satisfy you."

He turned again to Sholto MacKim.

"Give me your sword," he said. "'Tis better I should render it than you."

With great unwillingness the captain of the guard of Thrieve did as he was bidden. The Earl reversed it in his hand and held it by the point.

"And now, my Lord Chancellor, I deliver you a Douglas sword, depending upon the word of an honourable man and the invitation of the King of Scotland."

But even so the chancellor would not advance from

behind the cover of his soldiery, and the Earl looked around for some one to whom to surrender.

"Will you then appoint one of your knights to whom I may deliver this weapon? Is there none who will dare to come near even the hilt of a Douglas sword? Here then, Sholto, break it over your knee and cast it upon the board as a witness against all treachery."

Sholto did as he was told, breaking his sword and casting the pieces upon the table in the place where the King of Scots had sat.

"And now, my lords, I am ready," said the Earl, and his brother David stood up beside him, looking as they faced the unbroken ring of their foes the two noblest and gallantest youths in Scotland.

At this the King caught Lord William by the hand, and, lifting up his voice, wept aloud with the sudden breaking lamentation of a child.

"My cousin, my dear cousin Douglas," he cried, "they shall not harm you, I swear it on my faith as a King."

At last an officer of the Chancellor's guard mustered courage to approach the Earl of Douglas, and, saluting, he motioned him to follow. This, with his head erect, and his usual easy grace, he did, David walking abreast of him. And Sholto, with all his heart filled with the deadly chill of hopelessness, followed them through the sullen ranks of the traitors.

And even as he went Earl Douglas looked about him every way that he might see once more her for whose sake he had adventured within the portals of death.

CHAPTER XXXIV

BETRAYED WITH A KISS

THE earl and his brother were incarcerated in the lower chamber of the High Keep called David's Tower, which rose next in order eastward from the banqueting-hall, following the line of the battlements.

Beneath, the rock on which the castle was built fell away towards the Nor' Loch in a precipice so steep that no descent was to be thought of—and this indeed was the chief defence of the prison, for the window of the chamber was large and opened easily according to the French fashion.

"I pray that you permit my young knight, Sir Sholto MacKim, to accompany me," said the Earl to the officer who conducted them to their prison-house.

"I have no orders concerning him," said the man, gruffly, but nevertheless permitted Sholto to enter after the Earl and his brother.

The chamber was bare save for a *prie-dieu* in the angle of the wall, at which the Douglas looked with a strange smile upon his face.

"Right *à propos*," said he; "they have need of religion in this house of traitors."

David Douglas went to the window-seat of low stone, and bent his head into his hands. He was but a boy and life was sweet to him, for he had just begun to taste the apple and to dream of the forbidden fruit. He held his head down and was silent a space. Then suddenly he sobbed aloud with a quick, gasping noise, startling enough in that still place.

"For God's dear sake, David laddie," said his brother, going over to him, placing his hand upon his shoulder, "be silent. They will think that we are afraid."

The boy stilled himself instantly at the word, and looked up at his brother with a pale sort of smile.

"No, William, I am not afraid, and if indeed we must die I will not disgrace you. Be never feared of that. Yet I thought on our mother's loneliness. She will miss me sore, for she fleeched and pled with me not to come, yet I would not listen to her."

Sholto stood by the door, erect as if on duty at Thrieve.

"Come and sit with us," said the Earl William kindly to him, "we are no more master and servant, earl and esquire. We are but three youths that are to die together, and the axe's edge levels all. You, Sholto, are in some good chance to live the longest of the three by some half score of minutes. I am glad I made you a knight on the field of honour, Sir Sholto, for then they cannot hang you to a bough, like a varlet caught stealing the King's venison."

Sholto slowly came over to the window-seat and stood there respectfully as before, with his arms straight at his side, feeling more than anything else the lack of his sword-hilt to set his right hand upon.

"Nay, but do as I bid you," said the Earl, looking up at him; "sit down, Sholto."

And Sholto sat on the window-seat and looked forth

upon the lights leaping out one after another down among the crowded gables of the town as this and that burgher lit lamp or lantern at the nearing of the hour of supper.

Far away over the shore-lands the narrow strip of the Forth showed amethystine and mysterious, and farther out still the coast of Fife lay in a sort of opaline haze.

" I wonder," said William Douglas, after a long pause, " what they have done with our good lads. Had they been taken or perished we had surely heard more noise, I warrant. Two score lads of Galloway would not give up their arms without a tulzie for it."

" They might induce them to leave them behind, when they went out to take their pleasures among the maids of the Lawnmarket," said Sholto.

" Not their swords," said the Earl, " it needed all your lord's commands to make yours quit your side. I warrant these fellows will give an excellent account of themselves."

Presently the night fell darker, and a smurr of rain drifted over from the edges of Pentland, mostly passing high above, but with lower fringes that dragged, as it were, on the Castle Rock and the Hill of Calton.

The three young men were still silently looking out when suddenly from the darkness underneath there came a low voice.

" 'Ware window ! " it said, " stand back there above."

To Sholto the words sounded curiously familiar, and almost without thinking what he did, he seized the Earl and his brother and dragged them away from the wide space of the lattice, which opened into the summer's night.

"'Ware window!" came again the cautious voice from far below. Sholto heard the whistle and "spat" of an arrow against the wall without. It must have fallen again, for the voice came a third time—"'Ware window!"

And on this occasion the archer was successful, guided doubtless by the illumination of the lantern the guard had hung on a nail, and whose flicker would outline the lattice faintly against the darkness of the wall.

An arrow entered with a soft hiss. It struck beyond them with a click, and its iron point tinkled on the floor, the plaster of the opposite wall not holding it.

Sholto scrambled about the floor on hands and knees till he found it. It was a common archer's arrow. A cord was fastened about it, and a note stuck in the slit along with the feather.

"It is my brother Laurence," whispered Sholto. "I warrant he is beneath with a rope and a posse of stout fellows. We shall escape them yet."

But even as he raised the letter to read it by the faint blue flicker of the lantern, there came a cry of pain from within the castle. It was a woman's voice that cried, and at the sound of pleading speech in some chamber above them, William Douglas started to his feet.

The words were clear enough, but in a language not understood by Sholto MacKim. They seemed intelligible enough, however, to the Earl.

"I knew it," he cried; "the false hounds have imprisoned her also. It is Sybilla's voice. God in heaven— they are torturing her!"

He ran to the door and shook it vehemently.

"Ho! Without there!" he cried imperiously, as if in his own Castle at Thrieve.

But no one paid any attention to his shouts, and presently the woman's voice died down to a slow sobbing which was quite audible in the room beneath, where the three young men listened.

"What did she say?" asked David, presently, of his brother, who still stood with his ear to the door.

The Earl first made a gesture commanding silence, and then, hearing nothing more, he came slowly over to the window. "It is the Lady Sybilla," he said, in a voice which revealed his deep emotion. "She said, in the French language, 'You shall not kill him. You shall not! He trusted me and he shall not die.'"

Meanwhile Sholto, knowing that there was no time to lose, had been drawing in the cord, which presently thickened into a rope stout enough to support the weight of a light and active youth such as any of the three young men imprisoned in David's Tower.

But the sound of the woman's tears had thrown the Earl into an excitement so extreme that he hammered on the great bolt-studded door with his bare clenched hands, and cried aloud to the Chancellor and Livingston, commanding them to open to him. His first calmness seemed completely broken up.

Meanwhile Sholto, his whole soul bent on the cord which gave the unseen Douglases a chance of saving the lives of their masters, had drawn thirty yards of stout rope into the room. He fixed it by a double knot, first to a ring which was let into the wall, and afterwards to the massive handle of the door itself.

"Now, my lord," he whispered, as he finished, "be

pleased to go first. Our lads are beneath, and in the shaking of a cow's tail we shall be safe in the midst of them."

The Earl held up his hand with the quick imperative motion he used to command silence. The sound of the woman's voice came again from above, now quick and high, like one who makes an agonised petition, and now in tones lower that seemed broken with sobs and lamentations.

At first William Douglas did not appear to comprehend the meaning of Sholto's words, being so bent on his listening. But when the young captain of the guard again reminded him that the time of their chances for relief was quickly passing, and that the soldiers of the Chancellor might come at any moment to lead them to their doom, the Earl broke out upon him in sudden anger.

"For what crawling thing do you take me, Sholto MacKim?" he cried; "I will not leave this place till I know what they have done with her. She trusted me, and shall I prove a recreant? I would have you know that I am William, Earl of Douglas, and fear not the face of any Crichton that ever breathed. Ho — there — without!" and again he shook the door with ineffectual anger.

His only answer was the sound of that beseeching woman's voice, and the measured tread of the sentry, whose partisan they could see flashing in the lamplight through the narrow barred wicket, as he turned in front of their door.

And it was now all in vain that Sholto pled with his master. To every argument Lord Douglas replied, "I

cannot go — it consorts not with mine honour to leave
this castle so long as the Lady Sybilla is in their hands."

Sholto told him how they could now escape, and in a
week would raise the whole of the south, returning to
the siege of the castle and the destruction of the traitors
Crichton and Livingston. But even to this the Earl had
his answer.

"What — flee like a coward and leave this girl, who
has loved and trusted me, defenceless in their hands!
You yourself have heard her weeping. I tell you I cannot go — I will not go. Let David and you escape! My
place is here, and neither snivelling Crichton nor that
backstairs lap-dog Livingston shall say that they took the
Earl of Douglas, and that he fled from them under cloud
of night."

David Douglas had been standing by hopefully while
Sholto tied the rope to the rings. At his brother's words
he sat down again. William of Douglas turned about
upon him.

"Go, David, I bid you. Escape, and if aught happen
to me, fail not to make the traitors pay dearly for it."

But David Douglas sat still and answered not. Then
Sholto, desperate of success with his master, approached
David, and with gentle force would have compelled him
to the window. But, at the first touch of his hand, the
boy thrust him away, striking him fiercely upon the
shoulder.

"Hands off!" he cried, "I also am a Douglas and no
craven. I will abide by my brother to the end."

"No, my David," said the Earl, turning for a moment
from the door where he had been again listening, "you
shall not stay! You are the hope of our house. My

mother would fret to death if aught happened to you. This is not a matter which concerns you. Go, I bid you. On me it lies, and if I must pay the reckoning, why at least only I drank the wine."

"I will not;" cried the boy; "I tell you I will bide where my brother bides and his fate shall be mine."

Then Sholto, well nigh frantic with apprehension and disappointment, went to the window and leaned out, gripping the sill with his hands.

"They will not leave the castle," he whispered as loud as he dared; "the Earl will not escape while the Lady Sybilla remains a prisoner within."

"God in heaven!" cried a stern voice from below which made Sholto start, "we shall be broken first and last upon that woman. Would to God I had slain her with my hand! Tell the Earl that if he will not come to those that wait for him underneath the tower, I, Malise MacKim, will come and fetch him like a child in my arms, even as I did from under the pine trees at Loch Roan."

And as he spoke the strain of the rope and its swaying over the window-sill proclaimed that the mighty form of the master armourer was even then on the way upwards towards the dungeon of his chief.

"Go back, I command you, Malise MacKim," he said, "go back instantly. I have made up my mind. I will not escape from the Castle of Edinburgh this night."

But Malise answered not a word, only pulled more desperately on the rope, till the sound of his labouring breath and grasping palms could be heard from side to side of the chamber.

The Earl leaned further out.

"Malise," he said, calm and clear, "you see this knife. I would not have your blood on my hands. You have been a good and faithful servant to our house. But, by the oath of a Douglas, if you come one foot farther, I will cut the rope and you shall be dashed in pieces beneath."

The master armourer stopped—not with any fear of death upon him, but lest a stroke of his master's dirk should destroy their well-arranged mode of escape.

"O Earl William, my dear lord, hear me," he said in a gasping voice, still hanging perilously between earth and heaven. "If I have indeed been a faithful servant, I beseech you come with me—for the sake of the house of Douglas and of your mother, a widow and alone."

"Go down, Malise MacKim," said the Earl, more gently; "I will speak with you only at the rope's foot."

So very unwillingly Malise went back.

"Now," said the Earl, "hearken—this will I do and no other. I will remain here and abide that which shall befall me, as is the will of God. I am bound by a tie that I cannot break. What life is to another, honour and his word must be to a Douglas. But I send your son Sholto to you. I bid him ride fast to Galloway and bring all that are faithful with speed here to Edinburgh. Go also into Douglasdale and tell my cousin William of Avondale—and if he is too late to save, I know well he will avenge me."

"O William Douglas, if indeed ye will neither fleech nor drive, I pray you for the sake of the great house to send your brother David, that the Douglases of the Black be not cut off root and branch. Remember, your mother is sore set on the lad."

"I will not go," cried David, as he heard this; "by the saints I will stand by my brother's shoulder, though I be but a boy! I will not go so much as a step, and if by force ye stir me I will cry for the guard!"

By this time the young David was leaning half out of the window, and almost shouting out his words down to the unseen Douglases beneath.

"Go, Sholto," said the Earl, setting his hand on his squire's shoulder. "You alone can ride to Galloway without drawing rein. Go swiftly and bring back every true lad that can whang bow, or gar sword-iron whistle. The Douglas must drie the Douglas weird. I would have made you a great man, Sir Sholto, but if you get a new master, he will surely do that which I had not time to perform."

"Come, Sholto," said his father, "there is a horse at the outer port. I fear the Crichton's men are warned. As it is we shall have to fight for it."

Sholto still hesitated, divided between obedience and grief.

"Sholto MacKim," said the Earl, "if indeed you owe me aught of love or service, go and do that thing which I have laid upon you. Bear a courteous greeting from me to your sweetheart Maud, and a kiss to our Maid Margaret. And now haste you and begone!"

Sholto bent a moment on his knee and kissed the hand of his young master. His voice was choked with sobs. The Earl patted him on the shoulder. "Dinna greet, laddie," he said, in the kindly country speech which comes so meltingly to all Galloway folk in times of distress, gentle and simple alike, "dinna greet. If one Douglas fall in the breach, there stands ever a better behind him."

"But never one like you, my lord, my lord!" said Sholto.

The Earl raised him gently, led him to the window, and himself steadied the rope by which his squire was to descend.

"Go!" he said; "honour keeps the Douglas here, and his brother bides with him — since not otherwise it may be. But the honour of obedience sends Sholto MacKim to the work that is given him!"

Then, after the captain of his guard had gone out into the dark and disappeared down the rope, the Earl only waited till the tension slackened before stooping and cutting the cord at the point of juncture with the iron ring.

"And now, Davie lad," he said, setting an arm about his brother's neck, "there are but you and me for it, and I think a bit prayer would not harm either of us."

So the two young lads, being about to die, kneeled down together before the cross of Him who was betrayed with a kiss.

R

CHAPTER XXXV

THE LION AT BAY

THE morning had broken broad and clear from the east when the door of the prison-house was opened, and a seneschal appeared. He saluted the brothers, and in a shaking voice summoned them to come forth and be tried for offences of treason and rebellion against the King and his ministers.

William of Douglas waved a hand to him, but answered nothing to the summons. He wasted no words upon one who merely did as he was bidden. All night the brothers had sat looking out on the city humming sleeplessly beneath them, till the light slowly dawned over the Forth and away to the eastward Berwick Law stood dwarfed and clear. At first they had sat apart, but as the hours stole on David came a little nearer and his hand sought that of his brother, clasped it, and abode as it had been contented. The elder brother returned the pressure.

"David," he said, "if perish we must, at least you and I will show them how Douglases can die."

So when they rose to follow the seneschal who summoned them, as they left the chamber of detention and the clanking guard fell in behind them, Earl William put his hand affectionately on his young brother's shoulder and kept it there. In this wise they came into the

great hall wherein yestereven the banquet of treachery
had been served. The dais had been removed to the
upper end of the room, and upon it in the furred robes
of judges of the realm, there sat on either side of the
empty throne Crichton the Chancellor and Sir Alexander
Livingston. Behind were crowded groups of knights,
pages, men-at-arms, and all the hangers-on of a court.
But of men of dignity and place only the Marshal de
Retz, ambassador of the King of France, was present.

He sat alone on a high seat ranged crosswise upon the
dais. The floor in the centre of the hall was kept clear
for the entrance of the brothers of Douglas.

Crichton and Livingston looked uneasily at each other
as the feet of the guard conducting the prisoners were
heard in the corridor without, and with a quick, appre-
hensive wave of his hand Crichton motioned the armed
men of his guard closer about him, and gave their leader
directions in a hushed voice behind his palm.

The seneschal who had summoned them strode in first,
and then after a sufficient interval entered the young
Lords of Douglas, William and David his brother. The
elder still kept one hand affectionately on the shoulder of
the younger. His other was set as usual in the silken
belt which he wore about his waist, and he walked carelessly, with a high air and an easy step, like one that
goes in expectantly to a pleasant entertainment.

But as soon as the brothers perceived in whose presence they were, an air of pride came over their faces and
stiffened their figures into the sterner aspect of warriors
who stand on the field of battle.

Some three paces before the steps of the dais on which
sat the self-constituted judges was arranged a barrier of

strong wooden posts tipped with iron, and two soldiers
with drawn swords were on guard at either end.

The Douglases stood silent, haughtily awaiting the
first words of accusation. And the face of young David
was to the full as haughty and contemptuous as that of
Earl William himself.

It was the Chancellor who spoke first, in his high rasping creak.

"William, Earl of Douglas, and you David, called the
Master of Douglas," he began, "you are summoned hither
by the King's authority to answer for many crimes of
treason against his royal person— for rebellion also and
the arming of forces against his authority — for high
speeches and studied contempt of those who represent
his sovereign Majesty in this realm, for treasonable alli-
ances with rebel lords, and above all for swearing allegiance to another monarch, even to the King of France.
What have you to say to these charges?"

The Earl of Douglas swept his eyes across the dais
from side to side with a slow contempt which made the
Chancellor writhe in his chair. Then after a long pause
he deigned to reply, but rather like a king who grants
a favour than like one accused before judges in whose
hands is the power of life and death.

"I see," said he, "two knights before me on a high
seat, one the King's tutor, the other his purse-bearer.
I have yet to learn who constituted them judges of
any cause whatsoever, still less of aught that concerns
William Douglas, Duke of Touraine, Earl of Douglas,
hereditary Lieutenant-Governor of the realm of Scotland."

And he kept his eyes upon them with a straight

forth-looking glance, palpably embarrassing to the traitors on the dais.

"Earl Douglas," said the Chancellor again, "pray remember that you are not now in Castle Thrieve. Your six thousand horsemen wait not in the courtyard out there. Learn to be more humble and answer to the things whereof you are accused. Do you desire that witness should be brought?"

"Of what need are witnesses? I own no court or jurisdiction. I have heard no accusations!" said the Earl William.

The Chancellor motioned with his hand, whereupon Master Robert Berry, a procurator of the city, advanced and read a long parchment which set forth in phrase and detail of legality twenty accusations against the Earl,—of treason, rebellion, and manifest oppression.

When he had finished the Chancellor said, "And now, Earl Douglas, what answer have you to these things?"

"Does it matter at all what I answer?" asked the Earl, succinctly.

"I do not bandy words with you," said the Chancellor; "I order you to make your pleading, or stand within your danger."

"And yet," said William Douglas, gravely, "words are all that you dare bandy with me. Even if I honoured you by laying aside my dignities and consented to break a lance with you, you would refuse to afford me trial by battle, which is the right of every peer accused."

"'Tis a barbarous custom," said the Chancellor; "we will try your case upon its merit."

The Earl laughed a little mocking laugh.

"It will be somewhat safer," said he, "but haste you and get the sham done with. I plead nothing. I do not even tell you that you lie. What doth one expect of a gutter-dog but that it should void the garbage it hath devoured? But I do ask you, Marshal de Retz, as a brave soldier and the representative of an honourable King, what you have done with the Lady Sybilla?"

The Marshal de Retz smiled — a smile so chill, cruel, hard, that the very soldiers on guard, seeing it, longed to slay him on the spot.

"May I, in return, ask my Lord Earl of Douglas and Duke of Touraine what is that to him?" he said, with sneering emphasis upon the titles.

"It matters to me," replied William Douglas, boldly, "more than life, and almost as much as honour. The Lady Sybilla did me the grace to tell me that she loved me. And I in turn am bound to her in life and death."

The Chancellor and the tutor broke into laughter, but the marshal continued to smile his terrible smile of determinate evil.

"Listen," he said at last, "hear this, my Lord of Touraine; ever since we came to this kingdom, and, indeed, long before we left the realm of France, the Lady Sybilla intended nothing else than your deception and destruction. Poor dupe, do you not yet understand? She it was that cozened you with fair words. She it was that advised you to come hither that we might hold you in our hands. For her sake you obeyed. She was the willing bait of the trap your foes set for you. What think you of the Lady Sybilla now?"

William of Douglas did not answer in words, but as
the marshal ceased speaking, he drew himself together
like a lithe animal that sways this way and that before
springing. His right hand dropped softly from his
brother's shoulder upon the hilt of his own dagger.

Then with one sudden bound he was over the barrier
and upon the dais. Almost his blade was at the marshal's throat, and but for the crossed partisans of two
guards who stood on either side of De Retz, he had
died there and then by the dagger of William Douglas.
As it was, the youth was brought to a stand with his
breast pressed vainly against the steel points, and paused
there crying out in fury, "Liar and toad! Come out
from behind these varlets that I may slay thee with
my hand."

A score of men-at-arms approached from behind, and
forced the young man back to his place.

"Bring in the Lady Sybilla," said the marshal, still
smiling, while the judges sat silent and afraid at the
anger of one man.

And even while the Earl stood panting after his out-
burst of furious anger, they opened the door at the back
of the dais and through it there entered the Lady Sybilla.
Instantly the eyes of William Douglas fixed themselves
upon her, but she did not raise hers nor look at him.
She stood at the farther side at the edge of the dais,
her hands joined in front of her, and her hair streamed
down her back and fell in waves over her white dress.

An angel of light coming through the open door of
heaven could not have appeared more innocent and
pure.

The Marshal de Retz turned towards his sister-in-law,

and, with his eyes fixed upon hers and with the same pitiless chill in them, he said in a low tone, "Look at me."

The girl raised her eyes slowly, and, as it had been, reluctantly, and in them, instead of the meek calm of an angel, there appeared the terror and dismay of a lost soul that listens to its doom.

"Sybilla," hissed rather than spoke De Retz, "is it true that ever since by the lakeside of Carlinwark you met the Earl of Douglas you have deceived him and sought his doom?"

"I care not to hear the answer," said the young man, "even did I believe that which you by your power may compel her to say. Unfaith in another is not unfaith in me. I am bound to this lady in love and honour — aye, even unto death, if that be her will!"

"I have, indeed, deceived him!" replied the girl, slowly, the words seeming to be forced from her one by one.

"You hear, William of Douglas!" said the marshal, turning upon the young man, who stood still and motionless, never taking his eyes off the slender figure in white.

The marshal continued his pitiless questioning.

"At Castle Thrieve you persuaded him to follow you to Crichton and afterwards to Edinburgh, knowing well that you brought him to his death."

"It is true!" said the girl, with a voice like one speaking out of the grave itself.

"You hear, William of Douglas!" said the marshal.

"And at Castle Crichton you played the play to the end. With false cozening words you deceived this young man. You led him on with love on your lips and hate in your heart. You kissed him with the Judas kiss. You led his soul captive to death by the drawing of your eyes."

In a voice that could hardly be heard the girl replied, her whole figure fixed and turned to stone by the intensity of her tormentor's gaze.

"*I did these things! I am accursed!*"

The ambassador turned with a fleering triumph.

"You hear, William of Douglas," he said, "you hear what your true love says!"

Then it was that, with the calm air and steady voice of a great gentleman, William Douglas answered, "I hear, but I do not believe."

A spasm of joy passed over the countenance of the Lady Sybilla. She half sprang towards her lover as if to clasp him in her arms.

But in the midst, between intent and act, she restrained herself.

"No, I am not worthy," she said. And again, and lower, like a lamentation, "I am not worthy!"

Then, while all watched eagerly, the marshal rose from his seat to his full height.

"Girl — look at me!" he cried in a loud and terrible voice. But Sybilla did not seem to hear him.

She was looking at the Earl, and her eyes were great and grey and vague.

"Listen, my true lord, and then hate me if you will," she said; "listen, William of Douglas. Never before have I found in all the world one man true to the core. I did not believe that such an one lived. Hear this and then turn from me in loathing.

"For the sake of this man's life, forfeit ten times

over" (she pointed, as she spoke, at the marshal), "to whom, by the powers of hell, my soul is bound, I came at the bidding of the King of France and of this man, my master, to compass the destruction of the Earl of Douglas. Our King's son desired his duchy, and promised to this man pardon for his evil deeds. I came to satisfy them both. On my guilty head be the punishment. It is true that I cozened and led you on. It is true that at Castle Thrieve I deceived you, knowing well that which would happen. I knew to what you would follow me, and for the sake of the evil wrought by your fathers, I was glad. But afterwards at Crichton, when, in the woods by the waterside, I told you that I loved you, I did not lie. I did love you then. And by God's grace I do love you now — yea, before all men I declare it. Once for a season of glorious forgetting, all too brief, I was yours to love, now I am yours to hate and to despise. I tried to save you, but though you had my warning you would not go back or forget me. Now it is too late!"

As she spoke over the face of William Douglas there had come a glow — the red blood flooding up and routing the white determined pallor of his cheek.

"My lady," he answered her, gently, "be not grieved for a little thing that is past. That you love me truly is enough. I ask for no more, least of all for pity. I have not lived long. I have not had time allotted me wherein to do great things, but for your sake I can die as well as any! You have given me of your love, and of the flower thereof. I am glad. That you have loved me was my crown of life. Now it remains but to pay a little price soon paid, for a joy exceeding great."

But the Chancellor had had enough of this. He rose, and, stretching forth his hand towards the barrier, he said: "William of Douglas, you and your brother are condemned to instant death as enemies of the King and his ministers. Soldiers, do your duty. Lead them forth to the block!"

And with these words he left the dais, followed by Sir Alexander Livingston. The girl stood in the place whence she had spoken her last words. Then, as the men-at-arms went shamefacedly to take the Earl by the arm, she suddenly threw herself across the platform, leaped lightly over the barrier, and fell into his arms.

"William, once I would have betrayed you," she said, "but now I love you. I will die with you — or by the great God I will live to avenge you."

"Hush, sweetheart," said William Douglas, touching her brow gently with his lips, and putting her into the arms of an officer of the court whom her uncle had sent to remove her. "Fear not for me! Death is swift and easy. I expected nothing else. That you love me is enough! Dear love, fare thee well!"

But the girl heard him not. She had fainted in the arms that held her. Yet the Marshal de Retz had still more for her to suffer. He stood beside her and dashed water upon her till she awoke, that she might see that which remained to be done.

*   *   *   *   *   *

It was a scene dreary beyond all power of words to tell it, when into the courtyard of the Castle of Edinburgh they brought the two noble young men forth to die. The sun had long risen, but the first flush of broad morning sunshine still lingered upon the low platform on which stood the block, and beside it the headsman sullenly waiting to do his appointed work.

The young Lords of Douglas came out looking brave and handsome as bridegrooms on a day of betrothing. William had once more his hand on David's shoulder, his other rested carelessly on his thigh as his custom was. The brothers were bareheaded, and to the eyes of those who looked on they seemed to be conversing together of light matters of love and ladies' favours.

High above upon a balcony, hung like an iron cage upon the castle wall, appeared the Chancellor and the tutor. The young King was with them, weeping and crying out, "Do nothing to my dear cousins—I command you—I am the King!"

But the tutor roughly bade him be still, telling him that he would never reign if these young men lived, and presently another came there and stood beside him. The Marshal de Retz it was, who, with a fiendish smile upon his sleek parchment face, conducted the Lady Sybilla to see the end. But it was a good end to see, and nobler far than most lives that are lived to fourscore years.

The brothers embraced as they came to the block, kneeled down, and said a short prayer like Christians of a good house. So great was their enemies' haste that they were not allowed even a priest to shrive them, but they did what they could.

The executioner motioned first to David. An attendant brought him the heading cup of wine, which it was the custom to offer to those about to die upon the scaffold.

"Drink it not," said Earl William, "lest they say it was drugged."

And David Douglas bowed his head upon the block, being only in the fifteenth year of his age.

"Farewell, brother," he said, "be not long after me. It is a darksome road to travel so young."

"Fear not, Davie lad," said William Douglas, tenderly, "I will overtake you ere you be through the first gate."

He turned a little aside that he might not see his brother die, and even as he did so he saw the Lady Sybilla lean upon the balcony paler than the dead.

Then when it came to his turn they offered the Earl William also the heading cup filled with the rich wine of Touraine, his own fair province that he was never to see.

He lifted the cup high in his right hand with a knightly and courtly gesture. Looking towards the balcony whereon stood the Lady Sybilla, he bowed to her.

"I drink to you, my lady and my love," he cried, in a voice loud and clear.

Then, touching but the rim of the goblet with his lips, he poured out the red wine upon the ground.

*   *   *   *   *   *

And thus passed the gallantest gentleman and truest lover in whom God ever put heart of grace to live courteously and die greatly, keeping his faith in his lady even against herself, and holding death itself sweet because that in death she loved him.

CHAPTER XXXVI

THE RISING OF THE DOUGLASES

It was upon the Earl's own charger, Black Darnaway, that Sholto rode southward to raise to their chief's assistance the greatest and compactest clan that ever, even in Scotland, had done the bidding of one man.

The young man's heart was high and hopeful within him. The King's guardians dared not, so he told himself, let aught befall the puissant Douglases in the Castle of Edinburgh, without trial and under cover of the most courteous hospitality.

"Try the Earl of Douglas!" so Sholto thought within him. He laughed at the notion. "Why, Earl William could by a word bring a hundred thousand men of Galloway and the Marches to make a fitting jury."

So he meditated, his thoughts running fast and fiery to the beating of Black Darnaway's feet as he climbed the heathery slopes which led towards Douglasdale. Day was breaking as he rode down to the town of Lanark yet asleep and smokeless in the caller airs of the morn. At the gates of this frontier town he delivered his first summons of feudality. For the burghers of Lanark were liegemen of the Douglases of Douglasdale, and were (though not with much good-will) bound to furnish service at call.

Sholto had some difficulty in making himself heard

athwart the ponderous wooden gates, bossed with leather and studded with iron. At first he shouted angrily to the silences, but presently nearer and nearer came a bellow as of a brazen bull, thunderous and far echoing.

"Fower o' the clock and a braw, braw morning."

It was Grice Elshioner, watchman of the town of Lanark, evidencing to the magistrates and lieges thereof that he was earning his three shillings in the week — a handsome wage in these hard times, and one well able to provide belly-timber for himself and also for the wife and weans who, dwelling in a close off the High-street, were called by his name.

Sholto thundered again upon the rugged portal.

"Open there! Open, I say, in the name of the Earl of Douglas!"

"Fower o' the morning! Lord, what's a' the steer? In the name o' the Yerl o' Douglas! But wha kens that it isna the English? Na, na, Grice Elshioner opens not to every night-raking loon that likes to cry the name o' the Yerl o' Douglas ower oor toon wa'!"

And Grice the valorous would have taken him off with a fresh, sleep-dispelling bellow had it not been that he heard himself summoned in a voice that brooked no delay.

"Open, varlet of a watchman, or by Saint Bride I will have you swinging in half an hour from the bars of your own portcullis. I who speak am Sholto MacKim, captain of the Earl's guard. Every liegeman in the town must arm, mount, and ride this instant to Edinburgh. I give you fair warning. You hear my words, I will not enter your rascal town. But if so much as one be wanting at the muster, I swear in the name of my master that his house shall be burned with fire and razed to the ground, and his wife be a widow or ever the cock craw on another Sabbath morn!"

And without waiting for a reply Sholto laid the reins upon the neck of Black Darnaway and rode on southward up Douglas Water to the home nest of the lordly race.

And behind him, with a wail in it, blared through the narrow streets the stormy voice of Grice Elshioner, watchman of Lanark, "Wauken ye, wauken ye, burgesses a'! The Douglas hath sent to bid ye mount and ride."

The *birr* of the war drum saluted Sholto's ears ere he had turned the corner of the town parks. Then came the answering shouts of the burghers who thrust inquiring and indignant heads out of gable windows and turret speering-holes.

"*Birr!*" continued the undaunted and insistent town drum.

"Harness your backs! Fill your bellies, and stand ready! The Douglas has need o' ye, lieges a'!" cried the sonorous voice of the watch. Sholto smiled as he listened.

"I have at least set them on the alert. They will join the Douglasdale men as they pass by, or we will show them reason why. But they of Lanark are ill-set townward men, and of no true leal heart, save an it be to their own coffers. Yet will they march with us for fear of the harrying hand and the burning roof tree."

The sun rose fair on the battlements of Douglas Castle as Sholto rode up to the level mead, whereon a little company of men was exercising. He could hear the words of command cried gruffly in the broad Galloway speech.

Landless Jock was drilling his spearmen, and as the shining triple line of points dropped to the "ready to receive," the old knight and former captain of the Earl's guard came forward a little way to welcome his successor with what grace was at his command.

"Eh, sirce, and what has brocht sic a braw young knight and grand frequenter o' courts sae far as Douglas Castle? Could ye no even let puir Landless Jock hae the tilt-yaird here to exercise his handfu' in, and keep his auld banes a wee while frae the rust and the green mould?"

But even as the crusty old soldier spoke these words, the white anxiety in Sholto's face struck through his half-humorous complaint, and the words died on his lips in a perturbed "What is't — what is't ava, laddie?"

Sholto told him in the fewest words.

"The Yerl and Dawvid in the power o' their hoose's enemies. Blessed Saint Anthony, and here was I flighterin' and ragin' aboot my naethings. Here, lads, blaw the horn and cry the slogan. Fetch the horses frae the stall and stand ready in your war gear within ten minutes by the knock. Aye, faith, will we raise Douglasdale! Gang your ways to Gallowa' — there shall not a man bide at hame this day. Certes, we wull that! Ca' in the by-gaun at Lanark — aye, lad, and, gin the rascals are no willing or no ready, we will hang the provost and magistrates at their ain door-cheeks to learn them to bide frae the cried assembly o' their liege lord!"

Sholto had done enough in Douglasdale. He turned north again on a yet more important errand. It was forenoon full and broad when he halted before the little town of Strathaven, upon which the Castle of Avondale looks down. It seemed of the greatest moment that the

s

Avondale Douglases should know that which had befallen their cousin. For no suspicion of treachery within the house and name of Douglas itself touched with a shade of shadow the mind of Sholto MacKim.

He thundered at the townward port of the castle (to which a steep ascent led up from a narrow vennel), where presently the outer guard soon crowded about him, listening to his story and already fingering bowstring and examining rope-matches preparatory to the expected march upon Edinburgh.

"I have not time to waste, comrades; I would see my lords," said Sholto. "I must see them instantly."

And even as he spoke there on the steps before him appeared the dark, handsome face and tall but slightly stooping figure of William Douglas of Avondale. He stood with his hands clasped behind his back, and his serious thought-weighted brow bent upon the concourse about Sholto.

With a push of his elbows this way and that, the young captain of the Earl's guard opened a road through the press.

In short, emphatic sentences he told his tale, and at the name of prisonment and treachery to his cousins the countenance of William Douglas grew stern and hard. His face twitched as if the news came very near to him. He did not answer for a moment, but stood biting his lips and glooming upon Sholto, as though the young man had been a prisoner waiting sentence of pit or gallows for evil doing.

"I must see James concerning this ill news," he said when Sholto had finished telling him of the Black Bull's Head at the Chancellor's banquet-table.

He turned to go within.

"My lord," said Sholto, "will you give me another horse, and let Darnaway rest in your stables? I must instantly ride south again to raise Galloway."

"Order out all the horses which are ready caparisoned," commanded William of Avondale, "and do you, Captain Sholto, take your choice of them."

He went within forthwith and there ensued a pause filled with the snorting and prancing of steeds, as, mettlesome with oats and hay, they issued from their stalls, or with the grass yet dewy about their noses were led in from the field. Darnaway took his leave of Sholto with a backward neigh of regret, as if to say he was not yet tired of going on his master's service.

Then presently on the terrace above appeared lazy Lord James, busily buckling the straps of his body-armour and talking hotly the while with his brother William.

"I care not even whether our father—" he cried aloud ere, with a restraining hand upon his wrist, his elder brother could succeed in stopping him.

"Hush, James," he said, "at least be mindful of those that stand around."

"I care not, I tell you, William," cried the headstrong youth, squaring his shoulders as he was wont to do before a fight. "I tell you that you and I are no traitors to our name, and who meddles with our coz, Will of Thrieve, hath us to reckon with!"

William of Avondale said nothing, but held out his hand with a slow, determinate gesture. Said he, "An it were the father that begat us." Whereat, with all the impetuousness of his race and nature, James dashed his palm into that of his brother.

" Whiles, William," he cried, "ye appear clerkish and overcautious, and I break out and miscall ye for no Douglas, when ye will not spend your siller like a man and are afraid of the honest pint stoup. But at the heart's heart ye are aye a Douglas — and though the silly gaping commons like ye not so well as they like me, ye are the best o' us, for all that."

So it came to pass that within the space of half an hour the Avondale Douglases had sent men to the four airts, young Hugh Douglas himself riding west, while James stirred the folk of Avondale and Strathavon, and in all the courtyards and streets of the little feudal bourg there began the hum and buzz of the war assembly.

Lord William went with Sholto to see staunch Darnaway duly stabled, and to approve the horse which was to bear the messenger to the south without halt, now that his mission was accomplished in the west. When they came out Sholto's riding harness had been transferred to a noble grey steed large enough to carry even the burly James, let alone the slim captain of the archer guard of Thrieve.

In the court, ranked and ready, bridle to bridle were ranged the knights and squires in waiting about the Castle of Avondale, while out on a level green spot on the edge of the moor gathered the denser array of the townfolk with spears and partisans.

In an hour the Avondale Douglases were ready to ride to the assistance of their cousins. Alas, that Earl William would take no advice, for had these and others gone in with him to the fatal town, there would have been no Black Bull's Head on the Chancellor's dinner table in the banqueting-hall of Edinburgh Castle.

CHAPTER XXXVII

A STRANGE MEETING

It was approaching the evening of the third day after riding forth upon his mission when Sholto, sleepless yet quite unconscious of weariness, approached the loch of Carlinwark and the cottage of Brawny Kim. West and south he had raised the Douglas country as it had never been raised before. And now behind him every armiger and squire, every spearman and light-foot archer, was hasting Edinburgh-ward, eager to be first to succour the young and headstrong chief of his great house.

Sholto had ridden and cried the slogan as was his duty, without allowing his mind to dwell over much upon whether all might not arrive too late. And ever as he rode out of village or across the desolate moors from castle to fortified farmhouse, it seemed that not he but some other was upon this quest.

Something sterner and harder stirred in his breast. Light-hearted Sholto MacKim, the careless lad of the jousting day, the proud young captain of the Earl's guard, was dead with all his vanity. And in his place a man rode southward grim and determined, with vengeful angers a-smoulder in his bosom, — hunger, thirst, love, the joy of living and the fear of death all being swallowed up by deadly hatred of those who had betrayed his master.

Maud Lindesay was doubtless within a few miles of

Sholto, yet he scarcely gave even his sweetheart a thought as he urged his weary grey over the purple Parton moors towards the loch of Carlinwark and the little hamlet nestling along its western side under the ancient thorn trees of the Carlin's hill.

He rode down over the green and empty Crossmichael braes on which the broom pods were crackling in the afternoon sunshine, through hollows where the corn lingered as though unwilling to have done with such a scene of beauty, and find itself mewed in dusty barns, ground in mills, or close pressed in thatched rick. He breasted the long smooth rise and entered the woods which encircle the bright lakelet of Carlinwark, the pearl of all southland Scottish lochs.

With a strange sense of detachment he looked down upon the green sward between him and his mother's gable end, upon which as a child he had wandered from dawn to dusk. Then it was nearly as large as the world, and the grass was most comfortable to bare feet. There were children playing upon it now, even as there had been of old, among them his own little sister Magdalen, whose hair was spun gold, and her eyes blue as the forget-me-not on the marshes of the Isle Wood. The children were dressed in white, five little girls in all, as for a festal day, and their voices came upward to Sholto's ear through the arches of the great beeches which studded the turf with pavilions of green shade, tenderly as they had done to that of William Douglas in the springtime of the year.

The minor note, the dying fall of the innocent voices, tugged at his heartstrings. He could hear little Magdalen leading the chorus:

> " *Margaret Douglas, fresh and fair,*
> *A bunch of roses she shall wear,*
> *Gold and silver by her side,*
> *I know who's her bride.*"

It was at "Fair Maid" they were playing, the mystic
dance of Southland maidenhood, at whose vestal rites no
male of any age was ever permitted to be present. The
words broke in upon the gloom which oppressed Sholto's
heart. Momentarily he forgot his master and saw Maud
Lindesay with the little Margaret Douglas of whom the
children sang, once again gathering the gowans on the
brae sides of Thrieve or perilously reaching out for purple irises athwart the ditches of the Isle.

> " *Take her by the lily-white hand,*
> *Lead her o'er the water;*
> *Give her kisses, one, two, three,*
> *For she's a lady's daughter.*"

As Sholto MacKim listened to the quaint and moving
lullaby, suddenly there came into the field of his vision
that which stiffened him into a statue of breathing
marble.

For without clatter of accoutrement or tramp of hoof,
without companion or attendant, a white palfrey had
appeared through the green arches of the woodlands. A
girl was seated upon the saddle, swaying with gentle
movement to the motion of her steed. At the sight of
her figure as she came nearer a low cry of horror and
amazement broke from Sholto's lips.

It was the Lady Sybilla.

Yet he knew that he had left her behind him in
Edinburgh, the siren temptress of Earl Douglas, the
woman who had led his master into the power of the

enemy, she for whose sake he had refused the certainty of freedom and life. Anger against this smiling enchantress suddenly surged up in Sholto's heart.

"Halt there—on your life!" he cried, and urged his wearied steed forward. Like dry leaves before a winter wind, the children were dispersed every way by the gust of his angry shout. But the maiden on the palfrey either heeded not or did not hear.

Whereupon Sholto rode furiously crosswise to intercept her. He would learn what had befallen his master. At least he would avenge him upon one—the chiefest and subtlest of his enemies. But not till he had come within ten paces did the Lady Sybilla turn upon him the fulness of her regard. Then he saw her face. It broke upon him sudden as the sight of imminent hell to one sure of salvation. He had expected to find there gratified ambition, sated lust, exultant pride, cruelest vengeance. He saw instead as it had been the face of an angel cast out of heaven, or perhaps, rather, of a martyr who has passed through the torture chamber on her way to the place of burning.

The sight stopped Sholto stricken and wavering. His anger fell from him like a cloak shed when the sun shines in his strength.

The Lady Sybilla's face showed of no earthly paleness. Marble white it was, the eyes heavy with weeping, purple rings beneath accentuating the horror that dwelt eternally in them. The lips that had been as the bow of Apollo were parted as though they had been singing the dirge of one beloved, and ever as she rode the tears ran down her cheeks and fell on her white robe, and lower upon her palfrey's mane.

She looked at Sholto when he came near, but not as one who sees or recognises. Rather, as it were, dumb, drunken, besotted with grief, looked forth the soul of the Lady Sybilla upon the captain of the Douglas guard. She heeded not his angry shout, for another voice rang in her ears, speaking the knightliest words ever uttered by a man about to die. Sholto's sword was raised threateningly in his hand, but Sybilla saw another blade gleam bright in the morning sun ere it fell to rise again dimmed and red. Therefore she checked not her steed, nor turned aside, till Sholto laid his fingers upon her bridle-rein and leaped quickly to the ground, sword in hand, leaving his own beast to wander where it would.

"What do you here?" he cried. "Where is my master? What have they done to him? I bid you tell me on your life!"

Sholto's voice had no chivalrous courtesy in it now. The time for that had gone by. He lowered his sword point and there was tense iron in the muscles of his arm. He was ready to kill the temptress as he would a beautiful viper.

The Lady Sybilla looked upon him, but in a dazed fashion, like one who rests between the turns of the rack. In a little while she appeared to recognise him. She noted the sword in his hand, the death in his eye —and for the first time since the scene in the courtyard of Edinburgh Castle, she smiled.

Then the fury in Sholto's heart broke suddenly forth.

"Woman," he cried, "show me cause why I should not slay you. For, by God, I will, if aught of harm hath overtaken my master. Speak, I bid you, speak quickly, if you have any wish to live."

But the Lady Sybilla continued to smile — the same dreadful, mocking smile — and somehow Sholto, with his weapon bare and his arm nerved to the thrust, felt himself grow weak and helpless under the stillness and utter pitifulness of her look.

"You would kill me — kill *me*, you say —" the words came low and thrilling forth from lips which were as those of the dead whose chin has not yet been bound about with a napkin, "ah, would that you could! But you cannot. Steel will not slay, poison will not destroy, nor water drown Sybilla de Thouars till her work be done!"

Sholto escaped from the power of her eye.

"My master —" he gasped, "my master — is he well? I pray you tell me."

Was it a laugh he heard in answer? Rather a sound, not of human mirth but as of a condemned spirit laughing deep underground. Then again the low even voice replied out of the expressionless face.

"Aye, your master is well."

"Ah, thank God," burst forth Sholto, "he is alive."

The Lady Sybilla moved her hand this way and that with the gesture of a blind man groping.

"Hush," she said, "I only said that he was well. And he is well. As I am already in the place of torment, I know that there is a heaven for those who die as William Douglas died."

Sholto's cry rang sudden, loud, despairing.

"Dead — dead — Earl William dead — my master dead!"

He dropped the palfrey's rein, which till now he had held. His sword fell unheeded on the turf, and he flung himself down in an agony of boyish grief. But from her white palfrey, sitting still where she was, the maiden watched the paroxysms of his sorrow. She was dry eyed now, and her face was like a mask cut in snow.

Then as suddenly recalling himself, Sholto leaped from the ground, snatched up his sword, and again passionately advanced upon the Lady Sybilla.

"You it was who betrayed him," he cried, pointing the blade at her breast; "answer if it were not so!"

"It is true I betrayed him," she answered calmly.

"You whom he loved — God knows how unworthily —"

"God knows," she said simply and calmly.

"You betrayed him to his death. Why then should not I kill you?"

Again she smiled upon him that disarming, hopeless, dreadful smile.

"Because you cannot kill me. Because it were too crowning a mercy to kill me. Because, for three inches of that blade in my heart, I would bless you through the eternities. Because I must do the work that remains —"

"And that work is — ?"

"Vengeance ! !"

Sholto was silent, trying to piece things together. He found it hard to think. He was but a boy, and experience so strange as that of the Lady Sybilla was outside him. Yet vaguely he felt that her emotion was real, more real perhaps than his own instinct of crude slaying — the desire of the wasp whose nest has been harried to sting the first comer. This woman's hatred was something deadlier, surer, more persistent.

"Vengeance —" he said at last, scarce knowing what he said, "why should you, who betrayed him, speak of avenging him?"

"Because," said the Lady Sybilla, "I loved him as I never thought to love man born of woman. Because when the fiends of the pit tie me limb to limb, lip to lip, with Judas who sold his master with a kiss, when they burn me in the seventh hell, I shall remember and rejoice that to the last he loved me, believed in me, gloried in his love for me. And God who has been cruel to me in all else, will yet do this thing for me. He will not let William Douglas know that I deceived him or that he trusted me in vain."

"But the Vengeance that you spoke of — what of that?" said Sholto, dwelling upon that which was uppermost in his own thought.

"Aye," said the Lady Sybilla, "that alone can be compassed by me. For I am bound by a chain, the snapping of which is my death. To him who, in a far land, devised all these things, to the man who plotted the fall of the Douglas house — to Gilles de Retz, Marshal of France, I am bound. But — I shall not die — even you cannot kill me, till I have brought that head that is so high to the hempen cord, and delivered the foul fiend's body to the fires of both earth and hell."

"And the Chancellor Crichton — the tutor Livingston — what of them?" urged Sholto, like a Scot thinking of his native traitors.

The Lady Sybilla waved a contemptuous hand.

"These are but lesser rascals — they had been nothing

without their master and mine. You of the Douglas house must settle with them."

" And why have you returned to this country of Galloway ? " said Sholto. " And why are you thus alone ? "

" I am here," said the Lady Sybilla, " because none can harm me with my work undone. I travel alone because it suits my mood to be alone, because my master bade me join him at your town of Kirkcudbright, whence, this very night, he takes ship for his own country of Brittany."

" And why do you, if as you say you hate him so, continue to follow him ? "

" Ah, you are simple," she said ; " I follow him because it is my fate, and who can escape his doom ? Also, because, as I have said, my work is not yet done."

She relapsed into her former listless, forth-looking, unconscious regard, gazing through him as if the young man had no existence. He dropped the rein and the point of his sword with one movement. The white palfrey started forward with the reins loose on its neck. And as she went the eyes of the Lady Sybilla were fixed on the distant hills which hid the sea.

So, leaving Sholto standing by the lakeside with bowed head and abased sword, the strange woman went her way to work out her appointed task.

But ere the Lady Sybilla disappeared among the trees, she turned and spoke once more.

" I have but one counsel, Sir Knight. Think no more of your master. Let the dead bury their dead. Ride to Thrieve and never once lose sight of her whom you call your sweetheart, nor yet of her charge, Margaret Douglas, the Maid of Galloway, till the snow falls and winter comes upon the land."

CHAPTER XXXVIII

Sholto MacKim stood watching awhile as the white palfrey disappeared with its rider into the purple twilight of the woods which barred the way to the Solway. Then with a violent effort of will he recalled himself and looked about for his horse. The tired beast was gently cropping the lush dewy herbage on the green slope which led downwards to his native cottage. Sholto took the grey by the bridle and walked towards his mother's door, pondering on the last words of the Lady Sybilla. A voice at once strenuous and familiar broke upon his ear.

"Shoo wi' you, impident randies that ye are, shoo! Saw I ever the like aboot ony decent hoose? Thae hens will drive me oot o' my mind! Sholto, lad, what's wrang? Is't your faither? Dinna tell me it's your faither."

"It is more bitter than that, mither mine."

"No the Earl — surely no the Earl himsel' — the laddie that I hae nursed — the laddie that was to Barbara Halliburton as her ain dear son!"

"Mother, it is the Earl and young David too. They are dead, betrayed into the hands of their enemies, cruelly and treacherously slain!"

Then the keening cry smote the air as Barbara MacKim sank on her knees and lifted up her hands to heaven.

"Oh, the bonny laddies — the twa bonny, bonny laddies! Mair than my ain bairns I loved them. When
their ain mother wasna able for mortal weakness to rear
him, William Douglas drew his life frae me. What for,
Sholto, are ye standin' there to tell the tale? What
for couldna ye have died wi' him? Ae mither's milk
slockened ye baith. The same arms cradled ye. I bade
ye keep your lord safe wi' your body and your soul.
And there ye daur to stand, skin-hale and bane unbroken, before your mither. Get hence — ye are nae
son o' Barbara MacKim. Let me never look on your
face again, gin ye bringna back the pride o' the warld,
the gladness o' the auld withered heart o' her ye ca'
your mither!"

"Mother," said Sholto, "my lord was not dead when
I left him — he sent me to raise the country to his
rescue."

"And what for then are ye standin' there clavering,
and your lord in danger among his foes?" cried his
mother, angrily.

"Dear mother, I have something more to tell ye — "

"Aye, I ken, ye needna break the news. It is that
Malise, my man, is dead — that Laurence, wha ran frae
the Abbey to gang wi' him to the wars, is nae mair.
Aweel they are worthily spent, since they died for their
chief! Ye say that ye were sent to raise the clan —
then what seek ye at the Carlinwark? To Thrieve, man,
to Thrieve; as hard as ye can ride! To Castle Thrieve!"

"Mother," said Sholto, still more gently, "hearken
but a moment. Thirty thousand men are on their way to
Edinburgh. Three days and nights have I ridden without sleep. Douglasdale is awake. The Upper Ward

is already at the gates of the city. To a man, Galloway is on the march. The border is aflame. But it is all too late already, I have had news of the end. Before ever a man could reach within miles, the fatal axe had fallen, and my lords, for whom each one of us would gladly have died with smiles upon our faces, lay headless in the courtyard of Edinburgh Castle."

"And if the laddies were alive when ye rode awa', wha brocht the news faster than my Sholto could ride — tell me that?"

"I came not directly to Galloway, mother. First I raised the west from Strathaven to Ayr. Thence I carried the news to Dumfries and along the border side. But to-day I have seen the Lady Sybilla on her way to take ship for France. From her I heard the news that all I had done was too late."

"That foreigneerin' randy! Wad ye believe the like o' her? Yon woman that they named 'Queen o' Beauty' at the tournay by the Fords o' Lochar! — Certes, I wadna believe her on oath, no if she swore on the blessed banes o' Saint Andro himsel'. To the castle, man, or I'll kilt my coats and be there afore you to shame ye!"

"I go, mother," said Sholto, trying vainly to stem the torrent of denunciation which poured upon him; "I came only to see that all was well with you."

"And what for should a' be weel wi' me? What can be ill wi' me, if it be not to gang on leevin' when the noblest young men in the warld — the lad that was suckled at my bosom, lies cauld in the clay. Awa wi' ye, Sholto MacKim, and come na back till ye hae rowed every traitor in the same bloody windin' sheet!"

The foster mother of the Douglases sank on the ground

in the dusk, leaning against the wall of her house. She held her face in her hands and sobbed aloud, "O Willie, Willie Douglas, mair than ony o' my ain I loed ye. Bonny were ye as a bairn. Bonny were ye as a laddie. Bonny abune a' as a noble young man and the desire o' maidens' e'en. But nane o' them a' loed ye like poor auld Barbara, that wad hae gien her life to pleasure ye. And noo she canna even steek thae black, black e'en, nor wind the corpse-claith aboot yon comely limbs — sae straight and bonny as they were — I hae straiked and kissed sae oft and oft. O wae's me — wae's me! What will I do withoot my bonny laddies!"

It was with the sound of his mother's lament still in his ears that Sholto rode sadly over the hill to Thrieve. The way is short and easy, and it was not long before the captain of the guard looked down upon the lights of the castle gleaming through the gathering gloom. But instead of being, as was its wont, lighted from highest battlement to flanking tower, only one or two lamps could be discerned shining out of that vast cliff of masonry.

But, on the other hand, lights were to be seen wandering this way and that over the long Isle of Thrieve, following the outlines of its winding shores, shining from the sterns of boats upon the pools of the Dee water, weaving intricately among the broomy braes on either side of the ford, and even streaming out across the water meadows of Balmaghie.

Sholto was so full of his own sorrow and the certain truth of the terrible news he must bring home to the Lady of Douglas and those two whom he loved, Maud Lindesay and her fair maid, that he paid little heed to these wandering lanterns and distant flaring torches.

T

He was pausing at the bridge head to wait the lowering of the draw-chains, when out of the covert above him there dashed a desperate horseman, who stayed neither for bridge nor ford, but rode straight at the eastern castle pool where it was deepest. To the stirrup clung another figure strange and terrible, seen in the uncertain light from the gatehouse and in the pale beams of the rising moon.

The drawbridge clattered down, and sending his spurs home into the flanks of his tired steed, in a moment more Sholto was hard on the track of the first headlong horseman. Scarce a length separated them as they reached the outer guard of the castle. Abreast they reined their horses in the quadrangle, and in a moment Sholto had recognised in the rider his brother Laurence, pale as death, and the figure that had clung to the stirrup as the horse took the water, was his father, Malise MacKim.

Thus in one moment came the three MacKims to the door-step of Thrieve.

The clatter and cry of their arrival brought a pour of torches from every side of the isle and from within the castle keep.

"Have you found them — where are they?" came from every side. But Laurence seemed neither to hear nor see.

"Where is my lady?" he cried in a hoarse man's voice; and again, "Instantly I must see my lady."

Sholto stood aside, for he knew that these two brought later tidings than he. Presently he went over to his father, who was leaning panting upon a stone post, and asked him what were the news. But Malise thrust him back apparently without recognising him.

"My lady," he gasped, "I would see my lady!"

Then through the torches clustered about the steps
of the castle came the tall, erect figure of the Earl's
mother, the Countess of Douglas.   She stood with her
head erect, looking down upon the MacKims and upon
the dropped heads and heaving shoulders of their horses.
Above and around the torches flared, and their reek blew
thwartwise across the strange scene.

"I am here," she said, speaking clearly and naturally;
"what would ye with the Lady of Douglas?"

Thrice Laurence essayed to speak, but his ready tongue
availed him not now.   He caught at his horse's bridle to
steady him and turned weakly to his father.

"Do you speak to my lady — I cannot!" he gasped.

A terrible figure was Malise MacKim, the strong man
of Galloway, as he came forward.   Stained with the
black peat of the morasses, his armour cast off piecemeal
that he might run the easier, his under-apparel torn
almost from his great body, his hair matted with the
blood which still oozed from an unwashed wound above
his brow.

"My lady," he said hoarsely, his words whistling in
his throat, "I have strange things to tell.   Can you bear
to hear them?"

"If you have found my daughter dead or dying, speak
and fear not!"

"I have things more terrible than the death of many
daughters to tell you!"

"Speak and fear not — an it touch the lives of my
sons, speak freely.   The mother of the Douglases has
learned the Douglas lesson."

"Then," said Malise, sinking his head upon his breast,
"God help you, lady, your two sons are dead!"

"Is David dead also?" said the Lady of Douglas.

"He is dead," replied Malise.

The lady tottered a little as she stood on the topmost step of the ascent to Thrieve. One or two of the torch-bearers ran to support her. But she commanded herself and waved them aside.

"God — He is the God," she said, looking upwards into the black night. "In one day He has made me a woman solitary and without children. Sons and daughter He has taken from me. But He shall not break my heart. No, not even He. Stand up, Malise MacKim, and tell me how these things came to pass."

And there in the blown reek of torches and the hush of the courtyard of Thrieve Malise told all the tale of the Black Dinner and the fatal morning, of the short shrift and the matchless death, while around him strong men sobbed and lifted up right hands to swear the eternal vengeance.

But alone and erect as a banner staff stood the mother of the dead. Her eyes were dry, her lips compressed, her nostrils a little distended like those of a war-horse that sniffs the battle from afar. Outside the castle wall the news spread swiftly, and somewhere in the darkness a voice set up the Celtic keen.

"Bid that woman hold her peace. I will hear the news and then we will cry the slogan. Say on, Malise!"

Then the smith told how his horse had broken down time and again, how he had pressed on, running and resting, stripped almost naked that he might keep up with his son, because that no ordinary charger could long carry his great weight.

Then when he had finished the Lady of Thrieve turned

to Sholto — "And you, captain of the guard, what have you done, and wherefore left you your master in his hour of need?"

Then succinctly and to the point Sholto spoke, his father and Laurence assenting and confirming as he told of the Earl's commission and of how he had accomplished those things that were laid upon him.

"It is well," said the lady, calmly, "and now I also will tell you something that you do not know. My little daughter, whom ye call the Fair Maid of Galloway, with her companion, Mistress Maud Lindesay, went out more than twelve hours agone to the holt by the ford to gather hazelnuts, and no eye of man or woman hath seen them since."

And, even as she spoke, there passed a quick strange pang through the heart of Sholto. He remembered the warning of the Lady Sybilla. Had he once more come too late?

CHAPTER XXXIX

THE GIFT OF THE COUNTESS

It was the Countess of Douglas who commanded that night in the Castle of Thrieve. Sholto wished to start at once upon the search for the lost maidens. But the lady forbade him.

"There are a thousand searchers who during the night will do all that you could do — and better. To-morrow we shall surely want you. You have been three nights without sleep. Take your rest. I order you in your master's name."

And on the bare stone, outside Maud Lindesay's empty room, Sholto threw himself down and slept as sleep the dead.

But that night, save about the chamber where abode the mother of the Douglases, the hum of life never ceased in the great Castle of Thrieve. Whether my lady slept or not, God knows. At any rate the door was closed and there was silence within.

Sholto awoke smiling in the early dawn. He had been dreaming that he and Maud Lindesay were walking on the shore together. It was a lonely beach with great driftwood logs whereon they sat and rested ere they took hands again and walked forth on their way. In his dream Maud was kind, her teasing, disdainful mood quite gone. So Sholto awoke smiling, but in a moment he wished that he had slept on.

278

He lay a space, becoming conscious of a pain in his heart — the overnight pain of a great disaster not yet realised. For a little he knew not what it was. Then he saw himself lying at Maud's open door, and he remembered — first the death of his masters, then the loss of the little maid, and lastly that of Maud, his own winsome sweetheart Maud. In another moment he had leaped to his feet, buckled his sword-belt tighter, slung his cloak into a corner, and run downstairs.

The house guard which had ridden to Crichton and Edinburgh had been replaced from the younger yeomen of the Kelton and Balmaghie levies, even as the Earl had arranged before his departure. But of these only a score remained on duty. All who could be spared had gone to join the march on Edinburgh, for Galloway was set on having vengeance on the Chancellor and had sworn to lay the capital itself in ashes in revenge for the Black Dinner of the castle banqueting-hall.

The rest of the guard was out searching for the bonny maids of Thrieve, as through all the countryside Margaret Douglas and Maud Lindesay were named.

Eager as Sholto was to accompany the searchers, and though he knew well that no foe was south of the Forth to assault such a strong place as Thrieve, he did not leave the castle till he had set all in order so far as he could. He appointed Andro the Penman and his brother John officers of the garrison during his absence.

Then, having seen to his accoutrement and providing, for he did not mean to return till he had found the maids, he went lastly to the chamber door of the Lady of Douglas to ask her leave to depart.

At the first knock he heard a foot come slowly across

the floor. It was my lady, who opened the latch herself and stood before Sholto in the habit she had worn
when at the castle gateway Malise had told his news.
Her couch was unpressed. Her window stood open
towards the south. A candle still glimmered upon a
little altar in an angle of the wall. She had been
kneeling all night before the image of the Virgin, with
her lips upon the feet of her who also was a woman,
and who by treachery had lost a son.

"I would have your permission to depart, my Lady
Countess," said Sholto, bowing his head upon his breast
that he might not intrude upon her eyes of grief; "the
castle is safe, and I can be well spared. By God's
grace I shall not return till I bring either the maids
themselves or settled news of them. Have I your
leave to go?"

The Lady of Douglas looked at him a moment without speech.

"Surely you are not the same who rode away behind
my son William. You went out light and gay as David,
my other young son. There is now a look of Earl
William himself in your face — his mother tells you
so. Well, you were suckled at the same breast as he.
May a double portion of his spirit rest on you! That
lowering regard is the Douglas mark. Follow on and
turn not back till you find. Strike and cease not, till
all be avenged. I have now no son left to save or to
strike. Go, Sholto MacKim. He who is dead loved
you and made you knight. I said at the time that
you were too young and would have dissuaded him.
But when did a Douglas listen to woman's advice
—his mother's or his wife's? Foster brother you are

—brother you shall be. By this kiss I make you even as my son."

She bent and laid her lips on the young man's brow. They were hot as iron uncooled from the smithy anvil.

"Come with me," she added, and with a vehemence strangely at odds with her calm of the night before, she took Sholto by the hand and drew him after her into the room that had been Earl William's.

From the bundle of keys at her side she took a small one of French design. With this she unlocked a tall cabinet which stood in a corner. She threw the folding doors open, and there in the recess hung a wonderful suit of armour, of the sort called at that time "secret."

"This," said the Lady of Douglas, "I had designed for my son. Ten years was it in the making. His father trysted it from a cunning artificer in Italy. All these years has it been perfecting for him. It comes too late. His eyes shall never see it, nor his body wear it. But I give it to you. No Avondale shall ever do it upon him. It will fit you, for you and he were of a bigness. No sword can cut through these links, were it steel of Damascus forged for a Sultan. No spear-thrust can pierce it, though I leave you to avenge the bruise. Yet it will lie soft as silk, concealed and un-suspected under the rags of a beggar or the robes of a king. The cap will turn the edge of an axe, even when swung by a giant's hand, yet it will fit into the lining of a Spanish hat or velvet bonnet. This your present errand may prove more dangerous than you imagine. Go and put it on."

Sholto kneeled down and kissed the hand of his liege lady. Then when he had risen she gave him down the

armour piece by piece, dusting each with her kerchief
with a sort of reverent action, as one might touch the
face of the dead.   In Sholto's hands it proved indeed
light almost as woven cloth of homespun from Dame
Barbara's loom, and flexible as the spun silk of Lyons
which the great wear next their bodies.

With it there went an under-suit of finest and softest leather, that the skin should not be chafed by the
cunning links as they worked smoothly over one another
at each movement of the body within.

Sholto buckled on his lady's gift with a swelling
heart. It was his dead master's armour. And as piece
by piece fitted him as a glove fits the hand, the spirit
of William Douglas seemed to enter more and more into
the lad.

Then Sholto covered this most valuable gift with his
own clothing which he had brought from the house of
Carlinwark, and presently emerged, a well-looking but
still slim squire of decent family.

Then the Countess belted on him the sword of price
which went therewith, a blade of matchless Toledan
steel, but covered with a plain scabbard of black pigskin.

"Draw and thrust," commanded the lady, pointing at
the rough stone of the wall at the end of the passage.

Sholto looked ruefully at the glittering blade which
he held in his hand, flashing blue from point to double
guard.

"Thrust and fear not," said the Countess of Douglas the second time.

Sholto lunged out at the stone with all his might.
Fire flew from the smitten blue whinstone where the

point, with all the weight of his young body behind it, impinged on the wall. A tingling shock of acutest agony ran up the striker's wrist to the shoulder blade. The sword dropped ringing on the pavement, and Sholto's arm fell numb and useless to his side.

"Lift the sword and look," commanded the Lady Douglas.

Sholto did as he was bidden, with his left hand, and lo, the point which had bent like a hoop was sharp and straight as if just from the armourer's. "Can you strike with your left hand?" asked the lady.

"As with my right," answered the son of Malise the Brawny.

There was a bar at a window in the wall bending outward in shape like the letter U.

"Then strike a cutting stroke with your left hand."

Sholto took the sword. It seemed to him shortsighted policy that in the hour of his departure on a perilous quest he should disable himself in both arms. But Sholto MacKim was not the youth to question an order. He lifted the sword in his left hand, and with a strong ungraceful motion struck with all his might.

At first he thought that he had missed altogether. There was no tingling in his arm, no jar when the blade should have encountered the iron. But the Countess was examining the centre of the hoop.

"I have missed," said Sholto.

"Come hither and look," she said, without turning round.

And when he looked, lo, the thick iron had been cut through almost without bending. The sides of the break were fresh, bright, and true.

"Now look at the edge of your sword," she said.

There was no slightest dint anywhere upon it, so that Sholto, armourer's son as he was, turned about the blade to see if by any chance he could have smitten with the reverse.

Failing in this, he could only kneel to his lady and say, "This is a great gift — I am not worthy."

For in these times of peril jewels and lands were as nothing to the value of such a suit of armour, which kings and princes might well have made war to obtain.

The faintest disembodied ghost of a smile passed over the face of the Countess of Douglas.

"It is the best I can do with it now," she said, "and at least no one of the Avondales shall ever possess it."

After the Lady Douglas had armed the young knight and sped him upon his quest, Sholto departed over the bridge where the surly custodian still grumbled at his horse's feet trampling his clean wooden flooring. The young man rode a Spanish jennet of good stock, a plain beast to look upon, neither likely to attract attention nor yet to stir cupidity.

His father and Laurence were already on their way. Sholto had arranged that whether they found any trace of the lost ones or no, they were all to meet on the third day at the little town of Kirkcudbright. For Sholto, warned by the Lady Sybilla, even at this time had his idea, which, because of the very horror of it, he had as yet communicated to no one.

It chanced that as the youth rode southward along the banks of the Dee, glancing this way and that for traces of the missing maids, but seeing only the grass trampled by hundreds of feet and the boats in the stream dragging every pool with grapnels and ropes, two horsemen on rough ponies ambled along some distance in front of him. By their robes of decent brown they seemed merchants on a journey, portly of figure, and consequential of bearing.

As Sholto rapidly made up to them, with his better horse and lighter weight, he perceived that the travellers were those two admirable and noteworthy magistrates of Dumfries, Robert Semple and his own uncle Ninian Halliburton of the Vennel.

Hearing the clatter of the jennet's hoofs, they turned about suddenly with mighty serious countenances. For in such times when the wayfarer heard steps behind him, whether of man or beast, it repaid him to give immediate attention thereto.

So at the sound of hoofs Ninian and his friend set their hands to their thighs and looked over their shoulders more quickly than seemed possible to men of their build.

"Ha, nephew Sholto," cried Ninian, exceedingly relieved, "blithe am I to see you, lad. You will tell us the truth of this ill news that has upturned the auld province. By your gloomy face I see that the major part is overtrue. The Earl is dead, and he awes me for twenty-four peck of wheaten meal, forbye ten firlots of malt and other sundries, whilk siller, if these hungry Avondale Douglases come into possession, I am little likely ever to see. Surely I have more cause to mourn him — a fine lad and free with his having. If ye gat not settlement this day, why then ye gat it the neist, with never a word of drawback nor craving for batement."

Sholto told them briefly concerning the tragedy of Edinburgh. He had no will for any waste of words, and as briefly thereafter of the loss of the little maid and her companion.

The Bailie of Dumfries lifted up his hands in consternation.

"'Tis surely a plot o' thae Avondales. Stra'ven folk are never to lippen to. And they hae made a clean sweep. No a Gallowa' Douglas left, if they hae speerited awa' the bonny bit lass. Man, Robert, she was heir general to the province, baith the Lordship o' Gallowa' and the Earldom o' Wigton, for thae twa can gang to a lassie. But as soon as the twa laddies were oot o' the road, Fat Jamie o' Avondale cam' into the Yerldom o' Douglas and a' the Douglasdale estates, forbye the Borders and the land in the Hielands. Wae's me for Ninian Halliburton, merchant and indweller in Dumfries, he'll never see hilt or hair o' his guid siller gin that wee lassie be lost. Man, Sholto, is't no an awfu' peety?"

During this lamentation, to which his nephew paid little attention, looking only from side to side as they three rode among the willows by the waterside, the other merchant, Robert Semple, had been pondering deeply.

"How could she be lost in this country of Galloway?" he said, "a land where there are naught but Douglases and men bound body and soul to the Douglas, from Solway even to the Back Shore o' Leswalt? 'Tis just no possible — I'll wager that it is that Hieland gipsy Mistress Lindesay that has some love ploy on hand, and has gane aff and aiblins ta'en the lass wi' her for company."

At these words Sholto twisted about in his saddle, as if a wasp had stung him suddenly.

"Master Semple," he said, "I would have you speak more carefully. Mistress Lindesay is a baron's daughter and has no love ploys, as you are pleased to call them."

The two burgesses shook with jolly significant laughter, which angered Sholto exceedingly.

"Your mirth, sirs, I take leave to tell you, is most mightily ill timed," he said, "and I shall consider myself well rid of your company."

He was riding away when his uncle set his hand upon the bridle of Sholto's jennet.

"Bide ye, wild laddie," he said, "there is nae service in gaun aff like a fuff o' tow. My freend here meaned to speak nae ill o' the lass. But at least I ken o' ae love ploy that Mistress Lindesay is engaged in, or your birses wadna be so ready to stand on end, my bonny man. But guid luck to ye. Ye hae the mair chance o' finding the flown birdies, that ye maybes think mair o' the bonny norland quey than ye think o' the bit Gallowa' calf. But God speed ye, I say, for gin ye bringna back the wee lass that's heir to the braid lands o' Thrieve, it's an ill chance Ninian Halliburton has ever to fill his loof wi' the bonny gowden 'angels' that (next to high heeven) are a man's best freends in an evil and adulterous generation."

CHAPTER XL

FROM all sides the Douglases were marching upon Edinburgh. After the murder of the young lords the city gates had been closed by order of the Chancellor. The castle was put into a thorough state of defence. The camp of the Avondale Douglases, William and James, was already on the Boroughmuir, and the affrighted citizens looked in terror upon the thickening banners with the bloody Douglas heart upon them, and upon the array of stalwart and determined men of the south. Curses both loud and deep were hurled from the besiegers' lines at every head seen above the walls, together with promises to burn Edinburgh, castle and burgh alike, and to slocken the ashes with the blood of every living thing within, all for the cause of the Black Dinner and the Bull's Head set before the brothers of Douglas.

But at midnoon of a glorious day in the late September, a man rode out from the west port of the city, a fat man flaccid of body, pale and tallowy of complexion. A couple of serving-men went behind him, with the Douglas arms broidered on their coats. They looked no little terrified, and shook upon their horses, as indeed well they might. This little cavalcade rode directly out of the city gates towards the pavilion of the young

Douglases of Avondale. As they went two running
footmen kept them company, one on either side of their
leader, and as that unwieldy horseman swayed this way
and that in the saddle, first one and then the other applied with his open palm the force requisite to keep the
rider erect upon his horse.

It was the new Earl of Douglas, James the Gross, on
his way to visit the camp of his sons. As he approached
the sentries who stood on guard upon the broomy braes
betwixt Merchiston and Bruntsfield, he was challenged
in a fierce southland shout by one of the Carsphairn
levies who knew him not.

"Stand back there, fat loon, gin ye wantna a quarrel
shot intil that swagging tallow-bag ye ca' your wame!"

"Out of my way, hill varlet!" cried the man on horseback.

But the Carsphairn man stood with his crossbow
pointed straight at the leader of the cavalcade, crying
at the same time in a loud, far-carrying voice over his
shoulder, "Here awa', Anthon — here awa', Bob! Come
and help me to argue wi' this fat rogue."

Several other hillmen came hurrying up, and the little
company of riders was brought to a standstill. Then
ensued this colloquy.

"Who are you that dare stop my way?" demanded
the Earl.

"Wha may ye be that comes shuggy-shooin' oot o' the
bluidy city o' Edinburgh intil oor camp," retorted him
of Carsphairn, "sitting your beast for all the warld like
a lump o' potted-head whammelled oot o' a bowl?"

"I am the Earl of Douglas."

"The Yerl o' Dooglas! Then a bonny hand they hae

U

made o' him in Edinburgh. I heard they had only be-
headed him."

"I tell you I am Earl of Douglas. I bid you beware.
Conduct me to the tent of my sons!"

At this point an aged man of some authority stood
forward and gazed intently at James the Gross, looking
beneath his hand as at an extensive prospect of which
he wished to take in all the details.

"Lads," he said, "hold your hands — it rins i' my
head that this craitur' may be Jamie, the fat Yerl o'
Avondale. We'll let him gang by in peace. His sons
are decent lads."

There came from the hillmen a chorus of "Avondale
he may be — there's nae sayin' what they can breed up
there by Stra'ven. But we are weel assured that he is
nae richt Douglas. Na, nae Douglas like yon man was
ever cradled or buried in Gallowa'."

At this moment Lord William Douglas, seeing the
commotion on the outposts, came down the brae through
the broom. Upon seeing his father he took the plumed
bonnet from off his head, and, ordering the Carsphairn
men sharply to their places, he set his hand upon the
bridle of the gross Earl's horse. So with the two running footmen still preserving some sort of equilibrium in
his unsteady bulk, James of Avondale was brought to
the door of a tent from which floated the banner of the
Douglas house, blue with a bleeding heart upon it.

At the entering in of the pavilion, all stained and
trodden into the soil by the feet of passers-by, lay
the royal banner of the Stewarts, so placed by headstrong James Douglas the younger, in contempt of
both tutor and Chancellor, who, being but cowards

and murderers, had usurped the power of the king within the realm.

That sturdy youth came to the door of his pavilion half-dressed as he had lain down, yawning and stretching reluctantly, for he had been on duty all night perfecting the arrangements for besieging the town.

"James—James," cried his father, catching sight of his favourite son rubbing sleepily his mass of crisp hair, "what's this that I hear? That you and William are in rebellion and are defying the power o' the anointed king—?"

At this moment the footman undid the girths of his horse, which, being apparently well used to the operation, stood still with its feet planted wide apart. Then they ran quickly round to the side towards which the swaying bulk threatened to fall, the saddle slipped, and, like a top-heavy forest tree, James the Gross subsided into the arms of his attendants, who, straining and panting, presently set him on his feet upon the blazoned royal footcloth at the threshold of the pavilion.

Almost he had fallen backwards when he saw the use to which his daring sons had put the emblem of royal authority.

"Guid save us a', laddies," he cried, staggering across the flag into the tent, "ken ye what ye do? The royal banner o' the King o' Scots—to mak' a floor-clout o'! Sirce, sirce, in three weeks I shall be as childless as the Countess o' Douglas is this day."

"That," said William Douglas, coldly, indicating with his finger the trampled cloth, "is not the banner of Scotland, but only that of the Seneschal Stewarts. The King of Scots is but a puling brat, and they who usurp his name are murderous hounds whose necks I shall presently stretch with the rogue's halter!"

Young James Douglas had set an oaken folding chair for his father at the upper end of the pavilion, and into this James the Gross fell rather than seated himself.

His sons William and James continued to stand before him, as was the dutiful habit of the time. Their father recovered his breath before beginning to speak.

"What's this — what's this I hear?" he exclaimed testily, "is it true that ye are in flat rebellion against the lawful authority of the king? Laddies, laddies, ye maun come in wi' me to his excellence the Chancellor and make instanter your obedience. Ye are young and for my sake he will surely overlook this. I will speak with him."

"Father," said William Douglas, with a cold firmness in his voice, "we are here to punish the murderers of our cousins. We shall indeed enter the guilty city, but it will be with fire and sword."

"Aye," cried rollicking, headstrong James, "and we will roast the Crichton on a spit and hang that smug traitor, Tutor Livingston, over the walls of David's Tower, a bonny ferlie for his leman's wonder!"

There came a cunning look into the small pig's eyes of James the Gross.

"Na, na, foolish laddies, thae things will ye no do. Mind ye not the taunts and scorns that the Earl — the late Earl o' Douglas that is — put upon us a'? Think on his pride and vainglory, whilk Scripture says shall be brocht low. Think in especial how this righteous judgment that has fallen on him and on his brother has cleared our way to the Earldom."

The choleric younger brother **leaped** forward with an oath on his lips, but **his calmer senior** kept him back with his hand.

"Silence, James!" he said; "**I will answer our father.** Sir, we have heard what **you say**, but our minds are not changed. What cause to associate yourself with traitors and mansworn you **may have, we do not** know **and we do not care.**"

At his son's first words James the Gross rose **with a** sudden surprising access of dignity remarkable in one of his figure.

"I bid you remember," he said, speaking southland English, as he was wont to do in moments of excitement, "I bid you remember, sirrah, that I **am the Earl of Douglas** and Avondale, **Justicer of Scotland — and your father.**"

William Douglas bowed, respectful but unmoved.

"My lord," he said, "I forget nothing. I do not judge **you.** You are **in authority over our** house. You shall do what you will with these forces without there, **so be you** can convince them of **your** right. Black murder, whether **you** knew and approved it or no, has made you Earl of Douglas. But, sir, if you take part with my cousins' murderers now, or screen them from our just vengeance **and** the vengeance of God, I tell you that from this day you are a man without children. For in this matter I **speak not only** for myself, but for all your sons!" **He** turned to his brother.

"James," he said, "call in the others." James went to the tent door and called aloud.

"Archibald, Hugh, and John, come hither quickly."

A moment **after** three young men of noble build, little more than lads indeed, but with the dark Douglas allure

stamped plainly upon their countenances, entered, bowed
to their father, and stood silent with their hands crossed
upon the hilts of their swords.

William Douglas went on with the same determinate
and relentless calm.

"My lord," he said, very respectfully, "here stand
your five sons, all soldiers and Douglases, waiting to
hear your will. Murder has been done upon the chief
of our house by two men of cowardly heart and mean
consideration, Crichton and Livingston, instigated by the
false ambassador of the King of France. We have come
hither to punish these slayers of our kin, and we desire to
know what you, our father, think concerning the matter."

James the Gross was still standing, steadying himself
with his hand on the arm of the oaken chair in which he
had been sitting. He spoke with some difficulty, which
might proceed either from emotion or from the plethoric
habit of the man.

"Have I for this brought children into the world," he
said, "that they should lift up their hands against the
father that begat them? Ye know that I have ever
warned you against the pride and arrogance of your
cousins of Galloway."

"You mean, of the late Earl of Douglas and the boy
his brother," answered William; "the pride of eighteen
and fourteen is surely vastly dangerous."

"I mean those who have been tried and executed in
Edinburgh by royal authority for many well-grounded
offences against the state," cried the Earl, loudly.

"Will you deign to condescend upon some of them?"
said his son, as quietly as before.

"Your cousins' pride and ostentation of riches and

retinue, being far beyond those of the King, constituted
in themselves an eminent danger to the state.   Nay, the
turbulence of their followers has more than once come
before me in my judicial capacity as Justicer of the
realm.   What more would you have?"

"Were you, my lord, of those who condemned them
to death?"

"Not so, William; it had not been seemly in a near
kinsman and the heir to their dignities — that is, save
and except Galloway, which by ill chance goes in the
female line, if we find not means to break that unfortunate reservation.   Your cousins were condemned by my
Lords Crichton and Livingston."

"We never heard of either of them," said William,
calmly.

"In their judicial aspect they may be styled lords, as
is the Scottish custom," said James the Gross, "even as
when I was laird of Balvany and a sitter on the bed of
justice, it was my right to be so nominated."

"Then our cousins were condemned with your approval, my Lord of Douglas and Avondale?" persisted
his son.

James the Gross was visibly perturbed.

"Approval, William, is not the word to use — not a word
to use in the circumstances.   They were near kinsmen!"

"But upon being consulted you did not openly disapprove — is it not so?   And you will not aid us to avenge
our cousins' murder now?"

"Hearken, William, it was not possible — I could not
openly disapprove when I also was in the Chancellor's
hands, and I knew not but that he might include me in
the same condemnation.   Besides, lads, think of the mat-

ter calmly.   There is no doubt that the thing happens
most conveniently, and the event falls out well for us.
Our own barren acres have many burdens upon them.
What could I do ?   I have been a poor man all my life,
and after the removal of obstacles I saw my way to become the richest man in Scotland.   How could I openly
object ? "

William Douglas bowed.

"So —" he said, " that is what we desired to know!
Have I your permission to speak further ? "

His father nodded pleasantly, seating himself again as
one that has finished a troublesome business.   He rubbed
his hands together, and smiled upon his sons.

"Aye, speak gin ye like, William, but sit doon — sit
doon, lads.   We are all of one family, and it falls out
well for you as it does for me.   Let us all be pleasant
and agreeable together ! "

"I thank you, my lord," said his son, "but we will not
sit down.   We are no longer of one family.   We may be
your sons in the eye of the law and in natural fact.   But
from this day no one of us will break bread, speak word,
hold intimacy or converse with you.   So far as in us lies
we will renounce you as our father.   We will not, because of the commandment, rise in rebellion against you.
You are Earl of Douglas, and while you live must rule
your own.   But for me and my brothers we will never
be your children to honour, your sons to succour, nor
your liegemen to fight for you.   We go to offer our services to our cousin Margaret, the little Maid of Galloway.
We will keep her province with our swords as the last
stronghold of the true Douglases of the Black.   I have
spoken.   Fare you well, my lord ! "

During his son's speech the countenance of the newly made Earl of Douglas grew white and mottled, tallowy white and dull red in turns showing upon it, like the flesh of a drained ox. He rose unsteadily to his feet, moving one hand deprecatingly before him, like a helpless man unexpectedly stricken. His nether lip quivered, pendulous and piteous, in the midst of his grey beard, and for a moment he strove in vain with his utterance.

His eyes fell abashed from the cold sternness of his eldest son's glance, and he seemed to scan the countenances of the younger four for any token of milder mood.

"James," he said, "ye hear William. Surely ye do not hold with him? Remember I am your father, and I was aye particular fond o' you, Jamie. I mind when ye wad rin to sit astride my shoulder. And ye used to like that fine!"

There were tears in the eyes of the weak, cunning, treacherous-hearted man. The lips of James Douglas quivered a little, and his voice failed him, as he strove to answer his father. What he would have said none knows, but ere he could voice a word, the eyes of his brother, stern as the law given to Moses on the mount, were bent upon him. He straightened himself up, and, with a look carefully averted from the palsied man before him, he said, in a steady tone, "What my brother William says, I say."

His father looked at him again, as if still hoping against hope for some kinder word. Then he turned to his younger sons.

"Archie, Hugh, little Jockie, ye willna take part against your ain faither?"

"We hold with our brothers!" said the three, speaking at once.

At this moment there came running in at the door of the tent a lad of ten — Henry, the youngest of the Avondale brothers. He stopped short in the midst, glancing wonderingly from one to the other. His little sword with which he had been playing dropped from his hand. James the Gross looked at him.

"Harry," he said, "thy brothers are a' for leavin' me. Will ye gang wi' them, or bide wi' your faither?"

"Father," said the boy, "I will go with you, if ye will let me help to kill Livingston and the Chancellor!"

"Come, laddie," said the Earl, "ye understand not these matters. I will explain to you when we gang back to the braw things in Edinbra' toon!"

"No, no," cried the boy, stooping to pick up his sword, "I will bide with my brothers, and help to kill the murderers of my cousins. What William says, I say."

Then the five young men went out and called for their horses, their youngest brother following them. And as the flap of the tent fell, and he was left alone, James the Gross sank his head between his soft, moist palms, and sobbed aloud.

For he was a weak, shifty, unstable man, loving approval, and a burden to himself in soul and body when left to bear the consequences of his acts.

"Oh, my bairns," he cried over and over, "why was I born? I am not sufficient for these things!"

And even as he sobbed and mourned, the hoofs of his sons' horses rang down the wind as they rode through the camp towards Galloway. And little Henry rode betwixt William and James.

CHAPTER XLI

THE WITHERED GARLAND

MEANWHILE Sholto fared onwards down the side of the sullen water of Dee. The dwellers along the bank were all on the alert, and cried many questions to him about the death of the Earl, most thinking him a merchant travelling from Edinburgh to take ship at Kirkcudbright. Sholto answered shortly but civilly, for the inquirers were mostly decent folk well on in years, whose lads had gone to the levy, and who naturally desired to know wherefore their sons had been summoned.

In return he asked everywhere for news of any cavalcade which might have passed that way, but neither from the country folk, nor yet from hoof-marks upon the grassy banks, could he glean the least information pertinent to the purpose of his quest.

Not till he came within a few miles of the town did he meet with man or woman who could give him any material assistance. It was by the Fords of Tongland that he first met with one Tib MacLellan, who with much volubility and some sagacity retailed fresh fish to the burghers of Kirkcudbright and the whole countryside, giving a day to each district so long as the supply of her staple did not fail.

"Fair good day to ye, mistress!" said Sholto, taking off his bonnet to the sonsy upstanding fishwife.

"And to you, bonny lad," replied the complimented dame, dropping a courtesy, "may the corbie never cry at ye nor ill-faured pie juik at your left elbow. May candle creesh never fa' ou ye, red fire burn ye, nor water scald ye."

Tib was reeling off her catalogue of blessings when Sholto cut her short.

"Can you tell me, good lady," he asked, in his most insinuating tones, "if there has been any vessel cleared from the port during these last weeks?"

"'Deed, sir, that I should ken, for is no my ain sister marriet on Jock Wabster, wha's cousin by marriage twice removed is the bailie officer o' the port? So I can advise ye that there was a boat frae the Isle o' Man wi' herrin's for the great houses, though never a fin o' them like the halesome fish I carry here in my creel. Wad ye like to see them, to buy a dozen for the bonny lass that's waiting for ye? That were a present to recommend ye, indeed — far mair than your gaudy flowers, fule ballads, and sic like trash!"

"You cannot remember any other ship of larger size than the Manx fishing-boat?" continued Sholto.

"Weel, no to ca' cleared frae the port," Tib went on, "but there was a pair o' uncanny-looking foreign ships that lay oot there by the Manxman's Lake for eight days, and the nicht afore yestreen they gaed oot with the tide. They were saying aboot the foreshore that they gaed west to some other port to tak' on board the French monzie that cam' to the Thrieve at the great tournaying! But I kenna what wad tak' him awa' to the Fleet or the Ferry Toon o' Cree, and leave a' the pleasures o' Kirkcudbright ahint him. Forbye sic herrin's as are supplied

by me, Tib MacLellan, at less than cost price — as I
houp your honour will no forget, when in the course o'
natur' and the providence o' God you and her comes to
hae a family atween ye."

Sholto promised that he would not forget when the
time alluded to arrived. Then, turning his jennet off the
direct road to Kirkcudbright town, and betaking him
through the Ardendee fords, he made all speed towards
a little port upon the water of Fleet, at the point where
that fair moorland stream winds lazily through the
water-meadows for a mile or two, after its brawling
passage down from the hills of heather and before it
commits itself to the mother sea.

But it was not until he had long crossed it and reached
the lonely Cassencary shore that Sholto found his first
trace of the lost maidens. For as he rode along the
cliffs his keen eye noted a well-marked trail through the
heather approaching the shore at right angles to his
own line of march. The tracks, still perfectly evident
in the grassy places, showed that as many as twenty
horses had passed that way within the last two or three
days. He stood awhile examining the marks, and then,
leading his beast slowly by the bridle, he continued to
follow them westward till they became confused and lost
near a little jetty erected by the lairds of Cree and
Cassencary for convenience of traffic with Cumberland
and the Isle of Man. Here on the very edge of the foreshore, blown by some chance wind behind a stone and
wonderfully preserved there, Sholto found a child's
chain of woodbine entwined with daisies and autumnal
pheasant's eye. He took it up and examined it. Some
of the flowers were not yet withered. The inter-weav-

ing was done after a fashion he had taught the little
Maid of Galloway himself, one happy day when he had
walked on air with the glamour of Maud Lindesay's
smiles uplifting his heart. For that tricksome grace had
asked him to teach her also, and he remembered the lingering touch of her fingers ere she could compass the
quaint device of the pheasant's eye peeping out from the
midst of each white festoon.

Then a deep despair settled down on Sholto's spirit.
He knew that Maud Lindesay and the fair Maid of Galloway had undoubtedly fallen into the power of the
terrible Marshal de Retz, Sieur of Machecoul, ambassador of the King of France, and also many things else
which need not in this place be put on record.

CHAPTER XLII

In a dark wainscoted room overlooking that branch
of the Seine which divides the northern part of Paris
from the Isle of the City, Gilles de Retz, lately Chamberlain of the King of France, sat writing. The hotel
had recently been redecorated after the sojourn of the
English. Wooden pavements had again been placed
in the rooms where the barbarians had strewed their
rushes and trampled upon their rotting fishbones. Noble
furniture from the lathes of Poitiers, decorated with the
royal ermines of Brittany, stood about the many alcoves.
The table itself whereon the famous soldier wrote was
closed in with drawers and shelves which descended
to the floor and seemed to surround the occupant like
a cell.

Before De Retz stood a curious inkstand, made by some
cunning jeweller out of the upper half of a human skull
of small size, cut across at the eye-holes, inverted, and
set in silver with a rim of large rubies. This was filled
with ink of a startling vermilion colour.

The document which Gilles de Retz was busy transcribing upon sheets of noble vellum in this strange ink
was of an equally mysterious character. The upper part
had the appearance of a charter engrossed by the hand
of some deft legal scribe, but the words which followed

303

were as startling as the vehicle by means of which they were made to stand out from the vellum.

"𝕬nto 𝕭arran-𝕾athanas; 𝕷ord most glorious and puissant in hell beneath and in the earth above, 𝕴, his unworthy serbitor 𝕲illes de 𝕽etz, make my bows, hereby forever renouncing 𝕲od, 𝕮hrist, and the 𝕭lessed 𝕾aints."

To this appalling introduction succeeded many lines of close and delicate script, interspersed with curious cabalistic signs, in which that of the cross reversed could frequently be detected. Gilles de Retz wrote rapidly, rising only at intervals to throw a fresh log of wood across the vast iron dogs on either side of the wide fire-place, as the rain from the northwest beat more and more fiercely upon the small glazed panes of the window and howled among the innumerable gargoyles and twisted roof-stacks of the Hotel de Pornic.

Within the chamber itself, in the intervals of the storm, a low continuous growling made itself evident. At first it was disregarded by the writer, but presently, by its sheer pertinacity, the sound so irritated him that he rose from his seat, and, striding to a narrow door covered with a heavy curtain, he threw it wide open to the wall. Then through the black oblong so made, a huge and shaggy she-wolf slouched slowly into the room.

The marshal kicked the brute impatiently with his slippered foot as she entered, and, strange to relate, the wolf slunk past him with the cowed air of a dog conscious of having deserved punishment.

"Astarte, vilest beast," he cried, "have I not a thousand times warned you to be silent and wait outside when I am at work within my chamber?"

The she-wolf eyed her master as he went back towards

his table. Then, seeing him lift his pen, with a sigh of content she dropped down upon the warm hearthstone, lying with her haunches towards the blazing logs and her bristling head couched upon her paws. Her yellow shining eyes blinked sleepily and approvingly at him, while with her tongue she rasped the soft pads of her feet one by one, biting away the fur from between the toes with her long and gleaming teeth. Presently Astarte appeared to doze off. Her eyes were shut, her attitude relaxed. But so soon as ever her master moved even an inch to consult a marked list of dates which hung on a hook beside him, or leaned over to dip a quill in his scarlet ink, the flashing yellow eye and the gleam of white teeth underneath told that Astarte was awake and intently watching every movement of the worker.

Through the heavy boom of the storm without, the thresh of the rain upon the lattice casement, and the irregular whipping gusts which shook the house, the soft wheeze of the engrossing quill could be heard, the crackle of the burning logs and the heavy regular breathing of the couchant she-wolf being the only other sounds audible within the apartment.

Gilles de Retz wrote on, smiling to himself as he added line after line to his manuscript. His beard shone with a truculent blue-black lustre. For the moment the aged look had quite gone out of his face. His cheek appeared flushed with the hues of youth and reinvigorated hope, yet withal of a youth without innocence or charm. Rather it seemed as if fresh blood had been injected into the veins of some aged demon, moribund and cruel, giving, instead of health or grace, only a new lease of cruelty and lust.

x

Presently another door opened, the main entrance of the apartment this time, not the small private portal through which Astarte the wolf had been admitted. A girl came in, thrusting aside the curtain, and, for the space of a moment, holding it outstretched with an arm gowned in pure white before dropping it with a rustle of heavy silken fabric upon the ground.

The Marshal de Retz wrote on without appearing to be conscious of any new presence in his private chamber. The girl stood regarding him, with eyes that blazed with an intent so deadly and a hate so all-possessing that the yellow treachery in those of Astarte the she-wolf appeared kind and affectionate by contrast.

At the girl's entrance that shaggy beast had raised herself upon her fore paws, and presently she gave vent to a low growl, half of distrust and half of warning, which at once reached the ears of the busy worker.

Gilles de Retz looked up quickly, and, catching sight of the Lady Sybilla, with a sweep of his hand he thrust his manuscript into an open drawer of the escritoire.

"Ah, Sybilla," he said, leaning back in his chair with an air of easy familiarity, "you are more sparing of your visits to me than of yore. To what do I owe the pleasure and honour of this one?"

The girl eyed him long before answering. She stood statue-still by the curtain at the entrance of the apartment, ignoring the chair which the marshal had offered her with a bow and a courteous wave of his hand.

"I have come," she made answer at last, in the deep even tones which she had used before the council of the traitors at Stirling, "to demand from you, Messire Gilles de Retz, what you mean to do with the little Margaret

Douglas and her companion, whom you wickedly kidnapped from their own country and have brought with
you in your train to France?"

"I have satisfaction in informing you," replied the
marshal, suavely, "that it is my purpose to dispose of
both these agreeable young ladies entirely according to
my own pleasure."

The girl caught at her breast with her hand, as if to
stay a sudden spasm of pain.

"Not at Tiffauges—" she gasped, "not at Champtocé?"

The marshal leaned back, enjoying her terror, as one
tastes in slow sips a rare brand of wine. He found the
flavour of her fears delicious.

"No, Sybilla," he replied at last, "neither at Champtocé nor yet at Tiffauges — for the present, that is, unless
some of your Scottish friends come over to rescue them
out of my hands."

"How, then, do you intend to dispose of them?" she
urged.

"I shall send them to your puking sister and her
child, hiding their heads and sewing their samplers at
Machecoul. What more can you ask? Surely the young
and fair are safe in such worthy society, even if they
may chance to find it a little dull."

"How can I believe him, or know that for once he
will forego his purposes of hell?" Sybilla murmured,
half to herself.

The Marshal de Retz smiled, if indeed the contraction
of muscles which revealed a line of white teeth can be
called by that name. In the sense in which Astarte
would have smiled upon a defenceless sheepfold, so

Gilles de Retz might have been said to smile at his
visitor.

"You may believe me, sweet Lady Sybilla," said the
marshal, "because there is one vice which it is needless
for me to practise in your presence, that of uncandour.
I give you my word that unless your friends come wor-
rying me from the land of Scots, the maids shall not die.
Perhaps it were better to warn any visitors that even at
Machecoul we are accustomed to deal with such cases.
Is it not so, Astarte?"

At the sound of her name the huge wolf rose slowly,
and, walking to her master's knee, she nosed upon him
like a favourite hound.

"And if your intent be not that which causes fear to
haunt the precincts of your palaces like a night-devouring
beast, and makes your name an execration throughout
Brittany and the Vendée, why have you carried the little
child and the other pretty fool forth from their country?
Was it not enough that you should slay the brothers?
Wherefore was it necessary utterly to cut off the race of
the Douglases?"

"Sybilla, dear sister of my sainted Catherine," purred
the marshal, "it is your privilege that you should speak
freely. When it is pleasing to me I may even answer
you. It pleases me now, listen—you know of my devotion to science. You are not ignorant at what cost, at
what vast sacrifices, I have in secret pushed my re-
searches beyond the very confines of knowledge. The
powers of the underworlds are revealing themselves to
me, and to me alone. Evil and good alike shall be mine.
I alone will pluck the blossom of fire, and tear from hell
and hell's master their cherished mystery."

He paused as if mentally to recount his triumphs, and then continued.

"But at the moment of success I am crossed by a prejudice. The ignorant people clamour against my life—canaille! I regard them not. But nevertheless their foolish prejudices reach other ears. Hearken!"

And like a showman he beckoned Sybilla to the window. A low roar of human voices, fitful yet sustained, made itself distinctly audible above the shriller hooting of the tempest.

"Open the window!" he commanded, standing behind the curtain.

The girl unhasped the brazen hook and looked out. Beneath her a little crowd of poor people had collected about a woman who was beating with bleeding hands upon the shut door of the Hotel de Pornic.

"Justice! justice!" cried the woman, her hands clasped and her long black hair streaming down her shoulders, "give me my child, my little Pierre. Yester-eve he was enticed into the monster's den by his servant Poitou, and I shall never see him more! Give me my boy, murderer! Restore me my son!"

And the answering roar of the people's voices rose through the open window to the ears of the marshal. "Give the woman her son, Gilles de Retz!"

At that moment the woman caught sight of Sybilla. Instantly she changed her tone from entreaty to fierce denunciation.

"Behold the witch, friends, let us tear her to pieces. She is kept young and beautiful by drinking the blood of children. Throw thyself down, Jezebel, that the dogs may eat thee in the streets."

And a shout went up from the populace as Sybilla shut to the window, shuddering at the horrors which surrounded her.

The Marshal de Retz had not moved, watching her face without regarding the noise outside. Now he went back to his chair, and bending his slender white fingers together, he looked up at her.

Presently he struck a silver bell by his side three times, and the mellow sound pervaded the house.

Poitou appeared instantly at the inner door through which the she-wolf had entered.

"How does it go?" asked the marshal, with his usual careless easy grace.

"Not well," said Poitou, shaking his head; "that is, rightly up to a point, and then — all wrong!"

For the first time the countenance of the marshal appeared troubled.

"And I was sure of success this time. We must try them younger. It is all so near, yet, strangely it escapes us. Well, Poitou, I shall come in a little when I have finished with this lady. Tell De Sillé to expect me."

Poitou bowed respectfully and was withdrawing, too well trained to smile or even lift his eyes to where Sybilla stood by the window.

His master appeared to recollect himself.

"A moment, Poitou — there are some troublesome people of the city rabble at the door. Bid the guard turn out, and thrust them away. Tell them to strike not too gently with the flats of their swords and the butts of their spears."

Gilles de Retz listened for some time after the disappearance of his familiar. Presently the low droning note of popular execration changed into sharper exclamations of hatred, mingled with cries of pain.

Then the marshal smiled, and rubbed his hands lightly one over the other.

"That's my good lads," he said; "hear the rattle of the spear-hilts upon the paving-stones? They are bringing the butts into close acquaintance with certain very ill-shod feet. Ah, now they are gone!"

The marshal took a long breath and went on, half to himself and half to Sybilla.

"But I own it is all most inconvenient," he said, thoughtfully. "Here in Paris, in King Charles's country, it does not so greatly matter. For the affair in Scotland has set me right with the King and in especial with the Dauphin. By the death of the Douglases I have given back the duchy of Touraine to the kings of France after three generations. I have therefore well earned the right to be allowed to seek knowledge in mine own way."

"The service of the devil is a poor way to knowledge," said the girl.

"Ah, there it is," said the marshal, raising his hand with gentle deprecation, "even you, who are so highly privileged, are not wholly superior to vulgar prejudice. I keep a college of priests for the service of God and the Virgin. They have done me but little good. Surely therefore I may be allowed a little service of That Other, who has afforded me such exquisite pleasure and aided me so much. The Master of Evil knows all things, and he can help whom he will to the secrets of wealth, of power, and of eternal youth."

"Have you gained any of these by the aid of that

Master whom you serve?" asked the Lady Sybilla, with great quiet in her voice.

"Nay, not yet," cried the marshal, moved for the first time, "not yet — perhaps because I have sought too eagerly and hotly. But I am now at least within sight of the wondrous goal. See," he added, with genuine excitement labouring in his voice, "see — I am still a young man, yet though I, Gilles de Retz, was born to the princeliest fortune in France, and by marriage added another, they have both been spent well nigh to the last stiver in learning the hidden secrets of the universe. I am still a young man, I say, but look at my whitening hair, count the deep wrinkles on my forehead, consider my withered cheek. Have I not tasted all agonies, renounced all delights, and cast aside all scruples that I might win back my youth, and with it the knowledge of good and evil?"

Sybilla went to the door and stood again by the curtain.

"Then you swear by your own God that you will let no evil befall the Scottish maids?" she said.

"I have told you already — let that suffice!" he replied with sudden coldness; "you know that, like the Master whom I serve, I can keep my word. I will not harm them, so long as their Scottish kinsfolk come not hither meddling with my purposes. I have enough of meddlers in France without adding outlanders thereto! I cannot keep a new and permanent danger at grass within my gates."

The Lady Sybilla passed through the portal by which she had entered, without adieu or leave-taking of any kind. Gilles de Retz rose as soon as the curtain had

A BRIGHT LIGHT AS OF A FURNACE BURNT UP BEFORE HIM, AND THE
HEAT WAS OVERPOWERING AS IT RUSHED LIKE A RUDDY TIDE-RACE
AGAINST HIS FACE.

fallen, and shook himself with a yawn, like one who has
got through a troublesome necessary duty. Then he
walked to the window and looked out. The woman had
come back and was kneeling before the Hotel de Pornic.

At sight of him she cried with sudden shrillness, "My
lord, my great lord, give me back my child — my little
Pierre. He is my heart's heart. My lord, he never did
you any harm in all his innocent life!"

The Marshal de Retz shut the window with a shrug of
protest against the vulgarity of prejudice. He did not
notice four men in the garb of pilgrims who stood in the
dark of a doorway opposite.

"This is both unnecessary and excessively discompos-
ing," he muttered; "I fear Poitou has not been judicious
enough in his selections."

He turned towards the private door, and as he did so
Astarte the she-wolf rose and silently followed him with
her head drooped forward. He went along a dark passage and pushed open a little iron door. A bright light
as of a furnace burnt up before him, and the heat was
overpowering as it rushed like a ruddy tide-race against
his face.

"Well, Poitou, does it go better?" he said cheerfully,
"or must we try them of the other sex and somewhat
younger, as I at first proposed?"

He let the door slip back, and the action of a powerful
spring shut out Astarte. Whereat she sat down on her
haunches in the dark of the passage, and showed her
gleaming teeth in a grin, as, with cocked ears, she
listened to the sounds from within the secret laboratory
of the Marshal de Retz.

CHAPTER XLIII

MALISE FETCHES A CLOUT

THE four men whom the Messire Gilles, by good fortune, failed to see standing in the doorway opposite the Hotel de Pornic were attired in the habit of pilgrims to the shrine of Saint James of Compostella. Upon their heads they wore broad corded hats of brown. Long brown robes covered them from head to foot. Their heads were tonsured, and as they went along they fumbled at their beads and gave their benediction to the people that passed by, whether they returned them an alms or not. This they did by spreading abroad the fingers of both hands and inclining their heads, at the same time muttering to themselves in a tongue which, if not Latin, was at least equally unknown to the good folk of Paris.

"It is the house," said the tallest of the four, "stand well back within the shade!"

"Nay, Sholto, what need?" grumbled another, a very thickset palmer he; "if the maids be within, let us burst the gates, and go and take them out!"

"Be silent, Malise," put in the third pilgrim, whose dress of richer stuff than that of his companions, added to an air of natural command, betrayed the man of superior rank, "remember, great jolterhead, that we are not at the gates of Edinburgh with all the south country at our backs."

The fourth, a slender youth and fresh of countenance, stood somewhat behind the first three, without speaking, and wore an air of profound meditation and abstraction.

It is not difficult to indentify three out of the four. Sholto's quest for his sweetheart was a thing fixed and settled.   That his father and his brother Laurence should accompany him was also to be expected.   But the other and more richly attired was somewhat less easy to be certified.   The Lord James of Douglas it was, who spoke French with the idiomatic use and easy accentuation of a native, albeit of those central provinces which had longest owned the sway of the King of France.   The brothers MacKim also spoke the language of the country after a fashion.   For many Frenchmen had come over to Galloway in the trains of the first two Dukes of Touraine, so that the Gallic speech was a common accomplishment among the youths who sighed to adventure where so many poor Scots had won fortune, in the armies of the Kings of France.

Indeed, throughout the centuries Paris cannot be other than Paris.   And Paris was more than ever Paris in the reign of Charles the Seventh.   Her populace, gay, fickle, brave, had just cast off the yoke of the English, and were now venting their freedom from stern Saxon policing according to their own fashion. Not the King of France, but the Lord of Misrule held the sceptre in the capital.

It was not long therefore before a band of rufflers swung round a corner arm-in-arm, taking the whole breadth of the narrow causeway with them as they came. It chanced that their leader espied the four Scots stand-

ing in the wide doorway of the house opposite the Hotel
de Pornic.

"Hey, game lads," he cried, in that roistering shriek
which then passed for dashing hardihood among the
youth of Paris, "here be some holy men, pilgrims to the
shrine of Saint Denis, I warrant. I, too, am a clerk of
a sort, for Henriet tonsured me on Wednesday sennight.
Let us see if these men of good works carry any of the
deceitful vanities of earth about with them in their
purses. Sometimes such are not ill lined!"

The youths accepted the proposal of their leader with
alacrity.

"Let us have the blessing of the holy palmers," they
cried, "and eke the contents of their pockets!"

So with a gay shout, and in an evil hour for themselves, they bore down upon the four Scots.

"Good four evangelists," cried the youth who had
spoken first — a tall, ill-favoured, and sallow young man
in a cloak of blue lined with scarlet, swaggering it with
long strides before the others, "tell us which of you
four is Messire Matthew. For, being a tax-gatherer, he
will assuredly have money of his own, and besides, since
the sad death of your worthy friend Judas, he must
have succeeded him as your treasurer."

"This is the keeper of our humble store, noble sir,"
answered the Lord James Douglas, quietly, indicating
the giant Malise with his left hand, "but spare him and
us, I pray you courteously!"

"Ha, so," mocked the tall youth, turning to Malise,
"then the gentleman of the receipt of custom hath grown
strangely about the chest since he went a-wandering
from Galilee!"

And he reached forward his hand to pull away the cloak which hung round the great frame of the master armourer.

Malise MacKim understood nothing of his words or of his intent, but without looking at his tormentor or any of the company, he asked of James Douglas, in a voice like the first distant mutterings of a thunder-storm, "Shall I clout him?"

"Nay, be patient, Malise, I bid you. This is an ill town in which to get rid of a quarrel once begun. Be patient!" commanded James Douglas under his breath.

"We are clerks ourselves," the swarthy youth went on, "and we have come to the conclusion that such holy palmers as you be, men from Burgundy or the Midi, as I guess by your speech, Spaniards by your cloaks and this good tax-gatherer's beard, ought long ago to have taken the vows of poverty. If not, you shall take them now. For, most worthy evangelistic four, be it known unto you that I am Saint Peter and can loose or bind. So turn out your money-bags. Draw your blades, limber lads!"

Whereupon his companions with one accord drew their swords and advanced upon the Scots. These stood still without moving as if they had been taken wholly unarmed.

"Shall I clout them now?" rumbled Malise the second time, with an anxious desire in his voice.

"Bide a wee yet," whispered the Lord James; "we will try the soft answer once more, and if that fail, why then, old Samson, you may clout your fill."

"*His* fill!" corrected Malise, grimly

"Your pardon, good gentlemen," said James of Douglas aloud to the spokesman, "we are poor men and travel with nothing but the merest necessities — of which surely you would not rob us."

"Nay, holy St. Luke," mocked the swarthy one, "not rob. That is an evil word — rather we would relieve you of temptation for your own souls' good. You are come for your sins to Paris. You know that the love of money is the root of all evil. So in giving to us who are clerks of Paris you will not lose your ducats, but only contribute of your abundance to Holy Mother Church. I am a clerk, see — I do not deceive you! I will both shrive and absolve you in return for the filthy lucre!"

And, commanding one of his rabble to hold a torch close to his head, he uncovered and showed a tonsured crown.

"And if we refuse?" said Lord James, quietly.

"Then, good Doctor Luke," answered the youth, "we are ten to four — and it would be our sad duty to send you all to heaven and then ease your pockets, lest, being dead, some unsanctified passer-by might be tempted to steal your money."

"Surely I may clout him now?" came again like the nearer growl of a lion from Malise the smith.

Seeing the four men apparently intimidated and without means of defence, the ten youths advanced boldly, some with swords in their right hands and torches in their left, the rest with swords and daggers both. The Scots stood silent and firm. Not a weapon showed from beneath a cloak.

"Down on your knees!" cried the leader of the young

roisterers, and with his left hand he thrust a blazing
torch into the grey beard of Malise.

There was a quick snort of anger. Then, with a burst
of relief and pleasure, came the words, "By God, I'll
clout him now!" The sound of a mighty buffet succeeded, something cracked like a broken egg, and the
clever-tongued young clerk went down on the paving-
stones with a clatter, as his torch extinguished itself
in the gutter and his sword flew ringing across the
street.

"Come on, lads — they have struck the first blow.
We are safe from the law. Kill them every one!" cried
his companions, advancing to the attack with a confidence born of numbers and the consciousness of fighting
on their own ground.

But ere they reached the four men who had waited so
quietly, the Scots had gathered their cloaks about their
left arms in the fashion of shields, and a blade, long and
stout, gleamed in every right hand. Still no armour
was to be seen, and, though somewhat disconcerted, the
assailants were by no means dismayed.

"Come on — let us revenge De Sillé!" they cried.

"Lord, Lord, this is gaun to be a sair waste o' guid
steel," grumbled Malise; "would that I had in my fist
a stieve oaken staff out of Halmyre wood. Then I could
crack their puir bit windlestaes o' swords, without doing
them muckle hurt! Laddies, laddies, be warned and
gang decently hame to your mithers before a worse thing
befall. James, ye hae their ill-contrived lingo, tell them
to gang awa' peaceably to their naked beds!"

For, having vented his anger in the first buffet, Malise
was now somewhat remorseful. There was no honour in

such fighting. But all unwarned the youthful roisterers of Paris advanced. This was a nightly business with them, and indeed on such street robberies of strangers and shopkeepers the means of continuing their carousings depended.

It chanced that at the first brunt of the attack Sholto, who was at the other end of the line from his father, had to meet three opponents at once. He kept them at bay for a minute by the quickness of his defence, but being compelled to give back he was parrying a couple of their blades in front, when the third got in a thrust beneath his arm. It was as if the hostile sword had stricken a stone wall. The flimsy and treacherous blade went to flinders, and the would-be robber was left staring at the guard suddenly grown light in his hand.

With a quick backward step, Sholto slashed his last assailant across the upper arm, effectually disabling him. Then, catching his heel in a rut, he fell backward, and it would have gone ill with him but for the action of his father. The brawny one was profoundly disgusted at having to waste his strength and science upon such a rabble, and now, at the moment of his son's fall, he suddenly dropped his sword and seized a couple of torches which had fallen upon the pavement. With these primitive weapons he fell like a whirlwind upon the foe, taking them unexpectedly in flank. A sweep of his mighty arms right and left sent two of the assailants down, one with the whole side of his face scarified from brow to jaw, and the other with his mouth at once widened by the blow and hermetically closed by the blazing tar.

Next, Sholto's pair of assailants received each a mighty buffet and went down with cracked sconces. The rest, seeing this revolving and decimating fire-mill rushing upon them as Malise waved the torches round his head, turned tail and fled incontinently into the narrow alleys which radiated in all directions from the Hotel de Pornic.

Y

CHAPTER XLIV

LAURENCE TAKES NEW SERVICE

"Look to them well, Malise," said the Lord James; "'twas you who did the skull-cracking at any rate. See if your leechcraft can tell us if any of these young rogues are likely to die. I would not have their deaths on my conscience if I can avoid it."

First picking up and sheathing his sword, then bidding Sholto hold a torch, Malise turned the youths over on their backs. Four of them grunted and complained of the flare of the light in their eyes, like men imperfectly roused from sleep.

"Thae loons will be round in half an hour," said Malise, confidently. "But they will hae richt sair heads the morn, I'se warrant, and some o' them may be marked aboot the chafts for a Sabbath or twa!"

But the swarthy youth whom the others called De Sillé, he who had been spokesman and who had fallen first, was more seriously injured. He had worn a thin steel cap on his head, which had been cracked by the buffet he had received from the mighty fist of the master armourer. The broken pieces had made a wound in the skull, from which blood flowed freely. And in the uncertain light of the torch Malise could not make any prolonged examination.

"Let us tak' the callant up to the tap o' the hoose,"

322

he said at last; "we can put him in the far ben garret till we see if he is gaun to turn up his braw silver-taed shoon."

Without waiting for any permission or dissent, the smith of Carlinwark tucked his late opponent under his arm as easily as an ordinary man might carry a puppy. Then, sheathing their swords, the other three Scots made haste to leave the place, for the gleaming of lanthorns could already be seen down the street, which might either mark the advent of the city watch or the return of the enemy with reinforcements.

It was to a towering house with barred windows and great doors that the four Scots retreated.   Entering cautiously by a side portal, Malise led the way with his burden.   This mansion had been the town residence of the first Duke of Touraine, Archibald the Tineman. It had been occupied by the English for military purposes during their tenancy of the city, and now that they were gone, it had escaped by its very dilapidation the fate of the other possessions of the house of Douglas in France.

James Douglas had obtained the keys from Gervais Bonpoint, the trusty agent of the Avondales in Paris, who also attended to the foreign concerns of most others of the Scottish nobility.   So the four men had taken possession, none saying them nay, and, indeed, in the disordered state of the government, but few being aware of their presence.

Upon an old bedstead hastily covered with plaids, Malise proceeded to make his prisoner comfortable. Then, having washed the wound and carefully examined it by candlelight, he pronounced his verdict:

"The young cheat-the-wuddie will do yet, and live to swing by the lang cord about his craig!"

Which, when interpreted in the vulgar, conveyed at once an expectation of a life to be presently prolonged to the swarthy De Sillé, but after a time to be cut suddenly short by the hangman.

Every day James Douglas and Sholto haunted the precincts of the Hotel de Pornic and made certain that its terrible master had not departed. Malise wished to leave Paris and proceed at once to the De Retz country, there to attempt in succession the marshal's great castles of Machecoul, Tiffauges, and Champtocé, in some one of which he was sure that the stolen maids must be immured.

But James Douglas and Sholto earnestly dissuaded him from the adventure. How did they know (they reminded him) in which to look? They were all fortresses of large extent, well garrisoned, and it was as likely as not that they might spend their whole time fruitlessly upon one, without gaining either knowledge or advantage.

Besides, they argued it was not likely that any harm would befall the maids so long as their captor remained in Paris — that is, none which had not already overtaken them on their journey as prisoners on board the marshal's ships.

So the Hotel de Pornic and its inhabitants remained under the strict espionage of Sholto and Lord James, while up in the garret in the Rue des Ursulines Laurence nursed his brother clerk and Malise sat gloomily polishing and repolishing the weapons and secret armour of the party.

It was the evening of the third day before the "clout"

showed signs of healing. Its recipient had been conscious on the second day, but, finding himself a prisoner
in the hands of the enemy, he had been naturally enough
inclined to be a little sulky and suspicious. But the
bright carelessness of Laurence, who dashed at any
speech in idiomatic but ungrammatical outlander's
French, gradually won upon him. As also the fact
that Laurence was clerk-learned and could sing and play
upon the viol with surprising skill for one so young.

The prisoner never tired of watching the sunny curls
upon the brow of Laurence MacKim, as he wandered
about trying the benches, the chairs, and even the floor
in a hundred attitudes in search of a comfortable position.

"Ah," the sallow youth said at last, one afternoon as
he lay on his pallet, "you should be one of the choristers
of my master's chapel. You can sing like an angel!"

"Well," laughed Laurence in reply, "I would be indeed content, if he be a good master, and if in his house
it snoweth wherewithal to eat and drink. But tell me
what unfortunate may have the masterage of so profit-
less a servant as yourself?"

"I am the poor gentleman Gilles de Sillé of the household of the Marshal de Retz!" answered the swarthy
youth, readily.

"De Silly indeed to bide with such a master!" quoth
Laurence, with his usual prompt heedlessness of consequences.

The sallow youth with his bandaged head did not
understand the poor jest, but, taking offence at the tone,
he instantly reared himself on his elbow and darted a
look at Laurence from under brows so lowering and
searching that Laurence fell back in mock terror.

"Nay," he cried, shaking at the knees and letting his hands swing ludicrously by his sides, "do not affright a poor clerk! If you look at me like that I will call the cook from yonder eating-stall to protect me with his basting-ladle. I wot if he fetches you one on the other side of your cracked sconce, you will never take service again with the Marshal de Retz."

"What know you of my master?" reiterated Gilles de Sillé, glowering at his mercurial jailer, without heeding his persiflage.

"Why, nothing at all," said Laurence, truthfully, "except that while we stood listening to the singing of the choir within his hotel, a poor woman came crying for her son, whom (so she declared) the marshal had kidnapped. Whereat came forth the guard from within, and thrust her away. Then arrived you and your varlets and got your heads broken for your impudence. That is all I know or want to know of your master."

Gilles de Sillé lay back on his pallet with a sigh, still, however, continuing to watch the lad's countenance.

"You should indeed take service with the marshal. He is the most lavish and generous master alive. He thinks no more of giving a handful of gold pieces to a youth with whom he is taken than of throwing a crust to a beggar at his gate. He owns the finest province in all the west from side to side. He has castles well nigh a dozen, finer and stronger than any in France. He has a college of priests, and the service at his oratory is more nobly intoned than that in the private chapel of the Holy Father himself. When he goes in procession he has a thurifer carried before him by the Pope's special permission. And I tell you, you are just the lad to take his fancy. That I can see at a glance. I warrant you, Master Laurence, if you will come with me, the marshal will make your fortune."

" Did the other young fellow make his fortune?" said Laurence. Gilles de Sillé glared as if he could have slain him.

" What other?" he growled, truculently.

" Why, the son of the poor woman who cried beneath your kind master's window the night before yestreen'."

The lank swarthy youth ground his teeth.

" 'Tis ill speaking against dignities," he replied presently, with a certain sullen pride. "I daresay the young fellow took service with the marshal to escape from home, and is in hiding at Tiffauges, or mayhap Machecoul itself. Or he may well have been listening at some lattice of the Hotel de Pornic itself to the idiot clamour of his mother and of the ignorant rabble of Paris!"

" Your master loves the society of the young?" queried Laurence, mending carefully a string of his viol and keeping the end of the catgut in his mouth as he spoke.

" He doats on all young people," answered Gilles de Sillé, eagerly, the flicker of a smile running about his mouth like wildfire over a swamp. "Why, when a youth of parts once takes service with my master, he never leaves it for any other, not even the King's!"

Which in its way was a true enough statement.

" Well," quoth Master Laurence, when he had tied his string and finished cocking his viol and twingle-twangling it to his satisfaction, "you speak well. And I am not sure but what I may think of it. I am tired both of working for my father without pay, and of singing

psalms in a monastery to please my lord Abbot.   Moreover, in this city of Paris I have to tell every jack with
a halbert that I am not the son of the King of England,
and then after all as like as not he marches me to the
bilboes ! ”

"Of what nativity are you ? ” asked De Sillé.

"Och, I’m all of a rank Irelander, and my name is
Laurence O’Halloran, at your service,” quoth the rogue,
without a blush.   For among other accomplishments
which he had learned at the Abbey of Dulce Cor, was
that of lying with the serene countenance of an angel.
Indeed, as we have seen, he had the rudiments of the
art in him before setting out from the tourneying field at
Glenlochar on his way to holy orders.

"Then you will come with me to-morrow ? ” said
Gilles, smiling.

Laurence listened to make sure that neither his father
nor Sholto was approaching the garret.

"I will go with you on two conditions,” he said: "you
shall not mention my purpose to the others, and when
we escape, I must put a bandage over your eyes till we
are half a dozen streets away.”

"Why, done with you — after all you are a right
gamesome cock, my Irelander,” cried Gilles, whom the
conditions pleased even better than Laurence’s promise
to accompany him.

Then, lending the prisoner his viol wherewith to amuse
himself and locking the door, Laurence made an excuse
to go to the kitchen, where he laughed low to himself,
chuckling in his joy as he deftly handled the saucepans.

" Aha, Master Sholto, you are the captain of the guard
and a knight, forsooth, and I am but poor clerk Laurence

—as you have ofttimes reminded me. But I will show
you a shift worth two of watching outside the door of
the marshal's hotel for tidings of the maids. I will go
where the marshal goes, and see all he sees. And then,
when the time comes, why, I will rescue them single-
handed and thereafter make up my mind which of them
I shall marry, whether Sholto's sweetheart or the Fair
Maid of Galloway herself."

Thus headlong Laurence communed with himself, not
knowing what he said nor to what terrible adventure he
was committing himself.

But Gilles de Sillé of the house of the Marshal de
Retz, being left to himself in the half darkness of the
garret, took up the viol and sang a curious air like that
with which the charmer wiles his snakes to him, and at
the end of every verse, he also laughed low to himself.

CHAPTER XLV

But, as fate would have it, it was not in the Hotel de Pornic nor yet in the city of Paris that Laurence O'Halloran was destined to enter the service of the most mighty Marshal de Retz.

Not till three days after his converse with the prisoner did Laurence find an opportunity of escaping from the house in the street of the Ursulines. Sholto and his father meantime kept their watch upon the mansion of the enemy, turn and turn about; but without discovering anything pertinent to their purpose, or giving Laurence a chance to get clear off with Gilles de Sillé. The Lord James had also frequently adventured forth, as he declared, in order to spy out the land, though it is somewhat sad to relate that this espionage conducted itself in regions which gave more opportunities for investigating the peculiar delights of Paris than of discovering the whereabouts of Maud Lindesay and his cousin, the Fair Maid of Galloway.

The head of Gilles de Sillé was still swathed in bandages when, with an additional swaddling of disguise across his eyes, he and Laurence, that truant scion of the house of O'Halloran, stole out into the night. A frosty chill had descended with the darkness, and a pale, dank mist from the marshes of the Seine made the pair shiver as arm in arm they ventured carefully forth.

Laurence was doing a foolish, even a wicked, thing in thus, without warning, deserting his companions. But he was just at the age when it is the habit of youth to deceive themselves with the thought that a shred of good intent covers a world of heedless folly.

The fugitives found the Hotel de Pornic practically deserted. They approached it cautiously from the back, lest they should run into the arms of any of the numerous enemies of its terrible lord, who, though not abhorred in Paris as in most other places which he favoured with his visits, had yet little love spent upon him even there.

The custodian in the stone cell by the gate came yawning out to the bars at the sound of Gilles de Sillé's knocking, and after a growl of disfavour admitted the youth and his companion.

" What, gone — my master gone ! " cried Gilles, striking his hand on his thigh with an astounded air, " impossible ! "

" It was, indeed, a thing particularly unthoughtful and discourteous of my Lord de Retz, Marshal of France and Chamberlain of the King, to undertake a journey without consulting you," replied the man, who considered irony his strong point, but feebly concealing his pleasure at the favourite's discomfiture; " we all know upon what terms your honourable self is with my lord. But you must not blame him, for he waited whole twenty-four hours for news of you. It was reported that you were set upon by four giants, and that your bones, crushed like a filbert, had been discovered in the horse pond at the back of the Convent of the Virgins of Complaisance."

Gilles de Sillé looked as if he could very well have murdered the speaker on the spot. His favour with his lord was evidently not a thing of repute in his master's household. So much was clear to Laurence, who, for the first time, began to have fears as to his own reception, having such an unpopular person as voucher and introducer.

"If you do not keep a civil tongue in your head, sirrah Labord," — the youth hissed the words through his clenched teeth, — "I will have your throat cut."

"Ah, I am too old," said the man, boldly; "besides, this is Paris, and I have been twenty years concierge to his Grace the Duke of Orleans. I and my wife have his secrets even as you, most noble Sire de Sillé, possess those of my new master. You, or he either, by God's grace, will think twice before cutting my throat. Moreover, you will be good enough at this point to state your business or get to bed. For I am off to mine. I serve my master, but I am not compelled to spend the night parleying with his lacqueys."

Now the concierges of Paris are very free and independent personages, and their tongues are accustomed to wag freely and to some purpose in their heads.

"Whither has my master gone?" asked De Sillé, curbing his wrath in order to get an answer.

"He *said* that he went to Tiffauges. Whether that be true, you have better means of knowing than I."

The swarthy youth turned to Laurence.

"How much money have you, Master O'Halloran? I have spent all of mine, and this city swine will not lend me a single sou for my expenses. We must to the stables and follow the Sieur de Retz forthwith to Brittany."

"I have ten golden angels which the prior of the

convent gave me at my departure," said Laurence, with some pride.

His companion nodded approvingly.

"So much will see us through — that is, with care. Give them here to me," he added after a moment's thought; "I will pay them out with more economy, being of the country through which we pass."

But Laurence, though sufficiently headlong and reckless, had not been born a Scot for naught.

"Wait till there is necessity," he replied cautiously, "and the angels shall not be lacking. Till then they are quite safe with me. For security I carry them in a secret place ill to be gotten at hastily."

Gilles de Sillé turned away with some movement of impatience, yet without saying another word upon the subject.

"To the stables," he said; then turning to the concierge he added, "I suppose we can have horses to ride after my lord?"

"So far as I am concerned," growled Labord, "you can have all the horses you want — and break your necks off each one of them if you will. It will save some good hemp and hangman's hire. Such devil's dogs as you two be bear your dooms ready written on your faces."

And this saying nettled our Laurence, who prided himself no little on an allure blonde and gallant.

But Gilles de Sillé cared no whit for the servitor's sneers, so long as they got horses between their knees and escaped out of Paris that night. In an hour they were ready to start, and Laurence had expended one of his gold angels on the provend for the journey, which his companion and he stored in their saddle-bags.

And in this manner, like an idle lad who for mischief puts body and soul in peril, went forth Laurence MacKim to take up service with the redoubtable Messire Gilles de Laval, Sieur de Retz, High Chamberlain of Charles the Seventh, Marshal of France, and lately companion-in-arms of the martyred Maid of Orleans.

Now, before he went forth from the street of the Ursulines, he had laid a sealed letter on the bed of his brother, which ran thus: "Ha, Sir Sholto MacKim, while you stand about in the rain and shiver under your cloak, I am off to find out the mystery. When I have done all without assistance from the wise Sir Sholto, I will return. But not before. Fare your knightship well."

Laurence and Gilles de Sillé rode out of Paris by the Versailles road, and the latter insisted on silence till they had passed the forest of St. Cyr, which was at that time exceedingly dangerous for horsemen not travelling in large companies. Once they were fairly on the road to Chartres, however, and clear of the valley of the Seine and its tangled boscage of trees, Gilles relaxed sufficiently to break a bottle of wine to the success of their journey and to the new service and duty upon which Laurence was to enter at the end of it.

Having proposed this toast, he handed the bumper first to Laurence, who, barely tasting the excellent Poitevin vintage, handed the leathern bottle back to De Sillé. That sallow youth immediately, without giving his companion a second chance, proceeded to quaff the entire contents of the pigskin.

Then as the stiff brew penetrated downwards, it was

not long before the favourite of the marshal began to
wax full of vanity and swelling words.

"I tell you what it is," he said, "there would be
trembling in the heart of a very great man when the
nine cravens returned without me. For I am no shave-
ling ignoramus, but a gentleman of birth; aye, and one
who, though poor, is a near cousin of the marshal himself. I warrant the rascals who ran away would smart
right soundly for leaving me behind. For Gilles de Sillé
is no simpleton. He knows more than is written down
in the catechism of Holy Church. None can touch my
favour with my lord, no matter what they testify against
me. For me I have only to ask and have. That is why
I take such pride in bringing you to my Lord of Retz. I
know that he will give you a post about his person, and
if you are not a simple fool you may go very far. For
my master is a friend of the King and, what is better, of
Louis the Dauphin. He gat the King back a whole
province — a dukedom so they say, from the hands of
some Scots fool that had it off his grandfather for deeds
done in the ancient wars. And in return the King will
protect my master against all his enemies. Do I not
speak the truth?"

Laurence hoped that he did, but liked not the veiled
hints and insinuations of some surprising secret in the
life of the marshal, possessed by his dear cousin and
well-beloved servant Gilles de Sillé.

With an ever loosening tongue the favourite went on:

"A great soldier is our master — none greater, not
even Dunois himself. Why, he rode into Orleans at the
right hand of the Maid. None in all the army was so
great with her as he. I tell you, Charles himself liked

it not, and that was the beginning of all the bother of talk about my lord — ignorant gabble of the countryside I call it. Lord, if they only knew what I know, then, indeed — but enough.   Marshal **Gilles is** a mighty scholar **as well, and** hath Henriet the clerk — a weak, bleating ass that will **some day blab if my** master permit **me not to** slice his **gizzard** in time — he hath him **up to** read aloud Latin by the mile, all out of the books called Suetonius and Tacitus — such high-flavoured tales and full of — well, of things such as my master loves."

So ran Gilles de Sillé on as **the** miles fled back behind their horses' heels and the towers of Chartres rose grey and solemn through the morning mists before the travellers.

CHAPTER XLVI

THE COUNTRY OF THE DREAD

The three remaining Scottish palmers were riding due west into a sunset which hung like a broad red girdle over the Atlantic. All the sky above their heads was blue grey and lucent. But along the horizon, as it seemed for the space of two handbreadths, there was suspended this bandolier of flaming scarlet.

The adventurers were not weary of their quest. They were only sick at heart with the fruitlessness of it.

First upon leaving Paris they had gone on to the Castle of Champtocé, and from beneath had surveyed the noble range of battlements crowning the heights above the broad, poplar-guarded levels of the Loire. The Chateau de Thouars also they had seen, a small white-gabled house, most like a Scottish baron's tower, which the Marshal de Retz possessed in virtue of his neglected wife Katherine. In it her sister the Lady Sybilla had been born. Solitary and tenantless, save for a couple of guards and their uncovenanted womenkind, it looked down on its green island meadows, while on the horizon hung the smoke of the wood fires lit at morn and eve by the good wives of Nantes.

To that place the three had next journeyed and had there beheld the great Hotel de Suze, set like an enemy's fortress in the midst of the turbulent city, over against

the Castle of the King.   But the Hotel, though held like
a place of arms, was untenanted by the marshal, his
retinue, or the lost Scottish maids.

Next they found the strong Castle of Tiffauges, above
the green and rippling waters of the Sevres, void also
as the others.   No light gleamed out of that window of
sinister repute, high up in the cliff-like wall, from which
strange shapes were reported to look forth even at deep
midnoon.

North, south, and east the three had ridden through
the country of Retz.   There remained but Machecoul,
more remote and also darker in repute than any of the
other dwelling-places of Gilles de Retz.   As they rode
westward towards it, they became day by day more conscious of the darkening down of the atmosphere of fear
and suspicion, which, murky and lowering, overhung all
that fair land of southern Brittany.

The vast pine forests from which rose the lonely
towers of this the marshal's most remote castle could
now be seen, serrated darkly against the broad belt of
the sky.   The sombre blackness of their spreading
branches, the yet blacker darkness where the gaps between their red trunks showed a way into the wood, in-
creased the gloom of the weary travellers.   Yet they
rode on, Sholto eagerly, Malise grimly, and the Lord
James with the dogged resignation of a good knight who
may be depended on to see an adventure through, however irksome it may be proving.

James of Avondale thought within himself that the
others had greater interests in the quest than he — the
younger MacKim having at stake the honour of his
sweetheart Maud, the elder the life of his young

mistress, the last of the Galloway house of Douglas.

Yet it was with that jolly heart of his beating strong and loyal under his brown palmer's coat, that James Douglas rode towards Machecoul, only whistling low to himself and wishing that something would happen to break the monotony of their journey.

Nor had he long to wait. For just as the sun was setting they rode all three of them abreast into the little hamlet of Saint Philbert, and saw the sullen waters of the Étang de Grande Lieu spread marshy and brackish as far as the eye could reach, edged by peat bogs and overhung perilously by gloomy pines nodding over pools blacker than scrivener's ink.

As the three Scots looked into the stockaded entrance of the village, they could see the children playing on the long, irregular street, and the elder folk sitting about their doors in the evening light.

But as soon as the clatter of horses' hoofs was heard, borne from far down the aisles of the forest, there arose a sudden clamour and a crying. From each little sparred enclosure rushed forth a woman who snatched a baby here and there and drove a herd of children before her indoors, glancing around and behind her as she did so with the anxious look of a motherly barn-door fowl when the hawk hangs poised in the windless sky.

By the time the three men had entered the gate and ridden up the village street, all was silent and dark. The windows were shut, the doors were barred, and the village had become a street of living tombs.

"What means this?" said the Lord James; "the people are surely afraid of us."

"'Tis doubtless but their wonted welcome to their lord, the Sieur de Retz. He seems to be popular wherever he goes," said Malise, grimly; "but let us dismount and see if we can get stabling for our beasts. Did they not tell us there was not another house for miles betwixt here and Machecoul?"

So without waiting for dissent or counter opinion, the master armourer went directly up to the door of the most respectable-appearing house in the village, one which stood a little back from the road and was surrounded by a wall. Here he dismounted and knocked loudly with his sword-hilt upon the outer gate. The noise reverberated up and down the street, and was tossed back in undiminished volume from the green wall of pines which hemmed in the village.

But there was no answer, and Malise grew rapidly weary of his own clamour.

"Hold my bridle," he said curtly to Sholto, and with a single push of his shoulders he broke the wooden bar, and the two halves of the outer gate fell apart before him. A great, smooth-haired yellow dog of the country rushed furiously at the intruders, but Malise, who was as dexterous as he was powerful, received him with so sound a buffet on the head that he paused bewildered, shaking his ears, whereat Malise picked him up, tucked him under his arm, and with thumbs about his windpipe effectually choked his barking. Then releasing him, Malise took no further notice of this valorous enemy, and the poor, loyal, baffled beast, conscious of defeat, crept shamefacedly away to hide his disgrace among the faggots.

But Malise was growing indignant and therefore dangerous and ill to cross.

"Never did I see such mannerless folk," he growled; "they will not even give a stranger a word or a bite for his beast."

Then he called to his companions, "Come hither and speak to these cravens ere I burst their inner doors as well."

At this by no means empty threat came the Lord James and spoke aloud in his cheery voice to those within the silent house: "Good people, we are no robbers, but poor travellers and strangers. Be not afraid. All we want is that you should tell us which house is the inn that we may receive refreshment for ourselves and our horses."

Then there came a voice from behind the door: "There is no inn nearer than Pornic. We are poor people and cannot support one. We pray your highness to depart in peace."

"But, good sir," answered James Douglas, "that we cannot do. Our steeds are foot weary with a long day's journey. Give us the shelter of your barns and a bundle of fodder and we will be content. We have food and drink with us. Open, and be not afraid."

"Of what country are you? Are you of the household of the Sieur de Retz?"

"Nay," cried James again, "we are pilgrims returning to our own city of Albi in the Tarn country. We know nothing of any Sieur de Retz. Look forth from a window and satisfy yourself."

"Then if there be treachery in your hearts, beware," said the tremulous voice again; "for I have four young men here by me whose powder guns are even now ready to fire from all the windows if you mean harm."

A white face looked out for a moment from the casement, and as quickly ducked within. Then the voice continued its bleating.

"My lords, I will open the door. But forgive the fears of a poor old man in a wide, empty house."

The door opened and a curious figure appeared within. It was a man apparently decrepit and trembling, who in one hand carried a lantern and in the other a staff over which he bent with many wheezings of exhausted breath.

"What would you with a poor old man?" he said.

"We would have shelter and fodder, if it please you to give them to us for the sake of God's grace."

The old man trembled so vehemently that he was in danger of shaking out the rushlight which flickered dismally in his wooden lantern.

"I am a poor, poor man," he quavered; "I have naught in the world save some barley meal and a little water."

"That will do famously," said James Douglas; "we are hungry men, and will pay well for all you give us."

The countenance of the cripple instantly changed. He looked up at the speaker with an alert expression.

"Pay," he said, "pay — did you not say you would pay? Why, I thought you were gentlefolks! Now, by that I know that you are none, but of the commonalty like myself."

James Douglas took a gold angel out of his belt and threw it to him. The cripple collapsed upon the top of the piece of money and groped vainly for it with eager, outspread fingers in the dust of the yard.

"I cannot find it, good gentleman," he piped, shrill as an east wind; "alas, what shall I do? Poor Cæsar cannot find it. It was not a piece of gold — do tell me that it was not a piece of gold; to lose a piece of gold, that were ruin indeed."

Sholto picked up the lantern which had slipped from his trembling hand. The tallow was beginning to gutter out as it lay on its side, and a moment's search showed him the gold glittering on some farmyard rubbish. With a little shrill cry like a frightened bird the old man fell upon it, as it had been with claws.

"Bite upon it and see if the gold be good," said Sholto, smiling.

"Alas," cried the cripple, "I have but one tooth. But I know the coin. It is of the right mintage and greasiness. O lovely gold! Beautiful gentlemen, bide where you are and I will be back with you in a moment."

And the old man limped away with astonishing quickness to hide his acquisition, lest, mayhap, his guests should repent them and retract their liberality.

CHAPTER XLVII

CÆSAR MARTIN'S WIFE

PRESENTLY he returned and conducted them to a decent stable, where they saw their beasts bestowed and well provided with bedding and forage for the night. Then the old cripple, more than ever bent upon his stick, but nevertheless chuckling to himself all the way, preceded them into the house.

"Ah, she is clever," he muttered; "she thinks her demon tells her everything. But even La Meffraye will not know where I have hidden that beautiful gold."

So he sniggered senilely to himself between his fits of coughing.

It was a low, wide room of strange aspect into which the old man conducted his guests. The floor was of hard-beaten earth, but cleanly kept and firm to the feet. The fireplace, with a hearth round it of built stone, was placed in the midst, and from the rafters depended many chains and hooks. A wooden settle ran half round the hearthstone on the side farthest from the draught of the door. The weary three sat down and stretched their limbs. The fire had burnt low, and Sholto, reaching to a faggot heap by the side wall, began to toss on boughs of green birch in handfuls, till the lovely white flame arose and the sap spat and hissed in explosive puffs.

> *" Birk when 'tis green*
> *Makes a fire for a king !"*

Malise hummed the old Scots lines, and the cripple coming in at that moment raised a shrill bark of protest.

"My good wood, my fuel that cost me so many sore backs—be careful, young sir. Faggots of birch are dear in this country of Machecoul. My lord is of those who give nothing for naught."

"Oh, we shall surely pay for what we use," cried careless James; "let us eat, and warm our toes, and therewith have somewhat less of thy prating, old dotard. It can be shrewdly cold in this westerly country of yours."

"Pay," cried the old man, holding up his clawed hands; "do you mean *more* pay—more besides the beautiful gold angel? Here—"

He ran out and presently returned with armful after armful of faggots, while his guests laughed to find his mood so changed.

"Here," he cried, running to and fro like a fretful hen, "take it all, and when that is done, this also, and this. Nay, I will stay up all night to carry more from the forest of Machecoul."

"And you who were so afraid to open to three honest men, would you venture to bring faggots by night from yon dark wood?"

"Nay," said the old man, cunningly, "I meant not from the forest, but from my neighbours' woodpiles. Yet for lovely gold I would even venture to go thither—that is, if I had my image of the Blessed Mother about my neck and the moon shone very bright."

"Now haste thee with the barley brew," said Lord James, "for my stomach is as deep as a well and as empty as the purse of a younger son."

The strange cripple emitted another bird-like cachinnation, resembling the sound which is made by the wooden cogwheels wherewithal boys fright the crows from the cornfields when the August sun is yellowing the land.

"Poor old Cæsar Martin can show you something better than that," he cried, as he hirpled out (for so Malise described it afterwards) and presently returned dragging a great iron pot with a strength which seemed incredible in so ramshackle a body.

"Ha! ha!" he said, "here is fragrant stew; smell it. Is it not good? In ten minutes it will be so hot and toothsome that you will scarce have patience to wait till it be decently cool in the platters. This is not common Angevin stew, but Bas Breton — which is a far better thing."

Malise rose, and, relieving the old man, with one finger swung the pot to a crook that hung over the cheerful blaze of the birchwood.

The old cripple Cæsar Martin now mounted on a stool and stirred the mess with a long stick, at the end of which was a steel fork of two prongs. And as he stirred he talked:

"God bless you, say I, brave gentlemen and good pilgrims. Surely it was a wind noble and fortunate that blew you hither to taste my broth. There be fine pigeons here, fat and young. There be leverets juicy and tender as a maid untried. There — what think you of that?" (he held each ingredient up on a prong as he spoke). "And here be larks, partridge stuffed with sage, ripe chestnuts from La Valery, and whisper it not to any of the marshal's men, a fawn from the park of a month old, dressed like a kid so that none may know."

"I suppose that so much providing is for your four sons ? " said Sholto.

The cripple laughed again his feeble, fleering laugh.

"I have no sons, honest sir," he said; "it was but a weakling's policy to tell you so, lest there should have been evil in your hearts. But I have a wife and that is enough. You may have heard of her. She is called La Meffraye."

As he spoke his face took on an access of white terror, even as it had done when he looked out of the window.

"La Meffraye is she well named," he repeated the appellation with a harsh croak as of a night-hawk screaming. "God forfend that she should come home to-night and find you here ! "

" Why, good sir," smiled James Douglas, "if that be the manner in which you speak of your housewife, faith, I am right glad to have remained a bachelor."

Cæsar the cripple looked about him and lowered his voice.

"Hush!" he quavered, breathing hard so that his words whistled between his toothless gums, "you do not know my wife. I tell you, she is the familiar of the marshal himself."

"Then," cried James Douglas, slapping his thigh, "she is young and pretty, of a surety. I know what these soldiers are familiar with. I would that she would come home and partake with us now."

"Nay," said the old man, without taking offence, "you mistake, kind sir, I meant familiar in witchcraft, in devilry — not (as it were) in levity and cozenage."

The fragrant stew was now ready to be dished in great platters of wood, and the guests fell to keenly, each being provided with a wooden spoon. The meat they cut with their daggers, but the most part was, however, tender enough to come apart in their fingers, which, as all know, better preserves the savour.

At first the cripple denied having any wine, but another gold angel from the Lord James induced him to draw a leathern bottle from some secret hoard, and decant it into a pitcher for them. It was resinous and Spanish, but, as Malise said, "It made warm the way it went down." And after all with wine that is always the principal thing.

As the feast proceeded old Cæsar Martin told the three Scots why the long street of the village had been cleared of children so quickly at the first sound of their horses' feet.

"And in truth if you had not come across the moor, but along the beaten track from the Chateau of Machecoul, you would never have caught so much as a glimpse of any child or mother in all Saint Philbert."

At this point he beckoned Sholto, Malise, and the Lord James to come nearer to him, and standing with his back to the fire and their three heads very close, he related the terrible tale of the Dread that for eight years had stalked grim and gaunt through the westlands of France, La Vendée, and Bas Bretagne. In all La Vendée there was not a village that had not lost a child. In many a hamlet about the shores of the sunny Loire was

there scarce a house from which one had not vanished.
They were seen playing in the greenwood, the eye was
lifted, and lo! they were not. A boy went to the well.
An hour after his pitcher stood beside it filled to the
brim. But he himself was never more seen by holt
or heath. A little maid, sweet and innocent, looked
over the churchyard wall; she spied something that
pleased her. She climbed over to get it — and was not.

"Oh, I could tell you of a thousand such if I had
time," shrilled the thin treble of the cripple in their
eager ears, "if I dared — if I only dared!"

"Dared," said Malise; "why man — what is the matter with you? None could hear you but we three
men."

"My wife — my wife," he quavered; "I bid you be
silent, or at least speak not so loud. La Meffraye she
is called — she can hear all things. See — "

He made a sudden movement and bared his right
arm. It was withered to the shoulder and of a dark
purple colour approaching black.

"La Meffraye did that," he gasped; "she blasted it
because I would not do the evil she wished."

"Then why do you not kill her?" said Malise, whose
methods were not subtle. "If she were mine, I would
throttle her, and give her body to the hounds."

"Hush, I bid you be silent for dear God's sake in
whom I believe," again came the voice of the cripple.
"You do not know what you say. La Meffraye cannot
die. Perhaps she will vanish away in a blast of the fire
of hell — one day when God is very strong and angry.
But she cannot die. She only leads others to death.
She dies not herself."

" You are kind, gentlemen," he went on after a pause, finding them continue silent; " I will show you all. Pray the saint for me at his shrine that I may die and go to purgatory. Or (if it were to a different one) even to hell — that I might escape for ever from La Meffraye."

His hand fumbled a moment at the closely buttoned collar of his blue blouse. Then he succeeded in undoing it and showed his neck. From chin to bosom it was a mass of ghastly bites, some partially healed, more of them recent and yet raw, while the skin, so far as the three Scots could observe it, was covered with a hieroglyphic of scratches, claw marks, and, as it seemed, the bites of some fierce wild beast.

" Great Master of Heaven!" cried James Douglas. " What hell hound hath done this to you ? "

" The wife of my bosom," quoth very grimly Cæsar the cripple.

" A good evening to you, gentlemen all," said a soft and winning voice from the doorway.

At the sound the old man staggered, reeled, and would have swayed into the fire had not Sholto seized him and dragged him out upon the floor. All rose to their feet.

In the doorway of the cottage stood an old woman, small, smiling, delicate of feature. She looked benignly upon them and continued to smile. Her hair and her eyes were her most noticeable features. The former was abundant and hung loosely about the woman's brow and over her shoulders in wisps of a curious greenish white, the colour almost of mouldy cheese, while, under shaggy white eyebrows, her large eyes shone piercing and green as emerald stones on the hand of some dusky monarch of the Orient.

The old woman it was who spoke first, before any of the men could recover from their surprise.

"My husband," she said, still calmly smiling upon them, "my poor husband has doubtless been telling you his foolish tales. The saints have permitted him to become demented. It is a great trial to a poor woman like me, but the will of heaven be done!"

The three Scots stood silent and transfixed, for it was an age of belief. But the cripple lay back on the settle where Sholto had placed him, his lips white and gluey. And as he lay he muttered audibly, "La Meffraye! La Meffraye! Oh, what will become of poor Cæsar Martin this night!"

CHAPTER XLVIII

THE MERCY OF LA MEFFRAYE

It was a strange night that which the three Scots spent in the little house standing back from the street of Saint Philbert on the gloomy edges of the forest of Machecoul. The hostess, indeed, was unweariedly kind and brought forth from her store many dainties for their delectation. She talked with touching affection of her poor husband, afflicted with these strange fits of wolfish mania, in the paroxysms of which he was wont to tear himself and grovel in the dust like a beast.

This she told them over and over as she moved about setting before them provend from secret stores of her own, obviously unknown or perhaps forbidden to Cæsar Martin.

Wild bee honey from the woods she placed before them and white wheaten bread, such as could not be got nearer than Paris, with wine of some rarer vintage than that out of the cripple's resinous pigskin. These and much else La Meffraye pressed upon them till she had completely won over the Lord James, and even Malise, easy natured like most very strong men, was taken by the sympathetic conversation and gracious kindliness of the wife of poor afflicted Cæsar Martin of Saint Philbert. Only Sholto kept his suspicion edged and pointed, and resolved that he would not sleep that night, but

352

watch till the dawn the things which might befall in the
house on the forest's border.

Yet it was conspicuously to Sholto **that La Meffraye**
directed most of her blandishments.

Her ruddy face, so bright that it seemed almost as if
wholly covered with a birthmark, **gleamed** with absolute
good nature as **she** looked at him.   She threw off **the**
black veil **which** half concealed **her strange** coiffure of
green toadstool-coloured hair.   She placed her choicest
morsels before the young captain of the Douglas guard.

"'Tis hard," she said, touching him confidentially on
the shoulder, "hard to dwell here in this country wherein
so many deeds of blood are wrought, alone with a poor
imbecile like my husband.   **None cares** to help me **with**
aught, all **being too busy with their own affairs.   It falls**
on me **to till the fields, which, scanty** as they are, are
more than **my feeble** strength can compass unaided.
Alone I must **prune and** water the vines, bring in the
firewood, and **go out and in by** night **and day to** earn
a scanty living for this afflicted one and myself.   You
will hear, perchance, mischief laid to my charge in this
village of evil speakers and **lazy folk.   They hate** me
because I am no gadabout to spend time abusing my
neighbours at the village well.   But **the** children love
me, and that is no ill sign.   Their young hearts are open
to love a **poor** lone old woman.   What cares La Meffraye
for the sneers of **the** ignorant and prejudiced so long as
the children run to her gladly and search her pockets for
the good **things she never** forgets to bring them from
her kitchen ? "

So the old woman, talking all the time, bustled here
and there, setting **sweet** cakes baked with honey, confi-

2 ▲

tures and bairns' goodies, figs, almonds, and cheese before her guests. But through all her blandishments Sholto watched her and had his eyes warily upon what should befall her husband, who could be seen lying apparently either asleep or unconscious upon the bed in an inner room.

"You do not speak like the folk of the south," she said to the Lord James. "Neither are you Northmen nor of the Midi. From what country may you come?" The question dropped casually as to fill up the time.

"We are poor Scots who have lived under the protection of your good King Charles, the seventh of that name, and having been restored to our possessions after the turning out of the English, we are making a pilgrimage in order to visit our friends and also to lay our thanks upon the altar of the blessed Saint Andrew in his own town in Scotland."

The old woman listened, approvingly nodding her head as the Lord James reeled off this new and original narrative. But at the mention of the land of the Scots La Meffraye pricked her ears.

"Scots," she said meditatively; "that will surely interest my lord, who hath but recently returned from that country, whither they say he hath been upon a very confidential embassy from the King."

It was the Lord James who asked the next question.

"Have you heard whether any of our nation returned with him from our country? We would gladly meet with any such, that we might hear again the tongue of our nativity, which is ever sweet in a strange land — and also, if it might be, take back tidings of them to their folk in Scotland."

"Nay," answered La Meffraye, standing before them with her eyes shrewdly fixed upon the face of the speaker, "I have heard of none such. Yet it may well be, for the marshal is very fond of the society of the young, even as I am myself. He has many boy singers in his choir, maidens also for his religious processions. Indeed, never do I visit Machecoul without finding a pretty boy or a stripling girl passing so innocently in and out of his study, that it is a pleasure to behold."

"Is his lordship even now at Machecoul?" asked James Douglas, bluntly. The Lord James prided himself upon his tact, but when he set out to manifest it, Sholto groaned inwardly. He was never certain from one moment to another what the reckless young Lord might do or say next.

"I do not even know whether the marshal is now at Machecoul. The rich and great, they come and go, and we poor folk understand it no more than the passing of the wind or the flight of the birds. But let us get to our couches. The morn will soon be here, and it must not find our bodies unrested or our eyes unrefreshed."

La Meffraye showed her guests where to make their beds in the outer room of the cottage, which they did by moving the bench back and stretching themselves with their heads to the wall and their feet to the fire. Sholto lay on the side furthest from the entrance of the room to which La Meffraye had retired with her husband. Malise was on the other side, and Lord James lay in the midst, as befitted his rank.

These last were instantly asleep, being tired with their journey and heavy with the meal of which they had partaken. But every sense in Sholto's body was keenly awake. A vague inexpressible fear possessed him. He lay watching the red unequal glow thrown upwards from the embers, and through the wide opening in the roof he could discern the twinkling of a star.

Within the chamber of La Meffraye there was silence. Sholto could not even hear the heavy breathing of Cæsar Martin. The silence was complete.

Suddenly, from far away, there came up the howling of a wolf. It was not an uncommon sound in the forests of France, or even in those of his own country, yet somehow Sholto listened with a growing dread. Nearer and nearer it came, till it seemed to reverberate immediately beneath the eaves of the dwelling of Cæsar the cripple.

The flicker of the embers died slowly out. Malise lay without a sound, his head couched on his hand. Lord James began to groan and move uneasily, like one in the grip of nightmare. Sholto listened yet more acutely. Outside the house he could hear the soft pad-pad of wild animals. Their pelts seemed almost to brush against the wooden walls behind his head with a rustle like that of corded silk. Sholto felt nervously for his sword and cleared it instinctively of the coverture in which he was wrapped. Expectation tingled in his cheeks and palms. The silence grew more and more oppressive. He could hear nothing but that soft brushing and the galloping pads outside, as of something that went round and round the house, weaving a coil of terror and death about the doomed inmates.

Suddenly from the adjoining chamber a cry burst

forth, so shrill and terrible that not only Sholto but Malise also leaped to his feet.

"Mercy — mercy!   Have mercy, La Meffraye!" it wailed.

Sholto rushed across the floor, striding the body of James Douglas in his haste.   He dashed the door of the inner chamber open and was just in time to see something dark and lithe dart through the window and disappear into the indigo gloom without.   From the bed there came a series of gasping moans, as from a man at the point of death.

"For God's sake bring a light!" cried Sholto, "there is black murder done here."

His father ran to the hearth, and, seizing a birchen brand, the end of which was still red, he blew upon it with care and success so that it burst into a white brilliant flame that lighted all the house.   Then he, too, entered the room where Sholto, with his sword ready in his hand, was standing over the gasping, dying thing on the bed.

When Malise thrust forward his torch, lo! there, extended on the couch to which they had carried him two hours before, lay the yet twitching body of Cæsar the cripple with his throat well nigh bitten away.

But La Meffraye was nowhere to be seen.

CHAPTER XLIX

THE BATTLE WITH THE WERE-WOLVES

"Let us get out of this hellish place," cried James Douglas so soon as he had seen with his eyes that which lay within the bedchamber of the witch woman, and made certain that it was all over with Cæsar Martin.

So the three men issued out into the gloom of the night, and made their way to the stable wherein they had disposed their horses so carefully the night before.

The door lay on the ground smashed and broken. It had been driven to kindling wood from within. Its inner surface was dinted and riven by the iron shoes of the frightened steeds, but the horses themselves were nowhere to be found. They had broken their halters and vanished. The three Scots were left in the heart of the enemy's country without means of escape save upon their own feet.

But the horror which lay behind them in the house of La Meffraye drove them on.

Almost without knowing whither they went, they turned their faces towards the west, in the direction in which lay Machecoul, the castle of the dread Lord of all the Pays de Retz. Malise, as was his custom, walked in front, Sholto and the Lord James Douglas a step behind.

A chill wind from the sea blew through the forest. The pines bent soughing towards the adventurers. The night grew denser and blacker about them, as with the wan waters of the marismas on one side and the sombre arches of the forest on the other, they advanced sword in hand, praying that that which should happen might happen quickly.

But as they went the woods about them grew clamorous with horrid noises. All the evil beasts of the world seemed abroad that night in the forests of Machecoul. Presently they issued forth into a more open space. The greyish dark of the turf beneath their feet spread further off. The black blank wall of the pines retreated and they found themselves suddenly with the stars twinkling infinitely chill and remote above them.

They were now, however, no more alone, for round them circled and echoed the crying of many packs of wolves. In the forest of Machecoul the guardian demons of its lord had been let loose, and throughout all its borders poor peasant folk shivered in their beds, or crouched behind the weak defences of their twice barred doors. For they knew that the full pack never hunted in the Pays de Retz without bringing death to some wanderer found defenceless within the borders of that region of dread.

"Let us stop here," said Sholto; "if these howling demons attack us, we are at least in somewhat better case to meet them and fight it out till the morning than in the dense darkness of the woods."

In the centre of the open glade in which they found themselves, they stumbled against the trunk of a huge pine which had been blasted by lightning. It still stood

erect with its withered branches stretching bare and
angular away from the sea. About this the three Scots
posted themselves, their backs to the corrugations of the
rotting stump, and their swords ready in their hands to
deal out death to whatever should attack them.

Well might Malise declare the powers of evil were
abroad that night. At times the three men seemed
wholly ringed with devilish cries. Yells and howls as
of triumphant fiends were borne to their ears upon the
western wind. The noises approached nearer, and presently out of the dark of the woods shadowy forms glided,
and again Sholto heard the soft pad-pad of many feet.
Gleaming eyes glared upon them as the wolves trotted
out and sat down in a wide circle to wait for the full
muster of the pack before rushing their prey.

Sholto knew well how those in the service of Satan
were able to change themselves into the semblance of
wolves, and he never doubted for a moment that he
and his friends were face to face with the direct mani-
festations of the nether pit. Nevertheless Sholto Mac-
Kim was by nature of a stout heart, and he resolved
that if he had to die, it would be as well to die as became
a captain of the Douglas guard.

The blue leme of summer lightning momentarily lit up
the western sky. The men could see the great gaunt
pack wolves sitting upon their haunches or moving restlessly to and fro across each other, while from the denser
woods behind rose the howling of fresh levies, hastening to the assistance of the first. Sholto noted in especial one gigantic she-wolf, which appeared at every point
of the circle and seemed to muster and encourage the
pack to the attack.

ALL THE WILD BEASTS APPEARED TO BE OBEYING THE SUMMONS OF
THE WITCH WOMAN.

The wild-fire flickered behind the jet black silhouettes of the dense trees so that their tops stood out against the pale sky as if carved in ebony. Then the night shut down darker than before. As the soundless lightning wavered and brightened, the shadows of the wolves appeared simultaneously to start forward and then retreat, while the noise of their howling carried with it some diabolic suggestion of discordant human voices.

"*La Meffraye! La Meffraye! Meffraye!*"

So to the excited minds of the three Scots the wolf legions seemed to be crying with one voice as they came nearer. All the wild beasts of the wood appeared to be obeying the summons of the witch woman.

The strain of the situation first told upon the Lord James Douglas. "Great Saints!" he cried, "let us attack them and die sword in hand. I cannot endure much more of this."

"Stand still where you are. It is our only chance," commanded Sholto, as abruptly as if James Douglas had been a doubtful soldier of his company.

"It were better to find a tree that we could climb," growled Malise with a practical suggestiveness, which, however, came too late. For they dared not move out of the open space, and the great trunk of the blasted pine rose behind them bare of branches almost to the top.

"Your daggers in your left hands, they are upon us!" cried Sholto, who, standing with his face to the west, had a lower horizon and more light than the others. The three men had cast their palmers' cloaks from their shoulders and now stood leaning a little forward, breath-

ing hard as they waited the assault of foes whom they
believed to be frankly diabolic and instinct with all the
powers of hell. This required greater courage than
storming many fortifications.

Almost as he spoke Sholto became aware that a fierce
rush of shaggy beasts was crossing the scanty grass
towards him. He saw a vision of red mouths, gleaming
teeth, and hairy breasts, into the leaping chaos of which
he plunged and replunged his sword till his arm ached.
Mostly the stricken died snapping and tearing at each
other; but ever and anon one stronger than the rest
would overleap the barrier of dead and dying wolves
that grew up in front of the three men, and Sholto would
feel the teeth click clean and hard upon the mail of his
arm or thigh before he could stoop to despatch the brute
with the dirk which he grasped in his left hand.

The rush upon Sholto's side fortunately did not last
long, but while it continued the battle was strange and
silent and grim — this notable fight of man and beast.
As the youth at last cleared his front of a hairy monster
that had sprung at his throat, he found himself sufficiently free to look round the trunk of the blasted pine
that he might see how it fared with his companions.

At first he could see nothing clearly, for the same
strange and weird conditions continued to permeate the
earth and air.

For a moment all would be dark and then flash on
continuous flash would follow, the wild-fire running
about the tree-tops and glinting up through the recesses
of the woods as if the heavens themselves were instinct
with diabolic light.

As he looked, Sholto saw his father, a gigantic figure

standing black and militant against the brightest of it.
His hand grasped a huge wolf by the heels, and he
swung the beast about his head as easily as he was wont
to handle the forehammer at home. With his living
weapon Malise had swept a space about him clear, and
the beasts seemed to have fallen back in terror before
such a strange enemy.

But what of the Lord James? Overleaping the pile
of dead and dying wolves which his sword and dagger
had made, and from which savage heads still bit and
snarled up at him as he went, Sholto ran round to seek
the young Lord of Avondale. At the first flash after
leaving the tree trunk he was nowhere to be seen, but
a second revealed him lying on the ground, with four
shaggy beasts bending over him and tearing fiercely at
his gorget and breast-armour. With a loud shout Sholto
was among them. He passed his sword through and
through the largest, and in its fall the wounded monster
turned and bit savagely at the fore leg of a companion.
The bone cracked as a rotten branch snaps underfoot,
and in another moment the two animals were rolling
over and over, locked together in the death grapple.

Once, twice, and thrice Sholto struck right and left.
The rest of the beasts, seemingly astonished by the
sudden flank attack, turned and fled. Then, pushing off
a huge wounded brute which lay gasping out its life in
red jets upon the breast of the fallen man, he dragged
James Douglas back to the tree which had been their
fortress and propped him up against the trunk.

At the same moment a long wailing cry from the forest
called the wolves off. They retreated suddenly, disap-
pearing apparently by magic into the depths of the

forest, leaving their dead in quivering heaps all about the little bare glade where the unequal fight had been fought.

Malise the Brawny flung down the wolf whose head had served him with such deadly effect as a weapon against his brethren. The beast had long been dead, with a skull smashed in and a neck dislocated by the sweeping blows it had dealt its kin.

"Sholto! My Lord James!" cried Malise, coming up to them hastily. "How fares it with you?"

"We are both here," answered his son. "Come and help me with the Lord James. He has fallen faint with the stress of his armour."

After the disappearance of the wolves the unearthly brilliance of the wild-fire gradually diminished, and now it flickered paler and less frequently.

But another hail from Sholto revealed to Malise the whereabouts of his companions, and presently he also was on his knees beside the young Lord of Avondale.

Sholto gave him into the strong arms of Malise and stood erect to listen for any renewal of the attack. The wise smith, whose skill as a leech was proverbial, carefully felt James Douglas all over in the darkness, and took advantage of every flicker of summer lightning to examine him as well as his armour would permit.

"Help me to loosen his gorget and ease him of his body mail," said Malise, at last. "He has gotten a bite or two, but nothing that appears serious. I think he has but fainted from pressure."

Sholto bent down and with his dagger cut string by string the stout leathern twists which secured the knight's mail. And as he did so his father widened it out with his powerful fingers to ease the weight upon the young man's chest.

Presently, with a long sigh, James Douglas opened his eyes.

"Where are the wolves?" he said, with a grimace of disgust. Sholto told him how all that were left alive had, for the present at least, disappeared.

"Ugh, the filthy brutes!" said Lord James. "I fought till the stench of their hot breaths seemed to stifle me. I felt my head run round like a dog in a fit, and down I went. What happened after that?"

"This," said Malise, sententiously, pointing to the heaps of dead wolves which were becoming more apparent as the night ebbed and the blue flame rose and fell like a fluttering pulse along the horizon.

"Then to one or the other of you I owe my life," said Lord James Douglas, reaching a hand to both.

"Sholto dragged you from under half a dozen of the devils," said Malise.

"My father it was who brought you to," said Sholto.

"I thank you both with all my heart — for this as for all the rest. I know not, indeed, where to begin," said James Douglas, gratefully. "Give me your hands. I can stand upright now."

So saying, and being assisted by Malise, he rose to his feet.

"Will they come again?" he asked, as with an intense disgust he surveyed the battle-field in the intermittent light from over the marshes.

"Listen," said Malise.

The low howling of the wolves had retreated farther,

but seemed to retain more and more of its strange human character.

"*La Meffraye! La Meff—raye!*" they seemed to wail, with a curious swelling upon the last syllable.

"I hear only the yelling of the infernal brutes," said the Lord James; "they seem to be calling on their patron saint—the woman whom we saw in the house of the poor cripple. I am sure I saw her going to and fro among the devils and encouraging them to the assault."

"'Tis black work at the best," answered Malise; "these are no common wolves who would dare to attack armed men—demons of the nethermost pit rather, driven on by their hellish hunt-mistress. There will be many dead warlocks to-morrow throughout the lands of France."

"Stand to your arms," cried Sholto, from the other side of the tree. And indeed the howling seemed suddenly to grow nearer and louder. The noise circled about them, and they could again perceive dusky forms which glided to and fro in the faint light among the arches of the forest.

In the midst of the turmoil Malise took off his bonnet and stood reverently at prayer.

"Aid us, Thy true men," he cried in a loud and solemn voice, "against all the powers of evil. In the name of God—Amen!"

The howling stopped and there fell a silence. Lord James would have spoken.

"Hush!" said Malise, yet more solemnly.

And far off, like an echo from another world, thin and sweet and silver clear, a cock crew.

The blue leaping flame of the wild-fire abruptly ceased. The dawn arose red and broad in the east. The piles of dead beasts shone out black on the grey plain of the forest glade, and on the topmost bough of a pine tree a thrush began to sing.

CHAPTER L

THE ALTAR OF IRON

AND now what of Master Laurence, lately clerk in the Abbey of Dulce Cor, presently in service with the great Lord of Retz, Messire Gilles de Laval, Marshal and Chamberlain of the King of France?

Laurence had been a month at Machecoul and had not yet worn out his welcome. He was sunning himself with certain young clerks and choristers of the marshal's privy chapel of the Holy Innocents. Suddenly Clerk Henriet appeared under the arches at the upper end of the pretty cloisters, in the aisles of which the youths were seated. Henriet regarded them silently for a moment, looking with special approval upon the blonde curls and pink cheeks of the young Scottish lad.

Machecoul was a vast feudal castle with one great central square tower and many smaller ones about it. The circuit of its walls enclosed gardens and pleasaunces, and included within its limits the new and beautiful chapel which has been recently finished by that good Catholic and ardent religionary, the Marshal de Retz.

As yet, Laurence had been able to learn nothing of the maids, not even whether they were alive or dead, whether at Machecoul or elsewhere. At the first mention of maidens being brought from Scotland to the castle, or seen about its courts, a dead silence fell upon the

company of priests and singers in the marshal's chapel.
It was the same when Laurence spoke of the business
privately to any of his new acquaintances.

No matter how briskly the conversation had been
prospering hitherto, if, at Holy Mass or jovial supper
board, Laurence so much as breathed a question concerning the subject next his heart, an instant blight passed
over the gaiety of his companions. Fear momently
wiped every other expression from their faces, and they
answered with lame evasion, or more often not at all.

The shadow of the Lord of Machecoul lay heavy upon
them.

Clerk Henriet stood awhile watching the lads and
listening to their talk behind the carved lattice of Caen
stone, with its lace-like tracery of buds and flowers,
through which the natural roses pushed their way, and
over which the clematis tangled its twining stems.

"Stand up and prove on my body that I am a rank
Irelander," Laurence was saying defiantly to the world
at large, with his fists up and his head thrown back.
"Saint Christopher, but I will take the lot of you
with one hand tied behind me. Stand up and I will
teach you how to sing 'Miserable sinners are we all!'
to a new and unkenned tune."

"'Tis easy for you to boast, Irelander," retorted Blaise
Renouf, the son of the lay choir-master, who had been
brought specially from Rome to teach the choir-boys of
the marshal's chapel the latest fashions in holy song.
"We will either fight you with swords or not at all.
We do not fight with our bare knuckles, being civilised.
And that indeed proves that you are no true lover of the
French, but an English dog of unknightly birth."

2 B

This retort still further irritated the hot-headed son of Malise.

"I will fight you or any galley slave of a French frog with the sword, or spit you upon the rapier. I will cleave you with the axe, transfix you with the arrow, or blow you to the pit with the devil's sulphur. I will fight any of you or all of you with any weapons from a battering-ram to a toothpick — and God assist the better man. And there you have Laurence O'Halloran, at your service!"

"You are a loud-crowing young cock for a newcomer," said Henriet, the confidential clerk of the marshal, suddenly appearing in the doorway; "you are desired to follow me to my lord's chamber immediately. There we will see if you will flap your wings so boldly."

Laurence could not help noticing the blank alarm which this announcement caused among the youth with whom he had been playing the ancient game of brag.

It was Blaise Renouf who first recovered. He looked across the little rose-grown space of the cloister to see that Henriet had turned his back, and then came quickly up to Laurence MacKim.

"Listen to me," he said; "you are a game lad enough, but you do not know where you are going, nor yet what may happen to you there. We will fight you if you come back safe, but meantime you are one of ourselves, and we of the choir have sworn to stand by one another. Can you keep a pea in your mouth without swallowing it?"

"Why, of course I can," said Laurence, wondering what was to come next. "I can keep a dozen and shoot them through a bore of alder tree at a penny without missing once, which I wot is more than any Frenchman ever — "

" Well, then," whispered the lad Renouf, breaking in on his boast with a white countenance, "hearken well to me. When you enter the chamber of the marshal, put this in your mouth. And if nothing happens keep it there, but be careful neither to swallow it nor yet to bite upon it. But if it should chance that either Henriet or Poitou or Gilles de Sillé seize hold of your arms, bite hard upon the pellet till you feel a bitter taste and then swallow. That is all. You are indeed a cock whose comb wants cutting, and if all be well, we will incise it for your soul's good. But in the meanwhile you are of our company and fellowship. So for God's sake and your own do as you are bid. Fare you well."

As he followed Clerk Henriet, Laurence looked at the round pellet in his hand. It was white, soft like ripe fruit, of an elastic consistency, and of the largeness of a pea.

As Laurence ascended the stairs, he heard the practice of the choir beginning in the chapel. Precentor Renouf, the father of Blaise, had summoned the youths from the cloisters with a long mellow whistle upon his Italian pitch-pipe, running up and down the scale and ending with a flourished " A-a-men."

The open windows and the pierced stone railing of the great staircase of Machecoul brought up the sound of that sweet singing from the chapel to the ear of the adventurous Scot as through a funnel. They were beginning the practice for the Christmas services, though the time was not yet near.

" Unto God be the glory
  In the Highest;
Peace be on the earth,
  On the earth,
Unto men who have good-will."

So they chanted in their white robes in the Chapel of
the Holy Innocents in the Castle of Machecoul near by
the Atlantic shore.

The chamber of Gilles de Retz testified to the extraordinary advancement of that great man in knowledge which has been claimed as peculiar to much later
centuries. The window casements were so arranged
that in a moment the place could either be made as dark
as midnight or flooded with bright light. The walls
were always freshly whitewashed, and the lime was constantly renewed. The stone floor was stained a deep
brick red, and that, too, would often be applied freshly
during the night. At a time when the very word "sani-
tation" was unknown, Gilles had properly constructed
conduits leading from an adjoining apartment to the
castle ditch. The chimney was wide as a peasant's
whole house, and the vast fireplace could hold on its iron
dogs an entire waggon-load of faggots. Indeed, that
amount was regularly consumed every day when the
marshal deigned to abide at Machecoul for his health
and in pursuance of his wonderful studies into the deep
things of the universe.

"Bide here a moment," said Clerk Henriet, bending
his body in a writhing contortion to listen to what might
be going on inside the chamber; "I dare not take you
in till I see whether my lord be in good case to receive
you."

So at the stair-head, by a window lattice which looked towards the chapel, Laurence stood and waited. At first he kept quite still and listened with pleasure to the distant singing of the boys. He could even hear Precentor Renouf occasionally stop and rebuke them for inattention or singing out of tune.

> "*My soul is like a watered garden,*
> *And I shall not sorrow any more at all!*"

So he hummed as he listened, and beat the time on the ledge with his fingers. He felt singularly content. Now he was on the eve of penetrating the mystery. At last he would discover where the missing maidens were concealed.

But soon he began to look about him, growing, like the boy he was, quickly weary of inaction. His eye fell upon a strange door with curious marks burnt upon its panels apparently by hot irons. There were circles complete and circles that stopped half-way, together with letters of some unknown language arranged mostly in triangles.

This door fixed the lad's attention with a certain curious fascination. He longed to touch it and see whether it opened, but for the moment he was too much afraid of his guide's return to summon him into the presence of the marshal.

He listened intently. Surely he heard a low sound, like the wind in a distant keyhole — or, as it might be (and it seemed more like it), the moaning of a child in pain, it knows not why.

The heart of the youth gave a sudden leap. It came to him that he had hit upon the hiding-place of Margaret

Douglas, the heiress of the great province of Galloway. His fortune was made.

With a trembling hand he moved a step towards the door of white wood with the curious burned marks upon it. He stood a moment listening, half for the returning footsteps of Clerk Henriet, and half to the low, persistent whimper behind the panels. Suddenly he felt his right foot wet, for, as was the fashion, he wore only a velvet shoe pointed at the toe. He looked down, and lo! from under the door trickled a thin stream of red.

Laurence drew his foot away, with a quick catching sob of the breath. But his hand was already on the door, and at a touch it appeared to open almost of its own accord. He found himself looking from the dusk of the outer whitewashed passage into a high, vaulted chapel, wherein many dim lights glimmered. At the end there was a great altar of iron standing square and solemn upon the platform on which it was set up, and behind it, cut indistinctly against a greenish glow of light, and imagined rather than clearly defined, the vast statue of a man with a curiously high shaped head. Laurence could not distinguish any features, so deep was the gloom, but the whole figure seemed to be bending slightly forward, as if gloating upon that which was laid upon the altar. But what struck Laurence with a sense of awe and terror was the fact that as the greenish light behind waxed and waned, he could see shadowy horns which projected from either side of the forehead, and lower, short ears, pricked and shaggy like those of a he-goat.

Nearer the door, where he stood in the densest gloom, something moved to and fro, and as his eyes grew accustomed to the darkness Laurence could see that it was the

bent figure of a woman. He could not distinguish her
face, but it was certainly a woman of great age and bodily
weakness, whose tangled hair hung down her back, and
who halted curiously upon one foot as she walked. She
was bending over a low couch, whereon lay a little
shrouded figure, from which proceeded the low whimpering sound which he had heard from without. But even
at that moment, as he waited trembling at the door, the
moaning ceased, and there ensued a long silence, in
which Laurence could clearly distinguish the beating of
his own heart. It sounded loud in his ears as a drum
that beats the alarm in the streets of a city.

The figure of the woman bent low to the couch, and,
after a pause, with a satisfied air she threw a white
cloth over the shrouded form which lay upon it. Then,
without looking towards the door where Laurence stood,
she went to the great iron altar at the upper end of the
weird chapel and threw something on the red embers
which glowed upon it.

"*Barran — most mighty Barran-Sathanas, accept this
offering, and reveal thyself to my master!*" she said in a
voice like a chant.

A greenish smoke of stifling odour rose and filled all
the place, and through it the huge horned figure above
the altar seemed to turn its head and look at the boy.

Laurence could scarcely repress a cry of terror. He
set his hand to the door, and lo! as it had opened, so it
appeared to shut of itself. He sank almost fainting
against the cold iron bars of the window which looked
out upon the courtyard below. The wind blew in upon
him sweet and cool, and with it there came again the
sound of the singing of the choir. They were practising

the song of the Holy Innocents, which, by command of
the marshal himself, Precentor Renouf had set to excellent and accordant music of his own **invention.**

> "*A voice was heard in Ramah,*
> *In Ramah,*
> *Lamentations and bitter weeping,*
> *Rachel weeping for her children,*
> *Refused to be comforted :*
> *For her children,*
> *Because they were not.*"

Obviously there was some mistake or lack of attention
on the part of the **choir,** for the last line had to be repeated three times.

> "*Because they were not.*"

CHAPTER LI

THE MARSHAL'S CHAMBER

THERE came a low voice in Laurence MacKim's ear, chill and sinister: "You do well to look out upon the fair world. None knoweth when we may have to leave it. Yonder is a star. Look well at it. They say God made it. Perhaps He takes more interest in it than in the concerns of this other world He hath made."

The son of Malise MacKim gripped himself, as it were, with both hands, and turned a face pale as marble to look into the grim countenance which hid the soul of the Lord of Machecoul.

Gilles de Retz appeared to peruse each feature of the boy's person as if he read in a book. Yet even as Laurence gave back glance for glance, and with the memory of what he had seen yet fresh upon him, a strange courage began to glow in the heart of the young Scot. There came a kind of contempt, too, into his breast, as though he had it in him to be a man in despite of the devil and all his works.

The marshal continued his scrutiny, and Laurence returned his gaze with interest.

"Well, boy," said the marshal, smiling as if not ill pleased at his boldness, "what do you think of me?"

"I think, sir," said Laurence, simply, "that you have grown older since I saw you in the lists at Thrieve."

It seemed to Laurence that the words were given him. And all the time he was saying to himself: "Now I have done it. For this he will surely put me to death. He cannot help himself. Why did I not stick to it that I was an Irelander?"

But, somehow, the answer seemed like an arrow from a bow shot at a venture, entering in between the joints of the marshal's armour.

"Do you think so?" he said, with some startled anxiety, yet without surprise; "older than at Thrieve? I do not believe it. It is impossible. Why, I grow younger and younger every day. It has been promised me that I should."

And setting his elbow on the sill of the window, Gilles de Retz looked thoughtfully out upon the cool dusk of the rose garden. Then all at once it came to him what was implied in that unlucky speech of Laurence's. The grim intensity returned to his eyes as he erected himself and bent his brows, white with premature age, upon the boy, who confronted him with the fearlessness born of youth and ignorance.

"Ah," he said, "this is interesting; you have changed your nation. You were an Irishman to De Sillé in Paris, to the clerk Henriet, and to the choir at Machecoul. Yet to me you admit in the very first words you speak that you are a Scot and saw me at the Castle of Thrieve."

Even yet the old Laurence might have turned the corner. He had, as we know, graduated as a liar ready and expert. He had daily practised his art upon the Abbot. He had even, though more rarely, succeeded with his father. But now in the day of his necessity the power and wit had departed from him.

To the lord of the Castle of Machecoul Laurence simply could not lie. Ringed as he was by evil, his spirit became strong for good, and he testified like one in the place of final judgment, when the earthly lendings of word and phrase and covering excuse must all be cast aside and the soul stand forth naked and nakedly answer that which is required.

"I am a Scot," said Laurence, briefly, and without explanation.

"Come with me into my chamber," said the marshal, and turned to precede him thither.

And without word of complaint or backward glance, the lad followed the great lord to the chamber, into which so many had gone before him of the young and beautiful of the earth, and whence so few had come out alive.

As he passed the threshold, Laurence put into his mouth the elastic pellet which had been given him by Blaise Renouf, the choir-master's son.

The marshal threw himself upon a chair, reclining with a wearied air upon the hands which were clasped behind his head. In the action of throwing himself back one could see that Gilles de Retz was a young and not an old man, though ordinarily his vitality had been worn to the quick, and both in appearance and movement he was already prematurely aged.

"What is your name?"

The question came with military directness from the lips of the marshal of France.

"Laurence MacKim," said the lad, with equal directness.

"For what purpose did you come to the Castle of Machecoul?"

"I came," said Laurence, coolly, "to take service with you, my lord. And because I was tired of monk rule, and getting only the husks of life, tired too of sitting dumb and watching others eat the kernel."

"Ha!" cried Gilles de Retz, "I am with you there. There is, after all, some harmony between our immortal parts. For my part, I would have all of life, — husk, kernel, stalk, — aye, and the root that grows amid the dung."

He paused a moment, looking at Laurence with the air of a connoisseur.

"Come hither, lad," he said, with a soft and friendly accent; "sit on this seat with your back to the window. Turn your head so that the lamp shines aright upon your face. You are not so handsome as was reported, but that there is something wondrously taking about your countenance, I do admit. There — sit so, and fear nothing."

Laurence sat down with the bad grace of a manly youth who is admired for what he privately despises, and wishes himself well quit of. But, notwithstanding this, there was something so insinuating and pleasant about the marshal's manner that the lad almost thought he must have dreamed the incident of the burned door and the sacrifice upon the iron altar.

"You came hither to search for Margaret of Douglas," said the marshal, suddenly bending forward as if to take him by surprise.

Laurence, wholly taken aback, answered neither yea nor nay, but held his peace.

Then Gilles de Retz nodded sagely, with a quiet satisfaction in his own prevision, which to one less bold and reckless than the young clerk of Dulce Cor would have proved disconcerting. Then he propounded his next question:

"How many came hither with you?"

"One," said Laurence, promptly; "I came here alone with your servant De Sillé."

The marshal smiled.

"Good—we will try some other method with you," he said; "but be advised and speak. None hath ever hidden aught from Gilles de Retz."

"Then, my lord," said Laurence, "there is the less reason for you to put me to the question."

"I can expound dark speeches," said the marshal, "and I also know my way through the subtleties of lying tongues. Hope not to lie to me. How many were they that came to France with you?"

"I will not tell you," said the son of Malise.

The marshal smiled again and nodded his head repeatedly with a certain gustful appreciation.

"You would make a good soldier. It is a pity that I have gone out of the business. Yet I have only (as it were) descended from wholesale to particular, from the gross to the detail."

Laurence, who felt that the true policy was to be sparing of his words, made no answer.

"You say that you are a clerk. Can you read Latin?"

"Yes," said Laurence, "and write it too."

"Read this, then," said the marshal, and handed him a book.

Laurence had been well instructed in the humanities by Father Colin of Saint Michael's Kirk by the side of Dee water, and he read the words which record the cruelties of the Emperor Caligula with exactness and decorum.

"You read not ill," said his auditor; "you have been well taught, though you have a vile foreign accent and know not the shades of meaning that lie in the allusions.

"You say that you came to Machecoul with desire to serve me," the marshal continued after a pause for thought. "In what manner did you think you could serve, and why went you not into the house of some other lord?"

"As to service," said Laurence, "I came because I was invited by your henchman De Sillé. And as to what I can do, I profess that I can sing, having been well taught by a master, the best in my country. I can play upon the viol and eke upon the organ. I am fairly good at fence, and excellent as any at singlestick. I can faithfully carry a message and loyally serve those who trust me. I would have some money to spend, which I have never had. I wish to live a life worth living, wherein is pleasure and pain, the lack of sameness, and the joy of things new. And if that may not be — why, I am ready to die, that I may make proof whether there be anything better beyond."

"A most philosophic creed," cried the marshal. "Well, there is one thing in which I can prove, if indeed you lie not. Sing!"

Then Laurence stood up and sang, even as the choir had done, the lamentation of Rachel according to the setting of the Roman precentor.

"*A voice was heard in Ramah!*"

And as he sang, the Lord of Retz took up the strain,

THE PRISONERS OF THE WHITE TOWER.

and, with true accord and feeling, accompanied him to the end.

"Brava!" cried Gilles de Retz when Laurence had finished; "that is truly well sung indeed! You shall sing it alone in my chapel next feast day of the Holy Innocents."

He paused as if to consider his words.

"And now for this time go. But remember that this Castle of Machecoul is straiter than any prison cell, and better guarded than a fortress. It is surrounded with constant watchers, secret, invisible, implacable. Whoso tries to escape, dies. You are a bold lad, and, as I think, fear not much death for yourself. But come hither, and I will show you something which will chain you here."

With a kind of solicitous familiarity the Marshal de Retz took the lad by the arm and drew him to another window on the further side of the keep.

"Look forth and tell me what you see," he said.

Laurence set his head out of the window. He looked upon an intricate mass of building, composing the western wing of the castle, and it was some moments before he could distinguish what the Sieur de Retz wished him to see. Then, as his eyes took in the details, he saw on the flat roof of a square tower beneath him two maidens seated, and when he looked closer — lo! they were Margaret Douglas and, beside her, his brother's sweetheart Maud Lindesay. These two were sitting hand in hand, as was their wont, and the head of the child was bowed almost to her friend's knee. Maud's arm was about Margaret's neck, and her fingers caressed the childish tangle of hair. Presently the elder lifted the younger upon her knee and hushed her like a mother who puts a tired child to sleep.

Immediately behind this group, in the shadow of a buttress, Laurence saw a tall man, masked, clad in a black suit, and with a drawn sword in his hand.

The marshal looked out over the lad's shoulder.

"The day you are missed from the Castle of Mache-coul, or the day that the rest of your company arrives here, that sword shall fall, but in a more terrible fashion than I can tell you! That sentinel can neither hear nor speak, but he has his orders and will obey them. I bid you good night. Go to your singing in the choir. It is time for the chanting of vespers in the chapel of the Holy Innocents."

CHAPTER LII

THE JESTING OF LA MEFFRAYE

IT was in the White Tower of Machecoul that the Scottish maidens were held at the mercy of the Lord of Retz. At their first arrival in the country they had been taken to the quiet Chateau of Pouzauges, the birthplace of Poitou, the marshal's most cruel and remorseless confidant. Here, as the marshal had very truly informed the Lady Sybilla, they had been under the care of — or, rather, fellow-prisoners with — the neglected wife of Gilles de Retz, and at Pouzauges they had spent some days of comparative peace and security in the society of her daughter.

But at the first breath of the coming of the three strangers to the district they had been seized and securely conveyed to Machecoul itself — there to be interned behind the vast walls and triple bastions of that fortress prison.

"I wonder, Maudie," said Margaret Douglas, as they sat on the flat roof of the White Tower of Machecoul and looked over the battlements upon the green pine glades and wide seaward Landes, "I wonder whether we shall ever again see the water of Dee and our mother — and Sholto MacKim."

It is to be feared that the last part of the problem exceeded in interest all others in the eyes of Maud Lindesay.

2 o   385

"It seems as if we never could again behold any one we loved or wished to see — here in this horrible place," sighed Maud Lindesay. "If ever I get back to the dear land and see Solway side, I will be a different girl."

"But, Maud," said the little maid, reproachfully, "you were always good and kind. It is not well done of you to speak against yourself in that fashion."

Maud Lindesay shook her pretty head mournfully.

"Ah, Margaret, you will know some day," she said. "I have been wicked, — not in things one has to confess to Father Gawain, but, — well, in making people like me, and give me things, and come to see me, and then afterwards flouting them for it and sending them away."

It was not a lucid description, but it sufficed.

"Ah, but," said Margaret Douglas, "I think not these things to be wicked. I hope that some day I shall do just the same, though, of course, I shall not be as beautiful as you, Maudie; no, never! I asked Sholto Mac-Kim if I would, and he said, 'Of course not!' in a deep voice. It was not pretty of him, was it, Maud?"

"I think it was very prettily said of him," answered Maud Lindesay, with the first flicker of a smile on her face. Her conscience was quite at ease about Sholto. He was different. Whatever pain she had caused him, she meant to make up to him with usury thereto. The others she had exercised no more for her own amusement than for their own souls' good.

"My brother William must indeed be very angry with us, that he hath never sent to find us and bring us home," went on the little girl. "It is three months since we met that horrible old woman in the woods above Thrieve Island, and believed her when she told us that the Earl

had instant need of us — and that Sholto MacKim was
with him."

"None saw us taken away, Margaret," said the elder,
"and perhaps, who knows, they may never have found
any of the pieces of flower garlands I threw down before
they put us in the boats from the beach of Cassencary."

But the eyes of the little Maid of Galloway were now
fixed upon something in the green courtyard below.

"Maud, Maud, come hither quickly!" she whispered;
"if yonder be not Laurence MacKim talking to the singing lads and dressed like them — why, then, I do not
know Laurie MacKim!"

Maud came quickly now. Her face and neck blushed
suddenly crimson with the springing of hope in her
heart.

She looked down, and there, far below them indeed,
but yet distinct enough, they saw Laurence daring Blaise
Renouf to single combat and vaunting his Irish prowess,
as we have already seen him do. Maud Lindesay caught
her companion's hand as she looked.

"They have found us," she whispered; "at least,
they are seeking for us. If Laurence is here, I warrant
Sholto cannot be very far away. Oh, Margaret, am I
looking very ill? Will he think I am as — (she paused
for a word) — as comely as he thought me before in Scotland? Or have I grown old and ugly with being shut up
so long?"

But the Maid of Galloway heard her not. She was
pondering on the meaning of Laurence's presence in the
Castle of Machecoul.

"Perhaps William hath sent Laurence to spy us out,
and is even now coming from his French duchy with an

army. He is a far greater man than the marshal, and will make him give us up as soon as he finds out where we are. Shall I call down to Laurie to let him know that we are here?"

Maud put her hand hastily over her companion's mouth.

"Hush!" she said, "we must not appear to know him, or they will surely kill him — and perhaps the others, too. If Laurence is here, I wot well that help is not far away. Let us be patient and abide. Come back from the wall and sit by me as if nothing had happened."

But all the same she kept her own place in a spot where she could command the pleasaunce below, and looked longingly yet fearfully to see Sholto follow his brother across the green sward.

  *   *   *   *   *   *

"Sweet and fair is the air of the evening," purred behind them a low voice — that of the woman who was called La Meffraye. "It brings the colour to the cheeks of the young. But I am old and wise, and I would advise that two maids so fair should not look down on the sports of the youths, lest they hear and see more than is fitting for such innocent eyes."

The girls turned away without looking at their custodian, who stood leaning upon her little hand crutch and smiling upon them her terrible soft smile.

"Ah," she said, "proud, are you? 'Tis an ill place to bring pride to, this Castle of Machecoul. You will not deign to speak a word to a poor old woman now. But the day is not far distant when I shall have my pretty spitfire clinging about these old trembling knees,

and beseeching me whom you despise, as a woman either
to save you or kill you — you will not care which. *As
a woman!* Ha! ha! How long is it since La Meffraye
was a woman? Was she ever rocked in a cradle? Did
she play about any cottage door and fashion daisy chains,
as I have seen you do, my pretties, long ere you came to
Machecoul or even heard of the Sieur de Retz? Hath La
Meffraye ever lain in any man's bosom — save as the
tigress crouches upon her prey?"

She paused and smiled still more bitterly and malevo-
lently than before upon the two maidens.

"Did you chance to be awake yester-even?" she went on.
"Aye, I know well that you were awake. La Meffraye
saw right carefully to that. And you heard the crying
that rang out of yonder high window, from which the
light streamed all through the night. Wait, wait, my
pretties, till it is your turn to be sent for up thither,
when the shining knife is sharpened and the red fire
kindled. You will not despise La Meffraye when that
day comes. You will grovel and weep, and then will
La Meffraye spurn you with her foot, till the noise of
your crying be borne out over the forest, and for very
gladness the wolves howl in the darkness."

The little Maid of Galloway was moved to answer,
and her lips quivered. But Maud Lindesay sat pale and
motionless, looking towards the north, from which she
hoped for help to come.

"Our brother, the Earl of Douglas, will bring an army
from his dukedom of Touraine, and sweep you and your
castle from the face of the earth, if your master dares to
lay so much as a finger upon us."

La Meffraye laughed a low, cackling laugh, and in

the act showed the four long eye-teeth which were the
sole remaining dental equipment of her mouth.

"Oh, Great Barran —" she chuckled, "listen to the
pretty fool! Our brother will do this — our brother will
do that. *Our* brother will lick the country of Retz as
clean as a dog licks a platter. Know you not, silly fool,
that both your brothers are long since dead and under
sod in the castle of your city of Edinburgh. I tell you
my master set his little finger upon them and crushed
them like flies on a summer chamber wall!"

Maud Lindesay rose to her feet as La Meffraye spoke
these words.

"It is not true," she cried; "you lie to us as you have
done from the first. The Earl of Douglas is not dead!"

It was now little Margaret who showed the spirit of
her race, and put out her hand to clasp that of her elder
comrade.

"Do not let her even know that she has power to hurt
us with her words," she whispered low to Maud Lindesay.
Then she spoke aloud:

"If that which you say be true and my brothers are
dead — there are yet Douglases. Our cousins will deliver us."

"Your cousins have entered into your possessions,"
jeered the hag; "it is indeed a likely thing that they
will desire your return to Scotland in order to rob them
of that which is their own."

"We are not afraid," said the little maid, stoutly;
"there are many in the land of the Scots who would
gladly die to help us."

"Aye, that is it. They shall die — all die. Three of
them died yester-even, torn to pieces by my lord's wolves.

Fine, swift, four-footed guardians of the Castle of Machecoul — La Meffraye's friends! And one young cock below there of the same gang hath gone even now to my
lord's chamber. He hath mounted the stairs he will
never descend."

"Well," said the Maid of Galloway, "even so — we
are not afraid. We can die, as died our friends."

"Die — die!" cried the hag, sharply, angered at the
child's persistence. "'Tis easy to talk. To snuff a
candle out is to die. Poof, 'tis done! But the young
and beautiful like you, my dearies, do not so die at
Machecoul. No; rather as a dying candle flickers out
— falls low, and rises again, so they die. As wine oozes
drop by drop from the needle-punctured wine-skin — so
shall you die, weeping, beseeching, drained to the white
like a dripping calf in the shambles, yet at the same
time reddened and shamed with the shame deadly and
unnameable. Then La Meffraye, whom now you disdain
to answer with a look, will wash her hands in your life's
blood and laugh as your tears fall slowly upon the
latchet of her shoon!"

But a new voice broke in upon the railing of the hideous woman fiend.

"*Out, foul hag! Get you to your own place!*" it said,
with an accent strong and commanding.

And the affrighted and heart-sick girls turned them
about to see the Lady Sybilla stand fair and pale at the
head of the turret stair which opened out upon the roof
of the White Tower.

At this interruption the eyes of La Meffraye seemed
to burn with a fresher fury, and the green light in them
shone as shines an emerald stone held up to the sun.

The hag cowered, however, before the outstretched index finger of Sybilla de Thouars.

"Ah, fair lady," she whimpered, "be not angry — and tell not my lord, I beseech you. I did but jest."

"*Hence!*" the finger was still outstretched, and, in obedience to the threatening gesture, the hag shrank away. But as she passed through the portal down the steps of the turret, she flung back certain words with a defiant fleer.

"Ah, you are young, my lady, and for the present — for the present your power is greater than mine. But wait! Your beauty will wither and grow old. Your power will depart from you. But La Meffraye can never grow older, and when once the secret is discovered, and my lord is young again, La Meffraye is the one who with him shall bloom with immortal youth, while you, proud lady, lie cold in the belly of the worm."

       *   *   *   *   *   *

"It is true — all too true," said Sybilla de Thouars, sadly, "they are dead. The young, the noble were — and are no more. I who speak saw them die. And that so greatly, that even in death their lives cease not. Their glory shall flow on so that the young brook shall become a river, and the river become a sea."

Then in few words and quiet, she told them all the heavy tale.

But when the maids made as though they would cleave to her for the sympathy that was in her words and because of her tears, she set the palms of her hands against their breasts and cried, "Come not near one whom not all the fires of purgatory can purify — one who, like Iscariot, hath contracted herself outside the mercy of God and of our Lord Christ!"

But all the more they clave to her, overpassing her protestations and clasping her, so that, being deeply moved, she sat down on the steps of a corner turret which rose from the greater, and wept there, with the weeping wherewith women are wont to ease the heart.

Then went Maud Lindesay to her and set her hand about her neck, and kissed her, saying: "Do not be sorry any more. Confess to the minister of God. I also have sinned and been sorry. Yet after came forgiveness and the unbound heart."

Then the Lady Sybilla ceased quickly and looked up, as it had been, smiling. Yet she was not smiling as maidens are wont to smile.

"Pretty innocent," she said, "you mean well, but you know not what the word 'sin' means to such as I. Confess — absolve! Not even the Holy One and the Just could give me that. I tell you I have eaten of the apple of the knowledge of good and evil — yes, the very core I have eaten. I have the taste of innocent blood upon my lips. I have seen the axe fall, the axe which I put into the headsman's hands. I am condemned, and that justly. But one of you shall live to taste sweet love, and the crown of life, and to feel the innocent lips of children at her breasts. And the other — but enough. Farewell. Fear not. God, who has been cruel in all else, has given your lives to Sybilla de Thouars, ere in His own time He strike that guilty one with His thunderbolt."

And as she went within, the eyes of the maids followed her; but the masked man with the naked sword never so much as turned his head, gazing straight forward over the battlements of the White Tower into the lilac mist which hung above the Atlantic.

CHAPTER LIII

THERE stands a solitary rock at the base of which is a cave, on the seashore of La Vendée. Behind stretch the marshes, and the place is shut in and desolate. Birds cry there. The bittern booms in the thickets of grey willow and wet-shot alder. The herons nest upon the pine trees near by, till the stale scent of them comes down the wind from far. Ospreys fish in the waters of the shallow lake behind, and the scales of their prey flash in the sun of morning as they rise dripping from the dive.

In this place Sholto, Malise, and the Lord James Douglas were presently abiding.

It was but a tiny cell, originally formed by two portions of marly rock fallen together in some ancient convulsion or dropped upon each other from a floating iceberg. In some former age the cleft had been a lair of wild beasts, or the couch of some hairy savage hammering flint arrowheads for the chase, and drawing with a sharp point upon polished bone the yet hairier mammoth he hunted. But this solitary lodging in the wilderness had been enlarged in more recent times, till now the interior was about eight feet square and of the height of a man of stature when he stands erect.

The hearts of the three present cave-dwellers were sick and sad, and of them all the bitterest was the heart of

Sholto MacKim. It seemed to his eager lover's spirit, as he climbed to the top of the sand dunes and gazed towards the massive towers of Machecoul rising above the green woodlands, that hitherto they had but wandered and done nothing. The sorcerer had prevented them about with his evil. They had lost Laurence utterly, and for the rest they had not even touched the outer defences of their arch enemy.

Thrice they had tried to enter the castle. The first time they had taken by force two waggons of fuel from certain men who went towards Machecoul, leaving the woodmen behind in the forest, bound and helpless. But at the first gate of the outer hall the marshal's guard had stopped them, and demanded that they should wait till the cars were unloaded and brought back to them. So, having received the money, the Scots returned as they went to the men whom they had left in the forest.

After this repulse they had gone round and round the vast walls of Machecoul seeking a place vulnerable, but finding none. The ramparts rose as it had been to heaven, and the flanking towers were crowded night and day with men on the watch. Round the walls for the space of a bow-shot every way there ran a green space fair and open to the view, but in reality full of pitfalls and secret engines. From the battlements began the arrow hail, so soon as any attempted to approach the castle along any other way than the thrice-defended road to the main gate.

The wolves howled in the forests by night, and more than once came so near that one of the three men had to take it in turns to keep watch in the cave's mouth. But for a reason not clear to them at the time they were not again attacked by the marshal's wild allies of the wood.

The third time they had tried to enter the castle in their pilgrim's garb, and the outer picket courteously received them. But when they were come to the inner curtain, one Robin Romulart, the officer of the guard, a stout fellow, suddenly called to his men to bind and gag them — in which enterprise, but for the great strength of Malise, they might have succeeded. For the outer gates had been shut with a clang, and they could hear the soldiers of the garrison hasting from all sides in answer to Robin's summons.

But Malise snatched up the bar wherewith the winding cogs of the gate were turned, and, having broken more than one man's head with it, he forced the massive doors apart by main force, so that they were able all unharmed to withdraw themselves into the shelter of the woods. So near capture had they been, however, that over and over again they heard the shouting of the parties who scoured the woods in search of them.

It was the worst feature of their situation that the Marshal de Retz certainly knew of their presence in his territories, and that he would be easily able to guess their errand and take measures to prevent it succeeding.

Their last and most fatal failure had happened several days before, and the first eager burst of the search for them had passed. But the Scots knew that the enemy was thoroughly alarmed, and that it behoved them to abide very closely within their hiding-place.

The Lord James took worst of all with the uncertainty and confinement. Any restraint was unsuited to his jovial temper and open-air life. But for the present, at least, and till they could gain some further information as to the whereabouts of the maidens, it was obvious that they could do no better than remain in their seaside shelter.

Their latest plan was to abide in the cave till the marshal set out again upon one of his frequent journeys. Then it would be comparatively easy to ascertain by an ambush whether he was taking the captives with him, or if he had left them behind. If the maids were of his travelling company, the three rescuers would be guided by circumstances and the strength of the escort, as to whether or not they should venture to make an attack.

But if by any unhoped-for chance Margaret and Maud were left behind at Machecoul, it would at least be a more feasible enterprise to attack the fortress during the absence of its master and his men.

Alone among the three Scots Malise faced their predicament with some philosophy. Sholto ate his heart out with uncertainty as to the fate of his sweetheart. The Lord James chafed at the compulsory confinement and at the consistent ill success which had pursued them. But Malise, unwearied of limb and ironic of mood as ever, fished upon the tidal flats for brown-spotted flounders and at the rocky points for white fish, often remaining at his task till far into the night. He constructed snares with a mechanical ingenuity in advance of his age. And what was worth more to the company than any material help, he kept up the spirits of Sholto and of Lord James Douglas both by his brave heart and merry speech, and still more by constantly finding them something to do.

At the hour of even, one day after they had been a

fortnight in the country of Retz, the three Scots were
sitting moodily on a little hillock which concealed the
entrance to their cave. The forest lay behind them,
an impenetrable wall of dense undergrowth crowned
along the distant horizon by the solemn domes of green
stone pines. It circumvented them on all sides, save
only in front, where, through several beaker-shaped
breaks in the high sand dunes they could catch a
glimpse of the sea. The Atlantic appeared to fill these
clefts half full, like Venice goblets out of which the purple wine has been partially drained. To right and left
the pines grew scantier, so that the rays of the sunset
shone red as molten metal upon their stems and made
a network of alternate gold and black behind them.

The three sat thus a long time without speech, only
looking up from their tasks to let their eyes rest wistfully for a moment upon the deep and changeful amethyst
of the sea, and then with a light sigh going back to the
cleaning of their armoury or the shaping of a long bow.

It chanced that for several minutes no sound was heard
except those connected with their labour, the low whistle
with which the Lord James accompanied his polishing,
the *wisp-wisp* of Malise's arms as he sewed the double
thread back and forth through a rent in his leathern
jack, and the rasp of Sholto's file as he carved out the
finials of the bow, the notched grooves wherein the
string was to lie so easily and yet so firmly.

Thus they continued to work, absorbed, each of them
in the sadness of his own thought, till suddenly a shadow
seemed to strike between them and the red light of the
western sky. They looked up, and before them, as it
were ascending out of the very glow of sunset, they saw

a woman on a white palfrey approaching them by the
way of the sea.

So suddenly did she appear that the Lord James
uttered a low cry of wonder, while Malise the practical
reached for his sword. But Sholto had seen this vision
twice already, and knew their visitor for the Lady Sybilla.

"Hold there!" he said in an undertone. "Remember
it is as I said. This woman, though we have no cause
to love her, is now our only hope. Her words brought
us here. They were true words, and I believe that she
comes as a friend. I will stake my life on it."

"Or if she comes as an enemy we are no worse off,"
grumbled sceptical Malise. "We can at least encourage
the woman and then hold her as an hostage."

The three Scots were standing to receive their guest
when the Lady Sybilla rode up. Her face had lost none
of the pale sadness which marked it when Sholto last
saw her, and though the look of utter agony had passed
away, the despair of a soul in pain had only become more
deeply printed upon it.

The girl having acknowledged their salutations with a
stately and well-accustomed motion of the head, reached
a hand for Sholto to lift her from her palfrey.

Then, still without spoken word, she silently seated
herself on the grey-lichened rock rudely shaped into the
semblance of a chair, on which Malise had been sitting
at his mending. The strange maiden looked long at the
blue sea deepening in the notches of the sand dunes
beneath them. The three men stood before her waiting
for her to speak. Each of them knew that lives, dearer
and more precious than their own, hung upon what she
might have to say.

At last she spoke, in a voice low as the wind when it blows its lightest among the trees:

"You have small cause to trust me or to count me your friend," she said; "but we have that which binds closer than friendship — a common enemy and a common cause of hatred. It were better, therefore, that we should understand one another. I have never lost sight of you since you came to this fatal land of Retz. I have been near you when you knew it not. To accomplish this I have deceived the man who is my taskmaster, swearing to him that in the witch crystal I have seen you depart. And I shall yet deceive him in more deadly fashion."

Sholto could restrain himself no longer.

"Enough," he said roughly; "tell us whether the maidens are alive, and if they are abiding in this Castle of Machecoul."

The Lady Sybilla did not remove her eyes from the red west.

"Thus far they are safe," she said, in the same calm monotone. "This very hour I have come from the White Tower, in which they are confined. But he whom I serve swears by an oath that if you or other rescuers are heard of again in this country, he will destroy them both."

She shuddered as she spoke with a strong revulsion of feeling.

"Therefore, be careful with a great carefulness. Give up all thought of rescuing them directly. Remember what you have been able to accomplish, and that your slightest actions will bring upon those you love a fate of which you little dream."

"After what we remember of Crichton Castle, how can

we trust you, lady?" said Malise, sternly. "Do you now speak the truth with your mouth?"

"You have indeed small cause to think so," she answered without taking offence. "Yet, having no choice, you must e'en trust me."

She turned sharply upon Sholto with a strip of paper in her outstretched hand.

"I think, young sir, that you have some reason to know from whom that comes."

Sholto grasped at the writing with a new and wonderful hope in his heart. He knew instinctively before he touched it that none but Maud Lindesay could have written that script — small, clear, and distinct as a motto cut on a gem.

"*To our friends in France and Scotland,*" so it ran. "*We are still safe this eve of the Blessed Saint Michael. Trust her who brings this letter. She is our saviour and our only hope in a dark and evil place. She is sorry for that which by her aid hath been done. As you hope for forgiveness, forgive her. And for God's dear sake, do immediately the thing she bids you. This comes from Margaret de Douglas and Maud Lindesay. It is written by the hand of M. L.*"

The wax at the bottom was sealed in double with the boar's head of Lindesay and the heart of Margaret of Douglas.

Sholto, having read the missive silently, passed it to the Lord James that he might prove the seals, for it was his only learning to be skilled in heraldry.

"It is true," he said; "I myself gave the little maid that ring. See, it hath a piece broken from the peak of the device."

2 D

"My lady," said Sholto, "that which you bring is more
than enough. We kiss your hand and we will sacredly do
all your bidding, were it unto the death or the trial by fire."

Then, as was the custom to do to ladies whom knights
would honour, the Lord James and Sholto kneeled down
and kissed the hand of Sybilla de Thouars. But Malise,
not being a knight, took it only and settled it upon his
great grizzled head, where it rested for a moment, lightly
as upon some grey and ancient tower lies a flake of snow
before it melts.

"I thank you for your overmuch courtesy," the girl
said, casting her eyes on the ground with a new-born shy-
ness most like that of a modest maid; "I thank you,
indeed. You do me honour far above my desert. Still,
after all, we work for one end. You have, it is true, the
nobler motive, — the lives of those you love; but I the
deadlier, — the death of one I hate! Hearken!"

She paused as if to gather strength for that which she
had to reveal, and then, reaching her hands out, she
motioned the three men to gather more closely about
her, as if the blue Atlantic waves or the red boles of the
pine trees might carry the matter.

"Listen," she said, "the end comes fast — faster than
any know, save I, to whom for my sins the gift of second
sight hath been given. I who speak to you am of Brittany and of the House of De Thouars. To one of us in
each generation descends this abhorred gift of second
sight. And I, because as a child it was my lot to meet
one wholly given over to evil, have seen more and clearer
than all that have gone before me. But now I do fore-
see the end of the wickedest and most devilish soul ever
prisoned within the body of man."

As she spoke the heads of the three Scots bent lower and closer to catch every word, for the voice of the Lady Sybilla was more like the cooing of a mating turtle as it answers its comrade than that of a woman betrayed, denouncing vengeance and death upon him whom her soul hated.

" Be of good heart, then, and depart as I shall bid you. None can help or hinder here at Machecoul but I alone. Be sure that at the worst the unnameable shall not happen to the maids.   For in me there is the power to slay the evil-doer.   But slay I will not unless it be to keep the lives of the maids.   Because I desire for Gilles de Retz a fate greater, more terrible, more befitting iniquity such as the world hath never heard spoken of since it arose from the abyss.

" And this is it given to me to bring upon him whom my soul hateth," she went on.   " I have seen the hempen cord by which he shall hang.   I have seen the fire through which his soul shall pass to its own place. Through me this fate shall come upon him suddenly in one night."

Her face lighted up with an inner glow, and shone translucent in the darkening of the day and the dusk of the trees, as if the fair veil of flesh wavered and changed about the vengeful soul within.

" And now," she went on after a pause, " I bid you, gentlemen of the house of Douglas, to depart to John, Duke of Brittany, and having found him to lay this paper before him.   It contains the number and the names of those who have died in the castles of De Retz. It shows in what hidden places the bones of these slaughtered innocents may be found.   Clamour in his

ear for justice in the name of the King of France, and if
he will not hear, then in the name of the folk of Brittany.
And if still because of his kinship he will not listen, go to
the Bishop of Nantes, who hates Gilles de Retz.   Better
than any he knows how to stir the people, and he will
send with you trusty men to cause the country to rise in
rebellion.   Then they will overturn all the castles of
De Retz, and the hidden things shall come to light.
This do, and for this time depart from Machecoul, and
entrust me (as indeed you must) with the honour and
lives of those you love.   I will keep them with mine
own until destruction pass upon him who is outcast from
God, and whom now his own fiend from hell hath
deserted."

Then, having sworn to do her bidding, the three Scots
conducted the Lady Sybilla with honour and observance
to her white palfrey, and like a spirit she vanished into
the sea mists which had sifted up from the west, going
back to the drear Castle of Machecoul, but bearing with
her the burden of her revenge.

CHAPTER LIV

THE CROSS UNDER THE APRON

THE face of Gilles de Laval, Lord of Retz, had shone all day with an unholy lustre like that of iron in which the red heat yet struggles with the black. In the Castle of Machecoul his familiars went about, wearing expressions upon their countenances in which disgust and expectation were mingled with an overwhelming fear of the terrible baron.

The usual signs of approaching high saturnalia at Machecoul had not been wanting.

Early in the morning La Meffraye had been seen hovering like an unclean bird of prey about the playing grounds of the village children at Saint Benoit on the edges of the forest. At nine the frightened villagers heard the howl of a day-hunting wolf, and one Louis Verger, a woodman who was cutting bark for the tanneries in the valley, saw a huge grey wolf rush out and seize his little son, Jean, a boy of five years old, who came bringing his father's breakfast. With a great cry he hurried back to alarm the village, but when men gathered with scythes and rude weapons of the chase, the beast's track was lost in the depth of the forest.

Little Jean Verger of Saint Benoit was never seen again, unless it were he who, half hidden under the long black cloak of La Meffraye, was brought at noon by the

private postern of the baron into the Castle of Machecoul.

So the men of Saint Benoit went not back to their work,
but abode together all that day, sullen anger burning in
their hearts. And one calling himself the servant of the
Bishop of Nantes went about among them, and his words
were as knives, sharp and bitter beyond belief. And
ever as he spoke the men turned them about till they
faced Machecoul. Their lips moved like those of a Mos-
lemite who says his prayers towards Mecca. And the
words they uttered were indeed prayers of solemnest
import.

With his usual devotion at such seasons, Gilles de
Retz had attended service thrice that day in his Chapel
of the Holy Innocents. His behaviour had been marked
by intense devoutness. An excessive tenderness of conscience had characterised his confessions to Père Blouyn,
his spiritual director-in-ordinary. He confessed as his
most flagrant sin that his thoughts were overmuch set
on the vanities of the world, and that he had even sometimes been tempted of the devil to question the right of
Holy Church herself to settle all questions according to
the will of her priests and prelates.

Whereupon Père Blouyn, with suave correctness of
judgment, had pointed out wherein his master erred; but
also cautioned him against that undue tenderness of conscience natural to one with his exalted position and high
views of duty and life. Finally the marshal had received
absolution.

In the late afternoon the Lord of Retz commanded the
fire to be laid ready for lighting in his chamber aloft in
the keep of Machecoul, and set himself down to listen to

the singing of the choir, which, under the guidance of Precentor Renouf, rehearsed for him the sweetest hymns recently written for the choir of the Holy Father at Rome. For there the marshal's choir-master had been trained, and with its leader he still kept up a correspondence upon kindred interests.

Gilles de Retz, as he sat under the late blooming roses in the afternoon sunshine of the autumn of western France, appeared to the casual eye one of the most noble seigneurs and the most enlightened in the world. He affected a costume already semiecclesiastic as a token of his ultimate intention to enter holy orders. It seemed indeed as if the great soldier who had ridden into Orleans with Dunois and the Maid had begun to lay aside his earthly glories and seek the heavenly.

There, upon a chair set within the cloisters, in a place which the sunshine touched most lovingly and where it lingered longest, he sat, nodding his head to the sound of the sweet singing, and bowing low at each mention of the name of Jesus (as the custom is) — a still, meditative, almost saintly man. Upon the lap of his furred robe (for, after all, it was a sunshine with a certain shrewd wintriness in it) lay an illuminated copy of the Holy Gospels; and sometimes as he listened to the choir-boys singing, he glanced therein, and read of the little children to whom belongs the kingdom. Upon occasion he lifted the book also, and looked with pleasure at the pictured cherubs who cheered the way of the Master Jerusalemwards with strewn palm leaves and shouted hosannas.

And ever sweeter and sweeter fell the music upon his ear, till suddenly, like the silence after a thunderclap, the organ ceased to roll, the choir was silent, and out of the quiet rose a single voice — that of Laurence the Scot singing in a tenor of infinite sweetness the words of blessing:

> *"Suffer the little children to come unto Me,*
> *And forbid them not;*
> *For of such is the Kingdom of Heaven."*

And as the boy's voice welled out, clear and thrilling as the song of an upward pulsing lark, the tears ran down the face of Gilles de Retz.

God knows why. Perhaps it was some glint of his own innocent childhood — some half-dimmed memory of his happily dead mother. Perhaps — but enough. Gilles de Laval de Retz went up the turret stair to find Poitou and Gilles de Sillé on guard on either side the portals which closed his chamber.

"Is all ready?" he asked, though the tears were scarcely dry on his cheeks.

They bowed before him to the ground.

"All is ready, lord and master," they said as with one voice.

"And Prelati?"

"He is in waiting."

"And La Meffraye," he went on, "has she arrived?"

"La Meffraye has arrived," they said; "all goes fortunately."

"Good!" said Gilles de Retz, and shedding his furred monkish cloak carelessly from off his shoulders, he went within.

Poitou and Gilles de Sillé both reached to catch the mantle ere it fell. As they did so their hands met and touched. And at the meeting of each other's flesh they started and drew apart. Their eyes encountered furtively and were instantly withdrawn. Then, having hung up the cloak, with pallid countenances and lips white and tremulous, they slowly followed the marshal within.

*   *   *   *   *   *

"Sybilla de Thouars, as you are in my power, so I bid you work my will!"

It was the deep, stern voice of the Marshal de Retz which spoke. The Lady Sybilla lay back in a great chair with her eyes closed, breathing slowly and gently through her parted lips. Messire Gilles stood before her with his hands joined palm to palm and his white finger-tips almost touching the girl's brow.

"Work my will and tell me what you see!"

Her hands were clasped under a light silken apron which she wore descending from her neck and caught in a loose loop behind her gown. The fingers were firmly netted one over the other and clutched between them was a golden crucifix.

The girl was praying, as one prays who dares not speak.

"O God, who didst hang on this cross — keep now my soul. Condemn it afterwards, but help me to keep it this night. Deliver me — oh, deliver from the power of this man. Help me to lie. By Thy Son's blood, help me to lie well this night."

"Where are the three men from the land of the Scots? Tell me what you see. Tell me all," the marshal commanded, still standing before her in the same posture.

Then the voice of the Lady Sybilla began to speak, low and even, and with that strange halt at the end of the sentences. The Lord of Retz nodded, well pleased when he heard the sound. It was the voice of the seeress. Oftentimes he had heard it before, and it had never deceived him.

"I see a boat on a stormy sea," she said; "there are three men in it. One is great of stature and very strong. The others are young men. They are trying to furl the sail. A gust strikes them. The boat heels and goes over. I see them struggling in the pit of waters. There are cliffs white and crumbling above them. They are calling for help as they cling to the boat. Now there is but one of them left. I see him trying to climb up the slippery rocks. He falls back each time. He is weary with much buffeting. The waves break about him and suck him under. Now I do not see the men any more, but I can hear the broken mast of the boat knocking hollow and dull against the rocks. Some few shreds of the sail are wrapped about it. But the three men are gone."

She ceased suddenly. Her lips stopped their curiously detached utterance.

But under her breath and deep in her soul Sybilla de Thouars was still praying as before. And this which follows was her prayer:

"O God, his devil is surely departed from him. I thank thee, God of truth, for helping me to lie."

"It is well," said Gilles de Retz, standing erect with a satisfied air. "All is well. The three Scots who sought my life are gone to their destruction. Now, Sybilla de Thouars, I bid you look upon John, Duke of Brittany. Tell me what he does and says."

The level, impassive, detached voice began again. The hands clasped the cross of gold more closely under the silk apron.

"I see a room done about with silver scallop shells and white-painted ermines. I see a fair, cunning-faced, soft man. Behind him stands one tall, spare, haggard—"

"Pierre de l'Hopital, President of Brittany—one that hates me," said De Retz, grimly between his teeth. "I will meet my fingers about his dog's throat yet. What of him?"

The Lady Sybilla, without a quiver of her shut eyelids took up the cue.

"He hath his finger on a parchment. He strives to point out something to the fair-haired man, but that other shakes his head and will not agree—"

The marshal suddenly grew intent, and even excited.

"Look closer, Sybilla—look closer. Can you not read that which is written on the parchment? I bid you, by all my power, to read it."

Then the countenance of the Lady Sybilla was altered. Striving and blank failure were alternately expressed upon it.

"I cannot! Oh, I cannot!" she cried.

"By my power, I bid you. By that which I will make you suffer if you fail me, I command you!" cried Gilles de Retz, bending himself towards her and pressing his fingers against her brow so that the points dented her skin.

The tears sprang from underneath the dark lashes which lay so tremulously upon her white cheek.

"You make me do it! It hurts! I cannot!" she said in the pitiful voice of a child.

"Read—or suffer the shame!" cried Gilles de Retz.

"I will—oh, I will! Be not angry," she answered pleadingly.

And underneath the silk the hands were grasped with

a grip like that of a vice upon the **golden cross** she had borrowed from the little Maid **of Galloway**.

"Read me **that which** is written **on the** paper," said the marshal.

The Lady Sybilla began to speak in **a voice so low that** Gilles de Retz had to incline his ear very **close to her** lips to listen.

"Accusation against the great **lord and most** noble seigneur, Gilles de Laval de Retz, Sire de —"

"That is it — go on **after the titles**," said the eager voice of the marshal.

"Accused of having molested **the messengers** of his suzerain, the supreme Duke John **of Brittany**, accused of ill intent against the State; accused of **quartering the** arms-royal upon **his** shield; called to answer **for these offences in the city** of Nantes — and that is all."

She ended abruptly, like one who is tired and desires no more than to sleep.

Gilles de Retz drew a long sigh of relief.

"All is hid," he said; "these things **are less than noth-**ing. What does the Duke?"

"I cannot look again, I am weary," she said.

"Look again!" thundered her taskmaster.

"I see the fair-haired man take the parchment from the hand of the dark, stern man —"

"With whom I will reckon!"

"He tries to tear it in two, but cannot. He throws it angrily in the fire."

"My enemies are destroyed," said Gilles de Retz, "I thank thee, great Barran-Sathanas. Thou hast indeed done that which thou didst promise. Henceforth I am thy servant and thy slave."

So saying, he took a glass of water from the table and dashed it on the face of the Lady Sybilla.

"Awake," he said, "you have done well. Go now and repose that you may again be ready when I have need of you."

A flicker of conscious life appeared under the purple-veined eyelids of the Lady Sybilla. Her long, dark lashes quivered, tried to rise, and again lay still.

The marshal took the illuminated copy of the Evangelists from the table and fanned her with the thin parchment leaves.

"Awake!" he cried harshly and sternly.

The eyes of the girl slowly opened their pupils dark and dilated. She carried her hand to her head, but wearily, as if even that slight movement pained her. The golden cross swung unseen under the silken folds of her apron.

"I am so tired — so tired," the girl murmured to herself as Gilles de Retz assisted her to rise. Then hastily handing her over to Poitou, he bade him conduct her to her own chamber.

But as she went through the door of the marshal's laboratory she looked upon the floor and smiled almost joyously.

"His devil has indeed departed from him," she murmured to herself. "I thank the God of Righteousness who this night hath enabled me to baffle him with a woman's poor wit, and to lie to him that he may be led quick to destruction, and fall himself into the pit which he hath prepared for the feet of the innocent."

CHAPTER LV

THE RED MILK

Darkly and swiftly the autumn night descended upon
Machecoul. In the streets of the little feudal bourg there
were few passers-by, and such as there were clutched their
cloaks tighter round them and scurried on. Or if they
raised their heads, it was only to take a hasty, fearful
glance at the vast bulk of the castle looming imminent
above them.

From a window high in the central keep a red light
streamed out, and when the clouds flew low, strange
dilated shadows were wont to be cast upon the rolling
vapour. Sometimes smoke, acrid and heavy, bellied
forth, and anon wild cries of pain and agony floated
down to silence the footfalls of the home-returning rus-
tics and chill the hearts of burghers trembling in their
beds.

But none dared to question in public the doings of the
great and puissant lord of all the country of Retz. It
fared not well with him who even looked too much at
the things which were done.

The night was yet darker up aloft in the Castle of
Machecoul itself. In the sacristy good Father Blouyn,
with an air of resigned reluctance, was handing over to
an emissary of his master the moulds in which the tall
altar candles for the Chapel of the Holy Innocents were

usually cast and compacted. And as Clerk Henriet
went out with the moulds he took a long look through a
private spy-hole at the lads of the choir who were sitting
in the hall apportioned to their use. They were supposed to be busy with their lessons, and, indeed, a few
were poring over their books with some show of studious
absorption. But for the most part they were playing at
cards and dominos, or, in the absence of the master,
sticking intimate pins and throwing about indiscriminate
ink, according to the immemorial use of the choir-boy.

Clerk Henriet counted them twice over and in especial
looked carefully to see what did the young Scots lad,
who had so mysteriously escaped from the dread room
of his master. Laurence MacKim played X's and O's
upon a board with Blaise Renouf, the precentor's son,
and at some hitch in the game he incontinently clouted
the Frenchman upon the ear. Whereupon ensued trouble
and the spilling of much ink.

Henriet, perfectly satisfied, took up the heavy moulds
and made his way to his lord's chamber, where many
things were used for purposes other than those for which
they had been intended.

Upon the back of his departure came in the Precentor
Renouf, who laid his baton conjointly and freely about
the ears of his son and those of Laurence MacKim.

"Get to your beds both of you, and that supperless,
for uproar and conduct ill becoming two youths who
worship God all day in his sanctuary, and are maintained
at grievous expense by our most devout and worthy lord,
Messire Gilles of Laval and Retz, Seigneur and Lord!"

Laurence, who had of set purpose provoked the quarrel, was slinking away, when the "Psalta" (as the choir-

master is called in lower Brittany) ordered them to
sleep in separate rooms for the better keeping of the
peace.

"And do you, Master Laurence, perform your vigil of
the night upon the pavement of the chapel. For you are
the most rebellious and troublesome of all — indeed, past
bearing. Go! Not a word, sirrah!"

So, much rejoiced in heart that matters had thus fallen
out, Laurence MacKim betook himself to the Chapel of
the Holy Innocents, and was duly locked in by the irate
precentor.

For, upon various occasions, he had watched the Lord
of Retz descend into the chapel by a private staircase
which opened out in an angle behind the altar. He had
also seen Poitou, his confidential body-servant, lock it
after him with a small key of a yellow colour which he
took from his fork pocket.

Now Master Laurence, as may have already been
observed, was (like most of the youthful unordained
clergy) little troubled, at least in minor matters, with
scruples about such slight distinctions as those which
divide *meum* and *tuum*. He found no difficulty therefore in abstracting this key when Poitou was engaged
in attending his master from the chapel, in which
service it was his duty to pass the stalls with open lattice ends of carven work in which sat the elder choir-
boys. Having secured the key, Laurence hid it instantly
beneath the leaden saint on his cap, refastening the long
pin which kept our Lady of Luz in her place through the
fretwork of the little brazen key.

Presently he saw Poitou come back and look carefully here and there upon the floor, but after a while,

not finding anything, he went out again to search else-where.

The idea had come to Laurence that at the head of the stairway from the chapel was the prison chamber of Maud Lindesay and her ward, the little Maid Margaret of Galloway.

He told himself at least that this was his main object, and doubtless he had the matter in his mind. But a far stronger motive was his curiosity and the magic influence of the mysterious and the unknown upon the heart of youth.

More than to deliver Margaret of Galloway, Laurence longed to look again upon the iron altar and to know the truth concerning the strange sacrifices which were consummated there. And he yearned to see again that rough-eared image graven after the fashion of a man.

And the reason was not far to seek.

For if even the worship of the High God, according to the practice of the most enlightened nations, grounds itself upon blood and sacrifice, what wonder if, in the worship of the lords of Hell, the blood of the innocent is an oblation well pleasing and desirable.

Rooted and ineradicable is the desire in man's heart to know good and evil — but particularly evil. And so now Laurence desired to see the sacrifice laid between the horns of the altar and the image above lean over as if to gloat upon the sweet savour of its burning.

Long and carefully Laurence listened before he ventured forth. The Chapel of the Innocents was dark and silent. Only a reflection of the red light which burned in the keep struck through the clerestory upon the great cross which swung above the altar. This, being dis-

2 E

persed like a halo about the sign of Christ's redemption, rendered the corner where was placed the door into the secret stairway light enough to enable the youth to insert therein Poitou's key. The wards were turned with well-accustomed smoothness.

Carefully shutting the door behind him so that if any one chanced to enter the chapel nothing would be observed, Laurence set his feet upon the steps and began his adventure of supreme peril.

It was a narrow staircase, only wide enough indeed for one to ascend or descend at once. And the heart of Laurence sank within him at the thought of meeting the dread Lord of Machecoul face to face in its strait, black spirals.

He accomplished the ascent, however, without incident, and, passing through another low arch, found himself at the end of the passage over against the door with the curious burned hieroglyphics imprinted upon it. There was no light in the corridor, and Laurence eagerly set his hand to the latch. It opened as before and admitted him at a touch.

The temple-like hall was silent and dim. Only an occasional thrill as if of an earthquake passed across it, waving the heavy hangings and bringing a hot breath of some strange heady perfume to the nostrils. Laurence, with a beating heart, ensconced himself in a hidden nook behind the door. The niche was covered by a curtain and furnished with a grooved slab of marble placed there for some purpose he could not fathom.

Yet it was by no means wholly dark. A light shone into the Chapel of Evil from the opposite side, and through it he could discern shadows cast upon the floors

and striding gigantic across the roof, as unseen personages passed the light which streamed into the dusky
temple.

In the gloomiest part of the background, hinted rather
than seen, he could make out the vast dark figure domi-
nating the iron altar.

Then Laurence remembered that the chamber of the
marshal lay on the other side — the room with the im-
mense fireplace which he had once entered and from
which he had barely escaped with his life.

Little by little Laurence raised himself upon the
grooved slab until, standing erect, he could see some
small part of the whitewashed, red-floored chamber he
remembered so well! — only a strip, however, extending
from the door through which he looked to the great
fireplace whereon the heaped wood had already been
kindled.

At first all was confused. Laurence saw Henriet and
Poitou going hastily here and there, as servitors do
who prepare for a great function. Then came a pause,
heavy with doom. On the back of this he heard or
seemed to hear the frightened pleading of a child, the
short, sharp commands of a soldier's voice, a sound as of
a blow stricken, and then again a whimpering hush.
Laurence leaned against the wall with his face in his
hands. He dared not look within. Then he lifted his
head, and lo! in the gloom it seemed as if the huge
image had turned towards him, and in a pleased, confidential way were nodding approval of his presence.

He heard the voice of the Marshal de Retz again —
this time kindly, and even affectionate. Some one was
not to be frightened. Some one was to take a draught

from the goblet and fear nothing. They would not hurt him. They **had but** played with **him.**

Again Henriet and Poitou passed **and repassed,** and once Gilles de Sillé flashed across the interspace handing a broad-edged gleaming knife swiftly and surreptitiously to some one unseen.

Then came a short, sharp cry of agony, a gurgling moan, and black, blank, unutterable horror shut down on **Laurence's spirit.**

He sank down on **his** face behind the door and covered his eyes and ears with his **hands. So** he lay for a space without motion, almost without **sense,** upon the naked grooves of the marble slab. When **he** came to himself, **a** dusky light was diffused through **the** chapel. **As** he looked he saw La Meffraye come to the door and set her **face** within, like some bird of night, hideous and foul. Then she returned and Gilles de Sillé and Clerk Henriet came into the chapel bearing between them a great golden cup, filled (as it seemed by the care with which they carried it) to the very brim with some precious liquid.

To them, all clad in a priest's robe of flame-coloured velvet, succeeded the Lord of Retz himself. He held in his hand like a service-book the great manuscript written in red, which he had been transcribing at Sybilla's entrance, and as he walked he chanted, with a strange intonation, words that thrilled the very soul of the young man listening.

And yet, as Laurence looked forth from his hiding-place, it appeared that the black statue nodded once more to him as one who would say, "Take **note** and remember what thou seest; for one day thy testimony **shall be needful.**"

These were the words he heard in the chanting monotone:

"O great and mighty Barran-Sathanas — my only lord and master, whom with all due observance I do worship, look mercifully upon this the sacrifice of innocent blood; let it be grateful to thee — to whom all evil is as the breath of life!

"Hear us, O Barran-Sathanas! Thou hast been deaf in past days, because we served thee not without drawback or withholding, without sparing and without remorse. Because we hesitated to give thee the best, the delicatest, the most pitiful. But now take this innocentest innocence. Behold I, Gilles de Retz, make to thee the matchless sacrifice of the Red Milk thou lovest.

"The Red Milk I pour for thee. The Red Milk I bring thee. The Red Milk I drink to thee — that thou mayest be pleased to restore vital energy and new youth to my veins, to make me strong as a young man in his strength, and wiser than the wisdom of age. Hear me, O great master of all the evil of the universe, thou equal and coadjutor of the Master of Good, hear and manifest thy so mighty power. Hear me and answer, O Barran-Sathanas!"

Gilles de Retz took the cup from the hands of the servitors. He seemed so weak with his crying that he could hardly hold it between his trembling palms.

He lifted his head and again cried aloud:

"See, I am weak, my Satan — see how I tremble. Strength is departed from me. Youth is dead. Help thy faithful servant, aid him to lift up this precious oblation to thee!"

And as the great dusky image seemed to lean over

him, with a hoarse cry Gilles de Retz raised the cup and
held it high above his head.   As he did so a beam, sudden as lightning, fell upon it, and with a quick, instinctive horror, Laurence saw that it was filled to the
brim with blood fresh and red.

The marshal's voice strengthened.

"It is coming! It is coming! Barran manifests himself! O great lord, to thee I drain this draught!" cried
Gilles de Retz. "The Red Milk, the precious milk of
innocence, to thee I drink it!"

And he set the cup to his lips and drank deep and
long.

*   *   *   *   *   *

"It comes. It fills me. I am strong. O Barran, give
me yet more strength. My limbs revive. My pulse
beats. I am young as when I rode with Dunois. Barran, thou art indeed mightier than God. I will give thee
yet more and more. I swear it. I have kept the best
wine till the last — the death vintage of a great house.
The wine of beauty and brightness — I have kept it for
thee. Halt not to make me stronger! Help me — Barran, help — I fail — !"

His voice had risen higher and higher till it was well
nigh a scream of agony. Strangely too, in spite of the
fictitious youth that glowed in his veins and coloured his
cheek, it sounded like a senile shriek.

But all suddenly, at the very height of his exaltation,
the cup from which he had drunk slipped from his hand
and rolled upon the tesselated pavement of the temple,
staining it in gouts and vivid blotches of crimson.

"Hasten, ere I lose the power — I feel it checked.
Poitou, De Sillé, Henriet, go bring hither from the White

Tower the Scottish maids. Run, dogs — or you die! Quick, Henriet! Good De Sillé, quick! Fail not your master now! It ebbs, it weakens — and it was so near completion. Stay, O Barran, till I finish the sacrifice, and here at thy feet offer up to thee the richest, and the fairest, and the noblest! Bring hither the maidens! I tell you, bring them quickly!"

And the terrible Lord of Retz, exhausted with his own fury, cast himself at the feet of the gigantic image, which, bending over him, seemed with the same grimace sardonically to mock alike his exaltation and his downfall.

But Laurence heard no more. For sense and feeling had wholly departed from him, and he lay as one dead behind the door of the temple of Barran-Sathanas, Lord of Evil, in the thrice-abhorrent Castle of Machecoul.

CHAPTER LVI

THE SHADOW BEHIND THE THRONE

WITHIN the grim walls of Black Angers Duke John of Brittany and reigning sovereign of western France was holding his court. The city and fortress did not properly, of right and parchment holding, appertain to him. But he had occupied it during the recent troubles with the English, and his loving cousin and nominal suzerain Charles the Seventh of France had not yet been strong enough to make him render it up again.

The Duke sat in the central tower of the fortress of Black Angers, that which looks between the high flanking turrets of the mighty enceinte of walls. He wriggled discontentedly in his chair and grumbled under his breath.

At his shoulder, tall, gaunt, angular, with lantern jaws and a mouth like a wolf trap, deep-set eyes that flamed under bushy eyebrows, stood Pierre de l'Hopital, the true master of Brittany.

"I tell you I will go to the tennis-courts — the three Scots must wait audience till to-morrow. What errand can they have with me — some rascals whom Charles will not pay now that his job is done? They come to take service doubtless. A beggarly lot are all such outland varlets, but brave — yes, excellent soldiers are the Scots, so long as they are well fed, that is."

"Nay, my Lord Duke," said Pierre de l'Hopital, standing up tall and sombre, his long black gown accentuating the peculiarities of his figure. "It were almost necessary to see these men now and hear what they have to say. I myself have seen them and judge it to be so."

John of Brittany threw down the little sceptre, fashioned in imitation of that made for the King of France, with which he had been toying. The action was that of a pettish child.

"Oh," he cried, "if you have decided, there remains nothing for me but to obey!"

"I thank your Excellency for your gracious readiness to grant the men an interview," said Pierre de l'Hopital, having regard to the essential matter and disregarding the unessential manner.

Duke John sat glooming and kicking his feet to and fro on the raised dais, while behind his chair, impassive as the Grand Inquisitor himself, Pierre de l'Hopital, President of Brittany, lifted a hand to an unseen servitor; and in a few moments the three Scots were ushered into the ducal presence.

The Lord James in virtue of his quality stood a little in front, not by his own will or desire, but because Sholto and his father had so placed themselves that the young noble should have his own rightful precedence. For as to these things all Scots are careful by nature.

Duke John continued to keep his eyes averted from the men who sought his presence. He teased a little lop-eared spaniel, and nipped it till it yelped. But the President of Brittany never took his eyes off the strangers, examining them with a bold, keen, remorseless glance, in which, however, there was neither evil nor

the tolerance of it.   Not a man to make himself greatly
beloved, this Pierre de l'Hopital.

And little he cared whether or no.   In Brittany men
did his will.   That was enough.

James Douglas was nettled at the inattention of the
Duke.   He was of that large and sanguine nature which
is at once easily touched by any discourtesy and very
quick to resent it.

"My Lord of Brittany," he began in a loud clear
voice, and in his usual immaculate French, "I claim
your attention for a little.   I come to lay before you
that which touches your kin and kingdom."

Duke John continued to play with the lap-dog, and in
addition he formed his mouth to whistle.   But he never
whistled.

"His Grace of Brittany will now give you his undivided attention," said the President from behind, without moving a muscle either of his body or of his face,
save those necessary to propel the words from his vocal
cords.

The brow of Duke John flushed with anger, but he did
not disobey.   He raised his head and gazed straight at
the three men, fixing his eyes, however, with a studied
discourtesy upon Sholto instead of upon their natural
leader and spokesman.

Behind his chair Pierre de l'Hopital let his deep inscrutable eye droop once upon his master, and his spare
and sinewy wrists twitched as he held his arms by his
side.   He seemed upon the point of dealing ducal dignity a box on the ear both sound and improving.

"I am the Lord James of Douglas and Avondale,"
said the leader of the Scots with grave dignity, "and

I had three years ago the honour of breaking a lance with you in the tilt-yard of Poitiers, when in that town your Grace met with the King of France and the Duke of Burgundy."

At this John of Brittany looked up quickly.

"I do not remember you," he said, "and I never forget faces. Even Pierre will grant me that."

"Your Grace may possibly remember, then, the dint in your shoulder that you got from the point of a spear, caused by the breaking of the links of your shoulder-piece."

A light kindled in the Duke's eyes.

"What," he cried, "you are the young Scot who fought so well and kept his shield up day by day over the door of a common sergeant's tent, having no pavilion of his own, till it was all over dints like an alehouse tankard?"

"As were also the knights who dinted it," grimly commented Pierre de l'Hopital.

The Lord James of Avondale bowed.

"I am that knight," he said quietly and with gravity.

"But," cried the Duke, "I knew not then that you were of Douglas. That is a great name in Poitiers, and had we known your race and quality we had not been so ready with our shield-rapping."

"At that time," said James Douglas, "I had not the right to add 'of Douglas' to my titles. But during this year my father hath succeeded to the Earldom and estates."

"What—then is your father Duke of Touraine?" cried the Duke of Brittany, much astonished.

"Nay, my lord," said James Douglas, with some little

bitterness. "The King of France hath caused that to revert to himself by the success which attended a certain mission executed for him in Scotland by his Chamberlain, the Marshal de Retz, concerning whom we have come from far to speak with you."

"Ah, my cousin Gilles!" cried Duke John. "He is not a beauty to look at, but he is a brave man, our Gilles. I heard he had gone to Scotland. I wonder if he contrived to make himself as popular in your land as he has done in ours."

With a certain grave severity to which Pierre de l'Hopital nodded approval, the Lord James replied: "At the instigation of the King of France and Louis the Dauphin he succeeded in murdering my two cousins William and David of Douglas, and in carrying over hither with him to his own country their only sister, the little Countess of Galloway — thus rooting out the greatest house in Scotland to the hurt of the whole realm."

"But to your profit, my Lord James of Avondale," commented the hollow voice of Pierre de l'Hopital, speaking over his master's head.

The face of James Douglas flushed quickly.

"No, messire," he answered with a swift heat. "Not to my profit — to my infinite loss. For I loved my cousin. I honoured him, and for his sake would have fought to the death. For his sake have I renounced my own father that begat me. And for his sake I stand here to ask for justice to the little maiden, the last of his race, to whom by right belongs the fairest province of his dominions. No, messire, you are wrong. In all this have I had no profit but only infinite hurt."

Pierre de l'Hopital bowed low. There was a pleased look on his face that almost amounted to a smile.

"I crave your pardon, my lord," he said; "that is well said indeed, and he is a gentleman who speaks it."

"Aye, it is indeed well said, and he had you shrewdly on the hip that time, Pierre," cried Duke John. "I wish he could teach me thus cleverly to answer you when you croak."

"If you had as good a cause, my lord," said the President of Brittany to the Duke, "it were not difficult to answer me as sharply. But we are keeping these gentlemen from declaring the purpose of their journey hither."

The Lord James waited for no further invitation.

"I come," he said boldly, holding a parchment in his hand, the same he had received from the Lady Sybilla, "to denounce Gilles de Retz and to accuse him of many cruel and unrighteous acts such as have never been done in any kingdom. I accuse him of the murder of over four hundred children of all ages and both sexes in circumstances of unparalleled barbarity. I am ready to lead you to the places where lie their bodies, some of them burned and their ashes cast into the ditch, others charred and thrown into unused towers. I have here names, instances, evidence enough to taint and condemn a hundred monsters such as Gilles de Retz."

"Ah, give me the paper," came the raucous voice of the President of Brittany, as he reached a bony hand over his master's shoulder to seize it.

The Lord James advanced, and giving it to him said, "Messire, I would have you know that a copy of this is already in the hands of a trusty person in each of the towns and villages which are named here, and from which children have been led to cruel death by him whom I have accused, Gilles de Retz, Marshal of France."

The President of Brittany nodded as he almost snatched the paper in his eagerness to peruse it.

"The point is cleverly taken," he said, "as justly indeed as if you knew my Lord of Brittany as well as, for instance, I know him."

The Duke was obviously discomfited. He shuffled his feet more than ever on the dais and combed his straggling fair beard with soft, white, tapering fingers.

"This is wild and wholly absurd," he said, without however looking at James Douglas; "our cousin Gilles is in ill odour with the commonalty. He is a philosopher and makes smells with bottles. But there is neither harm nor witchcraft in it. He is only trying to discover the elixir of life. So the silly folk think him a wizard. I know him better. He is a brave soldier and my good cousin. I will not have him molested."

"My lord speaks of kinship," grated the voice of Pierre de l'Hopital. "Here are the names of four hundred fathers and mothers who have also a claim to be heard on that subject, and whose voices, if I judge right, are being heard at this moment around the Castles of Machecoul, Tiffauges, Champtocé, and Pouzages. I wot there is now a crowd of a thousand men pouring through the passages of the Hotel de Suze in your Grace's own ducal city of Nantes. And if there goes a bruit abroad, that your Highness is protecting this monster whom the people hate, and the evidences of whose horrid cruelty are by this time in their hands — well, your Grace knows the Bretons as well as I. They will make

one end of Gilles de Retz and of his cousin John, Duke
of Brittany."

"Think you so — think you so truly, Pierre?" cried
the unhappy reigning prince; "I would not screen him if
this be true.   But the King — what of the King?   They
say he hath promised him support with arms and men
for recovering to him and to Louis the Dauphin the
Duchy of Touraine."

"And think you, my lord, that the Dauphin will keep
his promise, if we show him good cause why he should
fare better by breaking it?" suggested Pierre de l'Hopital, with the grim irony which had become habitual to
him.

John of Brittany paused irresolute.

"Besides which," continued James Douglas, "I may
add that this paper is already in the hands of the Car-
dinal Bishop of Nantes, and if your Grace will not move
in the matter, his Eminence has promised to see justice
done."

"The hireling — the popular mouther after favour! I
know him," cried Duke John, angrily. "What accursed
demon sent you to him?   In this, as in other matters,
he will strive to oust me from the hearts of the folk of
Brittany.   He will be the people's advocate and will
gain great honour from this trial, will he? We shall
see. Ho! guards there! Turn out. Summon those that
are asleep. Let the full muster be called. I will lead
you to Machecoul myself. And these gentlemen shall
march with us.   But by Heaven and the bones of Saint
Anne of Auray, if in one jot they shall fail to substanti-
ate against Gilles de Retz those things which they have
testified, they shall die by the rack, and by the cord, and

by disembowelling, and by fire. So swear I, Duke John of Brittany."

"It is good," said James Douglas. And "It is good," accorded also Malise and Sholto MacKim.

"But before any dies in Brittany, Gilles de Retz or another, *I* will judge the case," commented Pierre de l'Hopital, President of Justice and Grand Councillor of the reigning sovereign.

CHAPTER LVII

THROUGHOUT La Vendée and all the country of Retz had run a terrible rumour. " The Marshal de Retz is the murderer of our children. He has a thousand bodies in the vaults of his castles. The Duke of Brittany has given orders that they shall be searched. His soldiers are forsaking him. The names of the dead have been written in black and white, and are in the hands of the headmen of the villages. Hasten — it is the hour of vengeance! Let us overwhelm him! Rise up and let us seek our lost ones, even if we find no more than their bones! "

And terrible as had been the gathering of the were-wolves in the dark forests around Machecoul upon the night of the fight by the hollow tree, far more threatening and terrible was the uprising of the angry commons.

In whole villages there was not a man left, and mothers too marched in that muster armed with choppers and kitchen knives, wild eyed and angry hearted as lionesses robbed of their cubs. From the deep glens and deeper woods of the country of Retz they poured. They disgorged from the caves of the earth whither the greed and rapacity of their terrible lord had driven them.

Schoolmasters were there with the elder of their pu-

2 F 433

pils. For many of the vanished children had disappeared
on their way to school, and these men were in danger
of losing both their credit and occupation.

Towards Tiffauges, Champtocé, Machecoul, the angry
populace, long repressed, surged tumultuously, and with
them, much wondering at their orders, went the soldiers
of the Duke.

But it is with the columns that concentrated upon
Machecoul that we have chiefly to do. Our three Scots
accompanied these, and here, too, marched John of
Brittany himself with his Councillor Pierre de l'Hopital
by his side.

Night fell as they journeyed on, ever joined by fresh
contingents from all the country round. In the van
pressed forward the folk of Saint Philbert, warm from
the utter destruction of the house of the witch woman,
La Meffraye, so that not one stone was left upon another.
Guided by these the Duke and his party made their way
easily through the forest, even in the darkness of the
night. And as they passed hamlet or cottage ever and
anon some frenzied mother would rush upon them and
fall on her knees before the Duke, praying him to look
well for her darling, and bringing mayhap some pitiful
shred of clothing or lock of hair by which the searchers
might identify the lost innocent.

As they went forward the soldiers pricked on ahead,
and caused the people to fall to the rear, lest any fore-
knowledge of their purpose might reach the wizard and
warn him to escape.

The woods of Machecoul were dark and silent that
night. Not the howl of a questing wolf was heard.
Truly the marshal's demons had forsaken him, or may-

hap they were all busy at that last carnival in the keep
of the Castle of Machecoul.

As the storming party approached nearer, and while
yet they were several miles distant, they became aware of
a great red light that gleamed forth above them. They
could not see whence it came, but the peasants of Saint
Philbert with affrighted glances told how it beaconed
only after the disappearance of some little one from
their homes, what strange cries were heard ringing out
from that lofty tower, and how for days after the smoke
of a great burning would hang about the gloomy turrets
of devil-haunted Machecoul.

Fiercer and ever fiercer shone the red glare, and the
faces of the soldiers were lit up so that Pierre de l'Hopital ordered them to keep to the more gloomy arcades of
the forest.

Then by midnight the cordon was drawn so closely
that none might pass in or out. And behind the soldiery the common folk lay crouched, anger in their hearts,
and their eyes turned towards the open windows in the
keep of Machecoul, from which flared the red light of
bale.

Then, covering their lanterns, the three Scots, with
Duke John, Pierre de l'Hopital, and a score of officers,
stole silently towards the tower by which the Lady
Sybilla had promised that an entrance should be gained
to the Castle of Machecoul.

It was situated at the western corner towards the
south, and was joined to its fellows at the corresponding
angles of the fortress by galleried walls of great height.
Ten feet above the ground was a little door of embossed
iron, but ordinarily no steps led to it when the castle

was in a state of defence. Yet when Sholto adventured into the angle of the wall, he stumbled upon a ladder that leaned against the little landing-ledge, above which was the entrance denoted on the plan.

Sholto ascended first, being the lightest and most agile of all. As he had expected, he found the door unlocked and a narrow passage leading within the tower. He lay a moment and listened, and then, being certain there was a light and the sounds of labour within, he crawled back to the ladder head, and whispered to the Lord James an order for total silence.

Whereupon, Sholto holding the ladder at the top, Duke John and his Councillor mounted like shadows, and with Malise and James Douglas to guard them they were presently crouched in the passage with the door shut behind them, and the officers keeping watch at the foot of the tower without.

These five listened to the sounds of busy picks within the tower. They could hear the ring of iron on stones and the panting of men engaged in severe toil.

"The marshal is preparing for flight," whispered the Duke, exultantly. "He is interring his treasures. He has been warned. But we will be overspeedy for him."

And he chuckled in his satisfaction so loudly that Malise, using no ceremony with Duke or varlet at such a season, put his hand over his mouth.

Then one by one they crawled along the narrow passage on their hands and knees, and presently from a little balcony, plastered like a swallow's nest on the inner wall of the tower, they found themselves looking down upon a strange scene.

A flight of steps led slantwise to the bottom, and at

the foot of the tower, stripped to the waist, they beheld
two men busily filling great sacks with a curious cargo.

The turret had never been finished. It contained
nothing whatever except the staircase. So far as Sholto
could see there was not even a window anywhere. The
door by which they had entered and another which evidently led into the interior of the castle were its only
outlets. The earth at the bottom had remained as it
had been left by the builders, who surely must have
thought that no madder architectural freak was ever
planned than this shut tower of the Castle of Machecoul
with its blank walls and sordid accoutrement.

But most strange of all, the original earth had been
covered to the depth of a foot or more with dark objects,
the true significance of which did not appear from the
distance of the little gallery where the party of five had
stationed themselves.

The two men at work below had brought torches with
them, which were fastened to the walls by iron spikes.
The smoke from these hung in heavy masses about the
tower, still further diminishing the clearness with which
the watchers aloft could observe what went on below.

One of the workmen was tall and spare, with the
forward thrust of head and neck seen in vultures and
other unclean birds. The other, who held the sacks
while his companion shovelled, was on the contrary
stout and short, of a notably jovial, rubicund countenance, in habit like the hostler of an inn, or perhaps
a well-to-do carrier upon the roads.

The two worked without speaking, as if the task
were distasteful. When one sack was full, both would
seize their picks and dig furiously at the floor of the

tower. Then when they had enough loosened, they would fall to shovelling the curiously shaped objects into the sacks again.

As Sholto looked down he heard a hissing whisper at his ear.

"These be Blanchet the sorcerer and Robin Romulart. But last week they took notice of my little Jean and praised him for a noble boy."

Sholto turned round, and there at his elbow, having followed them in spite of all orders and precautions, he discerned the woodman Louis Verger, whose little son had been carried off by the grey she-wolf.

Sholto motioned him back, and at a sign from the Duke, his father and he began to descend. So silently did they make their way down the stone steps, and so intent were the men upon their work, that in a minute after leaving the little gallery Malise stood behind the taller and Sholto stole like a shadow along the wall nearer to the little rotund man who had been called Robin Romulart.

The Duke held up his hand. Sholto and Malise each took their man about the throat with their left arms and pulled them backward, at the same time covering their mouths with their right hands. Blanchet never moved in the strong arms of Malise. But Robin, whose rotund figure concealed his great muscular development, might have escaped from Sholto had not the woodman Verger flung himself at the little man's throat and brought him to the ground. Then the Duke and the others descended, and as they did so they became conscious of a choking mephitic vapour which clung dank and heavy to the lower courses of the tower.

Suddenly a wild cry made all shiver. It came from

Louis Verger, who had sprung upon something that lay tossed aside in a corner.

"Silence, man—on your life! Silence!" hissed Pierre de l'Hopital. "Whatever you have found, think only of revenge and help us to it!"

"I have found him. He is dead! The fiends! The fiends!" sobbed Louis Verger, covering a small partially charred object with the curtmantle of which he had rapidly divested himself for the purpose.

Then it came upon those who stood on the floor of the tower that they were in the marshal's main charnel-house. These vague forms, mostly charred like half-burned wood, these scraps of white bone, these little crushed skulls, were all that remained of the innocent children who, in the freshness of their youth and beauty, had been seduced into the fatal Castle of Machecoul.

And what wonder that an appalling terror sat on the heart and mastered the soul of Sholto MacKim. For how did he know that he was not treading under foot at each step the calcined fragments of the fair body of Maud Lindesay?

Twenty sacks had been filled ready for transport, and as many more lay folded and empty in a heap in a corner. The marshal, uneasy perhaps as to the suspicions against him, and anxious to remove evidence from the precincts of his castle, had ordered this Tower of Death to be cleared. But truly his devil had once more forsaken him. The order had been given a day too late.

"God's grace, I stifle. Let us get out of this, and seize the murderer," quoth Duke John, making his way towards the door.

"Wait a moment," said Pierre de l'Hopital, "we must consider. We cannot let the commons see this or they will sack the castle from foundation to roof tree, and slay the innocent with the guilty. We must seize and hold for fair trial all who are found within. *And I, Pierre de l'Hopital, will try them!*"

"What then do you propose?" said the Duke, getting as near the door as possible.

"Let us bring in hither the officers and what soldiers you can trust — that is not my business," answered the President. "Then we will go through the castle, and after we have secured the prisoners and made sure of sufficient pieces of justificative evidence, of which we have infinite supply in these sacks, we may e'en permit the people to work their will."

As it was Sholto who had first entered, so it was Sholto who first left the Tower of Death. He it was also who, at the head of a strong band, surprised the marshal's sleepy inner guard, and helped to bind them with his own hands. It was Sholto who, at the foot of the stairs of the great keep, stood listening that he might know the right moment to lead the besiegers upward.

But even as he stood thus, down the stairway there came pealing a terrible cry, the shriek of a woman in the final agony, shrill, desperate, unavailing.

And at the sound Sholto flew up the stone steps in the direction of the cry, not knowing what he did, save that he went to kill.

And scarce a foot behind him followed the woodman, Louis Verger, and as they fled upward the red gloom grew brighter till they seemed to be rushing headlong into a furnace mouth.

CHAPTER LVIII

So at the command of the Marshal de Retz they sent to bring forth Margaret of Douglas and Maud Lindesay out of the White Tower, where they had been abiding. Margaret had gone to bed, and, as was her custom, Maud Lindesay sat awhile by her side. For so far as they could they kept to the good and kindly traditions of Castle Thrieve. It seemed somehow to bring them nearer home in that horrible place where they were doomed to abide.

"Give me your hand, Maud, and tell on," said little Margaret, nestling closer to her friend, and laying her head against her arm as she leaned on the low bedstead beside her.

Margaret was gowned in a white linen night-rail, made long ago for the marshal's daughter, little Marie de Retz, in the brighter days before the setting up of the iron altar. Catherine, his deserted wife, had been kind to the girls at Pouzages, and had given to both of them such articles of garmenture as they were sorely in need of.

"Tell on — haste you," commanded little Margaret, with the imperiousness of loving childhood, nestling yet closer as she spoke. "It helps me to forget. I can almost think when you are speaking that we are again

441

at Thrieve, and that if we looked out at the window we
should see the Dee running by and Screet and Ben Gairn
—and hear Sholto MacKim drilling his men out in the
courtyard. Why, Maudie, what is the matter? I did
not mean to make you cry. But it is all so sweet to
think upon in this place. Oh, Maudie, Maudie, what
would you give to hear a whaup whistle?"

Then drawing herself into a sitting posture, with her
hands about Maud's neck, she took a kerchief from under
the pillow and dried her friend's tears, murmuring the
while, "Ah, do not cry, Maud, my vision will yet come
true, and you shall indeed see Ben Gairn and Thrieve
—and everything. I was dreaming about it last night.
Shall I tell you about it, sweet Maud?"

Maud Lindesay did not reply, not having recovered
power over her voice. So the little Maid of Galloway
went on unbidden.

"Yes, I dreamed a glad dream yester-even. Shall I
tell it you all and all? I will — though you can tell
stories far better than I.

"Methought that I and you—I mean, dear Maud,
you and I, were sitting together in the gloaming at the
door of a little house up on the edges of the moorland,
where the heather is prettiest, and reddest, and longest.
And we were happy. We were waiting for some one. I
shall not tell you who, Maudie, but if you are good, and
stop crying, you can guess. And there was a ring on
your finger, Maud. No, not like the old ones — not
a pretty ring like those in your box, yet you loved it
more than them all, and never stopped turning it about
between your finger and thumb.

"They had let me come up to stay with you, and the

men who had accompanied me were drinking in the clachan. As we sat I seemed to hear their loud chorus, sounding up from the change-house.

"And you listened and said: 'I wish he would come. He is very long. It is always long when he is away.' But you never said who it was that was long away. And I shall not tell you, though I know. Perhaps it was old Jock Lacklands, who used to be captain of the guard, and perhaps grouting Peter, from the gate-house by the ford. But somehow I do not think so. Ah, that is better! Now do not cry again. But listen, else I will not tell you any more, but go off to sleep instead.

"Perhaps you do not want to hear the rest. Yet — it was such a pretty dream, and of good omen.

"You *do* want to hear? Well, then, be good!

"As we sat there we could hear the bumblebees scurrying home, and every now and then one of the big boom-beetles would sail whirring past us. We could hear the sheep crying below in the little green meadows so lonesomely, and the snipe bleating an answer away up in the sky above their heads, and you said, '*It is all so empty, wanting him!*'

"Then the maids brought in the cows, and milked them standing at the gable end, and we could smell the smell of their breath, sweet like the scent of the flowers they had been eating all day long. Then, after a while, they were driven out of the yard again, and went in a string, one after the other, back to their pastures, doucely and sedately, just like folk going to holy kirk on Sabbath days when it is summer time in Galloway.

"Then you said, 'I am weary of waiting for him!' And I answered, 'Why, — he has not been gone more than a day. Sometimes I do not see him for weeks, and *I* never fret like that!'

"Then you answered (it has all come so clear into my mind), 'Some day you will know, little one!' And you patted me on the head, and went to the house end to look into the sunset. You looked many minutes under your hand, and when you came back you said, as if you had never said it before, 'He is long a-coming! I wonder what can be keeping him.'

"Then the maidens told us that the supper was ready to put on the table, whereat you scolded them, telling them that it was too early, and that they must keep it hot against their master's coming. And to me you said, 'You are not hungry, are you?' And I answered, 'No,' though I was indeed very hungry — (in my dream, that is). Then you said again, sighing: 'It is strange that he should not come home! I cannot eat till he comes! Perhaps he has fallen into a ditch, or some eagle may have pecked out his eyes!'

"Then all the while it grew darker, and still no one came. Whereat you cried a little softly, and said: 'He might have come — I know right well he could have been here by this time if he had tried. But he does not love me any more.' And you were patting the ground with your foot as you used to do when — well, when he went away from Thrieve without coming out upon the leads to say 'Good-night.' Then, all at once, there was a noise of quick feet brushing eagerly through the heather, and some one (no, not Landless Jock) leaped the wall and caught me — *me* — in his arms."

"No, it was not you whom he caught in his arms!" cried Maud Lindesay, indignantly, and then stopped,

abashed at her own folly. But the little maid laughed
merrily.

"Aha!" she said, "*I* caught you that time in my trap.
You know who it was in my dream, though I have never
told you, nor so much as hinted.

"And he asked if you had missed him, and you made
a sign for me not to speak, just as you used to do
at Castle Thrieve, and answered, 'No, not a little bit!
Margaret and I were quite happy. We hoped you would
not come back at all this night, for then we could have
slept together.'"

Maud Lindesay drew a long, soft breath, and looked
out of the window of the White Tower into the dark.

"That is a sweet dream," she murmured. "Ah, would
that it were true, and that Sholto — !"

She broke off short again, for the maid clapped her
hands gleefully. "You said it! You said it!" she
cried. "You called him Sholto. Now I know; and I
am so glad, for he is nearly as good to play with as you.
And I shall not mind him a bit."

Little Margaret stopped short in her turn, seeing something in her friend's face.

"Why are you suddenly grown so sad, Maudie?" she
asked.

"It came upon me, dear Margaret," said Maud, "how
that we are but two helpless maids in a dreadful place
without a friend. Let us say a prayer to God to keep
us!"

Then Margaret Douglas turned and knelt with her
face to the pillow and her small hands clasped in front
of her.

"Give me your silver cross," she said, "I lent the

little gold one that was William's to the Lady Sybilla,
and she hath not returned it me again."

Maud gave her the cross and she took it and held
it in the palm of her hand looking long at it.   Then
she repeated one by one the children's orisons she had
been taught, and after that she made a little prayer of
her own.   This is the prayer.

"Lord of mercy, be good to two maids who are lonely
and weak, and shut up in this place of evil men.   Keep
our lives and our souls, and also our bodies from harm.
Make us not afraid of the dark or of the devil.   For
Thou art the stronger.   And do not forget to be near
us this night, for we have no other friend and sorely do
we need one to love and deliver us.   Amen."

It was true.   More bitterly than any two in the whole
world, these maidens needed a friend at that moment.
For scarcely had the childish accents been lost in the
night silence, when the outer door of the White Tower
was thrown open to the wall, and on the steps of the
turret stair they heard the noise of men coming upwards
to their prison-room.

But first, though the inner door of their chamber
was locked within, the bolts glided back apparently of
their own accord.   It opened, and the hideous face of La
Meffraye looked in upon them with a cackle of fiendish
laughter.

"Come, sweet maidens," she cried gleefully, as the
frightened girls clasped each other closer upon the bed,
"come away.   The Marshal de Retz calls for you.   He
hath need of your beauty to grace his feast.   The lights
of the banquet burn in his hall.   See the fire of burning
shine out upon the night.   The very trees are red with

it. The skies are red. All is red. Come — up — make yourselves fair for the eyes of the great lord to behold!"

Then behind La Meffraye entered Gilles de Sillé and Poitou, the marshal's servants.

"Make ready in haste — you are both to go instantly before my lord, who abides your coming!" said Gilles de Sillé. "Poitou and I will abide without the door, and La Meffraye here shall be your tirewoman and see that you have that which you need. But hasten, for my lord is instant and cannot be kept waiting!"

*   *   *   *   *   *

So they brought the Scottish maidens down from the White Tower into the night. They walked hand in hand. Their steps did not falter, and, as they went, they prayed to God to keep them from the dangers of the place. Astarte, the she-wolf, who must have kept guard beneath, stalked before them, and behind them they seemed to hear the hobbling crutch and cackling laughter of La Meffraye.

Across the wide courtyard of Machecoul they went. It also was filled with the reflection of the red tide of light which ebbed and flowed, waxing and waning above. Saving for that window the whole castle was wrapped in gloom and silence, and if there were any awake within the precincts they knew better than to spy upon the midnight doings of their dread lord.

The little party passed up the great staircase of the keep and presently halted before the inscribed wooden door by which Laurence had entered the Temple of Evil.

As Gilles de Sillé opened it for the maids to precede him, the skirt of Maud Lindesay's robe, blown back by the draught of the chamber, fluttered against the cheek

of Laurence MacKim as he lay on his face in the niche
of the wall. At the light touch he came to himself, and
looked about with a strange and instant change in all the
affections and movements of his heart.

With the coming in of the maidens, fear seemed utterly to forsake him. A clarity of purpose, an alertness
of brain, a strength of heart unknown before, took the
place of the trembling bath of horror in which he had
swooned away.

It was like the sudden appearance of two white angels
walking fearless and unscathed through the grim dominions of the Lords of Hell.

Incarnate Good had somehow entered the house of the
Demon, though it was in the slender periphery of two
maidens' bodies, and evil, strong and resistless before,
seemed in the moment to lose half its power.

IT WAS LIKE THE SUDDEN APPEARANCE OF TWO WHITE ANGELS WALK-
ING FEARLESS AND UNSCATHED THROUGH THE GRIM DOMINIONS OF
THE LORDS OF HELL.

CHAPTER LIX

AND as Laurence MacKim, crouched in the dim obscurity of the curtained doorway, looked forth, this is what he saw.

Maud Lindesay and Margaret Douglas advanced into the centre of the temple where was a slab of white marble let into the floor. As if by instinct the two maids stopped upon it, standing hand in hand before the iron altar and the vast shadowy image which gloomed above and appeared to reach forward in act to clutch them. After the first check in his hideous incantations, Gilles de Retz had returned to his own chamber, in which, after his entrance, the light gleamed brighter and more fiercely red than ever. As the maidens stood on the marble square La Meffraye went to the door and called certain words within, conveying some message which Laurence could not hear.

Then with an assured carriage and haughty stride came forth the marshal, his grey hair and blue-black beard in strong contrast with his haggard corpse-pale face, from which the momentary glow of youth half-restored had already faded, as fades a footprint upon wet sand.

Gilles de Sillé and Poitou bowed silently before him as men who have done their commission, and who retire to await further orders. But La Meffraye, once more apparent, stood her ground.

"Here are the dainty maids from the far land; no beggars' brats are they. No strays and pickings from the streets. No, nor yet silly village innocents who follow La Meffraye from the play-fields through the woodlands to the Paradise of our Lord Gilles! Hasten not the joy! Let these pearls of youth and beauteousness die indeed, but let them die slowly and deliciously. And in the last blood of an ancient race let our master bathe and find the new life he seeks. Hear us, O Barran-Sathanas, and grant our prayer!"

Then La Meffraye approached the maids and would have touched the dress of the little Margaret, as if to order it more daintily for the pleasing of her master's eye. But Maud Lindesay thrust her aside like an unclean thing.

Whereat La Meffraye laughed till her rusty black cloak quivered and rustled from hood to hem.

"Ah, my proud lady," she croaked, "in a little, in a very little, you too will be calling upon La Meffraye to save you, to pity you. But I, La Meffraye, will gloat over each drop of blood that distils from your fair neck. Aha, you shall change your tone when at the white throat-apple which your sweetheart would have loved to kiss, you feel the bite of the sharp slow knife. Then you will not thrust aside La Meffraye. Then you shall cry and none shall pity. Then she will spurn you from her knees."

"Out!" said Gilles de Retz, briefly, and like some inferior imping devilkin before the great Master of Evil, La Meffraye retreated hobbling to the doorway of the marshal's chamber, where she crouched nodding and chuckling, mumbling inaudible words, and mingling them ever with her dry cackling laughter.

Gilles de Retz stopped at the corner of the platform and looked long at Maud and Margaret where they stood on the great central square of marble. It was the Maid who spoke first.

"Dear Messire," she said sweetly and almost confidently, "you have a little girl of your own. I know, for I have played with her. I love her. Therefore you will not hurt us. I am sure you will not hurt us. You are going to send us back in a ship to our own country, because it is lonely here where Maud and I know no one!"

The marshal smiled upon her his inhuman inscrutable smile. He leaned against a pillar of strangely twisted design, and contemplated the two victims at his ease.

"Life is sweet to you, is it not?" he said at last; "you are truly happy, being young, and so have no need to be made young again."

"Oh, but I am very old," cried the Maid, gaining some confidence from the quiet of his voice, "I am nearly eight years old. And our Maudie here, she is — oh, a dreadful age! She is very, very old!"

"You would not like to die?" suggested Gilles de Retz, with a certain soft insinuation.

"Oh, no," said Margaret Douglas, "I am going to live long and long — till every one in the world loves me. I am going to help every one to get what he most desires. And you know I can, for I shall be very rich. And if what they say is true, and I am Princess of Galloway, I shall marry and be a very great lady. But I shall never marry any one who is not a Douglas."

The marshal nodded.

" I do not think that you shall marry any one who is not a Douglas!" he said, with a certain grave and not discourteous irony in his tones.

" Yes," the little Maid went on. She had lost all fear in the very act of speech. " Yes, and Maud, she is going to marry Sholto — and they will be very happy, for they love each other so. I know it, for she told me to-night just before you sent for us to come to your feast. That was kind of you to remember us, though it was past bed-time. But now, good marshal, you will send us back, will you not? Now, look kind to-night. You will be glad afterwards that you were good to two maids who never harmed you, but are ready to love you if you prove kind to them."

" Hush, Margaret," said Maud Lindesay. " It is use-less to speak such words to such a man."

The Marshal de Retz turned sharply to her.

" Ah," he said, with a curious bite in his speech, " then, my young lady, you would not love me, even if I were to let you go!"

" I should hate and abominate you for ever and ever, even if you helped me into Paradise!" quoth Maud Lindesay, giving him defiance in a full eye-volley.

" So," he said calmly, " I am indeed likely to help you into Paradise this very night. That is, unless Saint Peter of the Keys makes up his mind that so outspoken and tricksome a maid had best take a few thousand years of purgatory — as it were on her way upwards, *en passant.*"

A sudden lowering passion at this point altered his countenance.

" No," he thundered, standing up erect from the pillar

against which he had been leaning, and his whole voice and bearing changing past description, " it is enough — listen! I will be brief with you. I have brought both of you here that you may die. I cannot expect of you that you will understand or appreciate my motives, which are indeed above the knowledge of children. This is a temple to a Great God, and he demands the sacrifice of the noblest and most innocent blood. I do you the honour to believe that it is here to my hand. Also, your deaths will cause a number of people both in Scotland and elsewhere to sit easier in their seats. Lastly, I had sworn that you should die if your friends from Scotland came to trouble me. They have come, and Gilles de Retz keeps his word — as doth the Master whom he serveth!"

He bowed in the direction of the vast shadowy figure, which to Laurence's eye appeared to turn towards his niche with a leer, as if to say, "Listen to him. What a fool he is!"

The maids stood silent, not comprehending aught save that they were to die. Then suddenly Gilles de Retz cried out in his loudest military tones — " Henriet, Poitou, De Sillé, bind these maidens upon the iron altar, that Barran-Sathanas may feed his eyes on their beauty and rejoice!"

And as they stood motionless upon the square of white marble, the servitors came forward and led them to the great altar of iron. They lifted the maidens up and laid their bodies crosswise upon the vast grid, the bars of which were as thick as a man's arm, arranging them so that their heads hung without support over the bar next the shadowy image.

As they bound them rudely hand and foot, the long and beautiful hair of Maud Lindesay escaped from its fastenings and fell down till it reached the bath of red porphyry which extended underneath the whole length of the altar of iron.

Then through all the Temple of Evil there ensued sudden silence. Not a sob or a moan escaped from the doomed maidens, and the feet of the assistants fell silent and soft as the paws of wild beasts upon the ebon floor.

Gilles de Retz waited till his acolytes had retired to their appointed places, where they stood like carven statues watching what should happen. Then slowly and deliberately he ascended to the broad platform from which the iron altar rose, and stood with his arms folded over his flame-coloured robe, looking gloatingly down upon his innocent victims. Maud Lindesay was the nearer to him, and her unbound hair fell back and touched the peak of his pointed shoe of crimson Cordovan leather.

With a quick movement he caught up a handful of its rich luxuriance and allowed it to run through his fingers like sand again and yet again, with apparent delight in the sensation.

Even as he did so the dim figure of the horned demon above appeared to lean forward as if to touch him, and with a rushing noise the great hour-glass set upon a pedestal at the foot of the image turned itself completely over. Gilles with a startled air turned also, and seeing what it was he laughed a strange hollow laugh.

" It is indeed the hour, the hour of doom, fair maids," he said, looking down upon them as deferentially as if he had been paying his court in the great hall of Thrieve, "but it shall not pass without taking with it your souls to another, and I trust a higher, sphere!"

He paused, but no complaint or appeal reached his cruel and inexorable ear. The certain graciousness of Providence to those in extreme peril seemed to have blunted the edge of fear in the innocent victims. They lay still and apparently without consciousness upon the iron altar. The red glow played upon their faces, shining through from the inner chamber, and the figure of the marshal stood out black against it.

On the floor lay the goblet from which he had drunk the Red Milk.

"Give me the knife!" he cried, sudden as a trumpet that is blown.

And reaching a withered hand within the marshal's chamber as if to detach something from the wall, La Meffraye hobbled quickly across the altar platform, bearing in her hand a shining weapon of steel, broad of blade and curved at the point. She placed the ebony handle in the marshal's hand, who weighed it lovingly in his grasp.

Then for the first time since the men had bound her, the sweet childish eyes of little Margaret were unclosed and looked up at Gilles de Retz with the touching wonder of helplessness and innocence.

At that moment the image appeared to Laurence to beckon to him out of the gloom. A quick and nervous resolve ran through his veins. His muscles became like steel within his flesh. He rose to his feet, and, without pause for thought, rushed across the chapel from the niche where he had been hidden.

"Murderer! Fiend! I will kill you!" he cried, and with his dagger bare in his hand he would have thrown himself upon the marshal. But swifter than the rush of the young man in his strength there came another from the door of the inner chamber.

With a deep-throated roar of wholly bestial fury, Astarte the she-wolf sprang upon Laurence, and, though he sank his dagger twice to the hilt in her hairy chest, she over-bore him and they fell to the ground with her teeth gripping his shoulder. Laurence felt the hot life-blood of the beast spurt forth and mingle with his own. Then a flood of swirling waters seemed to bear him suddenly away into the unknown.

*   *   *   *   *   *

When Laurence MacKim came to himself he emerged into a chill world in which he felt somehow infinitely lonely and forsaken. Next he grew slowly conscious that his feet and arms were bound tightly with cords that cut painfully into the flesh. Then he realised that he, too, had taken his place beside the maids upon the altar of iron. Strangely enough he did not feel afraid nor even wish himself elsewhere. He only wondered what would happen next.

He opened his eyes and lo! they looked directly into the leering countenance of the monstrous image. Yet there seemed something curiously encouraging and even beneficent about the aspect of the demon. But so often as Gilles de Retz passed the triple array of his victims with his back to the image, the regard of the sculptured devil followed him, grim and mocking.

Words of angry altercation came to the ears of Laurence MacKim.

"I tell you," cried the voice of Gilles de Retz, "I will not spare them. Well nigh had I succeeded. Almost I was young again. I was tasting the first sweetness of knowledge wide as that of the gods. I felt the new life stirring within me. But I had not enough of the blood of innocence, which is the only worthy libation to Barran-Sathanas, who alone can bestow youth and life."

Then the Lady Sybilla answered him. "I pray you, Gilles de Retz, as you hope for mercy, slay not these maidens and this youth. Take me, and bind me, instead, for the sacrifice of death. I have wrought enough of evil! Take of my blood and work out your purpose. Let me give you the libation you desire. Gilles de Retz, if ever I have aided you, grant me this boon now. I beseech you, let these innocents go, and bind me upon the altar in their places."

Long and loud laughed Gilles de Retz, a hard, evil, and relentless laugh.

"Sybilla de Thouars an innocent maiden's sacrifice! Barran-Sathanas himself laughs at the jest. He would have no pleasure in your death. Soul and body you are his already. He desires only the blood and suffering of the innocent — of those on whom he has never set his mark. Nay, these three shall surely die, and in that bath of porphyry hollowed out under his altar I will lave me from head to foot in the Red Milk of innocence. I have no more need of you, Sybilla mine. You have done your work, and for your reward you can now depart to your own place. Out of my way, I say. Henriet, Poitou, quick! Remove this woman from before the altar!"

Then, struggling strongly in their hands, the servitors carried the Lady Sybilla to the farther end of the chapel, where they abode on either side, holding her fast. And as the last grains of sand began to swirl towards their fall and a little whirlpool to form funnel-wise in the midst of the hour-glass, the butcher was left alone with his victims upon the platform of the iron altar.

Gilles de Retz turned towards the image, and, lifting up his hand solemnly, he cried in a great voice, "O Barran-Sathanas, be pleased to behold this innocent blood spilled slowly in thine honour. As the red fount flows and the red fire burns, restore my youth and make me strong. Faithfully will I serve thee and thee alone, renouncing all other. O Barran-Sathanas, great and only Lord, receive my sacrifice. It is the hour!"

And so saying he laid hold of Maud Lindesay by the hair, and raised the curved knife on high.

Then from the end of the chapel to which the Lady Sybilla had been taken there came a sound. With a great despairing effort she burst from her captors' hands and ran forward. She knelt down on the marble slab whereon the maids had stood at their first entering, and as she knelt she held aloft a golden crucifix.

"If there be a God in heaven, let him manifest himself now!" she cried, "by the virtue of this cross of His son Jesus Christ, I call upon Him!"

Then suddenly all the place was filled with a mighty rushing noise. The last grains ran low in the hour-glass. It shifted in its stand and turned over. A tremor like that of an earthquake shook all the castle to its foundations. The solid keep itself rocked like a vessel in a stormy sea. The great image overturned, and by its fall

Gilles de Retz was stricken senseless to the earth. The next moment, like flood-gates burst by a mighty tide, the doors of the temple were opened with a clang, and through them a crowd of armed men came rushing in with triumphant shouts and angry cries of vengeance.

Sholto was far ahead of the others, and, as if led by the unerring instinct of love, he ran to the altar whereon his love lay white as death, but without a mark upon her fair body.

It was the work of a moment to cut their cords and chafe the numbed wrists and ankles. James Douglas took the little Margaret. Sholto had his sweetheart in his arms, while Laurence recovered quickly enough to aid his father in securing Gilles de Retz and his servants. La Meffraye they took not, for she lay dead within the inner chamber, where yet burned the great fire which was used to consume the bodies of the demon's victims. Two gaping wounds were found in her breast, in the same place in which the dagger of Laurence MacKim had smitten the she-wolf as she sprang upon him. But Astarte, woman witch or were-wolf, was never seen again, neither by starlight, moonlight, nor yet in the eye of day. Truly of Gilles de Retz was it said, "His demon hath deserted him."

Beneath in the courts and quadrangles, swarming through the towers and clambering perilously on the roofs, surged the press of the furious populace. It was all that Duke John and his officers could do to keep the prisoners in ward, and to prevent them from being torn limb from limb (as had perhaps been fittest), and tossed alive into the flaming funeral pyre of Castle Machecoul, which, lighted by a hundred hands, presently began to flame like a volcano to the skies.

For the hour that comes to every evil-doer had come to Gilles de Retz. And in that hour, as it shall ever be, the devil in whom he trusted had forsaken him.

But the Lady Sybilla stood on the garden tower that in happier days had been her pleasaunce, and beheld. And as she watched she kissed the golden crucifix of the child Margaret. And her heart rejoiced because the lives of the innocent as well as the death of the guilty had been given her for her portion.

" And now, O Lord, I am ready to pay the price!" she said.

CHAPTER LX

HIS DEMON HATH DESERTED HIM

THE soldiers of the Duke of Brittany stood with bared swords and deadly pikes around the Marshal de Retz and those of his servants who had been taken — that is to say, round Poitou, Clerk Henriet, Blanquet, and Robin Romulart. About them surged ever more fiercely the angry populace, drunk with the hot wine of destruction, having been filled with inconceivable fury by that which they had seen in the round tower wherein stood the filled bags of little charred remains.

"Tear the wolves into gobbets! Kill them! Burn them! Send them quick to Hell!" So ran the cry.

And twice and thrice the villagers of the Pays de Retz charged desperately as men who fight for their lives.

"Stand to it, men!" cried Pierre de l'Hopital. "Gilles de Retz shall have fair trial!

"*But I shall try him!*" he added, under his breath.

Never was seen such a sight as the procession which conducted Gilles de Retz to the city of Nantes. The Duke had sent for his whole band of soldiers, and these, in ordered companies, marched in front and rear. A triple file guarded the prisoners, and even their levelled pikes could scarce beat back the furious rushes of the populace.

461

It was like a civil war, for the assailants struck fiercely at the soldiers — as if in protecting him, they became accessory to the crimes of the hated marshal.

"*Barbe Bleu! Barbe Bleu!*" they cried. "Slay *Barbe Bleu!* Make his beard blood-red. He hath dipped it often in the life-blood of our children. Now we will redden it with his own!"

So ran the tumult, surging and gathering and scattering. And ever the pikes of the guard flashed, and the ordered files shouldered a path through the press.

"Make way there!" cried the provost marshals. "Make way for the prisoners of the Duke!"

And as they entered the city, from behind and before, from all the windows and roofs, rose the hoarse grunting roar of the hatred and cursing of a whole people.

But the object of all this rested calm and unmoved, and his cruel grey eye had no expression in it save a certain tolerant and amused contempt.

"Bah!" he muttered. "Would that I had slain ten millions of you! It is my only regret that I had not the time. It is almost unworthy to die for a few score children!"

During the journey to Nantes, Gilles de Retz kept the grand reserve with which, when he came to himself, he had treated those who had captured him. To the Duke only would he condescend to reply, and to him he rather spoke as an equal unjustly treated than as a guilty prisoner and suppliant.

"For this, Sire of Brittany," he said, "must you answer to your over-lord, the King of France, whose minister and marshal I am!"

The Duke would have made some feeble reply, but

Pierre de l'Hopital cut across the conversation with that stern irony which characterised him.

"My lord," he said, "remember that before you were made Marshal of France you were born a subject of the Duke of Brittany! And as such you shall be judged."

"I decline to stand at your tribunal!" said the marshal, haughtily.

"*Soit!*" said the President, indifferently, "but all the same you shall be tried!"

Duke John, knowing well that while his court was being held in the capital city of his province, and especially during the trial of Gilles de Retz, Nantes was no place for young maidens who had suffered like Maud Lindesay and Margaret Douglas, sent them under escort to the Castle of Angers.

Sholto MacKim and his father were allowed to accompany them, that they might not be without some of their own country to speak with during their sojourn in France. The Lord James, however, elected to abide with the court. For there were many ladies there, and, having nobility of address and desiring to perfect himself in the niceties of fashionable speech (which changed daily), he had great pleasure in their society, and rode in the lists by the side of the Loire with even more than his former gallantry and success.

For, as he said, he needed some compensation for the long abstinence enforced upon him by his habit of holy palmer. And right amply did he make himself amends, and was accounted by dames fair and free the lightsomest and properest Scot who had ever come into the land of France.

With him Laurence remained, both because his father

was still angry with him on account of his desertion of
them in Paris, and also because having been so long in
the Castle of Machecoul, there were important matters
concerning which in the forthcoming trial he alone
could give evidence.

Pierre de l'Hopital would have detained the Lady
Sybilla as a possible accomplice of the Sieur de Retz, but
by the intercession of the Scottish maidens, as well as by
the sworn evidence of Sholto and the Lord James, tes-
tifying that wholly by her means Gilles de Retz had
finally been caught red-handed, she was permitted to depart whither she would.

"I will go to my sister," she said to Sholto, who came
to know how he could serve her. "It matters little.
My work is nearly done!"

So, riding as was her custom all alone upon a white
palfrey, she passed out of their sight towards the south.

      *   *   *   *   *   *

In the city of Nantes the rumour of the taking of
Gilles de Retz had spread like wildfire, and as the
cavalcade rode through the streets, the windows rained
down curses and the citizens hooted up from the side-
walks. But the marshal kept his haughty and disdainful regard, appearing like a noble nature who perforce
companies for the nonce with meaner men. He sat his
favourite charger like a true companion of Dunois and
De Richemont, and, as more than one remarked, on this
occasion he looked like the royal prince and the Duke of
Brittany the prisoner.

So in the New Tower of the Castle of Nantes, Gilles
de Retz was placed to wait his trial. There is no need
to give a long account of it. The documents have been

printed in plain letter, and all the world knows how Clerk Henriet faltered under the stern questioning of Pierre de l'Hopital, and how finally he declared fully all these iniquities without parallel in which he had borne so cruel a part.

Poitou, more faithful to his master, held out till the threat of torture and the appeals of his friend Henriet broke him down. But the attitude and bearing of the chief culprit deserve that the historian should not wholly pass them over.

Even in his first haughty and contemptuous silence, Gilles de Retz was shifting his ground, and with a cool unheated intelligence orienting himself to new conditions. It soon became evident to his mind that the powers of Evil in which he trusted, and to whose service he had consecrated his life and fortune, had befooled and betrayed him.

Well — even so would he fool them — if, by the grace of God, there were yet any merit or hope in the service of Good. The priests said so. The Scripture said so, and they might be right after all. At least, the thing was worth trying.

For a cold and calculating brain lay behind the worst excesses of the terrible Lord de Retz. The religion of the Cross might not be of much final use — still, it was all that remained, and Gilles de Retz determined to avail himself of it. So once more he apostasised from Barran-Sathanas to Jehovah.

With an effrontery almost too stupendous for belief, he arrayed himself in the white robes of a Carmelite novice and spent his prison days in singing litanies and in private confession with his religious adviser.

2 n

When the great day of the trial at last arrived, the marshal, who had expected on the bench the weak kindly countenance of Duke John, was called upon to confront the indomitable judicial rectitude of Pierre de l'Hopital, President and Grand-Seneschal of Brittany.

Gilles de Retz appeared at his trial dressed in white of the richest materials and with all his military decorations upon him. But his judge, habited in stern and simple black, was not in the least intimidated.

Then came the great surprise. After the evidence of Henriet and Poitou had been read to him, the marshal was asked to plead. To the surprise of all, the accused claimed benefit of clergy.

"I have been a great sinner," he said, "I have indeed deserved a thousand deaths. But now I am a man of God. I have confessed. I have received absolution for all my sins. God has forgiven me, and my soul is cleansed!"

"Good!" answered Pierre de l'Hopital, "I have nothing to do with your soul. I must leave that, as you very pertinently remark, to God. But I am here to try your body, and if found guilty to condemn that body to suffer the penalties by law provided according to the statutes of Brittany."

Then Clerk Henriet was brought in to testify more fully of the crimes beyond parallel in the history of mankind.

The court had been hung round with black, and the only object which appeared prominent was a beautiful ivory crucifix with a noble figure of the Redeemer of Men carved upon it. This was suspended, according to the custom, over the head of the President of the Tribunal.

Henriet had not proceeded far with his terrible relation of well nigh inconceivable crimes when he stopped.

"I cannot go on," he said, in a broken appealing voice; "I cannot tell what I have to tell with That Figure looking down upon me!"

So, with the whole Court standing up in reverence, the image of the Most Pitiful was solemnly veiled from sight, that such deeds of darkness might not be so much as named in that holy and gracious presence.

And during the ceremony Friar Gilles of the order of the Carmelites stood up more reverently than any, for now, seeing that no better might be, he had definitely renounced Barran-Sathanas and cast in his lot with God Almighty.

*   *   *   *   *   *

"The sentence of this court is that you, Gilles de Laval, Lord of Retz, Marshal of France, and you, Poitou and Henriet, be carried to the meadow of La Biesse at nine of the clock on the morning of to-morrow, and that you be there hanged and burned till you be dead. And to God the Just One be the glory!"

The voice of Pierre de l'Hopital rang out through the silence of the hall of judgment.

"Amen!" said Friar Gilles, devoutly crossing himself.

And so in due course on the meadow of La Biesse, by the side of the blue Loire, the evil soul of Gilles de Retz went to its own place with all the paraphernalia of repentance and in the full odour of a somewhat hectic sanctity.

*   *   *   *   *   *

The day after the burning, a little company of riders left the city of Angers, journeying westward along the

Loire. It consisted of the maidens Margaret Douglas
and Maud Lindesay, with Sholto MacKim and a dozen
horsemen belonging to his Grace of Brittany. It had
been arranged that they were to be joined, upon an eminence above the river on the right bank, by the Lord
James, Malise, and Laurence, with the escort which was
to accompany them to the port of Saint Nazaire. There
(as was necessary in order to escape the troublesome navi-
gation of the swift and treacherous upper reaches) they
would find vessels ready to set sail for Scotland.

As the little cloud of riders left behind them the black
towers of Angers, they passed through woodland glades
wherein, in spite of the lateness of the season, the birds
were singing. The air was mild and delightsome. At
last, leaving the river, they struck away inland, having
the frowning towers of Champtocé on their left as they
rode. Presently they came to a forest, wherein in days
before the great cruelty, Gilles de Retz had often
hunted the wolf and the wild boar.

Here the woodland paths were covered deep with fallen
leaves, and the naked branches spoke of the desolation
of a dead year.

As the maids rode forward first of their company and
talked, as was natural, of that which had taken place
the day before at Nantes, they became aware of the Lady
Sybilla riding towards them on her palfrey of white.
She would have passed them without speech, with her
head downcast and her eyes fixed upon the dank ground
with its covering drift of dead autumnal leaves.

But Margaret, grateful for that which the Lady Sybilla
had done for them at Machecoul, spurred her steed and
rode thwartwise to intercept her.

"Sybilla," she said, "you will come with us to Scotland. I have many castles there, and, they tell me, a princessdom of mine own. We shall all be happy together and forget these ill times. Maud and I can never repay that which you have done for us."

"Yes, I pray you come with us," said Maud, a little more slowly, "we will be your sisters, and the ill times shall not come again."

The Lady Sybilla smiled a sad subtle smile and shook her head.

"I thank you. I thank you more than you know. It eases my heart that you should forgive a woman such as I for all the evil she has brought you and yours. But I am now no fit companion for you or any. I am become but a wandering shape, speaking to one who cannot answer, and seeking him whom I can never find."

The little Maid, being but a child, mistook her meaning.

"No, no," she cried, "your life is not done. If the one whom you love hath left you unkindly — well, bide awhile, and when the first smart is passed, we will marry you to some braver and more handsome knight. There are many such in Scotland. I pray you come with Maud and me even as we wish you. Why, there would not be three like us in all the land. I wager we will set kings by the ears between us. Though, as for me, I can only marry a Douglas!"

The smile of the Lady Sybilla grew ever sadder and ever sweeter.

"The man whom I loved, and who loved me, I betrayed to the death. There is no forgiveness for such as I in this life. Perhaps there may be in the next.

At least, *he* forgave me, and that is enough. He believed in me against myself, and I will wait. Till then
I go hither and thither and none shall hinder me or
molest — for upon Sybilla de Thouars God hath set the
seal of Cain!"

Margaret Douglas flicked her steed impatiently, caus-
ing the spirited little beast to curvet.

"I think it is very ill-done of you not to come to
Scotland with us," she said petulantly, "when we would
have been so good to you!"

"Too good, too kind," said the Lady Sybilla, very
gently; "such kindness is not for such as I am. But if
I may, while I live I will keep the golden cross you lent
me — the crucifix your brother gave to you on your
birthday!"

"Keep it — it is yours! I do not want it!" cried
Margaret, glad to have found some way of evidencing
her gratitude.

"I thank you," said Sybilla de Thouars; "some day I
may come to Scotland. And if I do, you shall come out
from Thrieve and meet me by the white thorns of the
Carlinwark at the hour when the little children sing!"

And so, without other farewell, she turned and rode
slowly away down the avenues of fallen leaves, till the
folding woodlands hid her from the sight of those two
who watched her with tear-blurred eyes and hearts
strangely stirred with pity for the fate of her whom
they had once hated with such good cause.

CHAPTER LXI

LEAP YEAR IN GALLOWAY

MORNING dawned fair over the wide strath of Dee. Cairnsmuir and Ben Gairn stood out south and north like blue, round-shouldered sentinels. Castle Thrieve rose grey in the midst of the water-meadows, massive and sombre in the early sunrise.

Andro the Penman and his brother John, with the taciturnity natural to early risers, were silently hoisting the flag which denoted the presence of the noble young chatelaine of the great fortress.

Sholto also was early astir, for the affairs of the castle and of the host were in his hand, and there was much business to be despatched that morning. The young Avondale Douglases were riding away from Thrieve, for word had come that James the Gross, seventh Earl of Douglas, was surely at death's door.

"Besides," said William Douglas, "wherefore should we stay — our work is done. No one will molest our cousin in her heritages now! We five have stood about her while there was need. But for the present Sir Sholto and his men can keep count and reckoning with any from the back-shore of Leswalt to Berwick bound."

"Aye, indeed," cried James Douglas, "we will go till the time come when the suitors gather, like corbies about a dead lamb!"

471

"That is not a savoury comparison," cried Margaret of Douglas, now grown older, and already giving more than a mere promise of that wondrous beauty which afterwards made her celebrated in all lands, "but after all, you, cousin James, have some right to make it. For, but for you and our good Sholto there, this little ewe lamb would have been carrion indeed!"

"Good-by!" cried James of Avondale. "Haste thee and grow up, sweet coz. Then will I come back with the rest of the corbies and take my chance of the feast. I will keep myself for that day."

But William Douglas sat square and silent on his charger.

The Maid of Galloway waved her hand gaily to the younger of the knights.

"You shall have your chance with the rest," she cried; "but you will not care about me then. Very likely I may have to fleech and cozen with you like a sweetie-wife at a fair before either of you will marry me. And you know I have sworn on the bones of Saint Bride to marry none but a Douglas of the Douglases!"

Then William Douglas saluted without a word, and turning his bridle-rein rode away with his face steadfastly set to the north. But James ever cried back farewells and jovial words long after he was out of hearing. And even on the heights of Keltonmuir he still fluttered a gay kerchief in his left hand.

Then Margaret Douglas went back within the gates, where her eyes fell upon Maud Lindesay, coming through the castle yard to meet her. For that morning she had not wished to encounter Sholto — at least not among so many. The two maidens walked on together, and which was the fairer, the black or the nut-brown, none could say who beheld them.

After a while Margaret Douglas sighed.

"I wonder which of them I like the best," she said.

Maud laughed a merry, scornful laugh in which was a world of superior knowledge.

"You do not like either of them very much yet, or you would have no difficulty about the matter!" said this wise woman.

"Well, I wonder which of them loves me best," she went on; "James tells me of it a hundred times every day and all day. But William says nothing. He only looks at me often, as if he disapproved of me. I am over light for him, I trow. He thinks not of me."

Then after a pause she said, again with her finger on her lip, "I wonder which of them would do most for my sake?"

"I know!" said Maud Lindesay, promptly.

*　　　*　　　*　　　*　　　*　　　*

With the young Avondales there had ridden forth Malise and his son Laurence on their way to the Abbey of Dulce Cor. Sholto went also with them to convoy them to the fords of Urr.

For Laurence was to be a clerk after all.

And this is the way he explained it.

"The Abbot cannot live long, and there is no Douglas to succeed him. Then your little Maid will make me Abbot, if that Maud of yours does her duty."

"She is not my Maud yet," sighed Sholto. For, as they say in Scotland, the lady had proved "driech to draw up."

"But she will be in good time," urged Laurence, "and

she must persuade the Lady Margaret of my many and surprising virtues."

"The Lady Margaret hath doubtless seen these for herself. Were you not bound beside her on the iron altar?" said Sholto.

"Yes, but I dirked the old witch-woman, or so they say. And that was no clerkly action!" objected his brother.

"Fear not," said Sholto, "you have all of her favour you need without working by means of another's petticoat. But how about marrying? You cannot wed or woo if you are a clerk.   You did not use to be so unfond of a lass in the gloamings along the sweet strand called the Walk of Lovers — you know where!"

"Pshaw," cried Laurence, "I never yet saw the lass I liked better than myself.   And I never expect to see one that I shall like better than the fat revenues of the Abbacy of Dulce Cor!"

He paused a moment as if roguishly considering some point.

"Besides," he went on, "wed I may not, but woo — that is another matter!   I have never yet heard that an Abbot —"

"Good-day!" cried Sholto, suddenly, at this point, "I will not stay to hear you blaspheme!"

And leaving his father and Laurence to ride westward he turned him back towards Thrieve.

"I will surely return to-morrow," cried Malise; "I must first see this gay bird safely in mew. Aye, and bid the Abbot William clip his wings too!"

So in the gay morning sunshine and with the reflection of the lift glinting dark blue from tarn and lakelet, Sholto MacKim rode towards the Castle of Thrieve.

He bethought him on all that was bygone. The Avondales were gone, James the Gross might die any moment —might even now be dead and William Douglas be Earl in his place!

He thought over William of Avondale's last words to himself, spoken with deep solemnity and in all the dignity of a great spirit.

"Sholto, you and yours have brought to justice the chief betrayer. The time is at hand when, having the power, I will settle with Crichton and Livingston, the lesser villains. And in that count and reckoning you must be my right-hand man. Keep your Countess, the sweet young Margaret, safe for my sake. She is very precious to me—indeed, beyond my life. And for this time fare you well!"

And he had reached a mailed hand to the captain of the Douglas guard, and when Sholto would have bent his head upon it to kiss it, William of Avondale gripped his suddenly as one grasps a comrade's hand when the heart is touched, and so was gone.

At the verge of the flowery pastures that ring the isle of Thrieve, Sholto met Maud Lindesay, wandering alone. At sight of her he leaped from his horse, and, without salutation of spoken speech, walked by her side.

"How came you here alone?" he asked.

Maud made her little pouting movement of the lips, and kicked viciously at a tuft of grass.

"I forgot," she said hypocritically, "I ought to have asked leave of that noble knight the Captain of Thrieve. We poor maids must not breathe without his permission —no, nor even walk out to meet him when we are lonesome."

Maud Lindesay lifted her eyes suddenly and shot at Sholto a glance so disabling, that, alarmed for the consequences, she veiled her eyes again circumspectly by dropping her long lashes upon her cheek.

" Did you really come out to meet me, Maud ? " cried Sholto, all the life flooding back into his cheeks, " in this do you speak truth and no mockery ? "

" I only said that we maidens were so much in fear of our Castle Governor, that we must not walk out even to meet him ! "

At this Sholto let his horse go where it would, and, as they were passing at the time through a coppice of hazel, he caught his saucy sweetheart quickly by the wrist.

"Mistress Maud, you shall not play with me ! " he said ; " you will tell me plainly — do you love me or do you not ? "

Maud Lindesay puckered her pretty face as if she had been about to cry.

" You hurt my arm ! " she said plaintively, looking up at him with the long pathetic gaze of a gentle helpless animal undeservedly put in pain.

Sholto perforce released the pressure on her arm. She instantly put both hands behind her.

" You did not hurt me at all — hear you that, Master Sholto," she cried, " and I do not love you — not that much, Sir Noble Bully ! "

And she snapped her finger and thumb like a flash beneath his nose.

" Not that much ! " she repeated viciously, and did it again. Sholto turned away sternly.

" You are nothing but a silly girl, and not worthy that

any true man should either love or marry **you!**" he said, walking off in the direction of the castle.

Maud Lindesay looked after him a moment as if not believing her eyes and ears. Then, so soon as she made sure that he was indeed not coming back, she tripped quickly after him. He was taking long strides, and it required a series of small hops and skips to keep up with him.

"Not really, Sholto?" she said beseechingly, almost running beside him now. He walked so fast.

"Yes, madam, really!" said that **young knight**, still more sternly.

She took a little run to get a step in front of him, so that she might advantageously look up into his face.

"Then you will not marry me, Sholto?"

Her hands were clasped with the sweetest petitionary grace.

"*No!*"

The monosyllable escaped from his lips with a snort like a puff of steam from under the lid of a boiling pot.

"Not even if I ask you very nicely, Sholto?"

"*No!*"

The negative came again, apparently fiercer than before, almost like an explosion indeed. But still there was a hollow sound about it somewhere.

At this the girl stopped suddenly and, drawing a little lace kerchief from her bosom, she sank her head into it in apparent abandonment of grief.

"Oh, what shall I do?" she wailed, "Sholto says he will not marry me, and I have asked him so sweetly. What shall I do? What shall I do? I will e'en go and drown me in the Dee water!"

And with her kerchief still held to her eyes — or at least (to be wholly accurate) to one of them — the despised maiden ran towards the river bank. She did not run very fast, but still she ran.

Now this was more than Sholto had bargained for, and he in turn pursued her light-foot, swifter than he had ever run in his life. He overtook her just as she reached the little ascent of the rocks by the river margin.

His hand fell upon her shoulder and he turned her round. She was still shaking with sobs — or something.

"I will — I will, I *will* drown myself!" she cried, her kerchief closer to her eyes.

"I will marry you — I will do anything. I love you, Maud!"

"You do not — you cannot!" she cried, pushing him fiercely away, "you said you would not! That I was not fit to marry."

"I did not mean it — I lied! I did not know what I said! I will do whatever you bid me!" Sholto was grovelling now.

"Then you will marry me — if I do not drown myself?"

She spoke with a sort of relenting, delicious and tentative.

"Yes — yes! When you will — to-morrow — now!"

She dropped the kerchief and the laughing eyes of naughty Maud Lindesay looked suddenly out upon Sholto like sunshine in a dark place. They were dry and full of merriment. Not a trace of tears was to be discerned in either of them.

Then she gave another little skip, and, catching him

by the arm, forced him to walk with her toward Castle Thrieve.

"Of course you will marry me, silly! You could not help yourself, Sholto — and it shall be when I like too. But now that you have been so stern and crusty with me, I am not sure that I will not take Landless Jock after all!"

* * * * * *

This is the end, and yet not the end. For still, say the country folk, when the leaves are greenest by the lakeside, when the white thorn is whitest and the sun drops most gloriously behind the purpling hills of the west, when the children sing like mavises on the clachan greens, you may chance to spy under the Three Thorns of Carlinwark a lady fairer than mortal eye hath seen. She will be sitting gracefully on a white palfrey and hearkening to the bairns singing by the watersides. And the tears fall down her cheeks as she listens, in the place where in the springtime of the year young William Douglas first met the Lady Sybilla.

THE END